# YOUR OWN FATE

Novels published by Midnight Fire Media

Your Own Fate
Night on Earth
Dreams Belong to the Night
ShadowWalk
Alarums of Reality
Afterglow Dust
Black Dragon
Falling
Thunder Road - Ice and Fire
Season of the Witch
Afterglow Rain

Anthology: Red Shadow and Other Stories

The Janus Clan series:

The Defenseless
The Slaves
Birds Flying in the Dark
At the End of the Rainbow
Lewis of Modern York

**Poetry:**

Amos Keppler: Complete Poems 1989 – 2003
Secrets - Descriptions of what cannot be described

(A few of the) novels to be published:

The Werewolf of Locus Bradle
Fangs and Claws of the Earth
Forsaken
Resurrection Dreams

For a «complete» list of current and current future Amos Keppler and Midnight Fire Media projects see the back of the book and the Midnight Fire/Midnight Fire Media web pages.

# Your Own Fate

## By

## Amos Keppler

**Midnight Fire Media**
2019

# Midnight Fire Media

http://midnight-fire.net/mfm
For more about Your Own Fate:
http://midnight-fire.net/yof


E-Mail:
ak13@midnight-fire.net
manofhood@yahoo.com

Cover, text, design, art, preprint and photos Amos Keppler

ISBN 978-82-91693-27-9

I will praise you, for I am fearfully and wonderfully made!
My soul knows how marvellous are your works.
You were aware when my very bones were formed,
Growing secretly inside my mother's body
As a plant's root grows beneath the earth.
You knew me before I was born.
The days of my life were all written in your book
Before they had ever begun.

psalm 139

The christian bible. Modern British English translation

# CHAPTER ONE

## SIX DAYS IN THE CITY OF ANGELS

Hot bitter air. The city's sour scent of exhaust and dust. For a moment he covered his mouth and nose, before he once again realized it was no use.

They had waited the entire day and started growing impatient. Eyes locked on to the worn-down building began swelling in the light from the setting sun. It had been early morning when they had crawled through the sewer to their present position, a leftover, unused pipe, where it seemed to them, incredibly enough, as if it smelled even worse than the path they had taken below the ground.

– He isn't coming, said the man staring exasperated through the binoculars.

– He hasn't shown up *yet,* that's for sure, the other man said, visibly frustrated. – We have people on all sides. The old plans show that the sewer does not pass under the building. If he's using subterranean access, he must have used a lot of time and resources at extending the stinking shit, and additionally paid off several public servants.

– He *does* have major resources at his command, the woman, Lieutenant Janet Caldwell, pointed out eagerly, grudgingly. – Whether he shows up or not, there's abnormally high activity inside. If we can't get the big fish, we'll be able to put major dents in his operation.

There was a minor break, virtually a vacuum. All three of them looked at the fourth person present, a man in modest, close to worn clothing. He seemed relaxed, and if they didn't know better, they would have believed he was bored.

– He will be here, he said dryly. They wondered once again, over the language, the accent and strange depths. – He doesn't hide. He never does.

– The way you talk, it sounds like you believe he would have come even if he had known we were here, Caldwell said, unable to hide her irritation.

– He isn't that crazy, the other one pondered. – But he would have made his presence known, in some way or another.

She was about to give an angry reply when the man with the binoculars grabbed her shoulder.

– A car is approaching, he said with audible excitement in his voice. – It's just the driver inside. I think it is him.

– It is him.

That was the man with worn clothes again. They realized, astounded that they didn't doubt his words.

– In an open car, the man with the binoculars cried incredulous, almost too loud. – By damn, who does he think he is?

Zahn didn't need binoculars. He didn't even have to open his eyes to see the demonic smile of the man behind the wheel. Suddenly he had trouble breathing. During the three years he had rarely been any closer than this.

– I saw your mother today.

It had started like that, an innocent, casual remark. *Do you know what? I saw your mother today.* There had been blue skies that day. No dark clouds. Not the slightest signs of any. But then someone had snapped their fingers and his life had fallen apart. He started sweating. It had been white hot all day, but he hadn't been sweating, not a drop. He had always been able to take heat well. Always.

The driver stopped the car softly and supremely relaxed. He left the car without closing the door and walked off without a worry in the world. They saw the dark storage facilities devour him. In spite of this, he seemed to crouch above it, like a giant.

*I've got you now. You won't get away this time.*

– Give the signal. Don't just sit there, damn it. HURRY UP

Nobody voiced a protest. They didn't dare. He suddenly looked quite insane.

*I can see and feel him, and know he can see and feel me…*

Hot bitter air. The city's sweet scent of exhaust and dust. Howling sirens. Long lines of patrol cars. Red and blue blinking lights. Heavily armed and well-armored figures dressed in blue flowed out of reinforced vehicles. It didn't take many minutes until the entire area, the very air itself seemed to be filled with red and blue lights, and sirens. An impressive display of what the city's official and semi-official police force could muster, a major display of power. The men and women looked uncertain at each other. They had expected heavy fire. Even armor-penetrating rockets hadn't been excluded during the pre-operational briefing. Everybody had been offered extra bonuses and the chance of pulling out, something that was close to unprecedented. Timothy Joyce had, during the time he had spent in Los Angeles made quite an impression on the city's governing elite. In fact, they had been so shaken that everybody from higher to lower circles of influence had joined forces to take him out.

Patrol cars surrounded the deserted factory area in two tight circles. A not inconsiderable number of uniformed people accessed the sewers. Choppers covered the air from a safe distance, but ready to move. Perhaps there had been larger united operations in LAPD history, but it wasn't very likely.

– I want to be among the first inside, Jeremy Zahn said, speaking his characteristic London dialect, with a voice, a behavior bordering on hysteria.

The international accent almost disappeared. He was already inside the walls, in the midst of the smoke, bullets and blood, like he had been for a long time. The sounds and sights and scents of past, present and future battles tore at his senses.

– That won't happen, Captain Lasko sniffed. – Forget it, pal! We're responsible for your safety. There will be tons of paperwork to take care of if you should croak.

*And you don't want anyone else to take the credit, «pal».* Zahn held back the sarcastic, hateful charge.

They stood on what was seen as a safe distance away. Zahn wasn't so sure about that, but it didn't really matter.

A six-door car with dark windows rolled up to them, close to silent, at least compared to the noise coming from the surroundings. Police Chief Arnold Springsteen enjoyed luxury.

He opened the door himself, and departed from the car, an impressive figure, with a powerful build, towering over everybody. The growing potbelly was the only thing diminishing the general impression.

– Everything's set here, sir, Lasko reported respectfully. – We've kept the building under constant surveillance and no one, I repeat, no one has left. Not a fly, not a goddamn microbe. To keep an eye on the place through a microscope is just about the only thing we haven't done, sir. Joyce - and his gang - is still in there. We've got them right where we want them, sir.

– I want to join the first line of attackers, sir, Zahn almost shouted.

– That's out of the…

– Oh, let him do it, Captain. Springsteen stopped the Captain's angry exclamation with an indifferent gesture. – He has followed his prey for three long years, all over the globe. He's entitled. There's no lack of people to do the paperwork, if necessary.

Zahn ignored them. He had already started dressing up in the protective gear and choosing weapons. One could say one thing about the LAPD: they had no lack of ordnance. All claims that the United States' police force was short on people and suffered from a supply shortage were obviously based on misinformation. The British policeman felt he could pick and choose. He had always been interested in weapons and could hardly contain his excitement. He limited himself to an upgraded M-16A2, with an M-305 rocket launcher, and also grabbed a Magnum 44' automatic… still among the best assault weapons available.

He was led through the many blockades, to the frontline. The coal black humor was evident in every pairs of eyes he met. The common policemen looked at him with scornful, cruel stares. He was perceived, right or wrong, as one of the brass, and one of the brass wasn't stupid enough to join the cannon fodder. Zahn was surprised how integrated the hierarchy was everywhere. All the places he had visited on his hunt for Timothy Joyce. The entire world.

Sergeant Flynn met him with a sharp, but not hostile look.

– I've been told you only have observer status, he said, very direct, – but I will ask you anyway: How do you wanna do this?

– Head on, Zahn said with a rough voice, – crushing everyone in our path. I prefer that Joyce is captured alive, but the creeps worshipping him you may take out at will.

– A man after my own heart. Flynn bowed. The others laughed good-humored and viciously – My thoughts exactly. Incidentally, that's also my orders.

– *The dance begins.* They heard Lasko's voice through the radio.

Shortly after that they also heard it through the giant speakers: –
TIMOTHY JOYCE, YOU'RE UNDER ARREST. YOU AND
YOUR ACCOMPLISHES HAVE ONE MINUTE TO LEAVE
THE BUILDING WITH YOUR HANDS ABOVE YOUR
HEAD. ANY FAILURE TO OBEY THAT COMMAND WILL
BE SEEN AS AN AGGRESSIVE ACT AGAINST US.

There was no answer, none whatsoever. Lasko glanced at his
watch. He did so several times. Someone fairly close by giggled.
Lasko glared to all sides in an attempt to catch the potentially
unfortunate officer.

It turned quiet. As quiet as it could be in a major city. The
deadline passed without any noticeable reaction from those inside
the building.

Then Lasko gave the signal, the go-ahead, and in the next
fifty minutes it was impossible to have a conversation in close
proximity to the storm's eye.

The police fired rockets and bullets from all sides, and after the
hail of bullets and explosions followed a barrage of attackers,
charging forward like ants attacking a hostile hill.

Zahn's right side hit the wall. He made it just in time, before
the bullets started flying from the inside. The rain hit several
patrolmen. Grenades fired by those defending the fortress
blew up even more. Satan! He had told Springsteen and the
entire hierarchy repeatedly the last twenty-four hours to bring
in units from the army, all the SWAT-teams, Special Forces,
anything available, told them that to fight Timothy Joyce could
be compared to that of challenging a small army. He was
no ordinary crook… or drug lord, but something far more
dangerous. Zahn still didn't know what he was or what made the
man tick, even after three years. Zahn wanted to. The admission
came easily, like a guilty pleasure. He knew he understood
Timothy Joyce better than any other human being, but it wasn't
enough. He had studied the man in detail, all accessible material,
but it wasn't enough.

Understanding shouldn't be a problem. Such men were hardly
difficult to understand. But Joyce was. And Zahn worried. And
that, in turn worried him more.

He fired one of the grenades in the launcher. The moment the
explosion rocked the enemy stronghold inside he threw himself

forward. The attackers charged into the building from all sides. Zahn shot a woman stumbling from behind a ruined cover. Several of her comrades in arms returned the fire or attempted to take cover. They were mowed down. The bloodthirsty excitement he had learned to know the last three years rose in him. Up to this point it had been fleeting, passing every time he had believed he had the prey in his net, before it had once more slipped away. But this time... Tonight even Timothy Joyce fought an overwhelming, superior force. His servants could be as loyal and well armed as humanly possible, but they couldn't number more than one tenth of the well-prepared attack force. One saw it clearly. They fought with a fanatical zeal Zahn never would understand, but they fought with their backs to the wall. It was a bloodbath. Policemen and women died left and right, front, center and behind. Zahn had prepared for it. It was inevitable. But it was worth it. Joyce had to be stopped.

Stopped!

An officer was hit and pushed Zahn with him when he fell. The large body rested on him and pushed him down. He pushed it off without exerting himself. A man fired at him, but missed, and hit a person further behind. Zahn killed him with one single shot in the head.

– You shoot damn well, the sergeant cried in acknowledgement, in a brief break behind a cover.

He ignored the sergeant. He knew how good he was, how good he had been forced to become, to get this far, to this night, this moment, what would come soon, any time now. He tasted the expectation in his mouth, letting it linger a second or two longer.

It cracked loud everywhere, like an eternal rolling stereo thundering in his ears. Dulled explosions on the opposite side of the building. Sharp, blinding on this one. He wanted to be on the opposite side, too, wanted to be everywhere Timothy Joyce might be.

And that could be anywhere.

– Let's get to the roof. I don't want him to get near a chopper.

Flynn nodded eagerly and signaled his men.

Followed by Flynn and four more Zahn started up the stairs. They met surprisingly little resistance. The bloodbath continued below, in an inferno of fire and pain. Death cries rose with the smoke and the heated air. Zahn knew shots were being fired, but he didn't hear them anymore. He left it behind, left that, too, behind.

A man appeared at the top of the stairs, and fired a lethal salvo. The rain of bullets hit Flynn and two others. Zahn leaned half outside the banister and fired as fast as he could at the indistinct figure. Lines of blood rose from the man's back and neck, and the man vanished from sight. Zahn advanced further with a gun in each hand. The two cops still breathing hesitatingly followed him.

The man laid dead right by the stairs. Glassy eyes stared at the ceiling. Zahn saw no one else. Except for the three standing and the dead the big room was empty, totally robbed of furniture, robbed of everything. On the walls there were woven carpets. Genuine Turkish style, Zahn noted. The bare walls were dark wood. The room seemed very luxurious… if one disregarded the missing furniture. All the emptiness screamed to be filled… by something.

– What the fuck is this? One of the policemen exclaimed nonplussed.

– It isn't shit, Zahn replied sharply. – Joyce is quite simply a raving lunatic. There's hardly any reason to what he's doing. Not to well-adapted, normal people. He's garbage, and should be treated thus.

Both nodded darkly. When one of them spoke it could just as well be the other. Zahn didn't recall if it was he who had spoken earlier, and didn't care.

– The way I see it, even the worst punishment available is insufficient in his case.

Joyce and his army had indeed made quite an impact in LA and among members of the city's proud police force.

On the opposite wall, about twenty steps ahead there were two closed doors, the only details interrupting the walls' conformity. The two dressed in blue looked uncertain at each other.

– Let's go, Zahn said in the commanding voice.

The voice of authority had spoken. They followed him and imitated his strolling, devil-may-care walk.

They reached the wall easily enough.

*He is in there somewhere. I can feel him. His cruelty, his deepfelt contempt for everything human.*

Zahn signaled to the officer in front to open the closest door. A slight hesitation and the man in blue obeyed. It was just a closet. There was a man with a machinegun in it. He made Swiss cheese of the officer. The already dead body was thrown backwards. Zahn stood there with weight evenly split on his feet, and filled the man in the closet with lead.

– You're one cold son of a bitch, the surviving officer exclaimed.

Zahn shrugged. What did he care about the dead? The body behind them was just another victim, another scalp in Timothy Joyce' belt. The Englishman shook his head, more than a bit annoyed, and went right ahead and kicked open the other door. He jumped inside, rolled across the floor, jumped to his feet with his weapon ready to fire, everything in one, fluid move. Nobody else here, nobody but the last representative of the Los Angeles Police Department in his close proximity. This room was an exact replica of the previous… except for the single door on the opposite side.

The best tactic would probably have been for the two of them to close in on it from opposite sides, but Zahn was sick and tired of following the star of reason. The volcanic rage building second by second didn't allow any form of hesitation. Ten steps from the door he fired a murderous salvo, looking forward very much to hearing the scream of pain from inside. That was stupid. He should have known better, *known better, known better*

There was a sound of metal against metal, a symphony in lead and steel. The bullets ricocheted almost straight back, missed Zahn and hit the police officer several times. He fell on his knees first, before falling forward, as he slowly stopped breathing. Zahn stood there paralyzed.

– You Satan, he said in a low voice.

– You Satan, he repeated louder.

He charged forward and kicked at the door. It stood just as unmovable. Naturally. He writhed in pain, and managed just about to hold onto his weapons.

Two steps forward, close to the wall. He pushed down the handle and pushed open the metal plate. The door slid open. No trouble. A hail of bullets heated the air where he could have been standing… if he had been stupid enough. The bullets whined harmlessly through the other door, back through the previous chamber. He threw away the machinegun, clutched the automag in both hands, threw himself around the corner, and fired an intense salvo at the gunman inside.

He hit a machinegun on a tripod, just as it fired again. The bullets hit the ceiling, the wall, the floor. The inanimate thing lay there, smoking and snarling.

The third chamber was exactly like the first two, except for it having no doors. There was one single opening, a further twenty steps away. Everything turned black. For a brief moment he imagined there was a huge poster on the other wall, saying

## WELCOME

and he sensed the rage and the insanity driving him turn even more rooted. He pushed on.

The illusion faded. He circled into a dark hall with all senses, with his entire being charged and ready. A small, scornful voice he had so far ignored told him that Joyce, if he had wanted to, could have killed him a long time ago. The madman had certainly had sufficient opportunity. Zahn wrote it off as luck. And luck did not last. Fate, or the chain of coincidences giving the illusion of fate, could absolutely remain on your side for a while, but then - suddenly - every moment of luck returned to you, like a fist in the face. He shook his head, shook himself awake, ready and dangerous. He could be just as deadly as Joyce. He had to be. If he wasn't, he had to become so. The endgame was near. He sensed it in every neural pathway, every synapse inside.

A lit room waited at the end of the corridor, beyond a line of darkened, well-equipped offices. Just before he reached it, there was a staircase leading further up. He chose the room first. It took time. Caution around every corner took time. Eventually he stood at the center of a room resembling an office. There was a desk and a chair slightly away from the wall, a TV and a DVD-player in a rack. A digital recorder four, close to five steps away from the desk. Joyce had a funny taste in decorations, but it was proven he had a funny taste for most things. He wasn't here either. Not physically. He was here.

Zahn heard noises from the floor above from a person who didn't bother being quiet or hiding. Zahn ran straight up the stairs, the taste of blood strong in his mouth. He had always thought it was an exaggerated, figurative way of speech, but now he did taste it, tasted it like hunger. He had chased his prey for three years. They had been near each other just a few times during that time, and Joyce had always had the advantage. This time was different. The trap, the fox trap had snapped close, and the prey waited in pain to be picked up.

The noise, the death down below seemed like something distant, unimportant now.

Now, this was what he called an office. It seemed to rise up around him, instead of him rising up to it. Not so big as the halls he had rushed through on his way here, but spacious. Persian carpets wall to wall. Bookshelves filled with hardback books. Two luxurious desks, deep chairs, even elegant stools. Heavy curtains. For quite some time now, he had pointed his gun at the man behind one of the desks.

– Now, this is what I call an office, Timothy Joyce said. – Welcome, Jeremy. You took your time. Is your taste in offices truly so different from mine? Since you have used such a long time getting here, that you have only reluctantly come here, I mean? Perhaps you would've preferred staying below and admired the decorations there?

– You're under arrest, Zahn snarled. – One wrong move, and I'll shoot you like a dog.

The burning need to pull the trigger almost overwhelmed him, but he kept himself in check.

– I can assure you of one thing, Jeremy. Joyce kept his hands flat on the desk as he rose from the chair, and kept them still when he started moving around the room. – Whatever you are, you're no dog.

– The attack force will be here soon, Zahn spoke in a hateful voice, – I can assure you, you won't get away. A snowball in hell has better odds than you.

– It will cost them time, effort and personnel to fight their way through my troops. We've got time, more than enough to speak about those things foremost on our mind.

Zahn changed his grip on the gun. He had clutched it so hard that his hands hurt.

– We've got nothing to talk about.

– Oh, come on, Jeremy. Don't insult us both with obvious lies. We both know you wouldn't be here, if you didn't want to talk. You want to *know*. We're not so different as you like to think. Of course not. Of course, you'll want to know. For what other reason would you follow me all over the globe the last three years?

Zahn attempted not to meet the other's eyes, but like the other times he was pulled into them. And he couldn't look away.

– You're a criminal and a murderer, you belong behind bars, in the electric chair, and I will make sure you receive whatever punishment society may decide for you, even though no punishment will be harsh enough.

He changed position on the floor, and lowered the gun to his hips. It didn't matter. He kept Joyce just as well covered, could take him out just as easily.

The laughter echoed through the room, throughout the building. Zahn heard the echo. Everything seemed to pause for a moment.

– If I am such a criminal, such a murderer, and I'm not saying I'm not, why, then, have I let you live all this time? You must admit that I've had plenty of opportunities to rid myself of such a nuisance like you?

– Why? He forced himself to say it.

– Because you're an interesting nuisance, Jeremy. You amuse me. Therefore, I let you live.

– Seems like you have fucked up royally, then. Saliva and poison flowed from Zahn's mouth. – The nuisance proved itself to be more trouble than you could handle.

– Heh, heh, it's certainly natural for you to think that way… But the confident aura surrounding you, is that fake, I wonder. I believe it is. It must have dawned on you that whoever is controlling our confrontations it isn't you?

Joyce picked a cigar from the biggest box on the table and lit it slowly, clearly enjoying himself. His eyes never left Jeremy.

– I told you you're amusing. That can be a lie, of course. Everything I've ever told you about my operations and my goals might be lies.

– I don't give a shit about your game. From now on you can play monopoly on death row.

– Mmmm, game, yes, of course it is a game, what isn't? Let me ask you a question then, my dear opponent…

– This is insane, Zahn mumbled.

A beyond insane bloodbath of a battle raged downstairs and they stood here, and had a conversation? He wished for the forces to come blazing. He wanted them to come *now*.

– That label, like all others, is a matter of viewpoint, Joyce said pleasantly. – It has no bearing in the real world. I'm assuming that you, as an intelligent being, can support that conclusion.

– Has it struck you that we're playing out the confrontation in… yeah, let's say an old James Bond movie? The super-villain thinks he holds all the cards and calmly explains the plot to the triumphant hero. The question is, naturally, who is the cliché and who is the reality.

– What do you expect to achieve? Zahn wanted so much to pull the trigger, pull, pull, pull, and never stop. – You must realize that the game is over.

It sounded so desperate, so pathetic.

– «The game is over, Blofeldt», Joyce cackled. – **Right before Bond dies in a hail of bullets.**

Jeremy felt like a boy again. The teacher asked triumphantly about today's lesson, and he was unable to respond.

– Back to my original question… Are you convinced I don't hold any cards, some you want to call?

Jeremy Zahn sensed the white-hot rage return. It always did when the sense of hopelessness was at its worst. He could hardly contain himself, stopping himself from charging the enemy.

– Where is Gwen? He almost shouted. – What have you done to her? You Satan, SATAN!

– The question, grammatically speaking is rather what *did* I do to her, but let that rest. To reply to your inaccurate question; as you have realized long ago, I did nothing to Gwen. I'm not doing anything. Gwen is here of her own free will, because she realized who she was, what she sees as important in life, what truly counts.

– You're lying… YOU'RE LYING

– She's here, she can tell you everything. You can hear everything from her mouth. What do you say, you little nuisance?

– H-here?

– Here, Joyce confirmed. – Don't be such a total hypocrite and pretend this is a surprise to you. You knew she would be in the line of fire, and you didn't care. That's typical for you.

The wave of distance and unreality kept growing in Zahn's line of sight. It threatened to devour him.

– I forgive you.

He heard the pleasant, well-known modulated voice, as if from far away. He hadn't heard her enter.

The weapon in his hand pointed at her, of its own volition, at the face he hardly recognized. It turned back and forth between the two targets, until he once more lowered it. She laughed softly.

Joyce spoke, and his words cut to the bone.

– Do you know what I told her before your timely arrival? «Say exactly what's on your mind». I knew what she would say anyway. I remember it well.

– What are you fucking TALKING about? Jeremy shouted.

Gwen spoke, and her words were soft like flower petals.

– I know you told the cops that everybody here, except Timothy, should be shot on sight. All the bugs.

– How do you KNOW? He screamed at her. – How can you know?

– A big, terrible bird told me, she replied soft and hard simultaneously. – What does it matter? You would've let them kill me, Jeremy. You've become that big and hard. And that's why I forgive you. Because you're about to grow up...

Joyce threw the cigar in his face. An attack that didn't just draw advantage of the fire Joyce had cultivated for minutes, but hit with such force in his temple that it made him dizzy. A kick and the gun flew from his hand. He struck out with his other hand and hit Joyce so hard that the other man flew across the room. Joyce dried the blood from his jaw, and rose with a satisfied grin.

– Not bad, he praised his opponent. – Can it be you don't know your own strength?

At the edge of his vision Zahn saw Gwen pick up the gun. She whistled while removing the clip, and then she threw it elegantly down the stairs.

– What... do you expect to achieve? Zahn wondered nonplussed. He turned to Gwen. – They're coming for you. You can kill me, and it won't serve you shit. YOU… you're just as guilty as him. You'll burn by his side.

– Poor Jeremy. She shook her head. – So little you understand, so little you know about yourself.

Jeremy threw himself at Joyce, snarling like a wild animal. They rolled over the floor. He struck and struck the enemy with fists heavy as sledgehammers. At some point he lost his body armor, and he hardly noticed. The fact that it fell off, totally ruined didn't surprise him, and even that realization failed to shock him. He kept pounding his opponent, hitting Timothy Joyce so hard, harder than he had ever hit anybody before, kicked anybody before, in a murderous attack beyond belief.

Joyce slapped him, pushed him away like he was a kid. Zahn landed hard, shook his head and fought his way up again. Joyce waited for him. Zahn feinted an attack and kicked out, fast as lightning with his left foot at the other's head. Joyce avoided it with a patronizing smile. If not for his bloody and swollen face one might have misunderstood, and believed he took a Sunday stroll. Zahn struck out again. Missed. And again. Missed again. Joyce grabbed him, lifted him up with one hand, and held him there. A cruel hit in the belly emptied his lungs of air. The other man shook him like a ragdoll.

– You don't have a chance in the world, Joyce thundered. – I know you'll see the light soon. I know. But you still need a lesson or two.

He threw Zahn through the air, across the room. Jeremy heard bones break. The soft carpet seemed to embrace him. First the carpet on the wall, then on the floor. How could Joyce be so strong? He wasn't that much taller, that much bigger. Jeremy felt a deep despair and shame. *I should've been dead. Why can't you just kill me?* Joyce kicked him. With his right foot. With his left foot. With his right foot again. Zahn raised his right arm in a desperate attempt to defend himself. Joyce kicked it at the wall. Tiny, desperate cries turned to one big scream. Joyce bent down. Strike followed strike, and it never seemed to end. Zahn didn't understand how he could still be alive, far less be more or less conscious. He gasped and sobbed in frustration and pain, and dull, distant joy while the beating kept going on and on and on.

Zahn crouched on the floor. Through pain, through mist he saw the two coconspirators bend down over him.

– I'll never join you, the beaten to a pulp heap spat. – Never, you ass…

Another strike.

– That statement isn't wrong, the large man commented, in yet another cryptic proclamation.

Like he always did, like he always was, a riddle, a devil in human form.

– You won't get away. To speak with the mouth filled with blood and skin demanded an impossible effort. Zahn didn't care. He had passed the stage, now, when such things mattered. – They'll take you and destroy you. He who laughs last, laughs best. Heh, heh.

A fist shot forward. Jeremy's head and neck were pulled up.

– You have great confidence in yourself and your place in the world. That's both a very right and very wrong observation.

Jeremy laughed and laughed. He was unable to stop.

– You're just an inflated ego, he laughed. – You're so crazy that you'll keep believe in your own infallibility when you sit on death row.

He stared defiant up into Joyce' terrible face, waited for death to come. The laughter faded, until it vanished completely. Didn't the face he knew so well, even better than his own… change? Didn't the wounds vanish as he watched? He was delirious. It was impossible, of course. But it seemed far less swollen to his foggy, crystal clear vision. Joyce smiled.

– You know I'll get away. It was a statement, very calm, but with a wrath Zahn never could have imagined. – You're shit under my heel, Jeremy, but you know that. I will quite simply walk out of here, and no one will stop me. Nobody can. Say it, Jeremy. Confession is good for the soul, everybody knows that. Say it. You'll feel better afterwards, I guarantee it.

The conviction came abruptly, like another blow to the head, with an uncomprehending expression in the wide-open eyes.

– You'll get away.

Jeremy started crying, and something was released within him. The crying shook his body, and pain haunted him.

Another pull, and the enormous face above him filled his entire vision. His eyes widened further. He gasped and stopped

breathing. For minutes, eternities, he died. The eyes above him…
*They changed color.* He saw it as clear as if he should have observed
it in full daylight, close up. The forehead seemed to expand. Just
a moment, before once more returning to normal. He wanted to
shake his head in shock. He didn't have the energy. Joyce smiled,
let go and rose. Eyes that had been green continued being blue.
Jeremy shook and shook his head. Everything whirled indistinct
in front of him. He had to be seriously injured, far more so than
he was willing to admit. Everything whirled and turned indistinct,
so terribly distinct. He hadn't seen Gwen for so long, and he still
didn't. She wasn't really here.

– Not much longer, now, she said huskily. He drowned in the
promise of her eyes. – Then we may be united once more.

– How can you live with him? He asked with a tortured voice. –
How can you? How can you?

– You're torturing yourself so, my Lord and Master. She patted
his hair. – Don't. Relax. Rest your troubled mind. It's time to
sleep, to sleep and dream….

He felt sick in his contempt. She seemed so wild and crazy, a
caricature of the woman he had known and loved. She would pay.
She would

Just then Joyce kicked him in the head, and everything turned
black.

A moment or an eternity, while he was drifting in and out of
consciousness, he heard them, he saw them.

– They're coming, my love.

She stood on her toes and kissed Joyce on the lips.

– We still got time, he said relaxed. He smiled pleasantly to
Jeremy. – Au revoir, old boy. I'm ready to start the great work.
There are just a few things I need to do first.

*He saw them, saw them disappear in a light in the air. He saw them wave
to him, and leave the room. He heard them walk down the stairs, no, he
heard steps ascend the stairs, trampling feet sounding too loud on the soft
carpet. He attempted to scream, but couldn't produce the slightest sound.*

Men and women in police uniforms rushed up the stairs and
spread out everywhere. His vision was filled with the sight of
uniforms. They stumbled around, kicked open doors to all rooms,
all closets.

– I've found our observer. One man knelt down while speaking in a radio and checked out the beaten body. – He looks like shit, but doesn't seem fatally wounded. Bring a stretcher anyway. Better safe than sorry, right.

– The room by the bookshelf, he said hoarsely. – I saw them walk in there. Joyce and… a woman.

Several officers looked at each other.

– There's no one there, now, one stated. – Not that it matters. If Timothy Joyce really is in the building, there's no way he'll get away.

– He'll get away…

He saw them glance at each other. It didn't matter. Nothing did.

Quite a while passed before they finally arrived with the stretcher. By then they had long since searched the building several times. It seemed like they had carried off absolutely everybody else, before they took care of him. Zahn sensed a bitter taste in his mouth. What if he had been critically wounded, goddamn it?

They carried him down the stairs, back the same way he had come with firespitting weapons so very long ago. How strange, he watched the patterns in the ceiling with perfect clarity. The scent, the stinking sweat, the stink of blood everywhere, of blood and death and life appeared to him with perfect clarity. He registered everything, but couldn't change anything. This was nothing new. This was the way it had always worked or not, for him. He had always showed great skill in demonstrating zero influence.

Jeremy Zahn fell, through the halls, down the final stairs, to one of the central halls, where the bodies rested in heaps.

Springsteen and Lasko waited outside, where the ambulances ran back and forth, left and arrived at an increasing number and speed. They said a few encouraging words every time another carcass was thrown into the hearse. A sign from the Chief, and Zahn's carriers stopped before the two.

– I see you made it, he grumbled. – That's good.

– What happened? Lasko asked.

Zahn opened and closed his eyes once.

– There was a bunch… coming at me from all sides. Joyce was there. I saw him…

– We haven't seen shit of him, Lasko complained, clearly nervous and very out of it. – People are still looking. They'll find him, just wait and see.

– Can he have escaped in a chopper? Zahn wondered tired.

– No choppers have departed where we haven't had complete control.

– He may have disguised himself and dressed like a cop…

– We're checking everybody leaving the area, and I mean everybody. Not a mouse gets out without security clearance.

– The bodies, too? The wounded?

– Now, you listen here… Lasko abruptly turned very red upstairs.

Springsteen stopped him with a hand. He turned towards the man on the stretcher.

– Some pal you've got. Good for you we have independent reports and photographic evidence of his presence. Otherwise you could have been in trouble, see?

He's not my friend, Zahn wanted to shout. He didn't have the strength.

– Instead it looks like you're the ones in trouble. Zahn managed a scornful grin. – Timothy Joyce is doing target practice on Los Angeles's finest - and walks away afterwards. Can you imagine the headlines tomorrow?

*I can.*

And he enjoyed himself so much that it hurt.

They threw him into the ambulance, fairly brutal. The door slammed shut. Two nurses, one female and one male started examining him in a professional, detached manner. Sirens filled the night. He stared at the ceiling. They injected him with painkillers. Icy pain was dulled in a distant mist. The pain didn't go away, but was just displaced. He didn't feel the pressure of the fabric below on his skin anymore. The world was a black hole. He didn't tailspin into it. He was there already. Sirens filled the night in the city of angels.

# CHAPTER TWO

## THREE YEARS BEFORE NOW - LONDON

He noticed the girl among countless others. The sun and the
night's flames showed in her hair, in her. So unlike him to express
himself… poetically, even in the mind. She stood out in a number
of ways. At least one way he couldn't name. She made him feel…
funny. A thoroughly strange feeling he didn't appreciate. He
was stuck in the morning traffic down from Piccadilly Circus.
She had placed herself at the corner outside the Plaza Cinema
Theater. The clear eyes scouted the area as if she was waiting for
someone. Not unreasonable that, with her looks. He noticed the
scar first, the small scar below the right eye. And he reacted to
that, in a good-natured way. She had an absolutely phenomenal
hair color, a mix of black and red/red blonde that was very
striking. And it seemed genuine, too. A stray thought only
enhanced when he came close enough to study her eyebrows.
They had the same color. Even the eyes had a special hue. All
in all she had extremely exotic features. Skin was fairly fair, but
clearly suntanned, a tan implying something quite different from
an early spring in London. That face and body, and he focused on
the scar, the defect.

She waved to him. No, that couldn't be right. She stared at
him with a smile radiating such heat that he lost his breath. He
shook his head in regret. He had Gwen, and she was more than
beautiful enough, but clearly a notch more ordinary.

The car in front of him stopped, and he was forced to stop
abruptly. He pushed the breaks so hard that his foot hurt. When
he looked back at the corner she wasn't there anymore. In many
ways it seemed like she had never been there. She had vanished
in smoke, in thin air, and no one else seemed to have seen it, seen
her.

She hadn't waved to him, of course, but to the man she was
about to meet, one on the sidewalk behind or to the side of the
car. He was suddenly quite relieved he hadn't returned her wave.
If the fiancée, or even worse, the husband had seen that, the guy

would probably misunderstand everything. It could have turned ugly, and that wouldn't do, especially not today, of all days.

Traffic didn't let up by the Nelson Monument at Trafalgar Square, not through Admirality Arch, or on the Mall by St. James's Park. It didn't let up, but there was progress, slow, uneven. There had been worse days. He drove along the park's left side on his way south. It was quite an ordeal of forced patience, until he could finally turn in on Broadway, and park in the VIP-garage at New Scotland Yard.

Tubbs, the desk Sergeant greeted him at the entrance, from his position behind the counter.

– I see you're early on the first day of your new job, sir.

Tubbs, a veteran close to retirement, could allow himself the slight sarcasm.

– I started out from home half an hour early, the other replied casually. – Better safe than sorry.

– That's just like you, sir. The Sergeant nodded without being too impressed.

Jeremy Zahn ignored the grumbling old man. He could do that, now, as the man made the youngest inspector in the annals of the British police.

The toilet was conveniently situated just before the major, inner hall. He walked there and stood before the mirror for a while, checking up on himself, taking his time righting and straightening the tie, brushing his suit and improving upon the details of his appearance. He made certain that the shave was sharp, and combed, once again, the dark brown hair.

He stopped in front of the door to the small office and admired the tag with his name on it. He opened the door and walked inside. Behind the desk sat a woman in uniform. He breathed in the sight of the corn-yellow hair, the fresh face color, the well-toned body when she rose. She had been pale and quite a wreck for days now. It happened every time she got her period. He dismissed the unpleasant memory and turned on the charm.

– You enjoy sitting there, he teased her.

– I'm so sorry, sir, I only wish to congratulate my new boss, the inspector.

– And I grant you that permission…

Gwen Talbot slipped into his arms and planted a wet kiss on his cheek.

He kissed her on her lips. She returned the kiss, hesitant at first, but then eagerly. She was still holding back a little, even when being alone with him, even in bed, but he would make her shape up. He had time and patience. And she was Superintendent Talbot's daughter.

– I'm so proud of you.

She glowed at him. She had clear, brown eyes.

He sat down behind the desk. It felt good, even better than he had imagined. She sat on the edge of the desk, looking at him.

– Do you know what?

– No, what?

– I saw your mother today.

He kept looking enigmatically at her.

– Oh, it wasn't really her, of course. A giggle, a nervous, but undeniably charming fix of a lock blocking her sight, before she continued, a bit tender. – But she looked a lot like her. The way she was before she… I almost doubted my own eyes. She would have been so proud of you today, Jeremy.

He nodded. The smile returned, first in him, then in her. She leaned heavily forward.

– So, what's the inspector's first order of business?

– The reception starts in half an hour or so, he said roguishly. – We can spare half that time, I reckon.

Eyes half closed. The mouth slackened. She moved closer to him. He pulled her to him, put her on her back on the desk. She put her arms around his neck and pulled him down.

The day turned out to be unusually successful. When the evening arrived and the two of them had dinner with Mr. and Mrs. Talbot, his prospective parents in law, it continued thus.

Abner Talbot had moved up in the world, and the family now lived in a luxurious apartment in Chelsea. Livery dressed servants served dinner. Everything proceeded extremely correct, with the exception of Abner on some rare occasions stealthily ate the birds holding them with his fingers. It fit well with Zahn's own experiences of the man. A thug remained a thug. Thoughts Zahn kept to himself, of course.

There were just the four of them, as Zahn had gathered. Mr. and Mrs. Talbot had warmed to his presence the last few months, but this was the final test. If they weren't pleased with what they saw, he didn't doubt they would break off the engagement. And Gwen wouldn't protest too much. She was an obedient and well-behaved daughter.

Mrs. Talbot didn't say much. She let Talbot speak. But she listened and evaluated all the more. All in all the setting was so old-fashioned one could easily and quickly go bananas. Zahn told himself he could take it. He had a career to protect.

– Unfortunately, I missed the ceremony today, Talbot rumbled, – but the way I heard it, it was both classy and beautiful.

– It most certainly was, sir, Zahn eagerly confirmed. – Everyone had something good to say about it afterwards.

The first course, a soup, was done. The dinner, the bird, was served. Wine was poured in the glasses. The bottles left at the table. The servants retreated for a while.

Abner attacked the large thighbone with knife and fork. He leaned over the table towards Jeremy.

– I have to say it pleased us all when your promotion came through, my boy, he said jovially. – Your future looks extraordinarily bright. Extraordinarily.

– Thank you, sir. Both Gwen and I are very happy.

– Understandable, it was chuckled. – Very understandable. And on that note, have you two thought more about giving us grandchildren?

The two youths exchanged looks.

– We have indeed thought about it, Jeremy replied, very relaxed. – Researched the matter, so to speak.

– We have decided that I will take a year's leave of absence, as soon as the opportunity and necessity presents itself, Gwen said, with slightly blushing cheeks. – We want children as soon as possible.

– Excellent, excellent. Abner turned into one big smile. – A pity the wedding is a whole month away, then. Well, well, patience will always be a virtue, I've always said.

The mother clutched her daughter's hand. Dessert was served. More bottles of wine were put on the table. All in all, a very nice evening. The end of a perfect day.

His future in-laws bid the happy couple farewell at the entrance. The lady kissed Jeremy motherly on the cheek. A servant drove their car to the gate. The two waved as they drove off, didn't blow the horn and suddenly found themselves in London's busy streets.

Gwen knocked her head at the soft seat pushing at her back.

– Jeez, I thought they would never let us go, she exclaimed.

– Let's not get too much into that, he admonished her. – We got our way. And even without giving obligatory promises. We have reason to be pleased.

She whined a few more minutes, but when he pulled her tight, and started kissing her when they stopped for a red light, she eventually softened completely.

– Where do we go tonight? She wondered with shining eyes.

– Why not take the town from east to west? Or north to south? Diagonally? All of the above?

– Let's go to the Magic Club, she said encouragingly.

– Okay, he said lightly. – Good idea.

Todd Winston, her ex boyfriend worked there. The two hadn't seen each other since the breakup. Jeremy had no reason to be jealous, no reason at all.

«Magic Club» was situated in Soho, in an adjacent street to Wardour Street. They left the car in a parking garage nearby and walked the short distance.

Friday night in London. People swarmed the streets. Spring hid in the shadows, right below the wet sidewalk. Suddenly high-spirited Gwen pulled close to him, and pushed her lips at his. A bit taken aback he held back. She laughed, quite pleased with herself.

A Chinese gang of juveniles stood at the corner by the entrance to «Chinatown». They leered at him.

– That's no way to treat a lady like that, the guy standing the closest, one step closer than the rest teased. – If she had been free…

Jeremy found his badge, and pushed it at the guy's face.

– Granted I am in a fairly good mood tonight, but not to the point that I can stand much of the bullshit you pale gooks are spouting. Is that a problem for you? Do you want to get on my bad side?

– Of course not, inspector, the other replied with a glaringly false respect. – Can't you take a joke? I was just kidding, damn it.

Jeremy left it at that. He imagined he heard their laughter long after they had disappeared, and almost regretted not having them arrested. The sarcastic glimpse in the eyes of the fucking gooks showed how little respect they had for coppers. That would change as he gained more influence, he promised himself that.

A uniformed patrolman stumbled towards him. He showed his badge once more.

– I only wanted to tell the youths a truth or two, constable, he said relaxed. – Nothing important.

– Yes, sir. The man stood straight. – Very well, sir.

Jeremy pulled himself together. His reaction had indeed been excessive. That some group of overconfident gook kids gave lip was just one of the big city's regrettable facts, nothing to blow steam over. He had far more important issues to deal with, far bigger grievances to overcome. He realized easily, searching himself, why he had reacted to such an overblown degree to such a trifle. The constant bowing and subservient behavior in relation to his future in-laws took its toll, more so than he had been willing to admit to himself.

He realized that the entire situation irritated him beyond belief. But he would have to hold out, at least for a considerable time ahead. In time alternative career-opportunities would reveal themselves. For the present time, more than ever, patience would pay off. Everything comes to those who wait. He had read that somewhere. It still sounded like a very good idea.

He patted Gwen's hair. It instantly led to the reaction he anticipated. She always melted easily. When she grabbed his hand and kissed it, her eyes shimmered anew.

The unrest stuck in his gut. It did that occasionally, to vanish quickly. Tonight, it stuck. He wondered if anybody followed them. If those triad recruits had decided to make him their special project, they would live to regret it.

They reached their destination, and a strange dizziness grabbed him. In the shimmering light everything seemed to float.

The light from Magic Club cast its shadow on the opposite sidewalk. In the alley, in the dark spot by the entrance he thought he glimpsed movement, a crouched figure. He thought about checking it out, but didn't find it worth it. A cab distracted him, and when he once again cast his attention at the alley, he saw nothing there. It had disappeared, now, what might not have been there at all. Arm in arm, side by side, the young couple walked through the door to Magic Club.

The foyer, even from the outside reeked even more of past elegance than Jeremy had imagined. The guard stood in the door. He opened it for Gwen with an elegant bow.

– Are you a member, sir? He asked Jeremy.

– It's all right, Gwen told him. – I'm a member.

She displayed her membership card. The receptionist looked at it, and handed it back with an amiable smile.

He stopped Jeremy when he wanted to walk by.

– Are you a member, sir? He asked, just as amiable.

– No! Jeremy snarled. – What's this, a scene from Jeremy Beadle Show?

– You may pass, sir. Have a nice evening.

Zahn mumbled something unintelligible. Sometimes he had an overwhelming feeling that the world had made it its project to *bother* him.

In the reception area everything went smoothly, though. The woman behind the counter showed herself to be the very incarnation of kindness. They wrote their names in the logbook, handed over their coats and could continue into the shadowy, smoke-filled locales.

The roulette tables were placed in a line on the right from the door, and far into the first room. To the left the line of blackjack tables stretched into the gray air. They did the scenic tour. In this house was also played Punto Banco, and at the back of the room - Poker. Jeremy stopped, almost subconsciously. He had no idea why, but he noticed one of the players there. Something was familiar about him. The man won big, but that wasn't why Jeremy had noticed him. That came later. Not the face either, hidden in shadows. Jeremy had no idea what had made him react, no idea at all.

Todd Winston met them in front of the stage, where tonight's entertainment was about to begin. He kissed Gwen on her cheek, and shook Jeremy's hand amiably. Very amiably.

– I want you to enjoy yourselves tonight, he emphasized. – I want you to see yourselves as my personal guests.

Time had flown today, Jeremy felt. Now, when night arrived, time seemed to float more. Everything turned more relaxed and laidback. But there were distractions. He observed the whirling fans in the ceiling. He could swear they were whirling at an ever-greater speed. The air pressure made hurricanes below them. He shook his head irritably. That had to be his overactive imagination.

– Two new players to table number ten, the floor manager declared. He shouted loud, but cultivated, and not the least with correct, very high-class Oxford English. – Two new players to table number ten.

– That's us, Todd said slick, very slick. He grabbed Zahn's arm. – I took the liberty of putting us on the list. You don't mind, darling?

– I don't play poker, Gwen replied sourly.

Jeremy sensed tendencies towards a charged mood within. He admitted that to himself. What he felt had to be anticipation. There was… something in the air. Something hidden. He couldn't identify it, but it was present, here in this room.

A woman walked elegantly down the stairs from the upper floor, where the private, extremely high stakes games were played. The skin-tight, revealing dress was like another layer of skin on the great, curvy body. It was *her,* the woman from the corner by Plaza Cinema Theater only a few, short hours ago.

There were four men at the table when Jeremy and Todd joined the game. No one made a formal presentation.

– We're playing traditional Five Card Draw at this table, Winston told him.

– That suits me fine, Zahn replied.

Informality dominated at these games. The four nodded to the newcomers, and that was that. The game continued. Jeremy sat right across the man he had noticed earlier. He couldn't focus on the game, on the wish to wipe the grin from Todd Winston's mouth. Something indefinite kept distracting him. Not firehair. Not Gwen's sour disposition behind his back. Of course not. Women or women's wiles had never distracted him.

– You're Timothy Joyce, he stated startled, while staring paralyzed at the man right across the table, a man who couldn't hide his size even while sitting.

He towered above everyone here. Those standing behind him seemed small in comparison. Everyone in the room did.

The man nodded with a humoristic smile.

– So, you, too, recognize our famous guest? Winston expressed with a surprised expression. – Isn't it exciting? I, for one have for quite some time, now, longed to play against him. It's said he's an excellent player.

– That isn't all that is being said about him, Gwen stated sarcastically.

Jeremy easily heard the brush of fear in her voice, and didn't object to that. Joyce had a reputation as a gambler, that was true. But it was totally subordinated to all his other dark acts and the other rumors flying around about him. Hidden by the insecure laughter by and around the table, Jeremy was shaking. He couldn't free himself from the impression that the walls were moving, that the air itself was shaking. First the walls, then the surroundings seemed to be fading. They sat by the entrance to a dark tunnel, and there was nothing behind them. Air floated in bright and dark smoke, the mood inside turned electric. The other three eventually introduced themselves. He forgot their names instantly.

Winston, like the perfect host, entertained and kept up the mood around the table, as the extremely articulate man he was. Zahn would have scowled at the asshole, but he didn't even react when Gwen bent down and kissed her former flame. He sensed Joyce's stare. This in spite of the fact that the infamous man hardly even looked in his direction. Not even when it was his turn to bet did the good Timothy send him more than a casual look.

But he stared anyway.

Jeremy had always been good at recognizing patterns, having an eye for details, something that had served him well on his way up the ladder in the London Police force.

– Goddamn, Winston conversed willingly, with a stinking cigar hardly leaving the broad and stinking gap, – we're living in interesting times. I mean, what *is* reality, and what *is* illusion? What *is* the difference between the extremes, and everything in-between?

– What do you mean? One of the players without a name asked.

– It goes like this… Winston shifted in his chair. – We live today in the most sophisticated age humanity has ever had the pleasure of experiencing. But it's certainly resulting in more than a few peculiarities. Case in point: The stories about aliens and flying saucers, and revenants, and similar. Perhaps there is something to them, perhaps not. My point, my claim, is that we never, *never* will be able to find conclusive evidence of their objective existence. Computer and communication systems have become so advanced, with such unforeseen possibilities that they can produce the incredible on an assembly line. And it's increasingly difficult to expose frauds. We're fucked, ladies and gentlemen. What if a humanoid octopus is levitating in the air before us right this moment? Levitating right there, in front of us. We can see and touch it, but we can't tell if it is an illusion, a fake.

Jeremy didn't really believe the man meant anything in particular with his words. He just enjoyed showing off.

Perhaps everything can be described as a kind of mirage, he thought. Perhaps not a fake, but definitely an illusion.

– The old gods? The host continued unabated, while winning a substantial amount of chips. – If there was any substance to the old stories, and they appeared today, they would hardly be more than ridiculous curiosities, an evening on a talk show, and then… good riddance.

– I, on my part, am interested in *people,* Timothy Joyce said lightly. – What's shaping us? Is it a chain of coincidences, or one single, fateful moment? Are we perhaps forming ourselves, our own fate?

– The majority are just sheep, following the leader. Winston chuckled.

– I don't necessarily disagree. Joyce nodded.

He stared at a point in the air for a moment, as if he was considering something.

– There are still places on Earth, where humans can be humans, he said distantly, as if tasting every word. – I've always been attracted to the desolate, remote places, where there can be no major human settlement.

Winston looked as if he very much wanted to comment on this, but he left it alone. The game hardened, and even he had enough to do focusing on it, instead of playing motormouth.

It was eventually clear to everybody that the true poker wasn't played with cards. Jeremy couldn't follow the cards. He lost constantly, and felt the sour taste of defeat in his mouth.

– You're not a completely unknown person, Todd, Joyce said

softly. – People are talking about you.

This would have to be some of the worst things one could say to Todd. The implication that he was nothing more than a moderately well-known person, all in all quite the mediocrity hit him hard. One could practically see how he fumed and shrank in the chair.

– What are you saying?

He did a lot of stuff that wouldn't stand the light of day. His... business partners would have a fit if they heard these activities were spoken about, even during a casual conversation.

– One of several rumors is that you have a twin brother stashed away somewhere. He's supposed to be stark, raving mad, the way I heard it.

– Oh, *that?* Todd blew his nose, visibly relieved. – There was actually a maniac claiming he was *me* a few years back. He won't be released among decent humans the first hundred years.

But Joyce had gotten under his skin. That grew increasingly clear, as the game progressed. The people standing around the table, following the game, could hardly take their eyes from Joyce. His reputation, the hypnotic personality caught them helplessly in his web. What was spoken about, concerning him, was more than most could take or even take in. What was whispered wasn't spoken about.

The three players without name pulled out within a ten-minute timeframe. By then they had on several occasions exchanged money for chips. Nobody took their place. The three seemed to just fade away in the smoke and the shadows. The game continued.

Half an hour after that Jeremy lost his last, few chips. He reckoned he should feel a certain pride because he had lasted as long as he had. The thought didn't make him feel any better.

Joyce and Winston kept playing. Jeremy remained by the table, unable to divert his attention from what was happening. Gwen made several failed attempts to get his attention, to «pull» him away from there. Sometimes, in isolated moments, he wasn't even sure she was actually there at all, even though his eyes did catch the beautiful female form occasionally. He followed, as if bewitched, what happened at the table. Joyce played strangely, just like Zahn wanted to play, like he would have played... if he had dared.

Joyce bluffed and teased, teased and bluffed. He could lose for a long time and seemingly be in a bind: But he always landed on his feet. When Winston was convinced that he was bluffing, he showed a superior hand. And when no cards were shown… nobody knew anything. No one was the wiser. Slowly, inevitably Todd turned edgy, shabby and uncertain in his play. Finally, he pushed, with a bitter, aggressive grimace, as an acknowledgment of defeat, his last stack of chips across the table, and they joined the opponent's giant heap.

– You were quite honestly lucky as a pig in a decisive moment, he exclaimed. – If you hadn't beaten my four tens, everything would have been different.

– Have you read «The Art of War» by Sun Tzu? Joyce wondered, in a light, hardly audible ironic voice.

– I don't waste my time reading stupid books, was the snarling reply.

– The quote in question is quite important in the philosophy of war, according to Sun Tzu, Joyce drawled.

He waited patiently, allowed Zahn to deliver the killing blow.

– «Every battle is won before it is fought», Jeremy said, filled with scorn.

Winston stood up, bowed, fooling nobody, and vanished behind a heavy curtain, striving to keep up appearances.

– He can afford to lose even this considerable amount of money, Joyce said, turning to Jeremy. – Money, when push comes to shove, when you get down to the fundamentals, means absolutely nothing.

The two of them were all alone there, by the table. The wind blew through the dark tunnel (weren't all tunnels dark?). Which way it blew Jeremy couldn't say.

Zahn wanted to shout with a mighty cry: «You're under arrest». Even in his mind it sounded silly and so very, very lame.

– And then there is you, Jeremy. You haven't lost that much. But you lose all the time, don't you? The way you play, you'll always lose.

– I haven't really had the time you've had to practice, Jeremy replied curtly.

(so very lame)

It sounded like he was apologizing.

Joyce smiled obligingly.

– You were hardly anything more than a nuisance throughout the game, Jeremy, and nuisances win nothing in this world.

– You trashed good ol' Todd, and he didn't exactly play it safe.

Zahn spoke aggressively, now. The trickle down his spine was cold, very cold, and for one moment he feared he wouldn't be able to hide it. For one moment, one moment there, he had forgotten he sat face to face with one of the most dangerous creatures on Earth.

Joyce laughed, a hard, rich laughter free of fear. The eyes, the hypnotic, desensitized/sensitized eyes caught Jeremy once more, and didn't let go.

– There's no discernible difference between small and big fights, the obviously brilliant man said even more kindly. Zahn sensed a sting of admiration he knew would always persist. – The game, our minor moment of pleasure, and the game of the world, is the same. There are ghosts and shadows. To succeed isn't difficult. You need to know who your enemies are - and act accordingly - that's all.

– And the Enemy is? Zahn wondered, his voice thick with sarcasm.

– Everybody working against you, and what you happen to see as your agenda, consciously or unconsciously. Your neighbor, your competitor - whoever might stand in your way. The entire world is your enemy.

– Not the most original viewpoint I've heard, Zahn stated.

He felt a little better. The other man's voice had a subtext of anger this time, and Joyce instantly seemed more human.

Joyce spoke again, and once again the impression was turned on its head.

– The *game* is the Enemy. Joyce sat still. It just appeared like he was leaning closer. – He or she who doesn't master it, who isn't playing one's own game is doomed to lose. You'll eventually realize this obvious truth.

He did indeed sit still, contrary to appearances and Jeremy's imagination. It didn't matter. He seemed just as threatening. But why? If Zahn hadn't known better, he would have claimed the notorious criminal had just given him a bit of advice, but that would have been even more insane?

Then he said something that had to make anyone's imagination run wild.

– Good ol' Todd was very much correct. The world is a puzzle, a whirl of impressions, a Chaos, where even Sherlock Holmes, if he had truly lived, would have had trouble seeing the big picture. This in spite of him clearly possessing the tool to do so.

Jeremy had been an «admirer» of Sherlock Holmes since childhood. «Do you mean the opium?» He wanted to throw at the other man.

But he was unable to utter a sound.

– What's reality and what's fantasy? The other man grinned. – Is there any objective criteria… or is everything a matter of viewpoint? Aren't most people fooled by an illusion, tricked into believing they have a useful life? Perhaps there's no substance behind it…

Zahn backed off figuratively. He forced himself to sit still, but he cringed inside. Didn't the snake sit there throwing metaphysics at him? Jeremy had always refused to even acknowledge such nonsense.

– You must be bored beyond words, he snarled.

The laughter haunted him while he sat still, and Joyce rose, and vanished in the smoke and shadows.

Zahn rose. He walked around for a while, without purpose. He didn't see Gwen anywhere. Or Joyce. Or Winston. And he didn't care. He hadn't even registered that Gwen had left the spot behind him. And he didn't care.

Todd had a lot going for him here, he had to admit that. Just to be licensed to operate an ordinary casino was hard enough, even though less-rigid rules had been implemented a few years back. But this was definitely beyond what the British Gaming Commission usually accepted. A casino with entertainment and such included. The owners, those pulling the management's strings clearly had a lot of power. Zahn sensed a quivering excitement when he sat down by one of the blackjack tables. The girl with the firehair sat down only two seats to his left.

He decided, without that much of an inner struggle, to make use of his reserves, and pulled two fifty-pounds notes from his pocket. He threw them at the table and got twenty-five-pounds chips in return. He placed one of them in a «shoe», and thereby participated in the game. It was that simple.

They played standard European casino blackjack. All players played against the bank. Aces counted one or eleven. Face cards ten. The bank had to draw on 16 or lower, stay on 17 or higher. The bank got one open card and each player two open cards each, before the players might get the opportunity, according to certain rules, to increase the bet.

It seemed simple and straightforward enough, even from a kid's point of view. Thus, it irritated him even more that he had never really mastered it.

Half an hour later he sat there sweating hard, and had to pull himself together for his hands not to shake. He had won over 150 pounds, and was well underway to win back what he had lost during the poker game. If he didn't make a fool of himself. He was so excited that he could hardly think.

He sensed her warm leg against his own. She sat so far away that it was impossible for her to reach him. He felt her leg anyway. She teased him with her toes, her eyes full of promise when he finally mustered the courage to meet them. She promised nothing, where she sat and treated everybody around her like empty air, like dirt under her feet. Her sovereign play, her patronizing attitude enhanced the sense of being just that, in the others. Jeremy had a painful hard-on. So bad that any position he tried out was highly uncomfortable. He pretended he was with her in a dark, closed off room. That was the only thing on his mind.

The game turned, and he just sat there, like an automaton, without independent thought. He lost. First, he lost everything he had won back, then his last hundred pounds. It had happened so quickly, in a whirl of smoke. Had he just lost fifteen games in a row without doing anything but sit there with a silly look on his face? Sixteen, thirty-two, what difference did it make? He was broke. Dusted. He would have to *walk* home. No cab tonight. He shook himself, raised his shoulders defiantly. This wasn't the end of the world. He had put aside quite substantial funds the last few years. One single evening of losing didn't matter. He would win it back the next time. What counted was losing or winning over time. And he had always been skilled in the game of patience, in the one stone at a time game.

He sat on a stool in the bar and drank. It didn't bother him. He had always been able to drink anybody else to oblivion. Even the strongest liquor faded like dew before the morning sun within him.

She sat down in front of him, on a stool strangely available. All the rest were taken. He saw that as damn strange, and suddenly felt even lighter in the head.

She had green eyes, not fire-colored, not like they had seemed in the caress of the setting sun. But fire still danced in them.

– You were a very naughty boy today. He drowned in the protuberances dancing around the beautiful head of hers, and didn't know what the hell she was talking about. – You didn't wave to me…

His eyes narrowed. She found a cigarette, and put it between her lips. He fumbled for his lighter, pulled himself together and lit the cigarette for her. He had no intention of keeping this up, of behaving like a starstruck teenager.

– You waved to me, he stated.

A moment he saw something in the dark look that could be interpreted as fear, and it comforted him. She wanted to play? That was all right as far as he was concerned. He didn't mind playing a bit. Not with her.

He put a hand on one of her muscular thighs.

– Remove the sweaty hand, she spat.

He didn't, and began to move it up and down. She didn't do anything to keep it from happening, and didn't say more. After a while she slipped down from the stool. The beast-like body pulled close to his. She grabbed the hard growth in his groin and tightened her grip, so clever, so devilishly skilled. He came, instantly. Helplessly, despairingly and bewitched.

The smile transformed her face when she, very pleased, wet her lips with a neat, tempting tongue. He breathed. She kissed him, just like he had wanted her to do, like a satanic true, redhead witch.

She led him off with her hand in his, and her consistent seductive smile.

They didn't go straight to the dark, closed-off room. She led him out on the dance floor, and he enjoyed dancing tight to the full, enticing body. They talked as well. All the time. In the dark lit theater hall. Just shadows there. On the stage and off. He enjoyed her company in a way he had previously been unable to imagine. She seemed to be sensing his thoughts and anticipating his needs before he thought them, and knew what he needed, far more understanding than Gwen had ever been.

Gwen saw somebody disappear around a corner, somebody she believed she recognized.

– Jeremy? She cried out, clearly uncertain.

She halted when she realized it was Timothy Joyce standing there. He stood with his back at the wall, with his arms folded across his chest. He didn't seem in any way threatening. She shivered.

– I've looked at you the entire evening, he said pointedly.

– Oh? I haven't noticed.

– You're playing the game, he laughed. – That's good. That makes me proud. I knew you weren't the cute, pure and virtuous girl everybody thinks you are.

– W-what do you mean?

The mask of superiority left her then, like the air in a punctured wheel.

– I can show you, he whispered aloud, and very seductive. – Come with me.

– No!

She shook her head hard. There was something about him, so familiar and terrifying.

But he just stood there, relaxed and non-threatening, so very calm. She trusted him.

What did he truly want from her? How could he want anything from her, an insignificance like her? He who had the entire world to choose from.

What did she have to lose anyway? They were alone here. Nobody would hear her if she cried for help. He could take her by force if he wanted. But he didn't. She stared at him with helpless fascination in her eyes.

The thought sneaked up on her.

What... did she want from him?

– You want to come with me, he stated, and there wasn't a sliver of doubt in his poignant voice, the entire terrifying creature.

– And learn all the world's secrets. You know you don't have anything to fear from me, and you know that after the mask of fear is removed from your eyes, you'll never want to return to your old life.

Her old life already. So quickly, so brutally everything was turned on its head. Nothing mattered. Nothing from her former, virtuous life. He was right. She knew him, like he knew her.

– I'm curious, she admitted, – but don't believe you have fooled me into anything.

He did nothing physical to make her obey. He turned and left. The short conversation was terminated. His laughter echoed within her, in the old, dusty hallways. She said goodbye to her old self, and followed him into the shadows.

The room smothered them, dark and tight. He glimpsed her and the bed. Nothing besides.

– My name is Jeremy, he said hoarsely. – What's yours?

– Your name is Jeremy, she sang. – Mine is Monica.

The sensuous grin filled his mind.

– It doesn't matter, now, does it? She said. – You know me, know how I feel, how I taste…

She pushed her tongue into his mouth, let him taste some more. She ascended and descended, while resting her hips at his groin. It had been wet and cold down there. Heat returned in a moment, raw, painful.

– … know how I touch, how it is when I tighten my cunt around you. You've always known.

He grabbed her arms and tightened his grip.

– Yes, take me! I want you to take me.

He pushed her away. She returned, fumbled his belt, while his arms fell down. He sensed it in every hair when she pulled his pants down his thighs.

– Little boy wants me anyway, I see. I thought so.

She writhed close to him, writhed out of the tight dress. He had been about to help her with it. Irritated he grabbed his own clothes, pulled in them, tore them off. They were torn several places. He fell back on the bed. She crawled on top of him, naked and hot. And the entire time he sensed the glimpse of contempt in the depth of her eyes.

He grabbed her arms, tightened his grip, and held her, while she nailed herself on him. A content, lazy look spread across the entire, oval-shaped face.

– Yes, little boy, she whispered, – let yourself go. Become a big boy.

They rolled gasping over on the side and remained that way, chest to chest, while tight muscles moved hips closer and farther away. It happened fast. She tightened around him, skilled and experienced, and he emptied himself, completely uncontrolled.

She put her head on his chest and sighed content.

– I'm good, I know you think so, she mewed in a deep, thorough state of satisfaction. – I know you want to keep me. The question is whether or not you'll be able to.

– Whore! He exclaimed. – Tramp.

– Thank you, she replied teasingly. – Spoken like a true bourgeois.

He threw her off him. So rough and brutal that she risked being seriously injured. He didn't care, and disappointment tore into him when she landed on the floor, elegantly on her feet. She started dancing in front of him, right away, taking her time, swinging her hips softly, pointing her nipples, her pouting lips at him, but the way he experienced it, it didn't take long until she was once more between his legs. Supple, strong hands started handling his soft limb. She lowered her mouth, sneaked her lips around the thudding head. His body tightened by itself. It wouldn't take long, before he would come in her warm, moist mouth. He sat up and pulled her head up after the firehair. He put her on her belly, and jumped on the supple body, pushing it down. She tried to pull away. He grabbed her harder, buried a fist in her hair and held a hand over her thick lips. She grabbed a bedpost, but if she attempted to get away, she didn't try very hard. He pushed himself into her. She moaned half choked. The body froze at first, but then it turned soft and compliant.

– Shut up, he snarled. – *Shut up!*

His body slipped back and forth over the sweaty thighs. She was clearly excited, it wasn't his imagination or wishful thinking, and that excited him horribly. He pushed forward. His grip slipped. He pushed even harder, and felt his control slip and grow simultaneously.

– *That's* more like it. Her voice sounded incredibly clear to him, in-between the gasps and the moans released through her lips. –

43

That's better. Much better.

No reason anywhere, it screamed inside him a few minutes later.

Hours, days, he couldn't tell at first. He rested alone on the bed, not recalling exactly when she had left him. Two insanely huge, wonderful green eyes still stared down at him in contempt. A horrible scream chased him out of bed. He pulled on his clothes and they got even more torn and rumpled. The tie was nowhere to be found and he gave up finding it, didn't give a fuck about it. He stumbled through the dark and fumbled along the wall until he found the door handle, and pushed himself out in the hallway. As he ran the corridor slowly turned brighter, but never bright. He heard *shots*. And more screams.

Shadows slipped close to him. He reacted slow, very slow. An amoeba with its soft limbs attempted to swim through quicksand and was stuck.

They grabbed him, pushed his head into the wall, and led him off. Dizziness overwhelmed him and paralyzed him. They had put him out of commission and had done so ridiculously easy. Blood flowed down his face from a cut on the forehead. He was taken to the main gambling hall, the biggest hall in the building. Everything was just white there, blinding white. The previously muted lighting had been supplanted with bright lamps. The entire emergency aggregate had been turned on. Flash. His vision glowed through red fluid. He blinked to clear his vision and realized what was happening. He didn't understand shit.

The casino was being robbed, and at the center of it all was Timothy Joyce, dominating the stage.

There was no reason anywhere. His associates had been posted all over the room. In all probability they had taken control of the entire casino. The confidence evident in every one of Joyce's moves, more than suggested the control was total. Though Jeremy imagined the man would show the same amount of confidence no matter the situation. Jeremy looked within, without, until he was able to see the two by the outlaw's side. Monica stood there proud, with her mouth formed in a smile. What was the point? There wasn't any, it couldn't be. Zahn was overwhelmed by a sense of total escapist paralysis. Nothing felt real or as if it was actually *happening*.

He saw Gwen, acknowledged her existence. Gwen was on the

outlaw's other side, and she in no way resembled a prisoner. That, in many ways, seemed like the most insane of it all.

She carried a gun, and a man crouched at her feet. Her entire attitude, her make up, the impression she gave away, had changed. She dressed the same, looked the same, and that made the transformation she had gone through in the short time since he had last seen her even more unbelievable. The face was, feature by feature, the same as he remembered. Even the sum of the parts hadn't changed. Zahn shook his head, and kept doing so, figuratively speaking, in the upcoming minutes.

– Ah, Jeremy, there you are, he heard Joyce cry out. – Then we're all here, I assume?

– We're all here, Monica confirmed.

Zahn didn't really listen. The brief interaction was just on par with the rest of the insanity transpiring here, everything intruding on his life this evening. He didn't really see the masked men and women carrying the heavy sacks filled with money, he just registered it in a way. It seemed like a sensible sight during a robbery. It was just that none of them seemed to be in a hurry of any kind. They even took their sweet time, it seemed. If there was any chance of police forces charging the premises, one saw no fear of that happening in the robbers' faces or body language.

They had thrown him on the floor with the other guests, he recalled. A dot of nothing, a sack too heavy to move, lost in a gray, blackish haze. He couldn't recall that he somehow had sat up.

Winston sat timidly and quietly a few people to the left. In this time and place Jeremy couldn't even send a few nasty thoughts in his direction. Not because of the man's lost arrogance, not for anything. He was merely another, random face in a cabinet of pale wax dolls. Timothy Joyce had them all in the palm of his fist.

Joyce alone. No one else was needed. He did it, by his own power. The man radiated a crushing confidence, a reddish aura, causing everybody else's to shrink.

Zahn blinked. What was he thinking? He shook his head in irritation. Aura? He had never seen such nonsense before, far less believed in it. The strangely blinding light, and the hit to his head, had made him quite dizzy. That was all there was to it.

– Honored guests… Joyce spoke softly. Everybody heard him. –

We have now filled most of our shopping carts. Just a few items now remain, until we can leave you in peace.

Jeremy stared at Gwen. He felt strangely calm, almost relaxed. That she stood there, with a gun in her hand, that she in strange ways had been somewhat… transformed into one of the robbers, he didn't see that as any stranger than anything else happening in this place, this… *cursed* place. So different from the street outside. It had always had a ghostly quality as far as Zahn was concerned, but nothing compared to here, now. So far outside time and space.

She approached him, the stranger. She stared at him, not unkindly, with an expression impossible to interpret, in the doll-like face. He couldn't do it, that's for sure. He would have said it was admiration, adulation… if he hadn't known better.

She stood at least ten steps away, but in spite of this, and all the noise, he heard her well the moment her lips moved.

– You don't understand at all, she said, filled with sorrow. Before turning more certain, happier. – But you will, I promise you that.

The insanity just kept building. Nothing had any meaning.

A signal from Joyce, a move with his little finger, and his people started moving. Jeremy was grabbed, with Winston and a few others, and led off. To another, smaller room. Jeremy hadn't been here before. It was probably exclusive to the employees. And… the casino's sentries. The video screens covered an entire wall. The mechanical eyes covered every spot and corner of the building, within and without. This was supposed to be one of the most secure casinos in London. Perhaps that's why Joyce had struck here. He certainly didn't need the money, but perhaps he had decided to teach somebody a lesson, a lesson in correct behavior. *Go and sin no more.*

The outlaw approached Winston.

– You're now going to give me the combination to your hidden safe, Todd, where most of today's and the week's income is stored. I'd say it's stupid of you not to get rid of the money the day you get it. Haven't you learned that banks are *the* most secure place in the world for storing money?

– Even if any of your somewhat far-fetched claims had any basis in fact, I would certainly not have told you anything, Winston replied with both shiver and contempt in his voice. He stared the other unexpectedly in the eyes. – Kill me, and you won't learn anything either. You don't have time to torture me. It looks like you will have to forget the bonus.

– I wonder what you will say if I first shoot you in one kneecap, and then the other. What will you say if I shoot off your BALLS?

Joyce did not raise his voice. It just sounded that way. He quite simply emerged like the incarnation of calm.

– GET ON TO IT, Winston howled, – GET ON TO IT, YOU DAMN…

He broke off. Not because any threatening move on Joyce's part. The outlaw quite simply turned his back on ol' Todd and left him.

Winston remained rigid. Everybody else held their breath. Joyce hadn't made any threatening move, but that could certainly come anytime, either from him or any of his coconspirators.

– Well, Joyce sighed, – it was fun for as long as it lasted…

Winston couldn't hold back a relieved and also triumphant smile.

– Time to open the damn vault. Get to it, boys and girls. Time is running out. You know the combination.

– WHAT!

Todd turned deadly pale. If there was something he hadn't expected, it was something like this. For some reason it hit him far harder than any threat of death and mutilation had done. He looked like he had fallen through the cracks. Jeremy knew that feeling well. He had hardly experienced it before tonight. Another rabbit, no, another *elephant* pulled out of the hat. Another psychological exercise in futility. Jeremy feared the next step. He did. Feared it.

Less than a minute later the remaining gang members re-entered the room, carrying sacks with the money from the vault. It wasn't… fraud. The sacks were transparent.

– How did you pull this off? Winston asked Joyce in bottomless despair. He seemed totally out of it. – We've just tested our new, rock solid security system.

– In all modesty, I *will* tell you one thing, Todd, Joyce replied pleasantly, – Presidents can be assassinated, and nations may fall. There isn't much I can't do, and not a single drop of rain falls in the world I'm not told about. Information is the key. Information is power.

Winston seemed to grow even paler after that. Jeremy actually felt kind of sorry for him just then.

– For the next post on the program.

Monica had placed herself by a closet, the place they stored chips and such. Suddenly everybody's attention was directed at her. Like a performing artist, with a swift, deliberate move, she opened the closet door.

The closet seemed empty, completely empty. There was nothing inside the eye could see. Jeremy saw Todd's eyes grow even wider, and froze, chilled to his depths.

– I will now do one last magic trick, Timothy Joyce declared, as pleasantly as ever. – The end of tonight's entertainment, I'm afraid.

And then he grabbed the dull, indifferent Todd Winston, dragged him to the closet, and threw him inside. The door closed with a bang. Winston *screamed*. It was the most horrible sound Jeremy Zahn had ever heard. The scream from the valley of death continued for a fraction of a second longer... until it seemed to be cut off. All in all, it had probably lasted about a second. Not more. Perhaps far less.

Zahn went nuts. He threw himself at Joyce with an insane howl hardly less impressive than the piece of art Winston had performed a second earlier. Jeremy had always believed it was just on film people behaved like this, this stupid. But here he did the same, making a fool of himself.

Joyce struck him down in an elegant, crushing move, so much bigger, stronger and supple.

– I stand corrected, we've got time for an encore.

Jeremy lay on his back, paralyzed, half unconscious. He glimpsed the barrel being pointed at him. But there was no fire. Did the huge man hesitate? That would truly be insane.

Joyce shot him twice in the chest. Pain cut through him. Why did he feel anything? He wasn't supposed to feel anything, feel such pain. He had always read that people with gunshot wounds didn't feel anything until a long time after the actual injury. To die was said to be painless. It was being alive that hurt.

People left the room. No more shots were fired. A few of the guests (of the casino that couldn't be robbed, like Titanic couldn't sink) remained after the robbers had left, but they didn't move.

48

They seemed just as dead as Zahn was convinced that he was. His final thought before he died was the closet. He stared at the closet. He stared inside it. Hardly saw anything else, sensed anything else. Almost overlooked the sight of Gwen leaving the room by Joyce's side. The closet was the death approaching him. The door had slid open, soundlessly, unnoticeable. There was nobody inside anymore, nothing there, except the stacks of chips Jeremy had always known had to be there. Todd Winston, no matter what one felt about the man… had vanished into thin air, dissolved into the thin haze rising from the gray blood flowing from Jeremy's body and onto the floor.

# CHAPTER THREE

## SIX DAYS IN THE CITY OF ANGELS

Again, once again, time and time again, he woke up to the sickening hospital smell. The bright sunlight through the open window merely enhanced the sense of total helplessness. The shock remained within. It clung to him like wet paper. He stayed in bed. Weak and depressed he rested, somewhat on his back, in a timespan feeling like hours, but was hopefully just a few minutes. Slowly, but not at all as painful as he had imagined, his body started to move, virtually of its own accord. He cursed it. His mouth moved in soundless spells. He shook and writhed in ever more intense movement, as if the wet paper was really there, as if it had substance, name and form. He tore off the hospital gown, tore off the wires and electrodes they had stuck to his body, probably setting off a silent alarm somewhere. It didn't concern him. Not in any way that mattered.

He crossed the floor, to the closet naked. He stood there for a while, leaning his head against the wall. Another while. He felt good. Unexpectedly so. He had been given a very rough treatment last night, but he realized that the problem was in his head, not in his body. He looked into the closet. Nobody but him had their personal belongings there, but he had. All his belongings.

He dressed quickly, without fuss. With the first, minor clothes in place he paused momentarily, taking stock of himself. A little bit of discolored skin, that's all, the only physical memory he had from the night before. He could hardly see anything else of injuries when placing his tall, skinny, powerful body in front of a wall mirror. It felt both exhilarating and a little strange.

Before leaving the room, he glanced at his medical chart. He picked it up from the bedpost, and almost instantly shook his head. This had to be a mistake. It said he had been admitted with broken bones and major internal bleeding. Somebody had fucked up royally. The description had to concern the man in the other bed. He looked really in a bad way. Actually, all other patients here seemed to be quite ill. None of them had woken up from the noise he had made. They hadn't merely switched his journal with another's, but also placed him in the wrong room to boot.

He entered the corridor, wasted several minutes waiting for the elevator, finally got fed up waiting, and used the stairs. He felt a certain stiffness in his limbs then. But not more than what was to be expected. Far less, actually. The way Joyce had beaten up on him he should have been half dead. He liked the thought of that, enjoyed the fact that he was able to take far more punishment now than three years ago. What sometimes felt like yesterday, other times like an eternity ago. Timelessness had haunted every one of his seconds since then.

A single female nurse sat behind the counter, tapping the keyboard. He told himself that this was necessary. If not, they would probably put him on a wanted poster or something, and he didn't need any more hassle than he already suffered from.

– I want to be discharged, he stated to her. He wasn't sure whether or not he did so with quiet confidence or a sickening servility. – The name is Zahn, Jeremy Zahn.

– Mr. Zahn, she noted hesitatingly, while tapping his name into the machine, retrieving information, any information. First there was a tiny wrinkle on her forehead, then her eyes widened hardly noticeable. Hardly noticeable to others, not to him. – Can you stand on your feet, sir?

He straightened unnoticeably, certain that she noticed.

– You saw me walk here, didn't you? You saw me walk down the stairs, right?

To this point she had seemed anonymous, very anonymous. He hadn't really looked at her, studied the woman behind the counter, cover. Now, he noted she was young and quite cute. Beautiful, he corrected himself. Or she would have been, if not for the professional mask that distorted her features. The way she sat there, all day long, she looked far more like a machine, a part of the machine she used than a living human being.

– Listen, he explained patiently, – you've screwed up royally with my journal. I can undress and you may examine me. A physician may examine me, but the only thing you'll find is some bruises and small wounds. It serves no purpose, to me, for you to compound your idiocy. I hope you realize this. You seem like a fairly smart doll, and it shouldn't be too difficult to realize what needs to be realized.

She nodded silently, attempted to hide behind a mask of justified indignation, but he saw straight through it, recognized the fear she had no chance of hiding. He didn't care if he had frightened her. The fear had served its purpose.

She handed him two copies of the discharge papers. He cast a casual glance at them. The basic information in the text was that the patient was well, and could leave the hospital by his own recognizance. He nodded. She hadn't attempted to get smart by attempting to make him sign a liability formula, something increasingly popular these days. He signed both and kept one for himself.

– What's your home address, sweetie? He felt like he overdid it a bit when he grabbed her under the jaw and forced her to meet his eyes.

She gave him her address, without the slightest hesitation. He left.

The paralysis remained, and he felt he was pulling his legs over the floor down the stairs, and out into «fresh air». The uncertainty still had its hooks in his flesh and mind, and he had no idea what he was supposed to do next. The temptation to go «home» rattled him. If only he had known where that was.

He had no place to go.

He could go wherever he wanted, but he didn't want to go anywhere.

The haze lingering above Los Angeles pushed him down, pushed inside him, and blew him apart from inside.

The four people stood a bit to the right on the parking lot. He recognized Caldwell, Russo and Wells. They had survived the attack on the bastion. That told him something, even though he couldn't say what. He didn't recognize the fourth, a younger man who couldn't hide flickering eyes. Not even inside the hood and robe covering most of his body.

– You don't look so bad, Caldwell commented. – According to rumors Joyce crushed every bone in your body, and then proceeded to ground them to powder, dancing on the remains.

– A few taps won't stop Zahn, the unknown stated.

Jeremy wondered. Didn't he hear... respect in those voices?

The first, initial assumption was clearly correct. He saw it in their eyes, in their very stance, the way they moved in his sphere. They waited for his word, his command, his actions, like the subordinates waited for the regent to acknowledge their presence.

He saw something new in Caldwell's eyes, too, a desperation that hadn't been there the day before. In a flash he realized why. She had had her feet kicked away from beneath her, lost faith in her most basic beliefs.

They all had.

Just during a few, short hours, a single night.

Or perhaps one single moment.

He didn't say anything. He waited.

– We intend to track down Joyce, she said suddenly and hotly, – and we intend to kill him. We… need you on the team, want you to join us. You've had more confrontations with our prey than anyone else, and you're still breathing.

– He plays a game with you, Russo said. – He lets you live just to amuse himself.

Zahn knew with just a look, that the man didn't really believe his own words.

– I don't believe that's it. Caldwell shook her head. – There's more to it. You're important in a way, but not because of that.

– That's right, Zahn said hoarsely. – Initially I, too, believed he wanted to play chess with me, but there's more to it. There has to be. All his plans, even though there are elements of spontaneity, are well prepared. In some unfathomable way I'm important to him.

He could smell the scents they released, the stink they conveyed to him, of fear, hatred and attraction.

– Let's find a less obvious spot, he told them, took command, leading them wherever the journey would lead them.

Downtown was a true cauldron of races, viewpoints and uncertainty. He enjoyed it here, especially since he knew his companions didn't share his view. The policewoman and men were visibly uncomfortable, while the fourth, which could hardly be called an adult, hardly cared about their whereabouts at all. Not ever.

They walked down Main Street. It was a long time since it had been any true main street. There were homeless and beggars thrown all over the sidewalk in large parts of the long stretch of road. Most of the buildings were derelict and could collapse at any moment.

Cars blew their deafening horns, spewing poison from their gaps. People moved back and forth from home to work with closed minds. This mood, or partly the lack of same, a heavy soup of depression and indifference... and potential explosive rage, seemed to linger in the very air.

Zahn recognized what he, in his more humorous moments, characterized as an uplifting mood within. His sensitivity towards the surroundings and individuals, the empathy he once upon a time hadn't known he possessed, seemed to have been even further developed since his arrival to the city of angels.

A place where devils lived and hunted.

The man he in a distant past perhaps had been, seemed like a distant dream now, another person.

They walked in a seemingly relaxed manner into a building looking from the outside like a large storage hall. When they were well inside it sort of went through a metamorphosis to a mix of hotel, tavern and market. Sweat, smoke and other, more exotic scents warred for dominance in the compressed air. The majority of those present remained completely indifferent to the new arrivals. The minority showing any reaction, big or small, showed hostility. This was caused, only in minor ways by the fact that new arrivals were cops, smelled and exposed in seconds. There were officers anonymously and openly under this roof. No, the hostility was general, something found in all places. Zahn had been many places that looked and didn't look like this. The décor changed, but the basics didn't.

Exactly a place where Timothy Joyce thrived. But he wasn't here, now, or any place nearby. Jeremy was convinced of that. He could smell the enemy miles away.

A nod from Zahn and Caldwell walked to the reception desk, a desk full of flowers and the man behind it, a florist, a hotel owner, in one package.

– We require a conference room, she told the florist and the hotel owner. – First class, please.

Such was much of life in the hypocritical, modern society, full of secrets no one - and everyone - knew.

– It may take a while, the man behind the counter said in a businesslike tone. – Would you care to wait on the couch for a few minutes?

Music flowed from hidden speakers. There was a couch, even a pleasant one, pleasant to sit on, if one cared about such shit. Zahn sat there relaxed, enjoying the music, the hidden music, while the others threw nervous glances around. While the florist's hidden eyes photographed them, thoroughly checked and identified them. Even though they had probably known who they were the moment they crossed the threshold, but they checked anyway. Some people were funny that way. They wanted to make sure there wasn't any new dangerous information available, and they didn't want *trouble*.

The Shadow Play. Everybody knew there was one, but still everybody played their part.

Caldwell stared at him, intensively, speculatively and challenging, a look he had already started getting used to. He sensed her eyes on his neck when they were led down a dark corridor. He sensed it warm without, within, when they stood in a less than perfect circle in a small, but «cozy» room. The word, merely the thought of it, made him smile ironically.

Oh, the room could easily be described as cozy. There would be those who came here for a moment of respite, of peace and leisure. And there was no surveillance. No microphones, video cameras or anything. Rumors of meetings held in this place always reached the outer world. But then the aim had never been lasting secrecy. Only the secret of what was actually discussed. Or that it actually took place, for as long as it took place.

Food was brought in, discreetly, quietly, but nobody attempted to sneak into the room. They just brought the food, and then left quickly, leaving the guests in peace.

Zahn focused on the unknown youth. As if on cue, a joint communication.

He had a slightly oriental look, but now, when he had removed his hood, it wasn't importunate.

– He KILLED my father, the boy cried silently. – My father and mentor lived when the revenant left him, but broken to a point that the final blow could just as well been deadly. He killed him by not killing him.

– Your father was Arthur Markham? Zahn stated it, didn't care about the subsequent nod from the hate-filled figure before him.

Jeremy had met Markham at a point definitely after the man's glory days and also traveled enough in the East for him to know the prevailing belief in honor that was so important there.

– He took your woman, the boy kept it up. – He could just as well have thrown her on a mule, and taken her away. He left you in the dust. You could just as well be dead…

Hatred, contempt, admiration. All this and more were present in the eyes staring at Zahn.

Zahn almost had to smile the way the boy behaved like a cliché of a young, vengeful oriental.

The two male cops didn't say anything. They just stared.

– We all have our reasons for wanting to destroy Timothy Joyce, Caldwell said softly.

– He has destroyed so many lives, Wells said. – He has long since passed the point of one life too many.

Echoes of agreement shook the room. This in spite of the fact that there shouldn't be any echo here. No microphones, no hidden rooms, they felt fairly certain of that. The owner couldn't risk or afford even the implication, suspicion of foul play, risking his reputation as a neutral «arranger». Both the economic and practical consequences would be… fatal.

The guy couldn't get much sleep at night. Zahn grinned to himself. He suspected that his new companions wouldn't exactly appreciate his sense of humor, quite ordinary as they were, after all.

– What do you say, shall we spend the night here… all of us? Caldwell wondered in a quiet, confidential moment a while later.

– Let's walk carefree through the streets, he replied, slightly distracted. – Show everybody we don't fear the Sleeping Wolf. Let's visit its den.

It led to a certain unrest among them. Especially the last sentence.

She nodded as if he was the second coming or something, stared at him with renewed respect. He wondered if she was aware of it, the shining admiration in her eyes. Probably not. Then she would have behaved far less withdrawn. Or… kept an even greater distance.

They walked the few blocks to the abandoned storage building, where there had been so much thunder and lightning the night before, the current highlight of what had been building for days.

The clean up continued. All the bodies had been removed during the night, but the crew kept «securing» the place, which in plain English meant that ever-higher number of servicemen and units from the army, kept looking for Timothy Joyce, combed the building for the thousandth time, searched through the sewers, x-rayed it, crawled through every corner of it within the closed-off area.

Zahn led his small group to the place where Joyce had first shown his mug in the city of angels, close to where the operation had been conducted from. He shook his head.

– It's funny how things turn out, he said. – It starts quietly, unnoticeable. A smaller group of youths, typical squatters, sneaks into an abandon building and sets up camp, screaming their rage at the world. After a few days the police come and throw them out. I wonder if they, both the youths and the cops, had any idea that the script wouldn't be followed this time, that quite a different fate awaited them all.

– Funny…? Caldwell didn't say more.

He ignored her. Like he usually did he saw the events play out before his eyes. He had watched the DVD, but he saw more now.

The case had gained a certain notoriety. The radical group «Beyond civilization» was known for aggressively supporting their political beliefs, and to not use velvet gloves in their handling of cops. So, LAPD showed up with fifty officers, as was common in most countries, to deal with twenty protesters. This happened whether or not the «unruly elements» were known to fight back. Media hadn't exactly swarmed the premises, but they had been there. Everything had been filmed. The officers had left their weapons in the holster, found their clubs and equipment. Behind the barricades stood people sympathizing with the squatters and raised their fists. They were ignored at this point. Several of the officers smiled in anticipation. The recordings revealed this expressively, and it was impossible to explain away afterwards. This anticipation wasn't exactly news either, and ordinarily no one would bother, but for some reason or another that, too, was changed this time.

– Let's get on with it. The chief of the operation waved to his subordinates. – Finish it before dinner.

Journalists, the recording crew and the neutral audience laughed. The Sergeant looked like John Wayne. Nice. Easy.

Normal, so very normal.

Suddenly everything changed, the world changed. Everybody heard it, the cracks from weapons being fired. As citizens of Los Angeles they had all heard it thousands of times before. This sounded different. A strange, hollow sound. And no matter if they had seen weapons being fired before, they had seen nothing compared to what they saw and experienced now. And what they saw were fifty police officers be mowed down in a hail of bullets. Lines of blood shot from their bodies and splashed on the concrete. A few managed to fire at the building, but during the course of a few seconds, ten, perhaps twenty, they all crouched on the ground, bleeding to death. Seven survived. Forty-three died. Before the audience had managed to run away it was over. There were frozen stares and bodies everywhere, also among those who hadn't even been hit.

Zahn saw it with open eyes, like shadows in red and black.

– There were no shots fired from the storage building? Not the first time?

– That's right, Caldwell confirmed. – Everybody was shot from behind.

He looked at the houses on the opposite side of the large, open area, at the streets and the narrow alleys.

– Every house was searched, Russo said. – We searched every house, every single room and closet. We found nothing. Nothing! Arrests were made. Somebody had to know something. Somebody! But there was no evidence, not even a shred of it, and in a high-profile case like that… that mattered. We had to let them go.

The youths from Beyond Civilization had been watched as they shortly afterwards had run in panic from the building. They had been picked up one by one during the following days.

– I interrogated one of those young creeps myself, Russo snarled. – None of them knew anything. If they did, they would have to be among the greatest actors ever to enter an interrogation room.

Sound, image, words, crying.

– W-we didn't f-fire, we had nothing to do with that. We fight a non-violent struggle. We aren't MURDERERS, do you hear me!

They were still incarcerated. But the charge was just «breaking and entering». Ridiculous!

And then had happened what had made Timothy Joyce society's Number One enemy in Los Angeles, leading to the later charge of the storage building. The ultimatum had been executed by one of Joyce's most trusted associates, Gwen Talbot. Jeremy was hardly able to recognize her, both features and attitude so changed from the time in London. Physically she was the same, but yet she was like transformed. She had warned that all police officers and military personnel that came within thirty steps of the building would be killed. Not necessarily there and then, but soon.

The two-hundred-man assault team had charged the building a few minutes after the message had been broadcast. They had been met by a murderous hail of bullets, had been forced to withdraw.

Now units from the LAPD and the army had full control in the area, but it had been costly. When the five walked through the building they easily smelled the blood and saw the remains, and that after the greatest cleanup operation in history. No matter how many times they attempted to clean away the blood, it would always be there.

– Nothing has happened today? Zahn asked the chief of operations. – Nothing unusual?

– Nothing, sir, the man replied tightly. – He hasn't made good on his threats, and if he tries, there's more lead waiting for him.

– Not yet, sergeant, Zahn said lightly. – Not that we know of.

For all they knew there could be hundreds of dead cops around town this minute they didn't know about. The sergeant had a very lively expression, and one could imagine that he, too, considered this possibility vividly. Zahn found some satisfaction in this.

– Is there anything more you can tell us, sergeant?

The man's eyes sharpened a bit. He wondered if he hadn't already answered that question.

– We… think we know how he got away, he replied, visibly pondering the options. – There's a hatch we… hadn't wielded shut, leading outside the siege.

– And how far did he have to swim in the dark and under water before reaching it, Sergeant? Caldwell wondered in a very sharp voice.

– Pretty far on one of the sides, and even longer on the other, the man replied, clearly on the defensive. – Uh… we've sent down divers…

– Send down more people, without any equipment. Caldwell sent him a pointed stare. – Well-trained people.

Several minutes underwater? A random hatch, which, even if Joyce and Gwen had known about it had to be hard to open. They couldn't use lights, as they would have been spotted instantly. Zahn shook his head.

– Let's go, he said. – There's nothing for us here.

They left the building, left its close vicinity, not much wiser than they had been before, or perhaps even a bit less wise.

They had a late lunch at Savoy, a smaller hotel close to the court building. Not because they needed to eat. They had eaten to the point of gorging during the little séance of enjoying the florist's hospitality. David Kelly, an English journalist, whom Zahn had had the doubtful pleasure of meeting a few times the last three years, treated them to the lunch. Kelly had an advantage over other journalists in this matter. He had followed Joyce and Zahn across the world.

Kelly paid, without it being necessary. It would have been easy for Zahn to make one single phone call. He didn't even have to call the mayor or the police Chief, to brag about his experience in hunting Joyce.

Yesterday's event had opened more than one fat wallet.

– It's you, the woman in the other end of the line had said in surprise and reluctant admiration. – I heard you were dead and buried.

– I need an account with unlimited credit, he had told her.

Ten minutes later he had received a collection of plastic cards that would have made even many wealthy people green with envy.

They could have paid for the «business lunch», but he didn't want that. Kelly's eagerness and generosity could have faded quickly if he realized that they were on a fishing trip and that he - and not they - was the fish.

– There's a reason for me making contact this time, Zahn told him straight up, and lied by telling the truth. – I don't want to hide from the bastard anymore, not in any way.

– So, you want him to come to you, Kelly nodded, in a sweeping movement. – That could work… I doubt it, but there's no point in leaving anything *untried,* right?

Zahn didn't move an eyelash, didn't even allow himself the luxury of fearing that Louis should barge out with a wrong remark, but kept staring impartially at Kelly.

Uncertainty flashed in the other man's eyes, inevitably, the way Jeremy had seen in so many others.

– He's still in town. That's what they keep saying, anyway. Now, the rumor of his presence is heard in many places, but I choose to believe there is substance in the rumors this time. My… sources, certainly not infallible, are normally far more believable than most others.

– He's not done here, yet, Zahn nodded.

Resulting in a rather prolonged period of unpleasant silence.

The talk went back and forth for a while. Zahn enjoyed himself. He knew he would win the battle of who would lose patience first. He could actually see how the bloodhound in front of him hung out his tongue to dry.

– My father was a great man, young Markham stated with pointed eyes, as a reply to a rather rude question. – Joyce caught him in a bad moment, that's all. Like a snake he encircled my father and bit while the prey looked away.

Kelly leaned back in his chair and took a very civilized sip of his British tea. And he took the bait. Zahn smiled.

– As I understand it, you're a kind of unofficial unit charged with hunting and catching Timothy Joyce, is that an accurate description, Mister Zahn?

– As far as it goes, David, Jeremy replied thoroughly. – We're one of several hundred groups, both secret, and others like ours, working openly. We have a wide range of authority, and can, if necessary, use the most extreme means…

The dark fell quickly, unexpectedly. There had been sunshine, and clear blue skies when they had taken to the streets again, not that long ago.

– Do you REALIZE what you just did? Kent Russo had

shouted enraged to him. – You've made every group of policemen into potential victims. And they'll become so paranoid eventually that they will fire at anything that moves. Why the fuck did you do it?

– And no one will dare not to move as part of a crowd of colleagues from this moment on, Zahn had grinned, before turning his head towards the policeman. – Are you sure you're in the right place?

Russo had blinked and figuratively speaking backed off.

– As if they're not his targets anyway, Zahn snarled, putting a stop to their last objections.

Downtown had been a seething cauldron for years now, and was that more than ever tonight. Nobody moved through here without being protected by a small army. Policemen or people attached to the police department didn't go here, without being a part of such a small army in full body armor.

Units from the US Army patrolled the streets now. The «cooperation» between military and civilian authorities had grown more pronounced the last few years, since a military officer, a so-called retired general, had been appointed «Drug Tsar», the person coordinating the government's so-called war against drugs. Soldiers were increasingly utilized against the nation's own citizens.

The two policemen, Dupond and Dupont, lurked behind Zahn and Caldwell. Young Louis rushed back and forth, front and center, and to the side of those he followed. A better… watchdog would be hard to find. Zahn suddenly shuddered down his spine without having the slightest idea why. It resembled the way he had learned to feel every time Joyce was close, but wasn't exactly like that. It dawned on him that Markham was dressed fairly similar to the way Joyce's henchmen had been on his many encounters with them during his endless hunt. Not so surprising perhaps. The older Markham had taught Joyce and such clothing was quite common in certain Martial Arts milieus.

In spite of this, the thoroughly logical and rational explanations he had given himself, he sensed the cold trickle up his spine. Up, not down. The heat that seemed to come from every cell in his body, every particle of the surroundings.

They cut into the Financial District, an area of Downtown

practically abandoned after five o'clock.

There was nothing instantly particular or threatening about the street before them. It wasn't filled with people and wasn't empty. A patrol from the army, accompanied by a group of cops had taken position at its center.

How fast the day had passed, how quickly the night had come. It was just twilight, but twilight had always been the beginning of night, right? Jeremy had taught himself that fact, and shuddered some more. Not down or up, but every spot simultaneously. Heat, cold, so hard to distinguish sometimes, wasn't it?

They sat by the sidewalk coffee shop at Seventh and Figuroa, by the 7+Fig building when it began. The night was a quiet one, peaceful enough. Patrols from the army and the crowd of police officers were close by. At least one had the illusion of peace. Something quite different from the neurotic, stressful activity they had witnessed in the same neighborhood during daylight.

The steam from the coffee rose in the air in very visible circles, strange patterns revealing themselves amazingly clear, almost like they were inside a freezer, but it wasn't cold, not even humid. The air stayed like it usually was in LA, hot and dry. So dry that Zahn felt downright weird in his throat. He had experienced similar things during his travels around the globe and hated it.

The steam rose, mixing with the air, mixing with the night.

Zahn sipped the coffee. He had acquired a taste for it the last three years. The foam from the Cappuccino stuck to his upper lip. It seemed to freeze, remain there, without reason, without rhyme, a state of things he had grown quite accustomed to.

It had, considering what had happened less than twenty-four hours ago been strangely quiet in this part of town all day, quieter than usual even, now, when most of the executives had left. But now the choir boiled and rose in the streets, and human minds and veins rose and boiled with the night.

Someone played a song from a car or an apartment somewhere, through an open window. An old, song, but its content, what it conveyed, seemed totally new and fresh.

Some people sang along. Sometimes, in-between the cracks Jeremy felt as if it was both sung and played. The singers did move their lips, but held no instruments in their hands. They might look like they were dancing, but one couldn't say for certain.

– I'll bet many here support Joyce, Dupond (or Dupont) sniffed.
– He's seen as a hero, like Robin Hood or Billy the Kid many places. What I most of all can't fathom is how he can retain that after what he did yesterday. And it isn't the first time he's sacrificed an entire pack of soldiers to get away.

Zahn smiled. He was confident that Wells didn't see the dark shadow in his face.

But he sensed it…

Jeremy didn't have to reply. Caldwell did it for him.

– What's being said, she interjected, – is that this is precisely the sacrificial fires igniting the ashes of the old kingdoms. And to remove the dead meat that blind, sheep-like followers represent, those who blindly and without hesitation and thought are willing to die for a cause, a leader. Those remaining will then be like the Messiah wants his subjects to be, independent and thinking individuals.

There was no need for Jeremy to conjure the face of Joyce in his mind. It was always there, from their first meeting in London, from Delphi, from the City of Angels, at the forefront in the time of the Crimson Tide. A shadow at the edge of the eye…

A group of dancers, singers and players seemed to be transformed from one step to another, and approached the group sitting around the small, round table. They never ventured close, but close enough for their presence to be known, to not be ignored, tantalizing, deceitful. Suddenly Jeremy froze, froze from a feeling he had learned to recognize as real, as meaningful.

– He's here!

He spoke so quietly that he didn't think anybody heard him, but everybody did.

The dancers didn't come any closer, but their song washed over the five like lukewarm slush a hot summer day, many voices sounding like one.

*For whose is the kingdom*
*The power, the glory*
*Forever and ever…*

Zahn noted a young female, a very womanly dancer. She definitely seemed to qualify as the urban legend type of the archetypal Joyce-disciple. The eyes matched that of the moves, direct and enticing. Zahn got a hard-on fast and painful. The reaction confused and irritated him, because he didn't understand it. He had experienced so much he didn't understand during the three short and eternal years.

The very night-air itself seemed to shimmer, turning into something it wasn't. He wanted to cackle at his own, confused thoughts. Three years ago, he might have done just that. But then he wouldn't have thought the way he now did.

Something hit him on the head. So light and fluffy that he would have claimed it was his imagination… three years ago.

He saw several others touch their heads in indulgence. There was no longer any doubt. Small objects fell from the sky, from the *sky*, far from the buildings. He looked down at the ground and imagined he saw a small squeaky creature jump away. The table was wet. He touched it with a steady hand. The middle of the street had turned wet. More squeaky creatures jumped all over the place. It wasn't a mirage if everybody experienced it. Surely not. It would have to be one of history's most extreme cases of mass suggestion or hallucination then. He registered that a waiter hurried to the table and dried it with a soft cloth.

– Excellent service here, Caldwell exclaimed dryly, too dryly. – The guides say so, the tourist brochures as well.

Sweaty hands fought to hold on to guns. Guns slipped out of hands while hearts hammered, and Jeremy Zahn sat there sweating as the shimmering, virtually invisible northern lights in the night air, in central parts of Los Angeles waxed and waned. All during a few, everlasting seconds.

Nobody danced anymore. There was no music in the streets. Timothy Joyce had paid a visit to this place, but not staying longer than a fraction of a second. He had touched Jeremy - again, not harder than fluttering butterfly wings in the dark. But *there*. Zahn remained convinced of that, even in the roaring silence afterwards. Jeremy imagined that he stood on the corner at the other side of the street, by the bus stop. He imagined that he, breathing hard pursued someone up the stairs close by, while almost puking because of the orange and green colors in the decorations. The entire Seventh/Figuroa seemed sickening to him.

He heard someone run up the stairs, saw the feet touch the

brown stairs, hands grab the green handles. And everything felt so real that the experience faded only very, very slowly.

They remained around the small, round table, outside the small, cozy coffee shop. Nothing happened. Nothing much had happened. Caldwell didn't dare meet his eyes. He didn't have to concentrate to smell the stench of her swollen cunt.

He sat there, and his thoughts sought backwards in time, in despair, in desperation. Not to the time before the Hunt began. He could no longer imagine Before. But to London, his final days there, before he had left the city forever. To his own twisted self, another person he had taught himself to hate.

# CHAPTER FOUR

## THREE YEARS BEFORE NOW

The shock stuck inside him, clung to him like wet paper. He felt like it was real, that instead of air, the wet paper covered him and pushed him down.

Abner Talbot charged into the room. In spite of looking a bit frazzled around the edges, he still behaved as if he owned the world.

– You were lucky as hell, he rumbled. – The bullets missed the heart by a hair. It's still a miracle that you survived.

– I don't feel very lucky, Jeremy commented, feeling very distant, remote from the world.

Talbot frowned, virtually unnoticeable.

– The nurses will soon be here to change your clothes, son, he said forcefully, in an attempt to regain lost authority. – They're even talking about changing the bedding already. You're sweating worse than a pig, they say, so much that the docs are actually worried.

– I don't sleep very well.

The doctors had also implied, more than once, what a miracle it was he was still breathing. It got old quite fast.

Female and male nurses entered the room to change him, and to change bedding, and interrupted Talbot's disapproving look, and whatever lecture he was about to give.

He didn't return until three days later, in the hope that Zahn had softened a bit.

Zahn hadn't. He sat upright in bed. It hurt, hurt bad a lot of the time, but he could look forward to an ever-longer period where the pain wasn't overwhelming. He didn't take... he refused to take painkillers. He feared he would go completely insane. But the fear never held him for long. Nothing but the fear for the enormous black hole he felt gnawing at his intestines.

Thoughts tumbled into one, haunting him, anointed him. Thousands of viewpoints, ways to keep going, almost too much. It didn't matter. They all boiled down to one.

When he once again encountered Abner Talbot, the last slices of respect he might have felt for him had vanished. It was just a mundane old man standing there, a bureaucrat who could be used and discarded.

– I assume he isn't rotting in a cell?

– He hasn't been seen at all during the time you've been here. We blocked every access point, and assume he's in hiding somewhere within the realm.

– He got away.

The mangled body leaned back in the bed, rested the head at the wall, in a moment's strength. The other man's ability to fool himself made laughter and malice boil within.

– There are procedures to be followed here, the old man stressed. – If procedures are followed, we'll eventually get our man. British police are the best in the world. People come here to learn our methods…

– I'll find him, Abner.

– If you intend to run off on your own, half cocked… The British Police can't support such an unwise venture.

– To hell with British Police, the man in the bed said quietly. – It's unable to help a fart after letting it out. I don't need your help either, Abner, I never did, but if you have the slightest shred of emotion behind the clown mask, I suggest you give me whatever help you can.

– If you travel abroad, without official backing, you can't expect official support. You'll be alone.

Jeremy slipped down in bed. It felt good to rest. He sensed sleep come virtually instantaneously. From that moment on, he ignored Talbot completely.

– I've always been alone…

When he spoke in the phone a few more days, a week later, it was raining outside, pouring evenly, without the slightest pause.

The doctor entered the room. Jeremy always thought of him as the doctor. His name had just always been totally meaningless.

– You're as good as recovered, the doctor commented. – Even though you probably should have remained in bed a few more days, I see no reason to keep you here against your will.

Zahn refrained from speaking. He browsed his notes. They looked completely unreadable, and had to be impossible to understand to others. An advantage to be sure, since he could use the waste bin without precautions.

He understood them.

– You see, Jeremy, the physician kept at it. – The miracle isn't merely in the fact that you survived, but how quickly you recovered. I've seen people with less extreme injuries remain in bed for months without really healing. Never. They've never become more than a shade of their old self.

Zahn threw the notebook in the bin, didn't need it anyway, recalling every little word on it, everything he needed to recall. It was as if it was burned into his memory.

– I-I suppose it's true what they say, that it depends on whether or not the patient wishes to recover.

– That, doc, is, in my opinion, more than a correct statement.

He even spoke differently from the way he had spoken before, moved differently. When he stood shaving before the mirror that night, a stranger returned his stare. He thought about what the doctor, the medical doctor had said. He would keep thinking about it in the times to come.

He pulled the gun from the shoulder holster. He pushed it between the belt and the waist, and drew it from there. It was a slow, rigid process. He had never done anything like this before, had seen it as foolish. For hours stretching into days he remained in front of the mirror, perhaps a couple of minutes all in all. This served no purpose. Not yet. Not even to the person he had been previously to the last few weeks in the hospital. He had a long way to go, he accepted that. It didn't matter anymore. He had time.

The night air made him lose footing a bit, before regaining it. All the eyes of the servicemen, guarding him, seemed to rest on him. A guard of honor. He didn't give a damn about them. Night turned to dawn, to day. Eventually, they left him more or less in peace.

His final weeks in London, he basically spent performing two tasks:

He started on his long, extenuating path to better physical and mental shape.

And he walked in Timothy Joyce's footsteps.

A policeman of oriental descent taught him Martial Arts. That wouldn't bring him very far. He knew that in advance and quickly confirmed it to himself. It was like playing chess. Learning to move the pieces wasn't hard, not hard at all. But the nice man teaching him couldn't teach him to develop the game itself, because he couldn't play it himself.

The post-noon hours he spent in the casino in the time before it opened. He went through the security, all the various routines, from top to bottom in the organization. To get the new chief of security, the entire new management to cooperate, was a surprisingly easy and satisfactory exercise.

– We've decided to run a tighter skip this time, Inspector Zahn, the man stated gruffly.

– That's fine, that's excellent. You don't need to tell me shit about the new security, the new routines. I just want full knowledge of the old. Full knowledge, is that clear?

No request, an order. Zahn saw the undefined fear in the other man's eyes.

Zahn searched for that undefined quality when looking at himself in the mirror, but didn't find it. Perhaps because it didn't scare him anymore.

He went through the personnel lists, the routines for transport and transfer of cash, knowledge of the system, codes, and all the probable and improbable things that could go wrong. He triple-checked everything, and kept checking, until he felt somewhat content that he knew everything by heart. He had talks with those who had been fired, with their wives, friends, lovers, bank affiliates. He repeated the procedure with those who hadn't been fired. Eventually it became impossible to complete the project, because he stepped on too many toes. The casino circles were thoroughly corrupt, from bottom to top in the Gambling Commission, but in spite of this, of hurdles in his personal investigation, he was forced to draw one, inevitable conclusion:

– Everything was in order, he told the new manager. – Firing people served no purpose.

– Oh, it did, the manager replied candidly. – Somebody had to be fired. Somebody had to suffer. If not, blood would have flowed, in this city and beyond, the next few months.

Zahn laughed a lot because of that the coming months.

The person he most of all had wanted to speak to, was naturally

Todd Winston. One might be tempted to use any cliché, in and out of the book, about what had happened to him… whatever it was. He had vanished without a trace, into thin air, faded like a ghost in daylight, evaporated like dew before the sun a spring morning. No one had seen him since his vanishing act inside the closet in the casino. Experts had investigated the case and the scene. There were no hidden doors, no hidden paths behind the wall. Nothing. Many still told the most amazing and absurd witness-accounts of the event. Most wisely kept their mouth shut. Zahn understood well why they didn't go to official or unofficial authorities with their story. As Timothy Joyce - or perhaps Todd Winston - would have said: It would be just another unconfirmed alien abduction story.

Timothy Joyce had executed another incredible feat, and since then nobody had seen or heard from him. His reputation grew even further.

Gwen Talbot had disappeared from the face of the Earth. Photos of her circulated in the media, in internal police circuits, and on the Internet. Nothing seen, nothing heard. Nobody had heard about the woman calling herself Monica. She didn't exist in any register or archives. Zahn watched the surveillance tapes of her with various experts. They did the rewind and play. They repeated it several times.

– She's not disguised, one of them said. – I would also say she has not undergone surgery. This is how she looks, her «natural» looks.

Wanted and hunted around the globe, and nobody had seen them anywhere.

There was one missing tape, though, from the hallway leading to the lavatories. Why that particular tape was missing or taken, no one could say or even speculate on. Nothing made sense.

Nothing made sense anywhere, not in any of it. The wind crawled on the ground and threatened to make him lose his footing, where he rushed forward, on the sidewalk, by the Eros Monument, in the midst of the endless, confused traffic on Piccadilly Circus. He moved towards the casino once again, was as if drawn to it.

He passed the phone booths on the right, moving up Wardour Street. A few steps after that one of the phones rang. He stopped and looked around. The phone, if it called to anyone, it would be him. He unhooked the receiver, pushed it at his ear. When he heard someone say his name, he couldn't tell if it was real, if it had been through the line… or if the hoarse, husky female voice came from *behind*. It itched painfully in his back, and he turned rapidly, in what was virtually a whirl of motion.

No one. Nothing. No people at all. No one close. Not even a hint of a shadow, an echo of a human figure fading as he locked his eyes on it.

He stood there, exactly like that, exactly on that spot. Finally, after a long, indefinite period of time, he crossed the street, the few steps to the casino. He stopped there, across the street opposite the entrance. The time was about two. The first guests joined the queue early these days. Now, close to opening time, there was a long line of guests waiting to get inside. It was said that the place had long since earned back the economic loss from the night Timothy Joyce had honored them with his presence. All casinos had gained a lot of new members, but naturally most of them sought this one, to walk in his shoes, to bask in the glory of his presence.

Dust whirled in the air. It shouldn't. Humidity lingered like mist in the air this clear, sunny day. Sufficient humidity to bind all dust, but not this. Wind blew from all sides, but the mist remained, blurring everything. His eyes locked on to a figure crouching in the narrow alley close to the entrance. Jeremy hardly recognized the man as he stumbled across the street and approached.

Todd Winston.

A Todd squinting his eyes at the sun, at the other man, like an old man. Stripes of gray mixed with the once so bright hair.

– Jeremy Zahn? The shaking lips formed words. – Is that you, kid? I haven't seen you for years. How are you, old boy? Heh, heh.

The maniac grabbed the inspector's collar. If not, he would probably have fallen. The minor unevenness between street and sidewalk would have made him lose his footing.

Jeremy looked at him, plagued by doubt. Was he wrong? It seemed so… unexpected. This couldn't be Todd Winston, could it? This wreck of a human being seemed ten, no, twenty years older than he had been at their last meeting. When Jeremy looked at the harried face, the empty stare, he felt the cold cut into him and stay there.

This was Todd Winston, but a completely different version compared to the one Jeremy had met a few short, long weeks ago.

– You're probably wondering what the hell happened to me, what Satan did to me? I trust you haven't forgotten?

Forget? How could he forget?

– Yes, I must confess I…

– He sent me to Hell, old sport, to HELL! I told everyone there my name, but nobody believed me. At least they pretended not to, the shitheads.

With a madman's strength Winston dragged Zahn into the closest pub. Zahn was unable to read the name on the sign, as if it hadn't been cleaned in twenty years.

Soon enough, they sat there, talking like old friends who hadn't seen each other for a long time. Zahn forced himself to keep hidden his almost infinite skepticism. He had to, if he should succeed in obtaining useful information from the man in front of him, a wreck that could collapse… or explode at any time.

– I was dreaming a night not long ago, did you know that? I saw you and… You didn't see me… I watched while you and Gwen entered the casino… again. You seemed dressed exactly like you had been that night many years ago, just as young and vital. Are you aware of what that *did* to me?

*The guy is completely bonkers,* Zahn thought.

– How was it… in hell? He asked carefully.

– It was Hell, I told you! They only played old music on the radio, and attempted to tell me that Todd Winston was a ten-year-old boy. Completely bonkers all of them. Do you know they sent *me* to the hospital and *not* the lying shit claiming I wasn't me?

Zahn recalled something then, pieces of a conversation, something important. For one moment it seemed like everything was clear, until it faded once more. More pieces. A puzzle spread by the winds.

As if by a miracle one of the case's most important witnesses had appeared right in front of him… and then the man in question was totally useless, both as a witness and human being.

– Joyce threw you into the closet, Zahn ventured, in a businesslike way. – No one saw you anywhere after that. What happened?

– Happened? Everything had changed. Everybody dressed different. I've heard that fashion can change overnight, but this was RIDICULOUS. I walked through the streets for hours before heading home. There was another name on my door. The key didn't fit. I hammered on the door, and a stranger opened it, and refused me access to my own home. I forced myself inside and froze there, by the door. Everything was changed. This was my house... But not my HOME. I didn't even hear the sirens growing louder, louder, louder. It didn't seem important... then.

The man sat there and cried, cried hard. Huge, salty tears flowed down the unshaven, unmade face, and made lines in the dirt.

– I must take a leak. The ghost Todd Winston rose from the deep chair. Even that seemed like a miracle. – Know that I'm very pleased to have finally met you, old boy. In all these years I've had only one goal... to re-experience, relive that last evening. I waited for you outside. You didn't see me, but I saw you. I couldn't stop you from entering. I couldn't stop anything from happening. Not a thing. Not even after learning the rules of the game. Too late, far too late. Everything stopped in me. Everything. I had to speak to you... before I... before I...

Zahn sat there, rubbing his eyes, long after Winston had gone. This... all this... it was just too much. He sipped all the fat beer-foam from the Guinness, and rose like a drunken man, suddenly filled with apprehension. Motion was slow. He hardly managed more than a stumbling walk. His feet quite simply didn't obey the mind. But he had almost reached his destination when the sharp, muted sound rolled through the building.

The door seemed to slide open in front of him. He stood there and stared.

Winston had taken no chances. He hadn't directed the barrel at the temple, but into his mouth. And pulled the trigger. It became impossible for Zahn not to freeze.

There was no reason anywhere. Not in any of it.


The train to Brussels raged through the Chunnel. Jeremy sensed the sea around him, its all-encompassing presence.

He once again walked through the huge, resplendent single resident building previously owned by Todd Winston. The housekeeper stared at him. He returned the stare, without making the slightest effort to hide the desire to break her neck like a twig.

– So there haven't been *any* changes since Winston disappeared?

– None, she assured him, eventually far more amenable.

The broker's office. Efficient, business-like. The broker. Efficient, businesslike, with only a slight worry visible at the edge of an eye.

– The house has had two owners previously to Mr. Winston, the broker curtly enlightened Zahn. – Both the second owner and Winston himself made extensive changes to the interior. Outside, however, it has only had minor maintenance done.

Abner, the old clown, beside himself with apathy. It was unexpectedly little energy directed at the attack on his previously upcoming son in law.

– He must have said *something?*

– Nothing making sense. Zahn had shaken his head, almost distracted.

Jeremy left, for the first time in his life the island kingdom of his birth and adolescence, never to return.

It felt fitting. He had waited so long with his first Journey. Perhaps, in order to catch up, he should make his new status permanent.

He lent his head back at the pillow at the top of the seat. It felt good. He didn't think he would have any trouble sleeping.


Amsterdam seemed like a perfect place to start the hunt. He didn't really have anything to go on, except a hunch. The city had for centuries had a reputation as a place where the most probable and improbable events happened, and actions were taken.

A man like Timothy Joyce couldn't help but enjoy such a place.

Jeremy Zahn stepped out from Central Station, on the broad main street, Damrak, early in the morning. He had slept well the entire night. The trip under the channel, the change of train in Brussels, it already felt like it had happened to a completely different person. That, too. He had slept, while awakening from the slumber he had suffered from his entire life.

Really funny. He pulled his lips in a tight smile, making a face. His entire life to this point had been an unreal dream, practically a nightmare, where everything was fixed, and there were no surprises. But this, these streets, this mood, didn't feel real either. There was something dreamlike here, something he couldn't quite grasp.

He followed the river of people into the tourist information office outside Central Station, further in, to the hotel reservation desk. He hadn't had any idea what to do when he came here, to the city, still hadn't, now, when being here. Some lofty ideas, stray thoughts. Nothing more. He replied mechanically to the woman behind the counter. Did he want a centrally placed hotel? One reasonably priced? Shower in the room? He couldn't recall what he said. A few minutes passed, until he found himself out between the tram-coaches, with a hotel reservation in his hand. Not long after that, he registered at the counter at Hotel Schirman, a place within walking distance and sight from the railway-station, right across the canal. The room was at the top floor, had white-painted walls and a bed, and the shower was in the hall just outside. The bed made up large parts of the space, but not more than expected. An okay place, he surmised.

Later that day he returned to the tourist information. Through speakers outside he and a lot of depressed travelers were told that Amsterdam was full. There were no longer available rooms anywhere. That made him glad he had arrived early.

He had dinner at a pizza restaurant on Damrak. An ancient, frail cat slept in a chair not far from where he sat. It didn't move, not the slightest. When he had stomach cramps and had to rush to the bathroom before he had consumed the entire pizza, the cat and the pizza remained on their respective spots when he returned. He had to wonder if the cat just didn't like pizza, or the flavor he had chosen, or if the animal had just died there in the chair. Perhaps it had happened only a short while ago, and no one had realized it yet. Or somebody had stuffed the wee beast and used it as a part of the interior. And it only looked like an old, frail cat.

The rest of the day, during the remains of daylight, he wandered aimlessly through the streets. Slowly, surely, he familiarized himself with the alien surroundings. Up streets, down streets. He had never walked so much in his entire life. Alleys, narrow alleys, everything started blurring to him, panning out… into infinity. He kept walking. Sometime during the day, he could never recall exactly when, a complete stranger approached him, wondering if he could spare some change. Zahn looked closer at him, a well-built man dressed in a military coat, probably from one of the army's surplus storage buildings.

– Sorry. Jeremy shook his head. – I'm pretty cleaned myself.
– C'mon, man, you must be able to spare something.

It dawned on Jeremy that the man treated him with a certain familiarity going beyond the techniques of the con game most beggars developed to get to befriend their victim. The jacket Jeremy wore could pass for a military jacket. He gave the man some Euros.

Twilight descended quickly on him. The low buildings suggested that the sun should be visible for quite some time in the evening, but some alleys were so narrow that the sun didn't reach them. Not as anything but a reflection in the windows on the other sidewalk. He realized he had stopped.

He stood in front of an Internet café. Weird, he smiled. A smile appeared between the days' long beard covering the face. He dimly recalled days and nights, and more nights he had walked these streets. But that wasn't possible. He looked at the date on the stables of newspapers outside a newsstand close by, on an electronic clock on the wall, on the computer screen in front of him. They all showed the same, the date the day he had first arrived in town. Weird, he smiled between the days' old beard. He had long since decided to establish an international email account and other sensors on the Web. He had surfed sufficiently to do it easily and quickly, and used no more than a few minutes on the first initial maneuvers. He had time.

The address was quite simply: JEREMYZAHN@HOTMAIL. COM

Microsoft owned hotmail. He knew well the various methods of registration they used, using so-called «cookies» and countless other methods.

He wanted to be seen, noticed.

He sat there, and felt sort of detached from himself, as if he wasn't truly sitting there, being in this place, tapping the keyboard. He had had many opportunities to doubt himself lately, doubt his very existence, but this was different. He really felt detached from the here and now, as if he was close to a place he couldn't see.

A feeling not lessening the coming seconds. He stared at the screen, couldn't take his eyes off it, as words filled the white space.

**HELLO, JEREMY, I HAVE BEEN WAITING FOR YOU TO SHOW, TO STUMBLE YOUR WAY HERE, SO TO SPEAK.**

For the first time, for the very first time in his life, Jeremy Zahn felt, truly felt the ice-cold trickle down his spine. He felt it, felt the nerve-endings tickle as the sensation moved from the neck to his ass. And it was such an overwhelming sensation that he sat there frozen, paralyzed.

He had entered his username and password, to receive his first mail. First there had been the welcoming message from Hotmail, but then as the second, in the same bulk, Timothy Joyce had sent him his message, one echoing far beyond the actual screen.

**I HEAR IT IS A WARM EVENING IN AMSTERDAM. UNFORTUNATELY, I CANNOT JOIN YOU TONIGHT, BUT PLEASE ENJOY YOURSELF ANYWAY.**

He read every word on the screen, as if someone had hypnotized him and he was unable to look away.

He shook, visibly. He looked around, at everybody else in a relatively thinly populated locale, the man, two rows away, the brunette by his side, the man behind the counter, the other, peripheral persons, and also the people passing by outside.

The message had to come from someone in the building. Or they had to be in league with someone sending the message. Or… Joyce wouldn't necessarily tell the truth, of course. As one of the world's foremost experts on disguises, he could sit three steps away, and Zahn couldn't be certain of recognizing him. Or…

He leaned back in the chair, just had to take it all to heart. There were hundreds of possible explanations, equally dissatisfactory, not even close to being satisfactory. He rose calmly from the chair, pushed it back, and left the place, even poorer on illusions. Lost in thought he rushed out on the street, while staring wildly around him. Did perhaps both, both actions/events inside, outside… happen simultaneously? Like he had just pointed out to himself: There were countless possible explanations and none of them had to be right.

Outside he suddenly found himself face to face with the beggar from early in the day.

– Hi, man, the man greeted him vigorously. – The world is a small place, huh? What do you say to us touring the town tonight, a grand tour the force of Amsterdam's bars?

– Sorry, I'm on a tight budget, Jeremy replied and added pointedly: – At least as long as you're around…

– Listen, man, I've done well for myself the last few days and am actually having a guilty conscience because of pulling the bread out of your pocket. In other words; it's on me.

Zahn looked closer at him, looked very close, and made no attempt at hiding it. Either the guy worked for Joyce or he didn't. Both possibilities felt okay right now.

– Ah, you're coming, the creature grinned in satisfaction. – I noticed it immediately, we're kindred souls.

As if to stress that, they chose the same direction of four possible from their current position. Jeremy reminded himself of the second law of paranoia: «the fact that you are paranoid, doesn't mean they're *not* out to get you».

– What shall we do first? Whores? Hookers? Prostitutes? Loose birds?

– Not whores, Jeremy said decisively. – Not hookers. Not prostitutes. Not loose birds.

– No? What then about eager call girls? He lifted his arms, as if deflecting the coming barrage. – Okay, I can take a hint…

Zahn caught himself in actually smiling. The guy had a charm belonging to another world. Slowly the shock, the sense of terror faded, or was at least delegated to a less important part of his consciousness. He wasn't convinced that was a good thing, but right now, he didn't care that much about it. He needed this… needed something in his life, not previously there.

From the first person he met, a beggar and homeless, a vagabond, without any home, anything to hold on to. Zahn shook his head in wonder. It didn't feel wrong. Several of those categories fit him as well, now.

They had been on their way into Red Light District. Now they turned back towards Central Station. After something that for Jeremy felt like idle wandering, they finally caught the Tram to their destination, a part of the town called Leidseplein, or

Leidse Square, «for our English-speaking friends». The place was evidently well known, both among the locals and the foreigners. Most left the Tram there, many, including Jeremy and company, without paying.

– It's no big deal. There are controls, but not very often. Those with money usually pay, and from those without it, there isn't much to gain anyway. Not that we really need the ride. As you'll discover it's quite possible to walk around the entire old city without straining oneself.

Jeremy laughed. He couldn't imagine where this devil-may-care laughter came from. It felt so long already, since he had visited the small café, and received the small, unique note from his «friend» Timothy Joyce, and the time in London, where he had lived his entire life. All that felt like a completely different existence.

They hit a pub, a classic English pub in execution, but different, without its limitations. They swallowed pint after pint of foaming Guinness, and when Jeremy, after the third round, started buying rounds, it dawned on him that he had been conned, after all, but he couldn't tell exactly how…

Music played close by, music seemingly playing itself, a peaceful scene, so much activity and fun. He didn't recall… didn't recall when he previously had felt anything similar.

– Listen to this. Rafe lifted a finger. Zahn squinted his eyes and listened carefully.

– In a tourist leaflet distributed in our lovely town, the police, among other things, warn against disturbing the people living in the Red-Light District at night. They claim that they, too, need their beauty sleep. And… they prohibit bathing in the canals.

– Prohibit bathing… in the canals? Zahn voice sharpened just a bit.

– HALLELUJAH!

He cried it out loud, not long afterwards, the moment before he joined Rafe in the dark water between the streets. There were lamps on all sides, casting a soft, ghostly illumination over the canal water.

He felt how the water closed around him, as he sank below the surface, into the murky depths. And everything changed and turned even ghostlier, stranger.

The two conspirators jumped out of the water and like pigs they howled their desires into the Amsterdam night. When the police finally arrived, they hid nude in a narrow alley and dried themselves with large towels.

And as if it had never happened, they found themselves back at the pub, the tavern. But they knew it had. The innocent, unimportant escapade showed in their eyes, in their every little movement, as they raised their glasses in yet another toast.

They sat there, and laughed themselves silly.

The lamps by the water, the dark water itself kept flashing in Zahn's fuzzy mind.

The time in the canal, the swimming, had happened so fast, lasted such a short time, that it seemed like it had never happened. That, too.

– So, what do you call yourself? He asked, quite intoxicated and happily. The people who had known him in London, the *amoebas*, would have been shocked beyond belief. – What's your... true name?

His drinking buddy looked up with eyes suddenly strangely sharp.

– Not an important issue, he apologized, fairly uncertain, with a huge smile. – I wanted to know your name, so I could tell my grandchildren, in a fifty years time that things are usually not like they seem at first glance.

– That, the other one nodded thoughtfully, – I believe, is a very accurate observation.

He reached out a hand.

– Rafe Charles, delighted to meet you.

– And I you. Hands met, and grasped. – I am...

– Jeremy Zahn. I know.

Jeremy couldn't fathom it. The room suddenly seemed so incredibly small. He still had the gun inside his jacket. Left hand. He had shaken hands with the left hand. The alcohol haze dissipated in a second. Even though the influence on his body didn't, couldn't, making it difficult to move, to move fast enough.

– You seek *him*, don't you? You want to find him more than anything.

– You know him? Jeremy asked.

Charles leaned back in the chair, closing his eyes for a moment.

– Know? I don't think anyone truly knows him. I had a few…
scraps with him some years ago.

He leaned forward again.

– I can tell you one thing about me. At the time I was a
completely different man than I am today. Lethal, able to strike
back at any individual stupid enough to… fuck with me. Not a
lightweight. At least that's what I thought. Until Timothy Joyce
decided I was worth his attention, until he fucked me over. No,
he didn't try to kill me. He didn't need to. I was left like a wet
cloth on the floor when he was through with me. He had killed
the most important in a human being, self-respect, and the belief
in oneself. I read about what happened to you and the others in
London. It's very similar to what happened to me.

A story. Not really a story, but random pieces of one, told
without passion, factual, almost without any resonance in the
voice.

They rose as if on cue, and left the place. Out in the streets
again, nothing changed. The surroundings, the stage, the
background, but nothing between the two of them.

The hotel room, the dark place, with walls that only looked
painted white. The neighbor typed on an old, fully mechanical
typewriter, while playing ancient ABBA songs. And it had to be
inspiring as hell, since he kept writing intensively for hours and
hours.

– I can still recall, vividly, how he looked like when he left me in
the dust, Charles said.

The alcohol had virtually paralyzed his vocal cords, but Jeremy
had no trouble understanding him.

– He said - and I quote: «I won't kill you now. If you had been
a fly, I might have, but you're not even that. One doesn't step on
shit in one's way, it's not proper». I didn't say anything, but he still
replied, as if he knew what I was thinking. «That's right, I really
don't care what's proper or not, but in this case I'm willing to
make an exception. I won't kill you, *now*. But know that I one day
or one night will return and kill you. You won't know the time or
the place, but I do».

Rafe leaned back in the squeaking bed, while hiding his face in
shaking hands.

– He turned his back to me, and walked away in a relaxed

manner. My gun was only two steps away. I had a fair chance of reaching it and shooting him, before he killed me, but... but I didn't do anything, not even the slightest pretence of an attempt. Then I knew that he was right, that I had already died, and all he had to do was to return at some predestined point in the future and bury me.

– Well, he doesn't even have to do that, the way you're talking, Zahn remarked sarcastically.

Something resembling a sharp flash appeared in the other's eyes.

– Have you heard about his... predictions? How they seem to be fulfilled? You must have, having dug in the man's life every day, every second for three months, an entire life...

– Do you believe in predestination, inevitability? That is what you're sitting here saying, right?

– I don't *know*, Charles said in bottomless despair. – I know I didn't use to. Every man creates his own destiny and all that shit... right?

– I don't believe it, Jeremy exclaimed. – I'll never believe it.

There was no answer. Nothing but a mumbling

– ... bury me.

Eyes remained open for a while, but they saw nothing. The totally loaded man slipped further back on the bed and remained there. Zahn waited a while to see if he would move, but he didn't. The chest heaved and pushed. Nothing more.

Zahn rose.

– You can't just sit on your ass, and wait for him to come, he said aloud.

He left. Went down the stairs, out in the streets.

It felt good this, to release the rage inside, to race through the streets in such an all-encompassing wild anger, a two-legged beast that murdered and molested. It dawned on him he would never let go of it. Others did, dying while still walking and breathing.

He drifted through the streets without aim, with purpose, until dawn caught up with him.

Even though Rafe had vanished when he returned to the room early in the morning, he bumped, as expected into him in front of Central Station later in the day. Charles seemed just as fresh and lively as he had been early the night before.

But now, when Zahn knew the demons riding the man, he realized they never truly left him.

– I ran, totally beside myself, he said, nodding, calm as death. – Until I eventually stopped, ending up here. It's not the worst place in the world.

A shrug, another sign of total surrender.

– Do you know the old story about the man being visited by Death?

– I know it, Zahn replied hoarsely.

– Death appears to the man and tells him to enjoy the time he has left, for the next day he will come and take him to the Kingdom of Death. The man waits until Death has left, before packing all his belongings, jumping on his horse, and rides the fastest he's able to the closest city. It's a hard journey. It takes all night and most of the next day. He has exhausted three horses and is totally spent himself when he finally arrives in Samara, the fortified city. At the city gate Death is waiting for him. «You idiot», Death says. «Death gives you the entire world and you throw it away». The man turns rigid in the saddle and falls dead off the horse.

They sat by a sidewalk café on the outskirts of Red-Light District. Charles didn't drink alcohol anymore. Perhaps there was hope for him.

– Listen, Zahn said, subdued and enraged, with a voice designed to convey contempt. – Perhaps you've resigned to your fate, but I haven't, so the least you can do is to help me take him out.

– Oh, you're one sneaky bastard. Charles laughed loudly and bitterly. – Perhaps you will get a shot or two at the Demon, if you live long enough. Don't worry, I'm not like your friend Winston, I won't kill myself.

But like Winston he was molded to dust, and as far down a human could go and still breathe.

– I've written a kind of mix between a dairy and scrapbook, Rafe Charles said unexpectedly. – It *might* teach you something useful. I don't think there has been anyone more obsessed with the good Timothy… until you came along. No matter how much there is about him in public records, it will always be insufficient, since the people there aren't personally involved. It's a job, a function. No matter how much they're taught to familiarize themselves with others' thoughts and behavioral patterns, they lack the most important: The drive flowing from a haunted heart.

*The guy is a poet.*

– What did you do, Rafe, when lightning struck?

– I and gang were trafficking in drugs, imports and sales in major ways.

Another shrug.

– That doesn't make sense, now, does it? He has stated his support for so-called «illegal substances», done it several times.

– About the substances. Not necessarily those earning big bucks on selling them. The big man bowed his head slightly. – And it can be a shitty thing. I see that, now, after he beat it into me, the suffering it might lead to.

Zahn concentrated, mentally turning thousands of pages.

– As far as I recall, he blames the authorities, and their official and unofficial policies, at least as much, for the suffering. There's no meaning in anything he does. Not this either. There's something strange, incomprehensible about his very existence, something I can't quite grasp.

They sat there for a while, in silence.

– Have you read Sherlock Holmes? Rafe wondered. – Do you know his most important theorem?

This time Zahn didn't need to think.

– Yes, it goes something like this: «If you eliminate the possible, and only the impossible remains, then that is, no matter how unbelievable and illogical the solution».

– Correct. The world is full of distractions, a puzzle, not with missing pieces, but with so many pieces not fitting in. Seemingly. Or said in another way: The world isn't a puzzle. There will never come a time when all pieces, in all puzzles, will fit. The world is chaos and unpredictability, an eternal enigma, disguised as something mundane, gray and boring. Joyce has realized this. He has embraced it and hides whom he truly is, hiding in plain view. To know him, to reach him, one must become him.

The insane and the completely sane warred in the large man's eyes.

They ventured into Red Light District in broad daylight. For some reason it felt safer to Jeremy than it would during the night.

Rafe talked endlessly, as if he had all this information in his head and had to get it out before it was too late.

– I have a chick here, he said. – I should really stay away from steady companionship, but I need someone to fuck, and I haven't money to pay even the cheapest whores on a daily schedule.

He kept changing between rationality and irrational madness.

– Hey, you, he suddenly shouted to a man passing by. – YES, YOU. Why are you following me? Do you have a special reason for it, or is it just a *hobby*?

After a period, actually several minutes, of unusual silence, he stopped and turned towards Zahn, sweating, with complete rationality visible in the bloodshot eyes.

– He's coming. I can feel it. He's coming for me.

More than anything, more than even Jeremy's fear that he himself, was about to crack up, the former inspector was scared by this rationality, this lack of doubt. It reminded him of what he had seen in Timothy Joyce or even in himself, in eyes, attitude and features. He laughed, a shrieking laughter, mad and chilling simultaneously.

And Rafe shrunk in fear under his ruthless contempt and onslaught.

Zahn rested on the couch at night. It was raining outside. In the bedroom Rafe and Antje kept it going. The way they kept at it one would think it would be impossible to sleep, but Zahn had slept. He had awakened half an hour ago, sweating, wide awake and scared to death not to find the gun. He had fumbled until he found it, and not let go of it since, while lying still, listening for sounds not fitting in, sounds that might fit other places, but not this one.

Antje, a big, tall nigger bitch had given him a warm welcome earlier in the day, perhaps too warm, since he had felt the results of it instantly. Rafe had suddenly turned extremely eager. They had disappeared into the bedroom, and kept at it ever since.

Zahn rose from the couch as quietly as possible, gritting his teeth, like an amateur. Wondering how long he would have to drag along the remains of his former life. He looked around the room, ensured himself no one was lurking inside it. The curtains covered the windows, keeping anyone from looking in. He dried sweat from his brow with the sleeve of his free hand, keeping the gun straight in front of him. The door to the hall was ajar. He attempted to recall whether it had been closed or not, before he had fallen asleep, but was unable to. Before really registering it, he was on his way across the room. Fingertips touched the door, pushing it open.

He slipped out in the hall. The darkness dominated out here, too, even more than in the living room. He had scanned for movement and he kept doing so, striving to sense the slightest change in the air. At least he had his socks on, but not his shoes. He doubted that was the case with a possible adversary.

On the other hand, an *adversary* would've had long practice in moving in something approaching silence.

Though in a city there was only relative silence. In the background cars always drove by, people talked or the city itself seemed to give away a permanent buzz. *That* he was fairly well versed in, separating important noises from those in the background. He had experience from homicide, where he had worked for a time on his way up. Everybody had told him that working in homicide was essential on the CV of anybody wanting a successful career.

He made a face at the darkness and the darkness made a face back. The large entrance hall seemed totally empty. Nothing moved, not even dust. He turned 180 degrees with his gun raised, holding it in both hands, frequently drying sweat from his brow, never letting go of the gun, not with either hand. Funny, the heat didn't really bother him. On the contrary, he was actually freezing ever so little.

And he had fired his weapon several times. On boards, on moving practice targets, and there had been occasions where he had participated in something resembling gun fights, but most of it had been done when he and the reinforcements had arrived. After releasing himself from the hospital, he had applied for transfer. When he started on his «leave of absence», he had yet to receive a reply.

And now it would probably never come, something that was just as well. The training he wanted, he needed they would never be able to give him. He could have applied for acceptance in SAS, the military Special Forces, but even there the training would be insufficient. He had to take the path Timothy Joyce had taken, had to become him in order to destroy him.

There was no one out here. Joyce would've known that without wasting time. Zahn leaned against the wall, filled with adrenaline, exhausted, putting the gun back in the holster.

He stood there, breathing in the dark, unable to stop breathing.

The shots were fired in a long series, from inside the apartment. He held the weapon without being conscious of having drawn it. He jumped without jumping, and kicked open the door. The bullets penetrated the wood, and struck exactly where he would have been if he had done as expected, and jumped inside after the first salvo. He fired through the door, blindly. A shout of pain, a yelp, on his right. He threw himself inside, rolled across the carpet. Chairs and tables turned over. He was fired at. The man leaned at the door to the bedroom. Blood flowed from wounds in his arm and side. Zahn fired and fired. The man, Rafe Charles, was hit several times in the chest, tumbled backwards into the bedroom and fell on his back. Jeremy mechanically changed clip with a frozen stare at the bloody body. He crawled, slipped over the floor, into the other room, where Rafe and Antje floated in pools of blood. He saw no one else, no matter how much he scouted. Antje didn't move. The pool of blood kept expanding on the floor beneath her. He didn't have to feel for her pulse to know she was gone, that she had died instantly.

– Rafe, what…

– No… mistake, Charles gasped. He yet lived, but he wouldn't for long. – I shot Antje, filled her with lead. Sorry. I fired at you, shot to kill, but you were far better than me, in spite of being a cherry. Damn you!

– But WHY? Jeremy knelt by his side, holding him, holding him tight.

– I'm… lethal, the dying man gasped in his usual dry manner, – a very dangerous individual. I exterminated an entire rival gang single-handedly once. He he. And you still took me out, that's… good.

He had trouble talking. His last words he gasped, yelped.

– I got away, I fooled him. Thank you…

He coughed once, and blood flowed from the penetrated lungs, out of the mouth, out everywhere.

Zahn rose, slowly, painfully. Everything had happened so fast, he had been unable to think, only act. Rafe had emptied a gun in Antje, before throwing it on the floor and started his attack on Zahn. Strangely enough the two guns had ended up side by side, under the window. The room did indeed resemble a slaugterhouse, with blood on the floor, on the walls and the ceiling. Blood everywhere. Zahn stopped between the bedroom and the living room. He stood there for a long time, before moving, leaving the place, and not looking back. He looked down on his hand, covered in blood. Sirens grew louder and noisy. He didn't care, but kept walking in a normal pace into the next alley, the moment the policemen rushed up the stairs to the apartment. Senses seemed to have been violently sharpened. All the senses, but most of all the non-obvious ones. The texture surrounding him, the patterns in the street and his path through them moved and changed from moment to moment. It seemed for a moment as if an elderly lady on the open square suddenly was right beside him. The trees closed in on him and distanced themselves once again. In the indistinct mirror image in the windows, he saw his own, unrecognizable face. He looked down on his hands, wet with blood. Now… Now, he had something tangible to hold on to.

# CHAPTER FIVE

## SIX DAYS IN THE CITY OF ANGELS

There, in Amsterdam's streets, after his insane and icy laughter, Rafe Charles had looked at him with fear in his eyes. The laughter had reminded him of something, someone.

A casual walk in narrow alleys gave way to whirlwinds of hands and feet, a body slipping in and out of view.

The two combatants seemed equal through the initial hits and kicks, the first few minutes of sliding movements, nude feet in the soft sand, the wave-like dunes. Until the bigger and more powerful man increased the speed and brutality, and drove the other backwards, until he lay on his back in the sand, with blood flowing from his mouth and bloody head wounds.

*Flowing thrusts, transitions, movements, like the wind that was always there, around them, around them all. Controlled aggression. Wrath.*

Zahn reached out a hand to Louis Markham, took the boy's hand, and pulled him on his feet.

– You're already back in shape, Zahn, Wells said, approaching them along with Caldwell and Russo.

Better shape, Zahn thought. Faster, stronger. Or is that just how it feels, after once again surviving, living?

He once again became aware of the surroundings, Venice Beach, California, USA. In truth he had been aware of them during the entire exercise. Overpowering the boy hadn't required his full attention, not even his half, and nothing of his wrath. He had been distracted most of the time, busy with thinking, observing the surroundings, observing himself. And the boy was good, he was damn good. He didn't let his own, smoldering rage block the fighter instinct, the way a cliché of a hot-blooded, vengeful oriental would. In spite of that he had been a pushover. Zahn had overwhelmed him, and could, if he had wanted to, have wrapped him up and sent him as a Christmas present.

Caldwell handed him his shirt and jacket. He slipped the clothes casually on his hardly sweating body. He picked up the shoes and socks he had left in the sand, but didn't wear them, but carried them with him in one hand. They entered the long promenade, walked down it.

The area was very changed compared to how it had been in the Sixties. Zahn hadn't been here then, of course, but it didn't take much imagination to more than sense the changes. The places that had been filled with rebels, musicians and artists, were now more or less only visited by tourists. People with money had bought the beach houses, and could enjoy the pale echoes of what had been. Real estate prices had soared and nobody with anything approaching a normal salary could afford to live here anymore. Some souvenir shops played The Doors, but that didn't keep it all from being horribly false and contrived.

An old man stood close by, supporting himself on his cane, outside the fenced tennis courts. The cane and the arm shook so violently that it looked like he could fall at any time. He stood with his cap in his hand, and it seemed doubtful that he could even hold onto that. The eyes in the wrinkled face stared at nothing. The sight incited in Zahn a horrible sense of undefined cold and rage.

They walked a while longer, until settling down by a table outside a café.

- You should clean your wounds, Caldwell told Louis.

- I can handle it, the boy replied with a shrug.

- You can handle it, Zahn nodded, - but you know better than walking around with them. Have them cleaned.

Louis nodded. After a brief fumble he found a box from his sack, and headed for the closest public restroom.

Caldwell looked enraged at Zahn. He smiled teasingly without even bothering to look in her direction, studying the scenery instead.

Venice had initially been planned as a copy of Venice in Italy, with canals and the works. Several had been built, before the idea, sensibly enough, had been abandoned. Now the streets were fairly normal, but it had kept its uniqueness as a mixture of European and American style. In the Sixties the hippies and artists had come here from all over the world. The present population was basically surfers, various eccentrics and tourists. But the place had kept its relaxed lifestyle. Zahn felt both attracted and repelled by the mood. But such was how he felt it in many places, the many places he visited and left.

A gang of boys and girls in their early twenties walked casually down the street, walked as if they owned it. They had trained in formal karate costumes close by on the beach where Zahn had enjoyed his exercise. In a very brief amount of time they had showered and changed, to a mix of sports outfits and something resembling gang uniforms. But they didn't really have much in common with traditional youth gangs he had encountered during his travels. Zahn saw instantly how economically, how purposely they moved, a clear sign of them having an immediate goal in mind. He remained laidback in the chair.

They stopped in front of him. Not in front of them. Of him. About three steps away, close enough to have a conversation, at a sufficiently safe distance. Safe enough. He smiled, a facsimile of the smile that had accompanied the laughter that had frightened to death Rafe Charles... and perhaps Arthur Markham.

- We watched you, the leader, a girl of middle height and visible muscles, nonchalant and patronizing - and with an underlying aggression impossible to truly hide stated. – You're good.

– Thank you very much, Zahn replied neutrally. – You're not bad yourselves.

– But not good enough…

– There are always bigger fish in the sea, he said.

– Joyce made you.

– He struck me down, and jumped up and down on me for a while, and then he got nasty.

– He's using you to measure himself, one of the boys said, very patronizing. – One day, when you're almost as good as him, he'll take you out permanently.

Zahn didn't say anything.

– But, the girl said, – there are things suggesting he might have miscalculated just a bit. He had help this time, didn't he?

– He had help, Zahn nodded. It was the truth, as far as it went.

– And yet he couldn't make you stay down. She nodded to herself.

The strange conversation ended. Without a word of goodbye, the youths turned away and left the place. Zahn sensed a pleasant warmth flow from a place inside his body.

– What was that about? Caldwell asked pointedly.

– We've just got ourselves another set of eyes and ears and scouts in this city, Zahn explained.

The wind. They could hear the wind, touch the wind.

– At least they're not superstitious, she commented, after a longer break, where the three of them sat and didn't say a word, – if they join up with… you, they don't believe the myth about our prey.

– You're thinking about his on the spot predictions?

– They're not on the spot, she said unexpectedly weakly, – but nothing but statements about events he's staging.

Silence reigned once again.

Louis returned, somewhat refreshed, somewhat whole.

Zahn researched the fight scenes in his mind, the way he hundreds of times had researched his bloody encounters with Timothy Joyce.

Louis had the fight, the heat and the moves in his blood. And it had been stimulated from an early age. And Zahn? If his hadn't been triggered early, it had been now. There had been something new and lethal in his fighting today, he hadn't noticed earlier. In attitude, muscles and body. A sharpened blade in the form of a man.

Words and images kept whirling in his thoughts. Full of meaning, devoid of understanding.

– What are we really doing here? Caldwell wondered. – I mean really doing here. It's a great place and all, but not exactly fit to find the tracks *we* seek.

He looked at her, gave her his complete attention, hardly managed to contain his irritation.

– You agreed to follow my orders, didn't you?

– Y-yes.

She noticed what was hidden, what showed in small nuances in his eyes, his voice and her facial skin paled visibly, even in the soft light of the afternoon sun.

Usually this sense of fear, of inferiority made her aggressive. Now it made her shrink further. He usually seemed so neutral, so emotionally cold, but sometimes, like now… To say he scared her was insufficient. It went far deeper than that. Like…

in the storage building forty-eight hours ago.

– Okay, then I won't hear anything like this anymore, is that clear?

– Clear, she squeaked.

– *Good!*

The others tried to not let themselves be marked by this short exchange of viewpoints, but they were. He more than sensed how hard he had shaken them.

Just what he had in mind. He knew fully, now, that there would be no more doubt about rank.

– I'm certainly willing to listen to reasonable suggestions from you, and to well-thought observations, if you should have any.

From then on, he treated them as if they didn't exist, didn't exist in his presence.

Gwen's face, Gwen herself, who he hardly had allowed himself to imagine, to think about, in three years, appeared before his inner eye. Gwen from the storage building and from the video he had seen at the central police headquarters.

That irritated him. He felt nothing else, nothing… except irritation.

His cell phone rang. The wrinkle between the eyes turned visibly deeper. He knew well that it was in moments like this, in his weak moments Joyce had used the opportunity to «contact» him. He found the phone in his pocket, but didn't hurry.

– Yes? He said. Seconds later he «hung up».

The others looked inquiringly at him.

– Message from Sergeant Martin, he told them. – The best-trained free divers didn't even reach the hatch before they had to turn around. As we thought that solution isn't more viable than hundreds of others.

And once again something touched the edge of his consciousness, before it slipped away, outside his reach. He tightened the muscles in his hand, before letting go.

Relaxing them. He rose abruptly, threw some bills on the table, and left. The others hurried after him.

He had been aware of the looks and interest from random people when sitting still. It was hard to avoid it. Now, when they were walking, and the senses were inevitably sharpened, it turned impossible. He had been notorious since the events in London, and especially since the equally noteworthy events in Calcutta and Asia the year before. The last couple of days his notoriety had outgrown any reasonable proportion. David Kelly had finally upgraded him from «interesting newbie» to the elite series. It actually amazed Zahn that Kelly still walked and breathed, that no one had removed him from the map yet. He had *irritated* many on his own way to fame. The obvious reason why was that he filled a need, like one of the many slugs in the present-day world.

Zahn had to admit to himself that he, too, had had use for him. To build his current status. What he used for his own purpose.

– Mr. Zahn. The cry came from behind somewhere, the next much closer. – JEREMY ZAHN

There was a slight question mark hanging after the last cry. Zahn turned and nodded to the big younger man stopping right in front of him, grabbed him with his eyes. There had been no need for the guy to cry out the way he had. He evidently sought a bit of publicity himself.

– I saw… observed you during your session on the beach, he said out of breath. – I was impressed. You see, I run a Martial Arts training center, and I was wondering if you needed more training partners, if you could spare a bit of your time, since you are in the neighborhood, to give my students a slice of the real world, so to speak?

He overdid it. Nobody used such formal language anymore. What was wrong with people these days? Did they think everybody enjoyed being famous?

– Truth to tell, I do have some time to kill, Jeremy Zahn nodded, seemingly relaxed. – I'm not sure you'll appreciate what I have to teach, though.

– We can take a little heat, he was assured.

– Do you have lots of space? Zahn asked cryptically.

– Lots, the young coach affirmed. – An abandoned car repair hall not far from here.

Truth to tell he was only marginally older than the other boys and girls. Everybody stared attentively at Zahn, with eyes filled with apprehension and expectation. Zahn ignored Caldwell's ironic grimace. As long as she was content with that, he saw no reason to act. Like he had counted on, she would never be more than a dubious ally.

Lines of light blew through the broken windows. The wind illuminated hot and cool bodies.

– Four and four, he told them nonchalant. – Go at me with everything you've got.

The buzz in the room buzzed even stronger.

– Why only four? A young boy, a young hothead wondered.

– The value beyond that number is rather limited, Zahn commented dryly.

After some rough handling and open rivaling the first four lined up for punishment. They greeted him in the traditional martial arts way, Zahn did not. And they got a glimpse of what was to come.

He spent the next half hour tearing countless boys and girls to shreds. It wasn't like with Louis, where he had taken his time. Here he played out all his aggressiveness, all his lethal skills from the first move. Some were so scared that they actually attempted to flee. He always caught them and roughed them up even more than he did the others, and none dared flee. And he hardly worked up a sweat. Some still glanced at the exits, but they remained on their spot. Scared, paralyzed and beaten up, and fascinated in spite of themselves, they remained.

He had their complete attention. Any move he made, any word he spoke, was hammered into their feverish minds.

– I've learned it's necessary to be ruthless and brutal when you want to make something work, he said, abruptly, without further introduction. – And when you want to make something big work, you must be even more ruthless and brutal. A person who does not use rough means will not get anything done and will eventually even risk burning out in very tangible ways because of inefficiency. Magical means, well thought-of plans or effective shadow play should never be underestimated, but ultimately, it's one's willingness or unwillingness to show strength in decisive moments that will eventually decide the outcome.

He noted with satisfaction that Caldwell stood there, using her arms to embrace herself, as if being cold. The others also revealed a similar subdued, receptive attitude.

– Oh, I'm certainly not underestimating the harmony between mind and body and all that shit. It's important, but is completely useless if one doesn't know how it may be used as a *weapon*. What I'm saying, what I'm telling you is that no form of combat should be excluded. Not well-thought-of strategy, not so-called non-violent resistance, not mental and physical violence.

He talked himself into a frenzy. There wasn't a trace of youthful eagerness and impatience in his voice, but it still burned with a passion he knew scared the living bearshit out of people. And these were no exception. They listened, in awe and respect. He didn't feel empty afterwards, but filled in a way he previously had only been able to imagine.

Smoke drifted in the air in the pub Stranger's Inn, under the ceiling, down at the floor between the guests' feet.

– It wasn't obvious, Caldwell said, – but you sounded like a revolutionary.

A girl danced on the desk, half clad, half unclad. Zahn studied her with a distant look in his eyes. He wasn't here. He was more here than he had ever been.

– I wasn't aware of that. He frowned. – I've never cared much for that stuff.

He had been traveling a lot the last three years, seen much more. He guessed one couldn't avoid noticing conditions here and there that were beyond, far beyond the need for critical comments. As long as one stayed in one place one grew accustomed to it - and one tended to close one's eyes to events that would make one sick, if everything was served simultaneously.

– They expected you to speak about Joyce, she said hesitatingly, cautiously. – And in a strange way, I don't think they were disappointed. You spoke about him without speaking about him, so to speak.

She didn't say what she most of all wanted to say. Didn't dare, both because she feared his reaction, and because of her own fear, fear of acknowledgment.

He grew distant. He saw tracks in snow, in a landscape of stone and mountains. Spread snow, hot summer. He looked into the woman's face, and what he saw there engraved, was Timothy Joyce's demonic features.

A group of boys raised their glasses in greeting. He raised his own, returning the greeting, relaxed, with burning eyes.

– I've heard that our man Joyce has his own cult in this state, one in which members worship him as a living god, Wells said gloomy. – Is there any substance to that?

– I've heard it, too, Jimmy Swain, the owner of the Martial Arts center said. He spoke slightly indistinct, because of a swelling on his left cheek. – I've never met any of them.

– California residents are nuts. Wells shook his head, he had moved here from New York the previous year. – No sense of life's realities.

– What do you mean? Russo asked interested, being born and raised in this state.

– I mean, Wells emphasized, shaking his head, – that everybody here is living right in the middle of an active earthquake area and they're virtually ignoring that fact. And then there's the San Andreas Fault Line.

– What about it? Louis asked curiously.

He had kept his youthful curiosity, his hunger for knowledge and everything.

– A relatively small bomb there… Wells struck out his arms, – and the entire state slides into the ocean. Arizona will get a lot of valuable seaside real estate. And the worst is that it might happen naturally, by itself. All Californians are walking suicides.

– But you, my good man, are also living here, Russo pointed out.

Wells reddened. There was laughter. End of discussion.

A TV was on somewhere. Zahn heard the words, didn't really need to see the images, saw them, looked at the screen very deliberately. They showed a car-chase scene. It was one of these countless programs where the police had the opportunity to show off their… their propaganda. Where car-chases were the order of the day. They always ended with one of two outcomes: Either the villain was caught and arrested, or the person in question suffered a gruesome death on the road after a series of bone breaking maneuvers.

– The Police, the show's host stated in a very patronizing tone, – allow these tapes to be shown for one reason only… they want an end to the attempts of bank robbers, outlaws and speeding violators to escape patrol cars. Here in California the authorities have choppers and drones at their disposal that can, at any time assist the very fast patrol cars on the ground and no one gets away. Violators are either caught or it all goes *wrong*, and the courts are saved the bother, saving a lot of the taxpayer's money. There's really only one option available to them and that's surrender.

Zahn laughed contemptuously. Caldwell looked curiously at him.

– What a laugh riot, he said aloud. – What a bunch of hot gas bubbles.

– It's a bit strange to hear you say that, another pointed out. – You are, after all, a cop yourself.

– I've come to see myself as an independent operator, Zahn grinned. – Besides, we should all realize that being a cop isn't keeping you from being stupid. It's true that this propaganda works wonders with most people, but now, with the last few days' incidents... People know that only sheep and idiots are adhering to rules and the law, know that crime does pay. And now, these days, they can't hide that fact to themselves anymore, the way they very much want to.

It didn't turn into a physical fight. The most important reason for this was that the present officers knew he could wipe the floor with them, and what was worse: That he would get away with it. Jeremy Zahn had an understanding with the authorities, with the powers that be, going far beyond ordinary police authority.

The last few years he had familiarized himself with the more unofficial parts of the establishment. And here, now, in the city of angels they had let him even closer to their halls of power.

Someone changed channels. The screen showed the Mayor, with his staff, and the Chief of Police and bunch, in front of the City Hall.

– We won't ACCEPT such RIFF-RAF in our town, he thundered. – Steps have been taken and are taken this moment to clean the city of both Joyce and his corruptive influence.

– What about the... considerable threats Joyce has uttered against the city police and government? A journalist asked.
– What measures are you prepared to take to keep him from executing them?

– We're in a FULL state of alert, it was replied instantly. – All the considerable power a modern society has at its disposal has been activated. Additionally, we've developed a flexible response, based on Mister Joyce's... unique behavioral pattern. We're not underestimating him, we're not falling into that trap, but he's just one man, after all, leader of a smaller group of people practically eradicated just days ago.

Zahn merely laughed this time. He chuckled for minutes.

He sat by a broad, round table, with Caldwell, Louis, and a host of interested parties.

– Many have claimed you're in league with him, a girl said, – that all of it is just a game, but that's bollocks. He emptied his revolver in your chest, damn it.

– Yeah, Zahn replied with a modest smile, – he's made a number of attempts to kill me, both in person and through proxies, and failed.

– But during those three years you've only come close to him twice, in London and here.

– I've always been close to him. The response was like a gust of wind, the proximity of a glacier. – Never more than a heartbeat, a corner away, but never closer than an arm's length.

– That's so poetic. The sigh came from another end of the larger table.

He wondered. Wasn't this voice exactly the same as the former speaker?

A heavy sigh. He more than sensed the awakened sexual excitement in both voices. He saw it in their eyes when he studied them. For the first time he gave them a closer scrutiny. The boredom let go. The two had braided their hair on opposite sides of the face. Aside from that the resemblance was uncanny. Identical twins. He noticed his own interest. Two blonde, tanned beach bunnies. Burning desire and paranoia rose simultaneously within him. It struck him that if he was so instantly turned on from meeting two unknown pieces of driftwood on a beach, then Joyce would... know he would be.

Then it didn't matter anymore. He threw the final remaining caution to the wind, something he had, in truth done long ago.

He met their eyes. Strange, since they sat on each their side of the table, that he could meet both their eyes simultaneously. Both drew breath sharp and deep. He heard that, sensed the changes in their bodies. It was unmistakable. He rose from the chair. When he left only the two of them followed him. A buzz rose from the assembly. He didn't care. Later he imagined he had seen Caldwell's face somewhere. It didn't matter. She, too, was merely nothing more than a painting on an exhibition, one he passed through without looking closer at any of the images.

– The key, please, he told the barkeeper.

The man behind the counter actually, unbelievably resembled a question mark. Zahn had always thought question marks looked silly.

– The... key? OH, YES! The guy handed it to him without the slightest resistance. – Number 3, sir, up the stairs.

Zahn didn't pay. It wouldn't have cost him anything, but he didn't care for doing it. That was all the reason he needed.

– I don't want to be disturbed, do you understand?

– I'll take care of it, the man coughed, both scared and conscientious, – take care of everything.

Fear, Zahn thought. Fear is the key.

He was strolling up the stairs. The girls giggled as they followed him. When he opened the door to the room and held it open, they rushed by without daring to look up.

He closed and locked the door behind him, and slipped the key into his pocket.

– I'm going to call you Left and Right, he declared.

– We've been called... one began.

– ... worse things, the other completed.

He undressed without delay, without hesitation. With even wider eyes they started undressing each other. It happened with such elegance, such dedication on delivery that it was obvious they had done it before. They started playing with each other, without ever taking their eyes off him.

– Right, you come here.

The writhing creature split in two and one part approached him.

– You're left, he stated.

– From your point of view perhaps, she chuckled.

She wore just a tight shirt. Nothing but a tiny piece of cloth was left on her body. He pulled it off her. She raised her arms above her head, very cooperative, while writhing against him, writhing her hips tight to his body. He turned her around, held her tight, while he enjoyed touching her neck and the heavy breasts.

– Mine is the only one that counts, he mumbled, and pushed her down on the bed.

Right hurried forward and stopped before him. He had no trouble reading the fear in her eyes, the slight shaking of her lips. He grabbed her around the jaw and pushed it up, kissed her hard, and kept her there. The resistance that might have been in her, in them, faded quickly. He pushed her down on the bed, to the sister and crawled onto it himself.

– Left, come to me.

And Left came, instantly.

He rotated a hand across her belly, in ever-wider circles. She awaited the inevitable, in expectation, knowing. Eyes about to close opened wide again, when he removed his hand. He pulled the other sister to him by the legs. They realized he would take his time. He handled them thoroughly and close to impassionate. They cried out their complains of desperate need, writhing and throwing their bodies back and forth close to him. He registered they were tanned all over the body, and that fact didn't fail to please him. They pushed themselves at him from two sides, while both reached for his growing cock. He slapped them on the cheek, one time each. They froze. He repeated it. Tears jumped from their eyes. They stared blindly at him, attentive now. He grabbed a breast in each hand… waited a bit, touched them, allowed it to sink in… before squeezing hard. They howled. He pushed them both forward. They stood on all fours, gasping and sniffing in misery, in need. Their butts raised up, ready for him.

When he pushed his hands against their already swollen cunts, his hands turning instantly wet. They gasped some more and then they released prolonged, lasting moans. He placed one sister on her back on the bed, the other on her belly on her. Chest to chest they writhed in his iron-hard grip. Then he couldn't wait any longer, and he slipped inside she who was on top. He didn't give a shit whether or not she was Left or Right.

But even now he sensed a certain distance to it all in himself. To him it remained a kind of exercise in control, and one very, very successful. Even when he lost it completely when he pumped up one of the twins. When he turned them and kept going on she who had previously been below. When he emptied himself into the other girl, when he emptied himself for the second time.

He remained on his knees above them, heaving for breath. He had no idea how long time had passed before sensing movement, looking down, and seeing the two grab his still pulsing, half hard cock from two sides. They looked up at him with two pairs of begging eyes, still foggy with an all-encompassing desire strangling any reason. Half in reflection, half instinctively he loosened their braids, observed how their hair flowed down shoulders and bodies. All thought of right or left, right or wrong, faded from his consciousness, and they fell down on the bed, tumbled around in a single hot embrace.

He walked through a long tunnel. There was no light at the other end, he knew that, only knowledge… and understanding, unlimited understanding. How long he had had this dream he didn't know. It felt Eternal, both backwards and forwards.

Dawn's light came to him, long before the actual sky brightened in the east. Light came from the land in the east, from between the low houses, until it at dusk descended in the western sea.

The morning after he started the day with a long surfing trip on a wind-board. He had tried it a few months earlier, and enjoyed it. It was enormously exerting. The person on the board had to move constantly. Turn left, turn right. Back, fast as lightning. To keep the balance, to keep the wind behind. The sail was big and hard to handle, and one was forced to keep changing position. He had been completely exhausted the first time he had tried it. Now it was like a breeze, and he took ever-greater risks, attempted ever more difficult combinations, to test himself.

He stood on the beach, stared at the sunrise, stared back at the sea, with all the eyes in the back of his head. Nobody could sneak up on him. If a mole-like creature burrowed towards him under the sand, he would sense the vibrations in the ground. Caldwell moved quietly. He still discovered her while she still was far away. He knew he could sense if someone aimed a rifle at him from the row of houses.

– I don't understand you. She slipped close to him, though not too close. – Every time I think I have figured you out, something new appears, throwing a monkey wrench in my observations.

– Frustrating isn't it, to encounter someone not fitting into any pattern?

– Why must you be like that? She asked fretfully. – So…

– Frustrating?

She left.

She returned later that day when he sat in an armchair.

– You're surfing, you're sitting here, relaxing, she commented aggressively. – That doesn't have to be bad, but isn't very productive in our situation, I would gather.

– Read aloud, he ordered and handed her the scrapbook, Rafe Charles's journal.

She did, suddenly strangely subdued.

– *He's planning something big. Perhaps his attacks on the drug-lords represent the same as his attack on everything does. It's meant to be taken literally, a warning, that once, not that far into future, he begins whatever he's about to begin, no one will escape his wrath.*

– He says about himself, something I've heard referred more than once: «In Los Angeles Timothy Joyce will be born and he will build the foundation for his life's work».

Caldwell threw the book back into Zahn's lap.

– Ambiguous and partly incomprehensible, as usual. She shook her head. – Does he mean the start of his career or the escalation we've seen the last week?

– Definitely the second, but I believe he means the first as well.

– But… that doesn't make sense. He has been a well-known figure on the world stage for years.

– No, it just seems like that, Zahn corrected. – It does make sense, somehow. We just can't see what kind. Rafe didn't either, no matter how hard and long he studied the man.

He turned towards her. To this point he had stared a bit to the side, away from her. Now he stared her right in the eyes.

– This is what you and gorillas, and blind followers don't get, meanings beyond the obvious, beyond words. You have no imagination. You must quite simply pull yourselves together for us to survive this, for you to be of any use to me.

He rose, shadowed her. It took a while for her to realize she had the sun at her back, that she was between him and the sun.

– I've sworn to bring you face to face with Timothy Joyce, he told her. She shivered under the onslaught of his intensity, in his eyes, voice, in his core. – I've hunted him for three years, you have for two days. It's my hope you will be able to support me, in my hunt, but as long as that doesn't happen, you should stay clear of me. You see, I can do well without males and females with an inferiority complex, especially when they constantly strive to compensate for it.

– What are you saying? How can you stand there and say something like that to me?

– Shut up, he said, just as relaxed. – Be honest, you mean, instead of the usual modesty and dishonesty?

She stood there with her head bowed. He unbuttoned her blouse, until the breasts had been completely uncovered. He started fondling them, totally insensitive. She didn't resist. He had crushed all resistance in her, he knew that. He could pluck her whenever he wanted.

He let go of her. She gasped in shock and fell to her knees.

– Sorry, he said, – you don't really turn me on.

– Oh, you're clever, she said. – You cut deep, punish in ways others can't even imagine.

– That's what you want, he said. – To be *punished*. But you won't fool me, won't catch me in your web, so you might just as well stop trying.

– You will lead us to him, Jeremy, she said. – I knew that from the very first time I saw you.

He stared at her and concentrated on getting his eyes as condemnable as possible. It worked badly. She wasn't bad at cutting herself. They were all perfect outcasts, a perfect team. Perhaps they truly had a chance of tracking down Timothy Joyce.

He turned away and started on the long walk off the beach. She remained in the same position, exposed and abandoned.

His shadow never leaving her.

His phone rang in the evening. He had expected it, expected something. He had really been waiting for three years or perhaps even longer. In a calm beyond peace, the end of all peace.

They had returned to Downtown LA earlier that day, back to the well-equipped suite at the top of the hotel. One hell of a safe place. Every floor was heavily guarded. All the neighbor buildings as well. An eventual approaching chopper would be shot down blocks away. Zahn had discussed the security measures with each and every guard, gone through it down to the smallest detail. Not so much because he felt it would help, if Joyce decided to strike, but perhaps it would weaken him sufficiently for the core group to have a fighting chance.

Before leaving Venice, they had given cell phones to a larger group of hopeful groupies.

– You will not use this phone, was Zahn's words of departure to them. – You will program it to receive messages for me to contact you. If you ever use it to do anything else, I'll know, and I will track you down, and kill you. If you need to contact me, you'll use a public phone booth. If I can't be contacted directly, I'll get the message fast and will contact you.

The twins, now impossible to tell apart looked shyly at him under lowered eyelashes. The others, too, looked at him with a wide range of contradicting emotions and flat on its face admiration, so close, so close to submission.

The phone rang a while after darkness had set in. The others looked at him, but didn't move. He walked to the phone and unhooked the receiver.

– Yes?

He said. Nothing more, nothing less.

– *I'm in West Hollywood,* Zahn heard Jimmy Swain's excited voice. *– I've seen him. Not long, but more than enough. You don't forget a face like that. He didn't look at me, not as anything but dirt beneath his heel. Unless he can read minds, he has no idea he has been spotted. I swear, I didn't blow it.*

– Nobody says you have, Jimmy. Zahn rubbed himself between the eyes. – Relax and give me the details.

– He had his lady with him, too, the blonde.

– WHAT?

– *It's true,* Jimmy assured him, even more nervously, *– She isn't a sight one forgets either. They visited a restaurant. You wouldn't believe they're wanted all over the globe. It looked more like they were taking a Sunday stroll... even if it's not Sunday.*

– Stay there, exactly there. Give me the address. We'll be right with you.

The other hardly managed to confirm that, before Zahn hung up.

– It's an obvious trap, Caldwell remarked, as he filled a bag with weapons.

She followed mechanically his lead.

– Yeah? And so what?

The city's wall of sound hit them on Van Nuys' Boulevard, still a very busy street, though not like in its heyday. The drive continued, to the more fashionable areas. They didn't drive through Beverly Hills, but they were close to it, so close they could smell money.

Like the others he could smell burned rubber every time he made a turn at high speed. They didn't use sirens, nothing like that. They had no escort, but traveled alone. They were five people adrift, on the eternal Journey.

He drove calmly, controlled, on the edge, always on the edge. In his former life he had been a moderate driver, never been driving on the edge of the possible. Now it happened ever more often, ever more impossible.

The car rolled the last few turns to the parking lot Swain had called from. They spotted him a few steps away from the phone booth, when he signaled that everything was okay. The car stopped, and they had stepped out, guns in hands, almost before the engine had been turned off.

– They're still inside. Swain spoke fast, nervously. – Pauline and Penny cover the back.

– Good work, Jimmy, Caldwell praised him. – You go to the girls, now, and then you will all disappear.

Swain looked at Zahn. He didn't move an inch until Zahn had nodded, but after that he ran off like the wind. They knew he wouldn't interrupt anything.

– We go straight inside, Zahn said to his companions. – Be prepared for major civilian losses. Don't worry about it. It's in our mandate, and will be accepted. Grudgingly, but joyfully, when we bring them the head of our adversary.

They moved. Short, rapid steps. Everything seemed to happen in slow motion, in infinite slow motion. For a moment or two Zahn imagined that they weren't moving or moving towards the restaurant at all, but away from it. They compensated instinctively by speeding up a bit, to no avail. It was like they moved for hours, moved through a maze of air and shadow, before they suddenly found themselves right in front of the building. The door opened and feet touched a soft, woven oriental carpet, a pattern of complexity taking their breath and attention away. Caldwell waved her badge in front of the bouncer at the door. They walked down a staircase, and were able to see everything they hadn't from the street. He, they weren't any place, were nowhere to be seen.

– He has disguised himself again, Caldwell said impatiently. – But it doesn't matter. We've got him this time.

The group remained on high alert.

– Now, that was quick. The manager met them as they fully entered the room.

The group looked at each other, not really comprehending anything, fearing the worst.

– We're looking for this man and woman. Dupond (Russo) held up two photos. – They were seen walking in here.

– It's them, the manager confirmed. – Even though they didn't look exactly...

His eyes widened to an uncanny degree.

– Are those the people I think they are? He twisted his hands nervously, and even more so, when they nodded and confirmed his suspicions. – I should have recognized them, I guess, but as I said they didn't look exactly like that... And they used the toilet... the same toilet... and vanished completely.

Before he had finished speaking, they had rushed on, thrown away their bags and charged into the toilet. Both toilets in the backroom. Wells kicked in the door. Russo threw himself inside. He could hardly stop himself pulling the trigger, until he saw there was no one inside. Very fortunate for any ordinary guests...

Zahn was still standing by the manager's side when Caldwell appeared lurking from «her» toilet. She shook her head.

– They ran off from the bill, the manager said. – They vanished into the toilet after having completed their meal, and that was the last we saw of them.

– And walked out?

– That's out of the question. That someone runs from the bill is so astonishing that we hardly experience it, but it does happen on rare occasions, and we do have a heavy guard standing duty at the back and front of the restaurant to combat such vile behavior. They can't have escaped that way.

Zahn and Caldwell exchanged looks. Was this guy for real?

– But he and his female companion are gone? Caldwell stated sweetly. – So, where did they go?

– I'm forced to conclude they have somehow reached the basement, and left through there, in spite of all doors being locked. Wasn't it Sherlock Holmes that supposedly said...

– Let's take a look downstairs, Caldwell said.

They did and found two doors locked and wielded shut. Nobody could get out or in, without a powerful cutting torch.

The doors, they were told hadn't been in use during the current management. There were no keys, or locks, no way out.

– Do we call for backup and for someone to break this open? Caldwell wondered, clearly doubting the validity of her own suggestion.

– Don't bother, Zahn cut her off.

– They walked to the toilet, stayed there for a while, and walked back out, left the place in disguise, Russo said *excitedly.*

– Even though I feel I've developed keen observational skills in my years in the profession and should have seen that people that didn't enter the restaurant indeed left it, I realize you're right, the manager said crestfallen. – You must be right. There is, quite simply, no other logical explanation.

They left the place, still edgy and fully alerted.

But they no longer had the necessary drive, and felt fear tear them apart as they approached the car.

– This isn't a setback, Caldwell stated. – Just more lack of progress. We should take it seriously.

He quite enjoyed her choice of words just then.

Zahn studied the surroundings, the terrain, the houses, the parking lot, the streets, without really caring. Everything happened instinctively, on autopilot. Nothing had changed since they left the car. It was still there, on the exact same spot. Swain was gone, as instructed. There was nothing suspicious about the stage, the tapestry unfolding before Zahn's eyes.

– Stop! He said softly.

They took one more step, two forward, before halting and turning towards him.

– What is it NOW? Caldwell asked, boiling over in irritation.

The car exploded in a violent firestorm. The four people right in front of Zahn were struck to the ground as if by an invisible hand. He felt the strength of the explosion, but stood straight. Caldwell looked up on him with an expression of boundless fear in her naked eyes. He stood there with the gun in his hand. The night air was suddenly not the slightest bit chilling. He sensed the heat in his face. The boundless heat pushing against him from all sides, also from behind, where there were no visible flames. In that one, single moment his clothes felt like they were soaked in sweat. In the next, like the desert wind was rushing in from all sides. He noticed he had major trouble breathing.

# CHAPTER SIX

## ONE YEAR BEFORE NOW

He ran in the warm, solid snow. White, everything was just white. His own tracks turned indistinct, like the tracks he chased. They faded in the snow, faded before his very eyes.

The man moving through the city streets, through the tight crowds, did point to himself. His walk was clearly determined, not necessarily towards a close target, but a target, nonetheless. He sought *something*. That was clear to all the raffle encountering him. Everything around him got to him. The heat and stink of Calcutta or Kolkata dug into limbs, bones, far beyond the nose's capacity for smell. His sense of smell, like every other obvious sense, was merely a pale manifestation of what was deeper, in humanity's moist wells.

Zahn shook his head, both tormented and cheerful. Two years earlier he would have done his very best to close his eyes to the suffering, to the suffering and insanity he found here. Shiva - the Destroyer disintegrated everything, but Vishnu the creative power, made new life from even the most burned out pile. Humans recreated themselves constantly from the ashes.

He had heard rumors, more or less confirmed, about a dark man and a blonde woman raging in Asian cities, sometimes accompanied by a dark, firehaired woman. He recognized the signs of a legend already gaining mythic proportions. For over a year now, he had, with minor interruptions, traveled across the southern parts of this enormous continent, fully aware of the risk that Joyce, Monica and Gwen had already left and gone elsewhere. But he couldn't ignore the information. It fit too well, too well to be merely rumors. The uncertainty concerned the age of the tales. Sometimes the trail was hot, other times cold.

During the sixties and seventies people from Europe and America and elsewhere had come here to seek peace and wisdom. They had clearly been quite naïve to not spot the entropy and corruption, the human waste decaying here. Everybody saw what they wanted to see, he assumed. To a certain point. The most stupid dreamers created their own illusions. He knew that well. In spite of his inborn cynicism he had been that way himself.

Some streets were filled with beggars. Toothless prostitutes offered themselves. Cows died on the streets because no one wanted to touch them. No one removed them because they didn't want to touch them. During the putrid night the homeless fought for crumbs. More often than not the loser died and was instantly eaten. Dead bodies, also those who had starved to death, could rot for days because no one knew how long they had been lying there. He had seen it happen and hadn't puked. Hadn't even felt sick. But, rather in a backward way, the hideous sight had strengthened him. Some people saw holy men here, signs of universal unity. He saw more, even more signs of a totally out of whack global society. And he should know, widely traveled as he was.

White travelers had their own places in this town, too, as they had in most «third world» cities, living like kings on «fortunes» that would hardly last a month in Europe, the United States, Australia and Japan. Most of them, without ambition as they were, were content with a small place, in the safer areas of the city.

River Ganges, the morning bath. The bus drivers drove like pigs every morning to and from the beach. Special tours for all foreigners. Get instant purification. The entire delta, both in India and Bangladesh, was seen as the holy river's end, so people weren't… picky.

Zahn felt purified, sort of, on his own recognizance. Men with hair and beard below the waist, bathed naked in the dirty river. He did it as well, precisely because it was ridiculous. One of the many limitations he had to overcome was his own views on «morality» and «correct» behavior, of socially accepted acts.

It did have a cooling effect, but two seconds after returning to shore, one was just as sweaty and felt just as dirty as ever. He preferred the air condition at the hotel room.

Then the insane drive back to the city created wonders, with its blasts of wind through the bus.

The hotel basement, a dive of a bar and casino, was a rough place, in absolutely all meanings of the word. Riff raff and curious bystanders gathered there throughout the week. The many guards kept a tight ship, but in spite of this mass fights erupted on a regular basis. The house had specific rules and counted among the more honest in town… to no avail. To call the participating male and female players «desperate» did in no way do them justice. Known troublemakers and cheaters were banned from the premises. There would always be more of them.

Chaos and Cosmos constantly waging war, as they always had.

The Poker game started early. People always queued up to participate. Zahn bullied himself forward, like one had to do, if one wanted to play. He had played with limited success since his departure from London. Won just enough, here and there, to create a bit of a surplus, one of several contributions to cover his ongoing expenses. He had, without success, attempted to increase his funds in various banks around the world. The largest account had, to this point, been in Geneva. He had transferred most of the money there the day before. If he didn't win soon and win big, he would have to move to even lesser green pastures.

The chair rocked and threatened to collapse. Seven players around the table. No non-combatants were allowed nearby. Small possibilities for organized cheating in this room. The humidity and steam in the air made use of binoculars impossible. Two or more could cooperate, naturally, signal to each other, with routines learned over months and years. Zahn automatically reckoned this was done. He didn't care. It was just another hurdle, another limitation he had to beat.

The game was Five Card Draw. It was played with hard cash, American dollars. Insane amounts could change owners during an evening. Zahn had seen it happen. He had also seen winners have their throat cut two steps outside the hotel entrance. That thought sharpened his concentration further. He could feel the pattern at the backside of the cards with his fingertips, the way he had read about for years, heard others relate. He had polished his fingertips with both fine sand and sandpaper for years, without tangible results. Tonight, he felt it, felt it all. He was able to sense the various layers in the air. The stinking cigarette smoke had always bothered him. Tonight, it didn't.

He lost the first hand. Something he usually did. It irritated him, in spite of the experience he had gained during the years telling him it didn't really matter. The first few minutes always worked as a stalemate, a way of measuring the opponents. A process that took even longer as far as the tougher opposition was concerned. One realized quickly who would drop out first. They threw down the cards, swore, and left the table after an hour or two.

It had only been ten minutes. He couldn't recall if it was the sixth or seventh hand. He never could tell things like that later on. Small change had trickled to the center of the table during the first games. One guy had won two (or three) of them. The rest were evenly split between three others. Seven players around the table, at least one too many. Thirty-five cards were dealt. Usually each player could exchange all the five cards, but now that was reduced to three by necessity. That wasn't a problem, since all seven never traded three cards during the same game. Zahn got two deuces and decided in a moment of devil-may-care attitude to bet on them, to call a bet. It cost him fifty dollars, quite a bit during the initial stages of the evening. The ante, what everybody needed to put up to participate in the game, was ten dollars. He was already a hundred behind.

Fifty more and it increased to hundred and fifty (he had always seen as lost what was put on the table).

Four participated further in the hand, in addition to the guy who had opened it, a large part of the players. Suddenly it was 320 dollars on the table. The opener didn't want cards. The others took two, one and three. Zahn's chances of winning the game weren't very high. He probably had the worst hand of the five. No matter, he would learn something by studying the others' play. The evening was yet young.

One of a gambler's old, tired expressions. He grinned.

He picked up the cards, looking at all three simultaneously, had never been very fond of ceremonies. Several of the others picked theirs up one by one and looked at them in the most incredible and ridiculous ways. He looked at his cards one more time, and had to suppress a need to do the smallest of ceremonies. One more deuce and two treys. A tiny house, but a house, nonetheless.

The opener started with fifty. Sensible. One wouldn't want to scare the others off this early in the game. All three before Zahn called. He raised to a hundred. The opener raised instantly to two hundred. The other three folded. Zahn put on five hundred more. His opponent needed three hundred more to call him.

Zahn thought a bit through the game. The guy could have a house as well. He probably had just a Straight or a Flush... but one could never be certain. If he raised again, Zahn knew that his own devil-may-care, lethal feeling would begin evaporating.

The guy put on the three hundred. Zahn revealed, without ceremonies, his hand. The man swore and threw away his cards. Zahn took the money. 1370 dollars, in an early game, over half of it a surplus.

The next game Zahn opened on a pair of jacks, and demanded fifty for the others to buy cards. Three joined in. He didn't buy cards, and bluffed them under the table by putting 100 in the pot. Nobody called. Not exactly a big win, but he had succeeded in a bluff, and had increased his advantage.

Smoke... rose to the ceiling. Descended on the table, on the floor. He could see droplets of sweat on the others' brows, sense how dry his own was. Minutes passed. He lost some pots, but won far more, and when he won, he won far higher amounts.

After an hour he who had won the first few games left the table. After another fifteen minutes he who had lost the first major pot left as well. Zahn's stack of American dollars kept growing bigger.

He... won. Here in a downtrodden dive far away from what he had previously known, he won and kept winning. Players went bust, swore, and left the table. Others took their place.

Time passed, raged on like seconds. To leave the table wasn't allowed for one who wanted to remain a contender. One couldn't go to the toilet, couldn't take a break, without losing one's place at the table. Time crawled. Seconds could seem like hours. A man peed on himself. He was promptly removed by two giant guards. His considerable pile of money was left on the table. It was split between the remaining players. A shower of tears had made the bills a bit wet. No big deal. The room's moisture penetrated everything anyway. A new player joined. No presentation, only a swift, nervous greeting. The guy went bust in half an hour. The new after that didn't say anything. He lingered for a while.

Time flowed. The spectators drank. And drank. The place earned a lot of cash on these séances, no doubt about that, like during the gladiator games of Old Rome. It attracted people far and wide, and no poor suckers were admitted. The place had class. A classy dive. Zahn chuckled to himself, openly and scary. And the madness glowing in his eyes kept worrying his opponents.

Time flowed. The cards flowed in and out of his hands. A new hand began, another game in the big, everlasting game. He had two kings, joined, and threw the three useless cards. He enjoyed himself, enjoyed playing Five Card Draw, the classic poker game.

He got another king, a seven of clubs and eight of spades.

– Holy three kings, he exclaimed, striking his thigh excitedly.

This had happened quite a few times by now, and the others didn't care anymore, with their rocky, unmoving faces. He had never been good at masking his feeling during the game, so he had chosen another tactic.

Less than a minute later he had lost a slow round to a straight. Lucky.

The game continued, the game without beginning, without end. He got two kings and discarded the three useless cards, including an ace.

And received two more kings and a deuce of spades.

– Holy three kings, he shouted and struck a flat hand at his thigh.

He was number three this round. No ideal situation, but it didn't really matter with this bunch. They were too experienced, most of them, to be drawn into common pitfalls, into traps fooling a newbie.

And in this moment, he and they were shepherds of the same bush. They were desperate and needed money in a rush… and precisely for that reason money didn't matter.

Two seats to the right a man opened the post draw round with five hundred dollars. Number two called. Zahn did that, as well. The need to raise was almost overwhelming, but he resisted the temptation. He didn't want to reveal himself at this point. Sooner or later he would have to, if the opportunity presented itself, but not now. Hopefully one player or more had a killer hand and would bet like hell.

It happened with number six, the man with the bushy eyebrows that Zahn saw as his toughest opponent. The man raised five hundred. The next player, the last in the circle, raised five hundred more. Number One, he who had bet first raised with another thousand… The player before Zahn folded. Zahn would have to put two thousand on the table to call, to stay in the game. He knew nobody could have four aces, since he had discarded one. The man to Bushy Brow's left hadn't drawn cards. He had either a hand of Straight, Flush or Straight Flush, where the third possibility was improbable and the first was not very probable.

It was time.

– I raise with five thousand, he said hoarsely and put seven thousand on the table.

People folded in droves. Two called. Zahn revealed casually, with almost a total lack of drama, his four kings.

Some swore. Others digested it silently. Everybody threw away their cards without showing them. Zahn took the money. He didn't care about counting the bills, had never seen the point in that.

The ante was increased. New cards were dealt. Bushy Brow opened. Hundred dollars. Zahn called, like all of the players. Zahn kept a seven and an eight (foolishly) and discarded three. He drew three even worse cards in return.

– Holy three kings, he exclaimed and struck his thigh with a flat hand.

He began dancing a waltz on the chair.

Bushy Brow bet five hundred. Another raised to thousand. Zahn put five thousand on the table.

Everybody glared at him. They folded one by one, until he remained, the winner of the hand. He threw away his card without revealing them.

– So, what did you have? Bushy Brow rumbled.

It was just a test. He knew perfectly well that no one would ever get to know what Zahn's cards had been.

Next time Zahn didn't shout «holy three kings», but kept dancing on his chair. No rhythm, no waltz anywhere. He opened with a thousand dollars. One raised to two thousand. Zahn raised with another three. Three called. He showed his flush. People swore aloud. Several pulled out. He had gained a psychological advantage. He had beaten them.

A while longer, and there were only five left around the table. Those who quit or went bust were no longer replaced. Those who remained drank only enough to not be dehydrated. Zahn feared that he, at any moment, would feel an irresistible need to pee. But it didn't happen. He ignored his fears, his burgeoning neurosis, and focused his energy on the tournament, the tournament of fear.

Night outside, night inside. Muted lights. Low music. Or didn't it just look that way, seem that way? Perhaps people still danced and bawled, dangerously close to collide with the table and tip it over. He knew precisely where his gun was, he always did.

Cold trickled down his spine, or at least he imagined it did. When looking at the cards. He had never had a Straight Flush in his entire life, but now 8, 9, 10, 11and 12 of clubs stared at him. Not really the jack and the queen supposed to have eyes, but the three others, who didn't.

He opened the closing gambit this time. Perhaps he shouldn't have. Perhaps he should have hoped for the others to have great cards or try a bluff. He bet five thousand. The bets had increased considerably the last hour. All the remaining players had far more than they had started out with. Two players called, but didn't raise. That was that. Probably the best cards he would ever have, and he pulled a lousy twenty grand. He could have kept betting until doomsday with these cards, but the circumstances hadn't been right for heavy betting. The others didn't feel like it or they just didn't have the cards.

It had served to conserve the others' belief in his infallibility, though, and could be useful later. Could be.

He smiled. Twenty grand. Half a day earlier it would have been a fortune. Still was. He sat here with several hundred thousand dollars in front of him. In an hour or two... or a few minutes from now, it would either be more than tripled or gone. He felt relaxed, had never felt exactly like this before.

He boiled inside.

Every card was counted in his head, almost subconsciously, effortlessly, but it took a bit from him every time. Tiny bits slowly sapping a player during an evening, a night. Any sort of gambling was an exercise in exhaustion. Usually one fell into bed the moment the game was done. It mattered less, now, though, when one didn't play against the house. Everybody around the table had the same problem, a limit beyond exhaustion they couldn't cross. Endurance, however, meant everything here. No rest, no end, before the game itself ended. Some preferred playing against the house, where the rules were clearly defined. Zahn had taken a liking to his present type of gambling. True gambling, as some old timers would call it.

One hour just flew away. A fairly even hour to Zahn. Patience was always one of a poker player's most important assets. Ages could pass without good or even playable cards. One created one's own luck, but only to a certain point. Sometimes minutes could pass for eternities.

But this time, this hour just flew away.

A quick look at the cards. He had three fours. But that wasn't really that good a hand without a clear improvement. Not in this game.

Even the initial betting was fresh this time. One or more had good cards… or wanted the opponents to believe that. He called.

Perhaps more than one joined in because there was a substantial amount in the pot. Even professional players let themselves be carried away like that. Zahn had always played as if the money he had put on the table was lost the moment he put them there, and didn't have that problem.

His two new cards didn't improve on his three fours. He decided to play anyway. A steady hand pushed five thousand to the center of the table, what was technically called «the table» in the game. It was raised to twenty by the next guy. Bushy Brow folded, the two remaining as well. Zahn had registered that the man betting had very little money left. He had to win this round. Good enough reason to follow him home. If the guy pulled a double bluff, Zahn would learn something. Zahn called the twenty.

The man threw away the cards. Up, for all to see, but he didn't really care to reveal them. He didn't even have a pair. He rose, bowed, and left the table. Zahn grabbed the money and hauled them in.

They had just been dealt the next hand, when they heard a shot being fired. Nobody reacted visibly to it. The game continued without delay.

Four. And then there were only four.

Zahn didn't really feel weakened, but on the contrary strengthened. For every new hand dealt.

Bushy Brow dealt the hand, quite handy with the cards. Zahn couldn't decide whether or not he dealt from under the deck. It didn't truly bother him. It was one advantage Bushy Brow might have. There were other factors. And those who cheated had to live with the risk of being discovered. Several hands (fleshy hands) were displayed on the walls at this place. Everything was recorded on video. Nothing was done without due process here. One hour old recordings were studied at this moment. No one in their right... or wrong mind would be stupid enough to cheat here. Zahn grinned, and then he grinned some more.

A vision of a narrow mountain valley came to him, and didn't distract him. He was easily able to be several places simultaneously, and still concentrate more on one place. He had learned to live with the small flashes of reality. Flashes short like day, long as night.

Bushy Brow lost. His three aces were crushed against Zahn three queens and pair, Zahn's house.

It hadn't been much of a game, really. But it gathered strength and momentum. Ragnarok waited out there, patiently, eternally.

A few hands later. Zahn dealt the cards. He felt them between his hands, their surface, their patterns. Sweat and heartbeats from those playing poker at the river Styx's shores. He wasn't really playing against those who sat around the table, but against Joyce, against himself. He smiled. One of the players threw down the cards and left the table. He died in a knife fight two days later.

And then they were three. And the game pushed the game on. Instantly. An island was ravaged in a storm, all the houses torn to pieces. The day after, before they had started on the reconstruction, they were hit by another Storm, far worse than the previous one. The island was abandoned, but life kept on pulsing, Living there.

Zahn dealt the hand. Bushy Brow opened. After a few seconds there were already ten thousand dollars in the pot. Bushy Brow doubled when it was his turn again. Zahn and his second opponent called. Bushy Brow didn't «buy» cards. Zahn bought two, on his three aces. The third man one. Irritation coursed through Zahn and he fought against it, counterproductive as it was. It always felt bad to have three aces when another player didn't buy cards, when he guaranteed had a better hand. Unless he was bluffing. The best bluff was always one made from the ground up.

But Zahn didn't think he did, that he was bluffing. This time Bushy Brow and the other guy had strong, fear-inducing cards. He felt it, felt it even stronger when he got his fourth ace, and wondered if Bushy Brow had Straight Flush. Wondered if the other had, as well. It was too far gone to think that they both had it. But it didn't truly matter. Any Straight Flush would beat Zahn's four aces. And it didn't truly matter anyway, any of it… because this was a hand that would be played to the end.

There was no hesitation in the first bets, raises and re-raises. After just one minute there were several hundred thousand dollars on the table. And the players' piles of cash started shrinking considerably. Zahn had most left and he put it all out, went «all in», to assure that the two others to call had to use all their remaining money. He did it with a wide grin, spreading all over his face. For the first time he saw signs of worry in Bushy Brow's face.

He went through bet by bet, card by card, in his head, as he had done the entire evening. This was the final hand. And he realized it didn't really matter if he lost or won, since he, on a deeper level, had already won. And that that was the way a poker player did think. And that's why he had won before the game began.

Bushy Brow revealed his three kings and pair of tens. The other his four jacks. Zahn showed his four aces and it was like an anticlimax. He was hardly breathing any harder. He sensed his blood boil, and it threatened to blow him apart.

The two bowed sitting, rose and left.

Half an hour, forty-five minutes passed, as video-recordings were studied. The game master finally approached the table.

— It has been a pleasure watching you play, Mr. Zahn, he said politely. — Perhaps we'll have the pleasure at a later day as well?

— I think you can count on it, Zahn replied dryly.

He rose and started gathering the money, all the money. Everything continued. The game without end.

He spoke loud and clear. His words carried far, farther than the voice itself.

— I'm waiting for all interested parties outside, he declared. — To everybody deciding to make an attempt to gain my hard-earned cash, I'll say this: The slyest among you will probably succeed, eventually, but that somebody shouldn't be among the first to make an attempt. I wouldn't be among the first hundred, if I were you.

He walked outside, in the fresh air. The air seemed infinitely fresh. The money belt burned around his waist, his slim, muscular waist. He sat down on the bench. A swing camouflaged as a bench. A bench camouflaged as a swing. He sat there, while being served Glenmorangie whiskey. The smile he sent the waitress made her run back inside in panic. Either the drink was poisoned, or she thought so, or she had amorous intentions. He waited there for exactly one hour. Then he looked at his watch, rose and left the place.

He heard a lot in the days and weeks to come, and he listened. And finally, he heard something interesting, something tangible. He left Calcutta, the city of the dead the coming day, but remained, in people's eyes, forever.

The times later, when he played, were never the same. Sometimes he won, other times he lost. He didn't give a damn. It was just passing time, anyway. If he wanted to win, he did. The greater game called.

Memories, flashes expanding his inner vision. Two men having a conversation on a café. A group of female tourists talking fear-struck and fascinated about a man they had heard of in the north, about a wise man somewhere teaching the lethal use of hands and body. As if it could really be taught.

He left Calcutta in the midst of the hot season, heading north, passing a confused mix of old temples and ruins. The dry desert-like landscape changed into steppes and forests, and eventually mountains. The train headed north, at a snail's «speed». He didn't care. He had time.

At the snail's speed, towards the Himalayas, his current goal, Katmandu, Nepal. It was an ordeal, turning worse by the minute, the infinitely long journey, even worse than he had feared… «feared». Occasionally, in wrath and a sudden drive, he felt an extreme need to jump off and start running alongside the train. It was so bad sometimes that he could actually see it happen, see himself doing it, so lively, so real. He meditated, both attempting to mute and increase the raging fires inside. He had always been at war with himself, he realized that, now, with his ever-expanding consciousness. Always warred with himself about direction and content, and never getting anywhere.

It felt hysterically funny sometimes…

On the train he had to look within, he didn't have any choice. Traveling by train through an unknown and beautiful landscape could probably be inspiring the first few hours, but then you started getting bored. Everything was quiet, and nothing quieter than the sound of the train itself. Everything moved, but not those on the train. Modern travel in a nutshell.

So much was clear to him, now. Questions he hadn't even asked himself two years ago were answered and amplified.

– BEHOLD, he declaimed like a stunt poet. – I REACH DOWN, INTO THE SEETHING SEA, CREATING MYSELF FROM NOTHING.

He was eventually left alone in the compartment. The train was absolutely full, there were even people on the roof, but the staff made sure no one joined him after the last had disappeared, except for one notable exception they probably didn't bother to warn off.

The train stopped at some station. He didn't recall its name. Very often they could stand still for hours, wherever they stopped, at a station or not. This time it didn't last more than a minute.

No one could see, by looking at him, that he focused then, focused further. All his weapons, whether he carried them on his body or not, could be reached with small, smooth moves. He didn't truly need to focus that much extra these days, since he was always in a state of high alert. Old, well-oiled habits made him go through the rituals in his head every time something unusual happened.

A man entered the compartment, not too slow, not too fast, a man evidently used to a life in danger. At least to a point that he knew how people living a life in danger thought. A tall, skinny guy, with graying hair and a silly hat on his head. Not as silly as the British Empire-inspired a selection of the Indian police and/ or army walked around with, but still.

– My god, he exclaimed, – Is that a white man I see and perhaps even a European?

Zahn didn't say anything.

– Jacques Malin, Monsieur, at your service.

He wasn't a typical Frenchman. He spoke, for one, English without a trace of French accent, and his behavior didn't fit the label either. Obviously, an international nomad, one who didn't stay long in the same place.

Zahn accepted the hand offered him. And the reason they started talking wasn't really the boring ride. There were several reasons, but definitely not that.

There was an unspoken communication between those traveling without a home, without any home to return to, except the Journey itself. Humanity's natural nomadic spirit burned stronger in such people. Zahn had met several on his own Journey. They didn't have to have anything in common, except that, but it was enough.

Perhaps it was the only thing that mattered.

Zahn didn't offer his name or the slightest information about himself.

– Call me a journalist, if you want, Malin kept blabbering. – But I'm not, really. If I should call me anything it is A Traveler in Stories. I travel, I find stories, I write about them. I earn enough money to travel on.

– Sounds exciting, Zahn commented dryly.

– Ah, you're not even pretending to be interested. I like that in a person…

A lone pig stood inside an enclosure by a shed. If Zahn had been a photographer, he would have had a long time to prepare for the shoot. Hell, if he had been a painter, he would have managed to paint it, and then wait for the paint to dry, before the object had vanished from sight.

– Slow train coming… Malin stated.

It had been hours now since the guy had entered the train. Not his fault, really. Zahn was, quite simply, not very keen on having a conversation.

– I must admit that it, my chosen «profession», isn't always that interesting, Malin kept going. – Even among people breaking away from mundane pursuits and routines there are, incredibly enough, mostly boring personalities. Take my destination this time, for instance. I'm on my way to the Asian mountain area to write about the «special» culture. It has been done countless times before, but in a world that has a «tendency» to commercialize and trivialize everything it touches, repetitions are not only useful, but also the very foundation of everything. As long as the orange isn't flattened and squeezed for all its remaining juice, it is «news». And I am a «freelancer», one making his livelihood by selling stories. It's just like a writer being told to write the same book over and over again, but it is a living. Now, this does seem fairly unimportant compared to the major issues of our age, to everything else that is wrong with the world, but if a person realizes that this, to a high degree is symbolic for what *is* wrong with the world, it isn't completely unimportant.

Zahn was interested, almost in spite of himself. The bloke spoke so well for himself, so eloquently, and it didn't seem like the usual hollow phrasing and wording.

And then... there was something else, something tingling inside of him before Malin continued.

– But sometimes coincidence is on one's side, right? An incredible chain of coincidences coincides, and gains a certain significance. It so happens that I am on my way to meet a white man who has made a home for himself in the Asian mountains. But not even that is interesting in itself.

He stopped and looked casually out of the window. An elephant went berserk and was about to ravage a small, dusty village.

– But in this case...?

Zahn bent forward, suddenly with ambitions of hearing the rest.

Malin grinned widely, and raised a bony, incredibly long index finger, clearly very intent on letting the other pay for his hours of relative silence.

– In this case the man I'm looking for is Arthur Markham. He has, in recent years encountered another very famous, very infamous person, and believe it or not, another, eventually just as famous... or infamous person by the name of Jeremy Zahn is on its way to find him.

– That's what's called synchronicity, Zahn nodded.

– Ain't that the truth?

The Frenchman (not that he resembled a Frenchman) smiled his most incredible, disarming smile.

Zahn wanted to push the barrel of a gun at the other's forehead and pull the trigger. He resisted the temptation.

The train continued on its course, on its trail. The surroundings, the landscape passed by, whirling like air outside.

– I've studied Joyce with interest for a while, now, Jacques Malin continued with a considerably lower volume in his voice. – Who wouldn't do that, with a lot of free time and inquisitiveness on his hands? Nothing is written anywhere. But I have an excellent memory and am ready if the chance should present itself, and the reward should be worth the risk.

– So, you've done an in-depth study of him?

– That is to go a bit far, I guess. One picks up things here and there, putting the pieces of the puzzle together. Good journalists and scribes can hardly avoid doing that, and I imagine I'm quite the skilled newshound.

– I've studied him thoroughly for two years now, Zahn said, – and I'm hardly closer to him than when I started out.

– I do suspect that that isn't entirely correct, Malin pondered. – You must have inevitably learned a lot, but you lack the decisive pieces of the puzzle. They're there, but you don't see them, because you're too interested, too obsessed, to discover them. By pulling back a little, the way I've been able to do, in my relative indifference, one can more easily see all the pieces. One can still not see it in its entirety, mind you, but one can see a larger part of the board.

– But you've never met him?

– No, Monsieur, Timothy Joyce has fortunately seen me as too insignificant to honor with his personal attention.

There was a pause, in fear, in apprehension. But it ended quickly. When Malin continued it was with visible eagerness.

– What I initially found most fascinating with him was his quite astonishing skill as a master of disguise.

Zahn listened. He had learned to listen. He would never have come here, to this point in his life, without that obvious skill. He looked constantly forward, while the train raged on, on its predestined course.

– I've heard it said, he said slowly, – that he's able to disguise himself as just about anybody. I can't confirm it, as I've never experienced that part of his… art close up.

– I can attest to that, Malin nodded. The slight excitement in his voice was impossible to conceal. – In Paris, ten years ago, I had coincidently the honor of being among the audience during a TV-show. A French variation of a talk-show or its just as bad equivalent. No matter... the host, Marc Delon, was world famous at the time.

Zahn laughed out loud, a sharp, rough laughter. Malin looked perplexed at him.

– My apologies... Zahn shook his head. – A private joke. By all means continue.

– Well, the *point* was/is that everybody knew his face. They knew his gestures. The details of his movements had been broadcast hundreds of times. He was a well-known figure. I still remember the gasp from the audience when Joyce pulled off his mask, changed himself to himself in front of our very eyes. The ruthless laugher when the true, false Marc Delon was pulled bound and gagged onto the stage.

– I remember, Zahn said. – I watched it.

A flash. Lights behind his eyes. Gwen. And then Joyce, all those years ago, before Zahn had the slightest idea that their paths would ever cross.

– May I ask for a bit of silence, please?

The laughter had continued unabated. Until the moment he had pulled forth the bloody knife. Then it had faded, as if by magic.

– To you, Ladies and Gentlemen, I will say the following: I won't kill this Fool crawling at my feet. You see, that would be redundant. He's already dead, but has yet to acknowledge that fact. It will be slow, but eventually he will simply stop breathing.

Jeremy Zahn laughed hard on the train to Katmandu ten years later.

– Marc Delon hanged himself last year, didn't he? Malin commented casually.

– He did. Jeremy dried his tears. – I'm sorry for laughing, but I think the entire «show» was awful. I laughed so much that I shook that night, and it still sticks, I guess.

– No problem, the journalist or «the traveler in stories» assured him. – But I must say you're not at all the way I pictured you. Considering what Joyce has done to you, you're taking it awfully... well?

– It's more or less gallows humor, really. Zahn stared at him. – Besides, I've developed a keen sense of life's irony the last two years. Believe me, I intend to show my appreciation for the great

Timmy when I catch him.

– He fascinates you, Malin stated. – I guess it's quite understandable. He's a fascinating man. You probably know where I'm going here, as well?

– I do have a suspicion…

– My main reason, namely, for focusing so much on this incident, is that it is Timothy Joyce's first appearance.

– His first public appearance.

– No, no, his first appearance *ever*. Until he appeared in Paris that night, this Timothy Joyce didn't exist. He came from nowhere. Where was he born? Where did he live as a child and through adolescence? There are no records, are there? No public or private, not anywhere?

– Not any I or Interpol have managed to dig up. Zahn kept his face impassive. – There are many who have that name around the world, of course. They've all been checked out of the case quite satisfactory. The «hunting» budget for his apprehension has grown quite big these days. In my experience money is no longer an obstacle. They were thoroughly checked and rechecked. I've also visited quite a few of them personally, and in spite of several of them obtaining court others «not to be bothered», I'm reasonably certain they check out. Even dead people have been dug up and identified. Nothing there. He has managed to hide his tracks well.

– Remarkably well, one should add. One could imagine that the Frenchman moved his hands in a Latin gesture, but the fact was that he didn't move them at all. – He has taken drastic steps to hide his background, his origin. He has never been arrested. There are no known medical journals anywhere. It seems clear that he has simply created his own identity, or am I wrong, that he has created the name and reputation of Timothy Joyce… created him… from nothing?

The Frenchman, who didn't behave like a Frenchman (but who did), leaned exhausted, but content back in the seat.

– International law enforcement cooperation has more or less eliminated the few of the world's people baptized Timothy Joyce, Zahn commented dryly. – Now, only the other billions remain. Funny, isn't it?

Jacques Malin leaned back forward.

– It's a matter of course that you're among the people outside his inner circle who know him best, you must have an extensive archive somewhere?

– Most of it is in my head. Jeremy smiled to the suddenly very eager journalist. – I have a few crucial notes on paper, though, just to be sure I don't miss anything.

– I would give a lot to see that, Malin sighed.

– I could have shown it to you, Zahn grinned. – But then I would have to kill you…

Malin slowly once more leaned back in the seat.

Two days after his first, legendary performance.

Timothy Joyce had walked into a bank twenty steps from the entrance to the TV-studio. The surveillance cameras had recorded him while he had shot down eight customers and three employees, all present in the locale, and as he calmly walked back out, with one bag of money in each hand. He had put the gun away, rounded a corner, and vanished, seemingly in open air. Three days after that again he had shown up at the hospital where the only survivor after the shooting incident was being treated for her wounds. He had walked relaxed into the trauma ward, lifted up the fifty-two-year old housewife and thrown her out of the window. She had fallen five floors, and been smashed against the sidewalk below. On his way back out, he had killed an overeager nurse, striking him, breaking his neck with one blow.

Jeremy could recite the list, the entire list from memory. He had gone through it a thousand times, at least as thorough as he had taken on the security system at the London casino.

Joyce had kept to his preferences for the spectacular also after this, and also expanded upon his actions both in quality and quantity. But the basics remained:

There was no reason, no common sense, or pattern, nothing with any meaning or sense. He moved on Earth like a… like a force of nature, spreading death and destruction. That was by the way one of the more popular and sensible metaphysical explanations put forward: That he was Wrath incarnated, created by Nature to bring vengeance on mankind. But if that was the case it wasn't spectacular enough. *Not yet.*

After thousand and three days and nights on the train they finally reached the city of Jaynagar at the Indian/Nepali border.

# CHAPTER SEVEN

## SIX DAYS IN THE CITY OF ANGELS

Somebody had raised a tent on the outskirts of an old movie factory.

There were remote areas in Hollywood, too. He had wandered through them, now, in something resembling an eternity, but that hardly could be more than a few hours.

Though remote… He imagined there were houses here, around him somewhere, but he couldn't actually see them.

He reached an open area. There were old, decrepit barracks and a few set pieces. But mostly sand, dust floating in the air and flashing in the night. Gold or fool's gold someone had left on this place? Wherever it was. He spotted the small tent almost by chance. Someone had raised it by a rusty fence, a small tent the same color as the night in Los Angeles, deep blue, with strong islets of gray.

The desert wasn't far away, away from Los Angeles. The city had actually been built on a desert, a desert made somewhat fertile by aqueducts and other human technology. But one could still smell the desert here, a scent far beyond the sense of physical smell; the sense of desperation and thirst and eternal Hunger, dried-out people chasing the path out of the sandpit.

Fog drifted in the air, but fog always drifted in the air in LA. Fog not fog, but smog, human-created poison that everybody was breathing in and out.

He walked where he sought and what he sought was the tent.

A tent pointing to itself in the barren landscape, as someone knew it would. For him? Not necessarily. A tent here would point to itself for any fool moving close to it, if the person in question spotted it, in the fog and the poison.

No amusement park, no other tents, no wheel of fortune. But destiny's wheel still turned. The door to its inside was open, the tent's flap, the thin veil of velvet had been pulled aside. He couldn't see anything in there. But two steps inside, on the other side of the veil, details started emerging. He hesitated a tiny fraction of time, before he consciously stepped inside. One step, two, and he found himself in a kind of velvet darkness.

– Step inside without fear and of your own, free will, a female voice seemed to come from nowhere.

He was already inside, wasn't he?

No, in this room there was nothing but air. The tent had another room beyond this. He pushed another veil aside. Inside, by, beyond a dark table sat a woman. On the table was a large shiny and foggy crystal ball. He stared fascinated at the indistinct image inside the ball, at the woman's face. A face basically hidden by scarves and veils. He knew he had never seen her before, though. This in spite of the flash of recognition he spotted in her eyes. She knew him, he didn't know her. He got a lot of that these days, the last three years.

– You want to know your fate. He couldn't say for sure whether or not she moved her lips. – Sit down.

He sat down. The chair pushed softly at his butt, the velvet in the air at the rest of the body. He couldn't sense the ground against his feet.

She had evidently been in trance since he had first entered, so long ago. Now, she fell even deeper, without him being able to see it on her.

– There's a man, she «chanted», in an unbelievably low voice, with shadowy, huge eyes. – He's shadowing you.

Oh, this was great. A great setting to end all great settings, and done with twisted mirrors. At least she didn't mention a «tall, dark man».

– A tall, *dark* man, she intoned. – The Other Man, which shadow you must appear from, in order to move on, is your Fate. In him you see yourself, and he sees himself in you. You're like mirror images. It's impossible to know who's the original and who's the echo.

– We're not alike, he said, clenching his teeth, – not in any way.

She put the cards, tarot cards on the table. She looked into the crystal ball, studied the whirling images, glanced at her guest in uncertainty… and fear?

– Your fates are linked, she assured him, assured herself, with a quivering voice. – I've actually never seen such similar diagrams, never ever.

– So, you're reading our horoscope, now, as well, without knowing us or knowing anything about us?

This was getting better by the second. He wanted to leave, but something kept him there. Fear, insecurity, curiosity.

– You're good, you're really good. This entire setting is damn convincing. The smoke, the fog, the entire shebang, but you'll have to do even better.

– You want me to tell you about Timothy Joyce, Jeremy? She opened her eyes. He shook in the chair, the chair that might not be a chair. – I've already done that. It just hasn't dawned on you yet.

– What hasn't dawned on me yet? He said curtly, striving to stay on an even keel. – I must say you surpass all other fortunetellers when it comes to speaking in riddles.

– You don't know yourself, Jeremy. You're torn between the extremes of your life, with an unruly inner life. This is often the case with those fighting with themselves about what direction their life should take. Each person is potentially many.

– What are you, fortuneteller or amateur therapist?

She laughed. He glimpsed shiny white teeth. Then, suddenly, a rotten gap, a skeleton almost clean of flesh.

– Timothy Joyce, she said, dwelling on the name, tasting it, slightly dramatic. – He moves across the Earth and through Time using the gates of mist and fire. He can be in any place, any time, merely by willing it. He can reach into the past, the present and the future, and gain a power others can hardly imagine.

He felt the cold crawl inside, even more rooted. He ignored it.

– I've already heard countless similar versions, but in the most common he is a magician, using spells and charms, communicating with the demons of the Earth…

– Anyone may use the gates. Perhaps he can sort of open them, control them, but they're also opening by themselves, spontaneously. He can see them, though, very few can do that and even fewer understand what they see. They can fall through them by accident or coincidence. A person walks on a sidewalk. Suddenly he finds himself in a different city… or in the same city the day before. Or fifty years before. Or a thousand years later. Most people can't handle such a hyper-reality and go totally insane. They *break*, never to recover.

She stared at him. He returned the stare with hatred in his eyes. Her lips started shaking and she lowered her eyes.

– There are so many rumors and fantasies about him, he said sarcastically. – How are your claims any better or trustworthier than those all the other nutters are spouting?

– That isn't for me to decide, she reproached him mildly. – I read only potential, probability, not Fate. We all decide our own destiny. Perhaps everything is true, perhaps nothing?

– I need facts. He leaned forward. – Not evasive crap. Let me put it this way: If you're really on the level, if you're genuine, you'll tell me what I need to know.

Then he saw it, a clear flash of worry in her eyes.

– With most people I can read clearly. She frowned. – If someone wants to know tomorrow's stock exchange facts, I can tell them that with reasonable certainty. But something… something concerning Timothy Joyce and yourself… there's something… *blocking* my Sight. I wasn't certain at first, but certainty is coming to me, turning to conviction. Creatures like you are described in one of my ancestor's Book of Shadows, referring to far older, forgotten writings… the Book of Fate, where horrible legends are described, about Lords of Order and Chaos.

Her voice turned more distant, more indistinct the longer she spoke.

– You're unique, singular beings. The Masters of Fate, living outside Time and Space. Only you and you alone can ever know Timothy Joyce. «To understand him you need only understand yourself».

The fortuneteller said.

He shook his head, a single time. His eyes turned sly and wicked.

– You're fond of uttering «prophecies», right?

He leaned forward, far forward, now, stared at her with fixed, burning eyes.

– That's what I do, what I'm good at.

The unrest in her eyes grew worse.

– Well, then you shall have one in return, he said pleasantly. – I had a vision just now, and in it you were dead as a doornail. There was nothing but the skeleton left. What do you say to that?

– You… threaten me, here, in my own Sanctum?

– Who says anything about threatening? He grinned. – I'm merely returning your sweet kindness, a bit less cryptic. You tell Joyce to stop playing hide and seek, stop fighting through all sorts of proxies.

– You claim I'm in league with him, she gasped. – You're paranoid and sick!

– You're dead, he said, without mercy. – It is not often I've had visions, but those I've had, are usually accurate.

And in that very moment he also admitted that terrible truth to himself.

– And I'm God, he grinned, even wider. – I don't need to threaten. My Power is far greater than yours can ever be.

Her eyes widened in fear, in countless nuances of fear. *She believes me.*

He rose abruptly, suddenly fed up, just had to get away. He listened, but didn't hear the chair hit the floor. When he backed out of the tent, he never took his eyes off her. But she still disappeared, faded into the nothingness. He heard a sound from behind, and whirled around. No one… nothing. He turned again.

– So, you wish to play GAMES, huh? Well, you will PAY for that.

Morning already. He imagined he saw shadows out there, people he could see right through in the weak light of the dawn, circus tents rising from nowhere. He walked on in a stupor, as he felt a gathering soreness in the throat after his powerful, insane howl.

Joyce had always had a masterful ability to push people's buttons, especially his. Zahn had it himself, he knew that, but Joyce had developed it into an art, to a fearsome level.

Jeremy felt thoroughly pushed, that much was certain. He couldn't say why he felt so hammered, but he couldn't deny that he did. Everything felt twisted inside him, turned inside out. He moved through the indistinct surroundings, as if in a stupor. Streets that in no way resembled those of Hollywood, but far more downtrodden areas. What happened then, happened automatically, without thought, without obvious consciousness. He cocked his head, started taking softer steps on the hard surface, and he listened. And he heard the steps. From behind? There was no one close, no one he could see, but he was convinced someone was following him. A few quick glances, and he started running, rushed into the nearest building. Two floors, short staircases. He found himself on the roof before it had really dawned on him that he had actually run through the door downstairs. The roof, a wilderness of sheds, and clothes hanging from brittle ropes. He looked back down on the street, where he had been only seconds earlier. Nothing. No one. He didn't hear the steps anymore. Understood why. The only reason he had heard them, was because the person making them wanted them to be heard. He clenched his teeth, knew he should charge back down, hunt, take the initiative, and also make sure he didn't spring the trap.

– Damn witch, he mumbled, close to delirious.

She had hurt him, hurt him bad, cut him open like butter.

He sat there, on the roof, the rest of the night. It wasn't like he moved much, but he listened, and heard nothing. Not even the sound of voices and cars starting up in the morning. Had he imagined it was morning already, when he left the amusement park?

Seconds passed away like hours as his sweat froze in the cold and made his body stiff and useless. When the morning sun finally thawed him, he could finally move, and the stiffness vanished as if it had never been there at all.

He returned the same way he had come, back to the amusement park. He heard the sound of it from far away, didn't even have to listen. And there it was, right before his eyes. Nothing mysterious about it at all. Only an... amusement park. In the middle of the bright day. A parking lot with green spots, surrounded by trees. Tents, wheels of fortune, entertainment. The mobile amusement park had been raised on the same spot that had been empty just a few hours earlier... The same spot that wasn't the same spot. He cackled. The sound sounded like one of utter insanity. He searched, but saw no signs of a fortuneteller tent, nothing resembling one. That, in itself, didn't necessarily signify anything. To pack and move a small tent, didn't take long. It didn't surprise him that it was gone... totally consistent as it was with everything else happening, everything insane. People stared at him. Or was he imagining that... as well? They followed his movements with fear in their circle-round eyes, doing their mundane pursuits in a relaxed and energetic manner. People stumbled around like there were no worries. At least that was how it looked to the untrained eye, to those that didn't have his training, his ability to look beneath the surface, the façade. Behind the mask of satisfaction people put on to hide the truth, their true emotions, to people around them, to themselves. Hide the truth of a life in degradation and insanity.

The drums started up almost imperceptibly. The sound grew around him, without him being able to tell where it originated. He didn't see the drums or the drummers. The sound seemed to reach him from all sides. No one else reacted to it. Had they seen the drums and the drummers? In that there wasn't anything strange about this. Two police officers patrolled the amusement park area. Everything seemed peaceful and easygoing. Not wrong. He shook his head. The drums, with their ghostly qualities were really insignificant in this case, merely one symptom of what waited beyond.

The insanity couldn't be seen, couldn't be heard, but was there, just beneath the surface, here, just like everywhere, fucking everywhere.

A boy lost his ice cream and it hit the ground with a silent thud. That was what most people saw, he assumed. Zahn, with his trained eye, saw a bullet strike the ice cream and push it out of the boy's hands, saw the ice cream hit the ground several steps away. He was already in hiding behind a box, with the gun in his hand. The two officers shook. One bullet hit one in the chest. The other was hit in the throat. Everything seemed so peaceful. A hail of bullets hit them. More people behind and around them were hit. Bodies fell to the ground. The spell broke. People screamed hysterically. Zahn held up his shield, the one he had been granted by LAPD. It worked. At least people didn't fire at him.

A man trembled at his spot on the ground and spoke frantically into his cell phone. No words, only the mouth moving. There were no more shots. Not yet, Zahn thought. People remained on the ground. They moaned. This included those who hadn't actually been hit, and didn't run panic-stricken from the place. Zahn waved to the man with the cell phone, signed for him to throw the phone to Zahn. The man looked at him with a face dominated by skepticism, as if the tool represented a lifeline, something crucial to him. But eventually he let go and threw the phone to Zahn. Zahn caught it in the air and instantly began hitting the number to Caldwell's phone. He waited impatiently to hear the ringing. Waited, until he realized there wasn't any. He attempted to get back the dialing tone, in vain. Had there been any in the first place, had the owner spoken in a stupor? Zahn resisted the temptation to throw the shit away. He twisted his body around, into a very uncomfortable position to get a handle on his situation, glancing, looking at the buildings on the opposite side of the open area. Where had the bullets been fired from, where had the drumbeats come from? He clenched his teeth. This looked more and more like yet another excellently orchestrated, insane Timothy Joyce happening.

Zahn saw movement across the street. Did he hear the sound of someone running? There had to be something about the terrain here making sound carry across longer distances, at least where the drumbeats were concerned. No one had heard the shots. No one had realized anything, until people fell to the ground, bleeding, until they hit the dust, bleeding to death.

He watched the carnage, understanding nothing. Then... there was a sound, something buzzing in his mind.

It dawned on him that no one had fired at him. If they had they had to be extreme bad shots... since not a single bullet had even come close to him. It dawned on him... and he rose, to shocked outcries from the people around him, and he started running, following the sounds of the steps and beating hearts.

The tall buildings surrounded him. The narrow alley embraced him. He filled it. For three years this bullshit, this insanity had been running his life. He ran on.

A bullet passed right by his head. He fired his gun. A loud, long scream penetrated the place. He didn't let it affect him, but threw himself behind a corner, a kind of cover. The bullets fell, fell like rain. More gunmen ahead, at least three. He fired again, heard once again the sound of a high velocity projectile hitting thin skin, a frail shell. He drew his other gun, loading his righthand gun with one hand. A sound from behind. He turned and fired. A man with a rifle was shaken by the three bullets hitting him, tearing him apart. Four shooters, at least, probably more. A wide opening in the wall, closing like a trap. They thought.

He felt pain somewhere. Blood dripped from the right little finger and ring finger. He tore open his skirt in the neck and took a look at it, at the wound. It was in the arm, a trifle he hardly noticed. The blood flow had already stopped, and it had closed. Again, he wondered about his sense of time. He hadn't been in here that long, had he, hadn't had the mini minotaurs buzzing around him more than a few minutes? Fast healing tissue, several medical doctors, both in London and several times since then had mumbled, rambled about. Did they have any idea, any idea at all, what they were talking about?

Moving wasn't a problem. The pain was hardly noticeable, and it certainly didn't slow him down. He rushed into the next alley, no longer directly chasing those he hunted, whether they were fleeing or not. But he knew he closed in on them. Not with his nose like a dog, nothing like that, but something far deeper. Humans, like most hunters, had always chased their prey without necessarily seeing it, looking into its eyes. In the three years he had hunted Timothy Joyce he had never had more than a few, fleeting glimpses of the man, had often arrived at a scene right after Joyce had left it, but he had been able to smell him, as if he was right around the next corner.

That was why he didn't need to convince himself that Joyce wasn't close now. Not even around the next corner. Joyce had just sent his attack-dogs at him, to irritate him, to rattle his chain.

He circled and circled. They did as well, not fleeing anymore. He heard distant sirens. So distant they were indistinct, vague, making it impossible to determine if they were coming closer or growing more distant. He envisioned the men, how they split up, spread out. Pulling back together, almost like a unit, like one being, conversing not only without words, but also without physical signs.

This entire block had probably been a part of a studio once. Not one of the great ones, but there was a scent of past greatness. Of decay, of rotting autumn leaves. The way he remembered it from England, not here.

They fired. What were they firing at?

– I saw him, he walked here, at this very spot.

Had he walked there? He thought he had, but that had been

minutes ago.

– He's a DEMON, one wailed. – A demon from the pit, sent by the Lord to test us.

Zahn had to grin then, sensing the rush of triumph, treacherous, lovely, already before he had stepped out from his cover with a fully loaded gun in each hand. He shot two before they had turned more than halfway around. Four whirled around. He fired and fired, and they fell like cones, like targets on a shooting range. It didn't help them that they fired as well. They missed.

Only one of the opponents was still standing on shaky legs, a young, blond boy, holding his bleeding arm, desperately attempting to pick up a gun just within range. Zahn pointed at him with both revolvers. He had at least three bullets left. Two of the bullets had missed, been wasted. It irritated him a bit. At such close range he should have been able to pick them all off, exactly like on a shooting range.

– THE LORD IS GREAT, the boy chanted. – The Lord be praised!

The body started shaking in violent cramps. He fell to the ground and lay still. Stone cold. Zahn wasn't confused. He knew the wounds hadn't been serious, and when he smelled almonds it didn't surprise him.

The others had died of their wounds, shot to pieces.

In a well-known scenario the rescue unit arrived ten, twenty seconds later, late. They recognized him, and he didn't have to show his badge.

Smoke drifted while the clean up and survey were conducted. It had always drifted, but now it practically filled the air. He had always had trouble regaining his breath during similar earlier battles, after such adrenalin shocks. Now, he only felt the rush, the boiling blood.

A man approached Zahn, doing so a bit hesitant.

– Inspector Zahn?

– That's me, Zahn confirmed good humored.

– Will you come with me, sir, there has been a… a development. Several actually. If you…

– … will come with you, yes, that's okay sergeant.

The journalists flocking the streets outside weren't just pushed, but virtually kicked and beaten, to make room for Zahn and the officers leaving the alleys and the area marked by the yellow ribbons.

Zahn was brought to the headquarters under a full escort. So dusty the first time he walked inside, so different now. The place had been turned upside down by all the activity, fear and hatred. The two last factors had always been there, but the completely frenetic activity had not seen its like since the building had been constructed.

Deeper, into the holier parts of the temple that hadn't been filled with people. The elite were present, a smaller number of people, the way it was everywhere. The fear and the hatred, though, seemed, reasonably enough, even more pronounced.

Caldwell was there. The three others of Zahn's task force had also been given temporary access to the halls of power. Captain Lasko, Chief Springsteen, they were all here. The fact that Springsteen was still here, in the same position, said a lot about his survival instinct, his ability to hold his head above water. Zahn saw him as a typical chameleon, a smooth surface not revealing anything. Most people did reveal something. Despair, quiet despair, indifference. Springsteen was the typical politician, reflecting only what people sent to him. A lipstick mark showed on his neck. Caldwell seemed obviously embarrassed, but he wasn't fazed by it, wasn't fazed by it at all.

Chairs rattled when people sat down. Springsteen stood by the enormous video-screen. He had a keyboard on the table in front of him.

– This message was sent to us through the Internet less than an hour ago, he said aloud. – Sent from an office building in Manila, the Philippines. The entire building was subsequently blown to smithereens, along with all the people present. They died in droves.

He pushed «enter», and the recording was played.

Monica's well-known face filled the screen, filled Jeremy's vision.

– Greetings, people of Los Angeles... The words were spoken, aided by an ice-cold smile, a glowing passion. – A few days ago, you were told that Los Angeles was yours no longer. The lackeys, the brutes, the thugs of the city's former masters, were also told not to approach our headquarters. They were warned that everybody breaking this command would die. Today we've taken another step forward to effectuate this process. Every single police officer in Los Angeles and surrounding area participated in the assault. Everyone will die soon. This entire city, by its very existence is an insult to us. It will suffer a cruel fate. Those who don't want to be a part of this fate, should leave, should leave *now*. You will only have time to pack a few personal belongings. Our advice to you is to not dawdle. There will be no further communication from our side on this.

It turned quiet. No one in the room had spoken during the time the recording had been played. Now… it turned quiet.

– During the day fifteen of our people have been killed in random incidents, Springsteen told them tightly. – There's little or no doubt that Joyce is behind it.

– But *how?* A man at the front spoke up. – All his people were killed days ago.

Zahn waited a bit before speaking, waited for the lingering silence to grow.

– There's little doubt that our massacre of a small part of his cohorts has enraged and inflamed his far greater numbers of remaining supporters, just like he counted on, just like he wanted.

Did Springsteen smile? Zahn had wondered if he had also seen the shadow of a smile on the Chief's face earlier, but it had to be his imagination.

– I believe Zahn is correct, Lasko said, very tightly. – We're dealing with a man that has no respect whatsoever for human lives or generally see the value of a life. He pulls people in from the street and is a master in manipulating their emotions and herding them in the directions he wants.

– He's running internment camps, isn't he? This was Frances, a young intern at the Chief's office. Zahn had heard Springsteen call her by name. – Hell camps, where he's teaching and brainwashing his soldiers?

– There are ongoing rumors, Caldwell pointed out. – They've never been proven or confirmed.

– But where does he get his people? He must get them from somewhere…

Suggestions and comments filled the room, until the buzz overwhelmed any attempt at a normal conversation. Fear and rage and other, less identifiable emotions blanketed the room in noise. Springsteen raised his arms in an attempt to calm the assembly, and slowly, painfully it did calm down. Nerves on edge turned slightly less edgy.

– Ladies and gentlemen, he began. – It's perfectly understandable that you're impatient, that you want to go out there and *do* something. I assure you that something will be done. There will be a reckoning. There will be a resolution. Someone will bleed. But we won't succeed without a definitive plan, a strategy, to combat this enemy, this threat to our life and liberty. I will again thank you for coming. You will be apprised of all progress and fluid, expanding strategy in the matter.

The breakup happened fast, disciplined. In spite of the impatience written in their scared and tested expressions they followed orders. The system of respecting the chain of command and obeying official and unofficial instructions was deeply rooted in them. Even the representatives from the army, which had been ordered to «assist» local authorities held their tongue.

They all filed slowly out of the room. Zahn remained. Caldwell, as well. Signals she had given him earlier grew distinct, cleared the muddy waters in the bottle, in her dog-like eyes. He rose and followed her into a darker, smaller room, her private, unofficial office, given to her by a grateful Springsteen. She seemed indisposed, almost flattened and exited simultaneously. She hadn't taken a shower since she and Springsteen had had their last, breathless coach moment.

– You've looked for this Monica all over the world, searched Interpol's archives, everybody has been looking for her?

Zahn nodded, wondering where she was headed with this.

– I made, on a hunch, a search through our archives...

She handed him a file. He studied her and saw very little triumph in her eyes, in her stance, but there was something there, indeterminate. He understood why, the moment he opened the file.

– The name «Monica» wasn't much to go on, so I searched on appearance.

He shook visibly when he looked at the photograph.

– Monica Valdez, Caldwell said. – Not yet twenty, recruit at the LAPD police academy.

He stared at the well known, but... incomplete face. She had dark hair, without the fire-like tone he remembered. That didn't necessarily matter, though. Not that.

– It isn't her, he said hoarsely. – She's way too young. There's no scar and she's much too skinny.

He remembered. Monica had been muscles and size and suppleness, everything in one frame.

– I know. Caldwell nodded. – So, I made further inquiries, and it is a mystery.

– There are similarities. Zahn nodded, too. – What about older relatives?

– Well, it isn't the mother, unless she's hiding beneath a considerable obesity… She has no known sisters or relatives even resembling her. And why should Monica… the Monica attached to Joyce, use the same name as a younger relative? It does seem unreasonable or at least unlikely.

– But not impossible, Zahn pondered. – Besides, there are so many crazy things concerning Joyce that this is just one more, minor detail. There has to be a connection.

Another coincidence, another piece of the puzzle.

– I agree, Caldwell said. – But probably not a very useful one. I'm sorry.

– Have you interviewed her?

– I wouldn't do anything until I had spoken to you… The Chief… when I consulted him… agreed. You're actually the only one we have available, who has been close enough to Monica… long enough, to be able to describe her in detail, who's able to recognize her. She's as much of a mystery, just as non-existing, as Joyce himself. There's no background, no past, no origin, until she appeared from nowhere, by his side.

He lifted a finger, thoughtful, in rising excitement.

– Have someone run a search on Joyce's physical characteristics. But… make him younger, smaller. As far as I know it hasn't been done before.

– I can do it, she offered.

– You will come with me. You will all come with me.

There was a certain casual habit in a society to look for a person the way he was. Not the way he had been or perhaps would be. Those habits were involved everywhere. An unpredictable, ruthless person like Timothy Joyce would inevitably take advantage of that.

They sat in the hotel room, reading autopsy reports. There were just the five of them, as it had always been.

The coroner had left, a few minutes earlier, after presenting his case, very cross, because he had been summoned, instead of them coming to him, as was the order of things. He hadn't cared for the ongoing smile Zahn sent him, either. Or the fact that he had been ordered from the top to hurry, prioritize these particular autopsies.

– So, you've decided to keep our small unit, in spite of it all, Zahn? Dupont (or Dupond) intoned.

– As long as you might be useful, Zahn countered happily.

– Most of your victims died of gunshot wounds, Zahn. The coroner's voice filled the room anew, as Zahn pulled it from memory. Impressions, memory had always been very visual to him, a skill only enhanced with his increasingly extended consciousness. – Except he who committed suicide. He was by the way the only one with a cyanide capsule in his mouth. Funny, isn't it?

It was funny. The good coroner had a point there. Another funny thing to file under T. Joyce. Cold buzzed and whirled in the warm room.

– They were all marked by recent hard and may I add harsh exercise. One of them still had a bad leg, probably because of an injury during a long march or such.

– He's running his people very hard, Wells nodded, without any notable compassion.

– I've heard about his boot camps, Louis said, his voice clearly shaking. – There's no mercy there, no compassion.

– Not all of them are brainwashed, after what I've heard, Caldwell said. – Not those joining him voluntarily. But he's ruthless against those he sees as future cannon fodder.

– Those I encountered were obvious sacrificial lambs, Zahn said curtly.

He wondered, hiding it, about the contradictory, undetermined quality in her voice.

But in spite of being among the lowest of the low in Joyce's organization, they had all been lethal still, lethal in their one track minded «approach». But that had also been what did them in. The ability they once might have possessed to think for themselves had been virtually eradicated. Joyce had sent them against the target, like the blind at the fire.

I'm the fire, Jeremy thought.

Only one man had had a poison pill in his mouth. There could be a number of reasons for this. He might know important details that for any price couldn't fall into an enemy's hands. Or he belonged to a suicide group within the organization. Or...

Joyce had known who would survive the shootout.

Cold no longer trickled down Zahn's back. He was far beyond that state.

He recalled the faces on the tables, the remains of the men and women they had once been. He kept memorizing their faces long after the impressions of them had faded from the retina, as he always did. Tracks crossed the road and each other in front of him, a bundle of blind tracks, a bundle of important tracks, so hard to separate, separate fact from fiction, relevance from garbage. Somewhere, contained in some kind of information, hid knowledge, the answer to the riddle that was Timothy Joyce.

The phone rang. Caldwell took it. She was excellently suited to the role of switchboard operator. Zahn exposed his fangs. She shrank in her tracks. This time she didn't have to be a mind reader to read his thoughts.

– Caldwell, she replied harshly.

She didn't say more, but listened with the phone at her ear. She hung up and turned towards Zahn.

– They didn't find anything, she told him.

Zahn experienced neither disappointment nor joy. It had, after all, been a virtual shot in the dark.

– What was that about? Russo asked sharply.

Zahn shrugged. They would get to know it from others, anyway.

– We did a search on Joyce on what he possibly looked like as a younger man, a late teenager.

– That wasn't bad, Russo exclaimed astonished. – Why has no one thought about it before?

In a spell of kindness Zahn didn't explain it to him.

He also blamed himself because he hadn't thought about it before, before Monica Valdez appeared. What else had he failed to think of, what other avenues had he not explored?

– Good ol' Joyce, by the way is even crazier than I thought, Wells mused, – if he truly believes he's going to pull off what he's saying he will pull off.

– He will undoubtedly make one hell of an attempt, Zahn replied thoughtfully. – If that's what he's truly planning.

– You believe he's bluffing? Well, since that was kind of my point, I definitely agree with you.

– Not bluffing exactly. Zahn turned towards Wells then. – But he has been known to reveal intentions he obviously doesn't care to go through with. It's one more method of obscuring his true intentions, another diversionary tactic. I can tell you one thing: I've followed the man through Europe, Africa, South America, Asia and Australia, all the heavily populated continents on the globe. I think he deliberately «saved» North America, saved it until last. He has recruited people, built an organization without members, without tracks, without history, left a bloody trail of nothing... No, whatever he's planning I don't believe he is bluffing.

Well's face turned unusually expressive just then, in a non-expressive way. He didn't comment on Zahn's monologue.

The phone, the hotel's room telephone, rang again. Caldwell got it.

– Caldwell.

She turned towards Zahn (again).

– It's for you, she told him.

Zahn rose and walked to the table, accepting the phone.

– Zahn here.

He didn't say more. The «conversation» didn't last many seconds. He hung up.

– I'm going out. You wait here. You don't leave the room unless something drastic happens.

They didn't protest. He left and closed the door behind him.

A car waited for him in front of the main entrance. Hands kept close to the guns at all times. He knew he hardly had to think in order to draw them in one single, explosive movement. The light body armor would also protect him fairly well against an attack, but he couldn't move around with a fortress on his body. No one could ever guard oneself against everything, against all possible dangers.

He was brought to a building that truly resembled a fortress, especially with the new security precautions in place. Normally, security was on «a discreet, reasonable level». Now the entire place stank of fear.

He quite enjoyed that.

The security at the gate inside easily surpassed that in the Langley headquarters of the CIA in Virginia, yet another important place he had paid a visit. He was checked, rechecked, and checked anew. Retina scanning, fingerprints, urine samples, blood testing. The works. He was relieved of the guns. He was undressed. They groped his ass, researched his teeth. A considerable time had passed before he could finally enter the elevator. The elevator that, he knew, only stopped on one single floor in the entire building.

Nobody met him twenty floors up. The elevator doors slid open. He stepped out in one single room. A group of people sat around a large table. All the faces were hidden in shadow. He had seen one of them in bright daylight before. The others he had only met here, like this.

– We chose to support you in your feud against Timothy Joyce… Zahn recognized the voice of Taylor Lowell, the industrial tycoon. – In return you were supposed to limit the damages to this town.

– Correct.

– We don't feel you've done such a great job in that regard.

Zahn didn't speak.

– But that wasn't why we've called for you, Lowell said curtly to him, like he would to a child. – You've seen the communication from Joyce, made by his harlot?

Zahn nodded, still not saying anything.

– It wasn't sent to Chief Springsteen, but to *us*.

– You've told him about us, you unfaithful rabid dog.

The screeching voice came from the other side of the room, almost from the end of the table.

Exclamations of agreement followed this statement.

Zahn strongly suspected by now that not everybody present could be said to be representatives for the peaceful business profession.

– But he started fucking with you before you contacted me,

Zahn pointed out. – That was the most important reason you accepted my advances, that you took pity on me.

The sarcasm didn't escape them. But it didn't matter, really, since they had never enjoyed a hearty relationship.

It turned silent. They glanced at each other. He smiled. Had they imagined he would break down and confess his crimes? They hadn't met with much resistance throughout their lives, not true resistance. They thought they could do anything without paying for it. And experience confirmed their expectation, naturally. People like them took what they wanted in this world. People like them thrived like fish in water in the present-day world.

– How, then, has that satanic piece of shit procured all that information about us, all the detailed information we've spent a lifetime removing from public records? Things we couldn't imagine could be known to anybody?

– I've often wondered about the same myself, Zahn said dryly. – You have my sympathies.

The mood in the room turned distinctly lighter. But also more hectic, excited.

– So, you're not on his list of useful fanatics. A female voice. – But you have hunted him for three years, isn't that so?

– Hah! Zahn spat.

– But he still knows you far better than you do him?

– I've never hidden that fact. Zahn felt both calm and worried at the same time and wondered why. – But he has personally attempted to kill me twice, and to have me killed on countless occasions, without succeeding. I would say he has a problem.

– «There are no problems, only solutions», the woman quoted joyfully.

With her own voice.

– What the hell…

Another widely known man, Clayton Powers, shook visibly. Zahn recognized him before the face was pushed into the light, before the bald head hit the table, without any visible attempt from the man to keep it from happening.

Zahn took a step forward, managed to take one more, before falling on his knees.

Everything went hazy. He saw through a fog how more heads hit the table, heard bodies fall to the floor. A blond wig levitated towards the floor, but never seemed to actually reach it. A lamp was turned towards a face, a face he recognized beyond doubt.

– All the others are knocked out by the gas, Jeremy, Monica said, nodding in acknowledgment. – But you're still holding out. What stamina you've gained for yourself. My compliments.

He fell forward. By a miracle he managed to lift his hands and catch himself, remain on all fours. He began… crawling. Towards her. He lifted one hand, moved it forward, pulled a leg. Lifted the other hand, moved it forward, pulled the other leg.

– A perseverance, a strength envied by gods. You're gonna need it.

He had to fight for every little progress forward, as if she stood at the top of a tall ledge, while his system fought against the poison flowing into his lungs, into his bloodstream. The thought about this being futile should have struck him, of course, that he was easy prey for her, that the prey was already caught, but he refused to think that thought. He refused.

Everybody turned indistinct, but he still saw her face clearly, without the slightest distortion.

There was a theatrical element here, somewhere, here, too. The thought flashed through his mind, forgotten the moment it appeared. He had only eyes for her, and he couldn't avoid wondering why he hadn't lost consciousness already. But he crawled and crawled closer to her, while she kept growing in his vision…

until she filled it completely.

– I love you, Jeremy, she cried passionately. – I love you so much!

He caught a tiny glimpse of the fast movement that was her foot, the moment before it hit the side of his head and made all his lights go out.

# CHAPTER EIGHT

## SIX DAYS IN THE CITY OF ANGELS

The insane choir, cries didn't wake him, only made him move from one state of consciousness to another. He imagined he heard the noise and torture forever, unable to escape it. He attempted to return to the abyss, but couldn't.

Suddenly he pulled his head up, wide awake.

Timothy Joyce stood above him. The brutal expression in the face wasn't softened by the broad smile.

– Ah, Jeremy, with us again, are you? Not exactly unexpected. The rage burns away all poison, doesn't it?

– What the hell is this place? Zahn snarled, while fearing the boiling rage within would tear him apart. He pulled the chains so the wall he was chained to shook, in vain. Naturally.

– Ah, so impolite of me. Know that you are welcome, Jeremy, to the Stable.

Zahn discovered he was stark nude, hanging there, from the chains. In one, raw move he fought himself up on two legs, while snarling wildly at Joyce, only a step or so away. So close, so far.

– What in the blackest hell are you doing?

– What a beautiful anger, what incredible black rage. Joyce shook his head in awe. – I'm never completely certain I've managed to retain it all.

Zahn stood there, breathing hard and labored. Slowly he started receiving impressions, to sense more than the cacophony of sound drumming at him from the entire room. There were several other nude men and women chained with him on the wall. This was a great hall, in something very much resembling a medieval castle. There was no electricity. Fires and torches lit the place and cast long shadows everywhere. Drums thundered from many places around them. The prisoners hung by a round… pit at the center of the hall. The prisoners found themselves between it and something very much resembling stalls. Stalls filled in droves with people shouting and roaring. Below a large window he spotted a throne. One empty, with two smaller thrones on each side. Gwen and Monica sat on the two smaller, very relaxed and pleased with themselves.

– By the way, Joyce said casually. – I didn't give you permission to rise…

And then he struck a cruel, well-aimed blow at Zahn's abdomen. Zahn fell back on his knees. Blood flowed out and down on the floor, between clenched teeth.

– Believe me, Jeremy, this hurts me as much as it hurts you.

In a red mist of pain and suffering, Zahn shook his head. The bastard sounded so honest, so damn honest and honorable.

– You must have been a priest in your previous life, Zahn spat, and more blood followed.

That made Joyce laugh himself silly.

Zahn still smelled the scent of Los Angeles, with his body, his mind, in spite of the short time he had spent there. At least it felt that way. And now he smelled this place, a totally alien environment, so far removed from his range of experience. He shook his head, as if to clear it. But there was no need for that. His head had cleared the second he opened his eyes, the very moment this hyper-reality stared him in the face.

He wasn't bleeding anymore. He still tasted the blood in his mouth, but there wasn't any more of it. In all sense he should have been mortally wounded, but it didn't feel that way. He felt, on the contrary, better than ever. Faster, healthier, stronger and lethal beyond words.

Eight people were chained to the wall. On the opposite side of the pit eight others were lined up. They wore no clothes either, but they weren't chained.

Gwen and Monica rose from the throne. A gasp rose from the assembly. The two descended the stairs, very conscious of the effect they created. Gwen had changed dramatically from the woman he had known. All shyness, all modesty had vanished, and that was also revealed in her features and attitude. The thin fabric she wore was filled by the firm, curvy and lethal muscular body.

The drums died, loud voices faded, it turned quiet.

The two walked behind what was surely new recruits, studied them mercilessly, passionately.

– What happens in the Arena? Gwen asked a muscular youth.

– You fight, Mistress, you win or die.

Zahn scowled at Joyce while attempting to think, to find ways to handle this. He couldn't think of any.

– You have ended up on the wrong foot in life, he cried aloud to Joyce. – You should have been a theater instructor.

– You're correct, Joyce conceded generously. – This can remind a person of theater. But if so, it's far more a «Theater of Blood» than the boring stuff so popular these days.

Laughter, hairy laughter from the stalls.

Gwen and Monica, his two consorts, stopped by his side.

– You look great, Jeremy, Gwen said, with fire in her eyes, eyes measuring him from head to toe. – Far closer to the person I've always imagined you to be.

Not only a theater, but a stage. One more of Joyce's pieces. Not necessarily truer than a mirage. Those present undoubtedly experienced it as real, and clearly it was. True blood, true death, everything real. The sham was on another level, as it was with all illusions, magic tricks. Those present, a television audience, the technical staff were all encouraged to look elsewhere, anywhere else, except the place where what was happening was in fact… happening.

All… this was the illusion. The magic itself occurred somewhere else.

In spite of this being a real castle. The rocks were real. The flesh, the blood, everything was real.

Everything drifted by him. Dots of mist, dancing colors. During his life he had actually done LSD. It was nothing compared to this. He even saw several of the dead people from the attack on the storage building. Did Joyce truly believe he was so stupid; that he would be fooled this easily, by some poison in the blood and elaborate make-up?

No, he didn't. Joyce wasn't stupid either… but he still did what he did. Because it didn't have any meaning? Or… because it had?

– Look at you, it really hurts to watch a man think in circles this way, Joyce grinned joyfully.

What did he mean? That Zahn fucked up by thinking in circles? Or that he thought in circles the wrong way? Or… that he thought that way at all? Yes… perhaps this was what he had done wrong the entire time. If he had done anything wrong at all. By focusing way too much on the scintillating task of… understanding Joyce, of attempting to understand his motivations, his endless, incomprehensible acts, instead of thinking, acting by himself, by his own force, he had wandered into a labyrinth, become, in fact, the donkey chasing the carrot, and thereby losing himself.

– Fabulous, isn't it? Joyce said to the air. And in that moment, he seemed even stranger than he usually did, as if he shared, as if he shared something fundamental with someone, as he with an incredible smile studied the contradictory changes in Zahn's face. – So incredibly fabulous.

Memory brought Jeremy back in time. Had he truly been himself… ever? Hadn't he always passively repeated the words and actions of others? If all people were nothing but dust blowing through eternity, he had truly perfected that technique. Until the day three years ago, when he, no matter the reason, had broken out of the circle.

– SAND WILL FLOW, Joyce shouted. – ROCKS WILL ROLL

He raised his arms above his head and accepted his underlings' accolade. He lowered them again, and once more, it turned quiet.

– Four recruits will join us tonight, he stated incredibly forceful. – Sixteen will be given the chance. We have eight volunteers, eight resisting. When the dust settles, we will know who are truly eager. Only the best of the best will be given the chance to join us. Only the elite of the elite will walk through the needle's eye. But first…

A sign, and a huge stone door opened. Eight ragged individuals were pulled and pushed into the hall. Zahn recognized Clayton Powers and Taylor Lowell from the tower, recognized them all, reckoned they had all been captured there. All were known society figureheads.

– Our blood sacrifices, Joyce declared. – Not much bragging about, really, but an excellent snack to whet our appetite.

They were all bound hand and feet. A gag covering half the face kept them from doing more than grunt in fear and heavenly protest.

They were pushed down on their knees in front of the eight volunteers. The gladiators were given swords in their right hand. They lifted the shiny metal in reverence to Joyce. He gave the signal - and the blood feast began. The eight pillars of society were chopped to pieces. It happened quickly, brutally, without hesitation. Heads were rolling, arms and legs flew through the air. Blood jumped around, coloring the marble floor and the sand in the pit red. The swords were once again raised in greeting to Joyce, before they were thrown away, in a rigid, ceremonial gesture.

– A pattern is forming in the madness, Joyce said to the air.

Jeremy shook all over his body. That was what he had considered saying, but he never got the chance. All his old insecurities returned.

– FRIENDS, Joyce shouted with raised arms. – There is a great day for you tomorrow, when you will fight and die. It's just reasonable that you will enjoy your final night.

Gwen stepped up on the stalls, stopped in front of a man.

– *What are we?*

He stood up, stared straight ahead and recited:

– We are The Dead. Death can come around the next corner, the next turn, as the next arrow. We don't fear it. Most people die from the moment of their first breath. We don't. We live!

Hammering at seats, trampling at the floor made the entire castle shake. Zahn sensed the energy through the floor, through the chains.

The first fight began. One jumped voluntarily, eagerly into the pit. The other was freed of chains and thrown into it. He fought against it, but it was no use. The woman dressed in Joyce's colors viciously attacked him before he had regained his balance. He fought, fought back, but automatically, mechanically. Her aggressiveness made his pale in comparison. She drove him backwards until he stood with his back to the wall, and could back off no longer, and struck out with a hard hand, right into the man's throat, digging in with her fingers, with her claws, pulled it back, and pulled out blood, skin and vital organs. The opponent grabbed his neck, in a ridiculous attempt to keep in place everything flowing out. He fell to the ground in the red spotted sand and died in a pool of his own blood.

The woman raised her arms above the head in a wild joydance. She drowned in a hail of boos and angry cries. It hadn't been much of a fight.

The two huge thugs freed Zahn from the chains. His opponent, a huge and wild fury already waited in the pit. Images from fight two flared through his mind. A rough and ruthless play, where the two combatants had practically killed each other, until one had collapsed from pure exhaustion and the other had taken advantage of it long enough to break his neck. The mood had risen to violent heights. Zahn fought against the two bruisers, but strikes against the body's vulnerable, vital parts zapped his strength. They pulled him along like a wet spot on the ground. But… something else also happened. Through a red haze growing in his vision, he felt the strength flow, through limbs, through will. He allowed himself to be led, until he once more stopped. Stopped abruptly. The two men lost their balance. He freed himself with a shift, a simple pull, grabbed the two heads like he would have two cabbages and smashed them at each other. The two skulls cracked, and the brains decorated the floor. Two bodies twisted, dying in cramps. He didn't look at them, where he stood on the edge, but stared at each and every one of those present, before jumping.

The fury attacked after just a brief hesitation. He flared a smile to her, the moment he sensed fear. She hit him with a wild kick to the head. Huge, beautiful eyes grew even larger when he just shrugged it off. He slapped her. It didn't hurt her, hardly gave her a black eye, but it made rage return to her eyes. She renewed her attack. He kicked her legs away from her and hit her hard in the head on her way down. She rolled away before he managed to give her a deadly kick. She was good, even great, but like nothing compared to him. What he felt had far less to do with confidence, than with pure certainty.

He didn't bother pushing her at the wall, but took two steps at her, grabbed a thigh and a shoulder, and broke her back on his knee. She crouched on the ground, expiring. He stepped hard on her neck, so hard that the head was split from the body. He kicked it in a contemptuous gesture, and it rolled across the sand.

The blood rush overwhelmed him. He didn't really do any take off, just jumped from the pit, practically flying through the air, at the throne, where Joyce sat, flanked by his two consorts.

He stopped, stumbled, sensed small darts penetrate his body, flashed the sentinels with blowpipes to his left and right. He managed to get a lot closer, but the forward motion eventually halted, abruptly, certain as death. The last thing he heard was the roar of a thousand cries.

Insane images passed by him, whirled and danced through the air, in his close proximity. The black nothing was everywhere around him. Zahn recalled again how he had detested the French talk show host, Marc Delon, how pleasing it had been when Joyce had slaughtered him.

Had he ever enjoyed the darkness? During early boyhood? He couldn't really remember that he had done anything but fear it.

– A man followed me, he said aloud, – on the dark road from the main road and back to the house. It scared me, scared me a lot.

Did he really have any air around him? Instead of a soft, impenetrable swamp imprisoning him forever and ever? He screamed, but there was no sound.

He remembered. He remembered quite well, except what he wanted to forget.

Soft threads held him. He could move, twist his body, but not much. Black, everything was black around him. His eyes were open, but he couldn't see anything.

Joyce smiled, as he always did.

– Ah, Jeremy, back from the dead, are we?

He was stretched out on a flat rock. No chains this time, but long, tough ropes. He could twist his body, there, on his back, but ankles and wrists were like glued to the rock beneath him.

– You've passed another trial, but many yet remain.

His vision returned. He had thought they had pulled a mask down on his head, but that wasn't the case. One moment he was unable to see, the next he saw beyond seeing, with an insane, unbelievable clarity. Compared to everything else happening, it hardly surprised him.

The other seven winners were tied to other slabs around him, tied like him, nude, bloody like him, with dirty skin like him. They were in a dark cellar, where tall fires reached up into an elaborate system of holes and pipes in the ceiling. Smoke and moisture made it almost impossible to breathe.

Joyce, Monica and Gwen towered above them all.

– We've brought you to the Shadow World, Monica said, – Taken you away from everything you knew.

– Welcome to the world, Gwen toned in and out, sounding

like echoes in his head, disappearing and appearing in his widely sensitive ears and wide-open mind.

– You've done well! Joyce congratulated them. – You're still alive. I salute you. But more trials await. You're still not the warriors you might become, that you must become, in order to survive the immediate future.

– The fighting is just a part of it all. Monica spoke with a quiet intensity. – The world is your stage, and the world may, at any time, destroy you. Not all of you will survive.

Zahn started laughing. He laughed so loud and so intense that the caves shook.

– You're truly priceless, he exclaimed. – You should all be actors… But excuse me, you already are.

The other seven stared incredulous at him. A smile crossed Monica's lips.

– Is this also a play, beloved?

Her words flowed from her lips like honey.

She started kicking him.

– Beloved, Beloved Jeremy, she breathed, while brutal kicks and strikes kept raining on the helpless prisoner.

Nothing remained of the sophisticated person, only the brutal beast. Zahn didn't lose consciousness, but he drifted back and forth above its abyss, embraced its paralyzing pain, its strengthening red haze.

Everything just floated away. When he finally came to again, he had no idea how long time had passed. Perhaps hours, perhaps only seconds. The three still stood close to him, to his flat rock, staring at him, giving him their complete attention. Monica, bloody and messy, had pulled a few steps back, though. Her eyes glowed in the insanity, the extreme reason he had always seen there.

What glowed even stronger in Joyce's eyes.

– As you've probably heard, Jeremy, we've recently issued an ultimatum to the Los Angeles police. Everybody even moving close to our selected home was in fact, from that moment on, given a death sentence. As you know this embargo was ignored. Yes, it was actually ignored to such a degree that it can hardly be believed. By virtually every single member of the city's proudest. Not exactly unexpected, but very, very stupid.

Zahn no longer doubted that Joyce truly wanted to kill every single policeman in town. The man didn't usually bluff. The question was how he intended to do it. He would certainly make a very good attempt.

– But I've also chosen to show mercy. We're all ruled by both our black and white shadows.

– Some of the rabid dogs will be given a choice, Gwen said. – Those found worthy will have a choice of instant death, or to die in our service.

– Frances here, for instance… Joyce walked to one of the tied-up women. – Ellen chose to join my cause, unconditionally, didn't you, Frances?

He patted her forehead, in a comforting gesture.

– Yes, she cried, she mumbled between swollen lips. – My life for you, please, please.

– So, this is how you select your volunteers? Zahn cackled and coughed. – What a brilliant system…

– One of several, Joyce stated. – An excellent system. And the great thing about it is that I can do it without contradicting myself. You see… Ellen is already dead. Now, she's aspiring to join The Dead.

– We… are… The Dead, she gasped. – Death can come around the next corner, as the next arrow. We don't fear it.

– Soon. He patted her cheek. – Not much longer now. Just a few more turns, and you're free.

Gwen handed him a soft club. He accepted it and started beating up on Frances. Slowly, thoroughly. He evidently went to great lengths to not cause her serious harm.

– You, who were Frances, rejoice. I baptize you Ellen and you will embrace your new life.

– Embrace, she gasped. – My life for you, Timothy, my life for you. I'm yours, now and forever.

He patted her more on the cheek, allowed her a few seconds break, waited until she looked at him with gratitude in her eyes, before he continued the relentless, ruthless torture.

The strikes seemed harsh, but they didn't break anything, did no serious harm. But they hurt, and she was kept awake all the time, was denied the escape into unconsciousness, while the insanity kept going. The screams eventually stopped. In the end there

158

were only hoarse, desperate gasps. The voice had disappeared during the torture.

But there was hardly any blood. Blood had flowed from Zahn, during Monica's administration of enraged affection… hadn't it? Zahn suspected he could be disqualified when it came to evaluate the beating he had received, compared to what the others were given. But his distinct impression was that Monica had thrown all caution to the wind. She hadn't cared whether she killed him or not.

But… he was still alive. And… he didn't feel too bad. Not considering the circumstances. Rage boiled within him, and when he pulled the ropes, tightened all the muscles in his body, it hardly hurt anywhere.

The séance continued. The remaining six were also methodically and cruelly beaten and brutalized. It ended, eventually. It just didn't feel that way.

Zahn «rested» there, in a stupor. Again and again a voice resounded out of the darkness, the way he must have heard it, hours, years earlier.

– DON'T BELIEVE WE'VE FORGOTTEN ABOUT YOU, JEREMY

And then she came at him with a hot burning torch, pushing it at his belly. He stared blindly right ahead and to the side, as he twisted his body wildly, in a desperate attempt to escape the horrible pain, but there was no escape, no escape anywhere. The flames rose as his skin caught fire. And then she attacked him again. AND AGAIN. And he screamed and screamed, until he was able to scream no more.

And the pain didn't let up, not an inch, in his feverish twists and turns the coming hours and days.

– Good healing tissue, he cackled, with a horrifying imitation of a voice. – GOOD HEALING TISSUE

Cackled insanely.

– This is merely the beginning, Gwen said, when she, as the last of the troika, left the hot and moist cellar. – Prepare yourselves, steel yourselves, for what's to come.

Silence. Moans and howls of pain. Unconsciousness. Silence. Hours, days passed. The triumvirate didn't return.

Perhaps he was fantasizing. Perhaps he had died, and had yet to realize that fact. It was a reasonable assumption considering the horrendous treatment he had been given. He couldn't understand, couldn't fathom how he could still move, breathe.

He wondered what plan Joyce had for the world. Joyce had a plan, that was a given, and he had never done anything halfway. He killed randomly and ruthlessly, but what was behind it all? What motivation, what purpose? The entire set up looked like a distorted version of Nietzsche's writing. Joyce hadn't mentioned Nietzsche. There had been no need.

Rule number one: Nothing was ever what it seemed as far as Timothy Joyce was concerned.

Nothing had any meaning… if one looked at it with the twenty-first century's narrow and dull vision.

Jeremy opened his eyes, eyes that had always been open. Stared into the fire above, on what didn't look like any century, but timelessness.

He looked at his surroundings, caught the others' staring, horrified eyes, and it was him they were staring at.

A rumble rose from the depths. A sound always there, but now making itself known. Did the castle shake beneath him, or was it only he who was shaking? He writhed on the slab and it dawned on him that he had never stopped moving. The ropes cut into his skin, but he kept pulling them. And the roar rising from the depths was his own.

And it mixed with something tearing, something breaking. The ropes broke like strings when he pulled himself up. He pulled some more and the remains of the ropes binding him seemed to break in pieces. Muscles twitched and swelled under the skin. He felt incredibly vigorous and powerful, as if fire flowed through his veins, and he imagined that smoke and steam rose from him. The ankles were still stuck. Two more pulls and he was free. So easy, so effortless.

During the next two, three seconds he considered freeing the others and decided against it, decided he wouldn't expose himself to more treachery. They meant so little anyway, in the great scheme of things.

He rushed through dark hallways. Up, up. In spite of the rage coursing through him, reason held him back. What was crucial at this stage was to get out of and away from here. No matter how many guns he could get hold of he wouldn't have a snowball's chance in hell alone, against the legion of the damned. He moved quietly. Only the echo of his steps was heard in the old castle. He reached the great hall, the large window. The very air seemed to shimmer somewhere ahead. An exit? He saw no people. Lucky. He had been lucky who had managed so far without resistance. It wouldn't last. He didn't have time to look for the castle gate. His vision turned increasingly misty. If he hadn't felt like a million bucks, he would have thought he was about to faint. He threw himself through the window. Fire and mist seemed to flow around him. The right foot twisted when he landed on the hard ground. He moved on, limping. Soon he ran full throttle through the city of angels. The pain in the foot faded with those still lingering after the beating. The beating? Hah, he had become master of understatement as well.

The neighborhood he ran through reminded him of a remote storage area, but nothing similar to what had been Joyce's very temporary headquarters, what he had declared as his territory. Zahn hardly saw or felt anything around him, so he couldn't be absolute certain he had not encountered people so far, but it seemed reasonable to believe he hadn't. Even though he was fully aware of the fact that the way he looked no one would dare give notice if they saw him. A notion turning to certainty when he stopped in front of a dirty window. When he froze, horrified and fascinated. He touched his belly carefully, with a remote look in his eyes. There was no pain, as he brushed away soot and crust. It itched, but there wasn't really any pain. He shook his head, but it didn't clear. Under the crust and the ash, new, fresh, slightly inflamed skin appeared, shockingly clean compared to the blood and the shit covering the rest of his body, the savagery erupting from his very being.

He ran on. If he met anyone, met the police, there would be questions, questions he didn't have time for. Something had been driving him since he left the castle, across green fields, through deep forests, and dirty streets. The running calmed down, turning less wild, more directed. He slowed down when he reached something resembling a residential area. There was no wash hanging from any outside clothesline in this area, something that would have been a hopeless task here. The clothes would have quickly turned dirtier than before the wash, stained by dust and pollution. He broke into a cellar under a four-flat house. After ravaging most of the rooms, he finally found a clothesline with fairly dry clothes. A bit of moisture wouldn't matter, as it would dry in a matter of minutes in the smoldering heat, become impregnated with his sweat, his flowing body juices.

Whatever ruled his instincts drove him on. The tight clothes caused him a bit of a problem, clearly smaller as they were than what he had believed during his quick estimation, but they would do. He looked like a homeless person, and that was quite okay. Nobody noticed the homeless. They were hardly even ghosts in people's daily lives, something seen on TV, something passing good people on the street. He felt like a ghost now, not a homeless person. Nobody seemed to notice him. Everybody else certainly looked like revenants to him. He entered a bus. At least he believed he did. The driver threw him a single glance, and lost all nerve, all need to utter protests against his presence. Or perhaps he was dreaming. Zahn… or the driver.

He ran. Zahn ran through dusty streets.

He didn't run, but moved like he had all the time in the world. And he had. He would reach his destination soon enough.

The sun shone from a blue, cloud-free sky. But everything looked red, dark, as if he was wearing shades. But he wasn't. He stopped under a tree, in the shade, a totally ordinary day, staring at a house across the street. The address was like glowing letters in his vision. He «read» word by word, from the file Caldwell had shown him, recalling the pictures, his memory burning like the hot wind hitting his skin.

Monica Valdez, nineteen years old lived here, an LAPD officer in training. No remarkable results at school. Nothing remarkable anywhere. She resembled the Monica he knew, but only as a pale shadow.

Mother: Esmeralda. Mexican ancestry. No siblings, no other relatives on record. No father on record. Probably Caucasian. Dark, black hair. No sign of red or fire-colored hair. She was almost of the same height as Monica, but significantly slimmer. The information was correct. Caldwell had included the information about checking and double-checking of background, the policewoman to be, from cradle to the previous day. She had been born in this city, gone to school here, visited doctors here, attended the police academy here. Everything documented, checked and rechecked. Nothing mysterious about her life. Nothing suspicious.

Dark, bright day. The door to the entrance in the house across the street was opened. A young woman in police uniform danced down the stairs. She continued down the sidewalk in a relaxed walk. But it was mostly a sham. Someone with his experience could easily see that something was troubling her. He followed her, followed her like a shadow. In a flash she turned, and he saw her, saw her face. He kept walking calmly a few steps behind her. She turned her head. Suddenly he had bridged the distance between them. He grabbed her hair. She gasped and attempted to kick him. It touched harmlessly his thigh. He hit her in the abdomen, paralyzing her, pulled her with him to the nearest entrance. There were no other people around. There was no sound, except her labored breathing.

He pushed her at the wall, shaking her like a rag doll.

– You're not much worth, now, are you, «beloved»? Not on your own. How does it feel to be at the opposite end of hammering fists? Answer me, you damn…

She attempted to talk, attempted to breathe, near death in fear. He held her up by the neck. She kicked about, her feet not touching the ground. Her movements had already slowed down, like the wings of a dying butterfly.

The red haze danced in front of him, and made the world look incredibly clear and transparent. He saw her as she was, late developed, a skinny and unpolished girl, a mosaic not yet complete.

He let go of her. She landed on her feet, but swayed for seconds before standing somewhat steady, paralyzed like a statue. She never took her eyes off him. She coughed repeatedly, but her eyes never left the creature towering over her. The creature not so much taller, but infinitely bigger.

– You're not… her… I was… wrong.

She didn't have Monica's physique and not her height. Monica reached him to his forehead.

He had almost blacked out when he had seen… when he had spotted… spotted the scar, the tiny scar below the eye, a cruel coincidence in an insane world.

He grabbed her, and dragged the skinny body further into the building. She didn't resist. At least he didn't sense any resistance from her. He knocked on the first door he found, one of several apartments on this floor. Knocked, not hammered.

– Y-yes? A huge, powerful built man opened.

– You live in this apartment?

– Yes, what is it to you?

– I need to use this apartment until tomorrow morning. If I am disturbed the slightest, by noise or intruders, or anybody, I'll hunt you down and kill you. Do you understand this?

The last remaining traces of opposition left the man's face, flowed through his toes. He hurried outside. Without any clothes other than what he wore, without taking his time to bring shoes.

Zahn was alone with the girl in the small apartment.

– He believed you, she said. – He won't be back.

Even the voice was similar. It lacked the boundless passion, the rough edges, but there were similarities. Like a second or third generation echo.

– Miss Valdez, he said formally. – I'm associated with the Los Angeles police department…

– I know who you are, she stated.

– Miss Valdez, you've been the subject of an internal, informal investigation. You have a striking likeness to an international terrorist by the name of Monica.

A shadow clouded her face, one of fear and incredulity.

Then she spoke, with a thin and shaking voice.

– We all have a twin, isn't that what they say?

He studied her, from top to bottom, completely undaunted. He felt alienated, so infinitely closer to himself, his own core.

– You don't really believe I am her, do you? There was despair in her voice. – I've read about her. There's only a drawing of her, a drawing made from your description, right?

– You're not her, he stated.

– I don't understand this. She waved her hands in a typical Latin gesture. – You can't possibly believe I have anything to do with her. I'm a totally insignificant person. I have no siblings. My mother has no siblings. And why does she call herself Monica, that's truly insane.

– We don't believe you've got anything to do with her, he said, – but I do. And I follow no procedures or rules. I've been on his heels for three years, and I'm starting to lose my patience, Monica.

She froze, as paralyzed as when he had had his hands around her throat.

This apartment was buried halfway below the ground. The window was only just sticking up above the ground outside. And that was also how he felt, half buried, on his way up from and out of the darkness.

– Won't you sit down? She offered kindly.

– What a breach of protocol, he said cheerfully. – I'll have to inform you that I'm the host and you're the guest. The guest doesn't ask the host to sit down in his own house.

– I'm s-sorry, she stuttered. – I…

– I'm very familiar with the tactics you learn to calm a violent person in a hostage situation, he snarled. – It won't work with me.

She fell silent, shrinking under his burning stare, his very presence. He was right. He was calm now. His words were made calmly, well considered.

– Why not let me go? She said weakly.

– That's out of the question. You're connected to everything going on, in some way or another, and I won't let you go until I've found out how.

He stopped before her.

– I'll never let you go, he stated.

He took her around the jaw and pushed it up, let her have every chance of resisting, to express her enmity. He pushed his lips at hers. She didn't push back. He kissed her, wildly, uncompromisingly. She returned the kiss, suddenly, shockingly.

She gasped, backing off in shock.

– What did you do, what are you d-doing to me?

– Nothing you don't desire, he snarled. – Everything you've ever dreamed about.

He once more covered the distance between them, once more kissing her. He began undressing her, tearing apart the uniform piece by piece, pulling the tight pants down her thighs, and she no longer made any attempt to free herself from him, from his ruthless grip. She was breathing clearly faster, as she dug her nails

deep into his shoulders, clutching him, clutching him hard. He
threw her on her back on the bed. The black hair covered her
face. She crouched there, breathing and twitching, during the few,
long seconds it took him to undress and join her in bed.

She attempted to avoid looking at the growing, pulsing thing he
pointed at her, but her eyes were pulled to it, pulled irresistibly,
until she could no longer look away.

He knelt, his hands exploring her, exploring her as intimately as
they possibly could do. Her cunt grew wet and swollen. She bit
her lower lip, bit herself until she bled.

– Ah, mother's virtuous girl has tasted forbidden fruit…

She released a prolonged, desperate moan, writhing and
throwing herself on the bed, under his direction.

– Yes, she moaned, – yes.

No misunderstanding, no wishful thinking on his part.

He had her, had her good, but took his time, time, to enjoy
himself, to please himself, as he moved back and forth within
her. Even her body looked like Monica's. Skinnier, not so robust,
not so deadly. Like everything concerning her, merely a seed of
something more.

He watered her, and she screamed, in desire and delight.

He played with the hair in her groin afterwards. Black, curly
hairs twisting themselves around his fingers. She pulled tight
to him, as tight as she could possibly come, playing with his
cock, waiting for more, wanting more. And when he started
growing again almost instantly, she started kissing him, wild and
demanding.

– You've broken me, she whispered darkly. – Broken me in little
pieces. Put me back together. I'm yours. Make me yours, your
Monica.

She begged him, with a sweet, weak voice, like that of a little
child. He laughed harshly and scornfully, and she shrank, shrank
further.

– You misunderstand, like I knew you would, he laughed. – Like
any mediocre sheep, letting herself be shepherded, without doing
anything but bleating. I've got no plans making you mine. You
shall do it all. You shall be yours.

His waves hit her shores anew. And the sand turned to dust,
and the dust blew across the sea. She was on all fours, while

he clutched her hair and pumped her up from behind, violent, unstoppable, without holding back the slightest. She gasped constantly, tiny, brief breaths, almost without sound. As if she couldn't get sufficient air. She was filled time and time again, but wanted ever more.

Her entire body, the entire her, was filled. He sensed it. He filled himself countless times, grew to many times his former size. The sound grew then, a sound born in pain, violent birth pains, making the Earth shake.

He let go of her hair, threw her away like garbage. She collapsed on the bed. Her hips pointing up, while she remained in the position he had placed her. He enjoyed the sight of her butt sticking up like that, always ready, always available. He lay down beside her. She blinked repeatedly, slipping unresisting into sleep. He noticed that his own eyes started blinking, but he didn't fight it. He allowed it to happen, encouraged it. Sleep was Change, metamorphosis. He dreamed himself, like everybody does. But when he awakened the next morning he didn't do like most people, attempting to return to the person he had been the night before, but embraced this new, this hidden, that had always been waiting below the surface, patiently, for its time.

During the sleep he registered every single sound in the room, every change in the air. If she had attempted to escape, he would have known. But she didn't move, not really, only twisting her body without control, and mumbling and moaning in her fever-hot dreams.

He was still sleeping when she left the bed and started moving around in the kitchen. A few minutes and he scented the smell of food. He didn't need to fight himself out of his sleep. He quite simply decided to wake up, and he did, gaining an awareness without equal. Two worlds, one world became one.

He glimpsed her, out there, in the kitchen, glimpsed her hair, her butt.

It didn't take long after he had opened his eyes, and she arrived with the food tray. She had timed it very well, anticipating his needs perfectly.

– I suspected you were awake, she said, with a shadow of a smile present in her expressive, expressionless face. – I *sensed* it.

She put the tray in his lap, and crawled into bed, crawled to his side, pulled her naked body close to his.

– I knew you would be hungry, she said. – I'm hungry, very hungry.

She started munching the sandwiches, after pushing more than half over to his side of the tray. He started eating, without really using the opportunity to enjoy the great sandwiches.

– You're good, he praised her. – Your mother has taught you something useful.

– Yeah, she acknowledged. – Everything that will make me a good wife for someone.

As he had suspected there was more than a touch of bitterness in her voice.

– Do you know anything about your father? He wondered.

She stopped eating. He felt her turn rigid.

– Tell me everything you know.

His wish was her command. She obeyed instantly.

– I just know he left mother before I was born. She has never been willing to reveal more than that.

Zahn held up a sandwich, held it up before her mouth. She took a bite. He kept it in the same position. She took another bite, and another, and then she ate the rest in one mouthful.

– I love it when you feed me, she said, suddenly huskily, approaching seductively. – It makes me so horny. Please do it more. Please.

He fed her the remaining sandwiches. She ate faster and faster, bit hard, right by his fingers. His cock started twitching, and it grew large and hard from one moment to the next. She smiled and grabbed the tray as she placed herself on her knees. It gave away only a slight bump as it hit the carpet. She crawled onto his lap and sat down with one knee on each side of his thighs. He grabbed a swollen breast and started squeezing it. She moaned in need. He grabbed her hips and moved her effortlessly closer, held her above his groin, lowered her. Let her go. She started rocking instantly. Up and down. Up and down.

– I... have... never... felt it... like this... before, she gasped. – You fill me up, fill me up everywhere. Aaaaahhh

He started pushing then, unable to hold back any longer. Her hips slipped so fast up and down that there were just pushes and pulls, with no discernible difference between them. She moved her head back and forth. Her hair was pushed forward, pulled back, to the left, to the right, and pulled and pushed in all directions.

He saw her only in a haze after that, until they rested entwined in the blanket, in each other, a non-measurable time later. He twined her hair around his index finger.

In the silence he heard steps from the hall. Nothing special about that. He had heard it all night, even deep into sleep.

– You like my hair, that's for sure, she stated. – You're touching it all the time.

– It's… special, he nodded.

Curly and smooth simultaneously.

– Just like *hers?*

He nodded, not trusting his voice.

– When did you get the scar? He asked her.

– A month ago, she replied. – A sleaze cut me with the point of a knife.

He nodded. The photo he had seen had been about a year old.

– Now, I want you to remove the fake hair color, he said. Her eyes widened. – Remove everything, that covering your cunt as well. And the fucking colored contact lenses.

She hurried to the bathroom, halted a bit, looked back at him for a moment, looked like she wanted to say something, but she stayed silent, and hurried to the bathroom.

He sat on the bed, with his back to the wall. He would have thought the need to watch her, watch her in her task would be unbearable, but he felt completely relaxed. That, too, pleased him. He listened to the sound of the running water, saw her through the steam in the mirror, and the way he saw her then was identical to the way he saw her when she dried her hair and left the bedroom. Many of the hairs had a natural black color, but now the shades of fire clearly appeared. Her groin looked like it was burning. Flames danced around the dark skin on the shoulder, the belly and the breasts. The green eyes perfectly completed the sight.

– I didn't get it all off, she complained. – It will eventually disappear, though.

She walked to a window, looking out through a chink in the curtains.

– Mommy was behind this as well, as you've probably guessed. She has colored my hair for as long as I can remember, until she forced me to do it on my own. She inspected me every day, like she would a mare, every day for years. She insisted I should look like a «pureblooded» Mexican.

– Racism and its idiocy are prevalent everywhere, of course, Zahn commented dryly.

She turned around, while rubbing her back at the wall, at the curtains, with slow, sensuous moves. She displayed herself to him, suddenly very self-conscious.

– Do you know what? It feels good, so good to walk around like this, naked like this, especially in the morning, especially since it's evening…

He didn't comment on that. She was right. He had just never thought about it that way.

Darkness descended on them. Real darkness, seductive nuances in shadows.

He had some more food. The guy, whose apartment they had «crashed», had one of the best filled fridges he had ever seen. A huge, smoking hot beef waited on the plate before him. She ate merely a small part of the tempting meal. The hunger didn't yet gnaw in her like it did in him.

– I know that people training much and hard need considerably more food, she said giggling, – but you beat everything I've seen to this point.

They both sat nude by the table. It eventually felt quite natural, even though he was very conscious of how his cock moved from thigh to thigh as he moved on the chair. Desire burned on a low flame. He could have satisfied it just by reaching out a hand, but he let it burn, burn on a low flame.

The steak was consumed in an orgy of food, just as intense as the series of hot embraces they had enjoyed. A few bones were left on the plate, nothing more.

He walked to the closet then, finally. As expected, it was just as well outfitted as the rest of the apartment, both in terms of male and female clothing.

– It's just fair you're the one finding me some new clothes, you know, she joked solemnly. – You tore my sole uniform to shreds, my strong, dark Jeremy.

He looked at her, looked at the person beneath the words, beneath the exterior.

– Do you like the Academy? He wondered, not casually.

– I don't dislike it. She shrugged. – It's far better than many other things I've been forced to endure. I was very happy when I was accepted. It's a way out and away, an opening to something better. To Latinos in the ghetto becoming an officer of the law is often the only way out.

She gave him a quick kiss on the lips, before shyly pulling back.

Zahn dressed slightly irritated. He had been convinced the clothes would be the right size. The owner had seemed both tall and big enough. But only the clothing of extra width and length, fabric that wasn't supposed to cling to the body fit somewhat.

– You're so big, she whispered. – You can't expect a random chosen pretender to be truly useful. But the clothes will do, won't they? Until we can find you something better.

She dressed, as well, then, while constantly, consciously and subconsciously, posing for him.

– This coat is me, don't you agree?

Covering a blouse, tight pants, she pulled on a dark, distinct coat.

– It's okay, he shrugged.

She had a burning need for his acceptance.

Exactly as she was supposed to.

– Did you learn anything at all… at the academy?

– We learned about mediating, negotiating and stuff, she replied eagerly. – I like it.

– A LAPD classic, he grinned. – First you beat them senseless, and then you negotiate with them.

She popped like a balloon, so very transparent.

At least on the surface, but below it boiled and burned. He searched and probed there.

Dive. Dive into the abyss of oneself, one's own fate.

He walked to the door, opened it, turned around and looked back at her.

– Are we going out *now*?

– Why not? It's a great night, a great night for a walk.

– This neighborhood is virtually overrun with violent gangs and such, she said, clearly evasive.

– That's totally irrelevant, he stated. – The question is not what others might do, but what you want. Exist like the cute Madonna for the rest of your life, always submitting to others' will… or find your true face, your true will, also beyond the confines of four walls.

He walked outside and let go of the door. Before it closed, she had caught it, and hurried after him.

– *Diablo*, she hissed hot and intense at him. – You think it's that simple, do you, that you can get me where you want by using reverse psychology on me?

He turned like lightning, and grabbed her, grabbed her with fingers like claws. His eyes paralyzed her, just as much as the painful grip.

– You're nothing but clay I can mold, form in my own image.

He let go of her, and kept walking. She followed a few steps behind him, gasping and breathing hard, before she once more returned to his side.

– I was referred to your «speech» in Santa Monica, she said, looking down, with shivering lips, with a shred of despair. – The entire academy was. Your entire philosophy, your view on mankind… it's so wrong. We can be violent. We are not violent.

– Nothing wrong about dreaming, Sweet Madonna, he said. – I'll actually claim that present day humans dream too little, or they allow others to steer their dreams into a track fitting to those others. Those in charge, those dominating today's world, today's very perception of what a human being is. They love it when people walk around with blindfolds, that their subjects create a world in their mind completely different from the reality. This in spite of everybody observing the true reality every day. Stupid, isn't it?

He kept strolling ahead, without casting as much as a glance at her.

– You're completely wrong, Sweet Madonna. We are violent. We will always be violent. Fortunately so. The violence is a part of our aggression, what will always be there. We need the rage, need the strong drive inside, in order to resist and eradicate all the assholes that would want to enslave us, the type of individuals sustaining and supporting a society destroying all life, all fire.

– I've never met anyone like you, she said weakly. – I feel so small, so very small.

– Sweet Madonna wishes to be a Demon, he stated. – Grow big and strong.

– Yes, she whispered, almost inaudible. – Yes!

They arrived at a windblown, downtrodden tennis court. She realized they had been on their way here all the time, that they couldn't have ended up anywhere else.

– Take off your coat. We don't want to ruin your new, fine coat.

She threw it on the ground in contempt and attacked him, seemingly very aggressive. She would have terrified an ordinary bank robber or street trash. But he saw the fundamental uncertainty locked in her every move, experienced it as an echo of himself not so long ago. He locked her arm in a painful grip, and gave her a light tap on the jaw. Blood flowed from her mouth. She backed several steps while shaking her head. She circled him, while he stood still, even when she was behind him.

– Show me, he teased her. – Show me what you're capable of.

She attacked. He avoided her advances easily.

– You shouldn't be ashamed of your skills, he said. – There's nothing wrong with them, with the technical part of them. You need to strengthen your upper arms, your shoulders and thighs and hips, but the physical training isn't the most important.

She attacked from the side. He bent slightly forward and threw her far away, almost to the other side of the court. She landed hard on the dusty asphalt. He was at her in an instant and gave her a light kick in her side. She gasped, and jumped away from him, jumped up, virtually on all fours, stared at him like a tiny wounded animal.

– You need to develop your killer instinct, he said softly. – This is true even more for you than all others, because it will be of such immense use to you.

She surprised him then, like she always surprised him. When she renewed her attack, he had expected that, been well prepared. He pulled his head aside, but she still managed to hit him with a hard kick. Blood filled his mouth, a trifle he didn't let bother him, one that he, in truth hardly noticed. But still. She shouldn't have been able to touch him at all.

They kept it going for a while longer, until she was thoroughly beaten. And he hardly breathed harder. Though without her being seriously injured or even having much in the way of visible wounds.

– Let's go. I have what I need, now, have seen enough, to build on.

– Is the clay sufficiently warm and malleable, my Lord and Master?

Eyes glowed in defiance.

– Exactly how I want it, he stated.

They moved into a very troubled area. She kept silent, while she kept looking nervously around.

– «Don't be scared. Then they will just keep scaring you».

– That's easy for you to say, she snarled.

– Is it? He returned enraged. – *Is it?*

– No, she whispered. – I'm sorry, I… no.

She put a hand on his shoulder, for a brief moment. But the sense of touch lingered. She pulled closer to him, and stuck his arm into his.

– There was a moment I sensed… something, she whispered. And her whisper sounded totally different, now, compared to her whisper only moments ago. – A few minutes, a day with you, have taught me infinitely more than the entire time at the academy.

Green fire danced in her eyes.

– You can teach me so much, Jeremy.

He saw her stare up at him, eager, expectant, with the same desperate despair he had sensed in her from the beginning. And the voice… He froze slightly, so little that she probably didn't notice. But she was bright. Her voice, when she said his name… the intonation, everything, was very similar to Monica. Or was he just imagining that?

They reached a corner, crossed an invisible threshold. He sensed it, subconsciously began stretching, softening his limbs. Nothing obvious, but he prepared himself. He sensed the pulse beat faster. He stoked the embers, more than sensed the hidden flames.

Once again, a notion, a flare passed by. A word, a memory. Something about the «improbable». And it felt pretty improbable in itself. Redundant, at least. He had long since realized the improbability, the total insanity, about the last years' events.

Layer upon layer of disinformation and important information haunted him. This was about finding the essence, dividing it from the surrounding confusion.

The boys' gang appeared, and he was distracted, once again. Time failed him - again.

She turned visibly rigid and pensive. She knew these boys and not favorably.

– Hola, Monica, the leader greeted her.

– Hello, she replied casually.

But she fooled nobody.

– I see you've colored your hair like a *gringo*. If that's all you learn by wearing blue, you should truly quit.

– This is my natural color, she said, throwing a challenge at him.

They never had time to reply. Zahn took two steps forward and suddenly stood right in their midst. He attacked with a raw explosion of wrath, waltzing through them as if they were *nothing*. Nothing but frail paper tigers, pulled over skin, filled with blood. Monica never had time to count them. She knew their numbers from previous experience, but nothing rational worked in her mind right now.

One of them *howled* in fear, and made an escape attempt. Zahn pulled him back and struck him to the ground in one single swing. Those still standing attacked him, in desperation, in despair, because they had no other choice. He took them on, one on one, and all at once. They hit him with a few blows, but it didn't faze him. Not in any other way than to piss him further off. And they realized what a mistake they had made by irritating him, by being in the same street as Jeremy Zahn. Breathless and spellbound Monica couldn't do anything but stare, stare, stare.

The leader was suddenly there, in front of her. He had some bruises, but no substantial problems with staying sharp, and didn't seem considerably reduced in any way. She didn't think, but jumped at him, kicked him in the face. Another came at her from behind. She snarled and grabbed his head, pushed it at the wall. The leader attacked. She turned halfway around, and kicked him again, a whirling kick hitting at the side of the head. He went down on all fours, and remained there, shaking his head helplessly. She kicked out again, in his groin this time. She smiled, and before he hit the ground, she struck him again.

And then she sensed a horrible, ruthless rationality flow through her. And she was breathless no more.

– So easy, she said contemptuously. – So very simple. You haven't seen the true me before, have you, Raoul?

She bent down and lifted the pulped head by the hair. She pulled hard. He moaned.

– I can kill you, now, she said softly. – I will kill you if you ever come *near* me again. And you will welcome death.

He couldn't utter a word. The sudden, shocking fear held him in its grip. The big, powerful body shook.

She lifted him a bit further from the ground and struck a violent, painful blow to his ribs. He gasped and turned completely limp. She let the limp body fall to the ground. She straightened. And then she kicked him, using first her right foot, then the left. Kicked the head and upper body back and forth. He lay still. Blood flowed from his mouth.

– He didn't stand a chance, she marveled, turned to Zahn. – And you hadn't weakened him when you offered him to me. I can hardly believe I feared the bastard. I was so stupid.

– You made the same mistake as everybody else, he said. – You saw them as a single entity, instead of individuals. You're awake now, and look at the world with new eyes.

– Awake… she stated.

Silence ruled anew, a buzz beyond hearing, the immediate consciousness.

Her eyes were shining, her entire body seemingly glowing.

She stood by his side, in a chaos of twisted and beaten two-legged wolves and her fire seemed to brighten the entire dusty street, the gray neighborhood, brightening the entire world.

# CHAPTER NINE

## SIX MONTHS BEFORE NOW

The railway station in Jaynagar. Old trains breathed steam and smoke, both up and sideways, steam trains and also old fuel trains. The dust never really settled. The surrounding area had a natural fertility, but here, too, the air was thick with particles. Jacques Malin and Jeremy Zahn coughed all the way from the railway station.

– That list… Malin opened. – Even if I am very conscious of walking on risky ground here, I must insist on seeing it.

– There's no list. Zahn grinned. – Everything is in my head.

They had a few hours until the next departure. After a few minutes search they sat down by a sleepy sidewalk café. They were served what was claimed to be the local, traditional cuisine, but probably had a more international origin. A «white» course or a traditional, local meal, mixed with the intruders' preferences. Even here, at one of the world's outskirts, there was no rest from the world's mediocrity.

– Perhaps not so strange, Malin smacked. – considering your fabulous memory.

– Now, you sound downright suspicious, Zahn warned. – I'm starting to wonder what you haven't caught with that inquisitive mind of yours.

– One picks up things here and there. A shrug. – What might seem of minor importance at first, might be crucial in hindsight.

Zahn knew what was coming. One didn't need a crystal ball to see the obvious.

– You're denied access to casinos all over the world, are you not? You're too good. You're able to count the cards in blackjack from virtually the first to the last card in the deck. It's bad advertising for the casinos to deny you access, but they don't have any choice.

Zahn began to feel seriously *known*.

– But I, on the other hand, know very little about you, he pointed out.

It looked like Malin considered this.

– To this point I've avoided the infamy of those I write about, he said.

Zahn wolfed down the food. And when he had totaled the first, generous plate, he impatiently ordered another. He had developed an incredible, uncanny appetite lately.

The food burned in him afterwards, as it was consumed in his smoldering insides.

An older boy approached their table. He had stood in the shade, waiting, for a while. Zahn put the napkin away, and turned towards him.

– You're looking for Master Arthur? He asked them in English.
– Arthur Markham? I can take you to him.

– That won't be necessary, Malin assured him. – We're going to Katmandu, and it won't be difficult to find him there.

– Master Arthur no longer resides in Katmandu, but somewhere north of the border, not far away.

– How did you know we sought this person? Zahn asked sharply.

– I heard you speak about him. The boy shook lightly. – I can lead you to him.

He spoke excellent English, though with a distinct accent.

They crossed the border not long afterwards. The Indian army guarded the borders quite zealously, but this wasn't one of the unruly areas, where border disputes and guerillas made mincemeat of them. They had most of their northern force, most of their force, period, at the Pakistani border. Zahn, Milan and their guide just walked across, without any sophistication or fuss.

Tight forest, ever-higher terrain, more ruins and destroyed statues of gods and holy men, built in gigantic proportions. Zahn saw representations of Shiva and Vishnu. The Destroyer and the Preserver. And of Kali, the many-armed, reaching in many directions.

There were countless gods, there were none.

Layer upon layer of falseness, designed to seduce humanity into slavery and servitude.

Suddenly their guide had disappeared. They had walked for an hour, perhaps fifteen minutes more than that. He seemed to vanish, to dissolve into smoke, from one moment to the next. A person familiar with the surroundings could do that. Fuck. Zahn swore. One moment of divided attention, and anything could happen.

A memory virtually assaulted him, suddenly, crystal clear. He had chased Joyce and one of his groups in Norway's mountains, over snow and rocks. Had closed in on them, had been convinced he had truly glimpsed them, convinced he would see them around the next turn. But... there had been no one there.

And he had sensed heat, a heat reminding him of Calcutta, of India.

– Have we just experienced one of Joyce's tiny teasing slaps on the cheek? Malin wondered.

– I don't know, Zahn replied introspectively. – He does things like this.

– Can you find your way back to town?

– I can find the way down, there's never any problem finding the way down. But I suggest we do the opposite.

– Into the jungle? Malin exclaimed incredulous.

He was sweating harder already, like a reflexive reaction.

He clutched the camera in one hand and the machete in the other. Zahn walked first. He pushed himself through the tangle of trees and branches, without looking either left or right. If Malin had fallen and injured himself, he couldn't say for certain if the possessed man would have stopped.

It couldn't be called jungle exactly, what they fought their way through, with brief periods of rest crossing open spaces. But it was natural for a non-native to think that, in the tight forest.

They found the man they were looking for, without that much bother, after doing their utmost to stay the course and keep to a more or less straight line. He sat on the porch of a simple hut, on a height under the mountain. Malin turned and looked behind. There was no sign of civilization anywhere. He could hardly believe they had found their way here.

The man on the porch, in the creaking chair, gave no sign of having seen them, of having discovered that there were other people nearby. The skinny, sunken figure rocked in his chair. Aside from that he wasn't moving. Not with the body, not the eyes.

– Arthur Markham? Zahn cried aloud.

No reaction.

– Arthur Markham? Zahn asked again. – My name is Jeremy
Zahn. With me is Jacques Malin. We're here to talk with you
about Timothy Joyce.

Sunken eyes moved then, slowly, in pain.

– I'm Markham, he acknowledged with a weak and hoarse voice.
– Timothy Joyce has certainly crossed my path.

– He was your student, a few years back, wasn't he? Malin asked.

– An unusually gifted student, Markham nodded.

– Listen, Zahn said curtly, – we're not here to listen to the
uppity, polite version. We're here to hear about *Timothy Joyce*.

Silence reigned. Even the usually noisy surroundings of the
wilderness seemed to turn quiet, and its visuals to fade away. A
moment it looked like the man in the chair had returned to his
close to catatonic state, but then he moved his head, looked up.
At Zahn, not the Frenchman.

– You've come to the right place, to the right man, he said and
pulled back, visibly upset. – I can speak with some authority
regarding Timothy Joyce. I'm one of the few who can.

He clapped his hands. The boy from the station appeared. They
saw no signs of him recognizing them, he gave them no reason
to think that.

– This is Frank, my sole remaining servant.

They sat down on the wooden bench opposite the chair.
Markham remained in his place. Frank (or whatever the hell his
name was) served tea. Later they were served Cantonese roasted
duck, with rice and vegetables. Zahn ate with chopsticks as if he
had been born with them. Malin needed western cutlery.

Paper lamps were hung from the porch ceiling and lit. The three
remained on the porch during the evening, during the darkness.
«Frank» only appeared to serve, to remove plates and utensils.

– He was my student… I had no initial reservations about
teaching him, in spite of the fact that the training should really
begin during early childhood. He had an eagerness like a child and
considerable experience, also in the techniques I was teaching. He
was so quick to learn that he mastered the basic techniques after
just a few thrusts, in spite of a certain initial clumsiness… one
quickly vanishing. Even his muscles had a certain… softness, an
elasticity usually only found in children. That's the main reason

the teaching start as early as childhood. Both mind and body are considerably more elastic, malleable then. A person starting the training as an adult is running a higher risk of both physical and… mental injuries.

The jungle remained distant, its sounds hardly reaching their ears.

– So I agreed to train him. And he was truly open like a child. I was almost transfixed on occasions. I was tempted to imagine he had just been born, born as an adult, with speed and lethal skills far superior to ordinary humans. He couldn't compete with me, of course, but there was no acknowledgement of this in his moves, his attitude. He had no respect. This was something I reproached him for on numerous occasions. I thought he would learn it eventually, as my teaching was beaten into him… but it never happened. I touched often upon the subject of… misuse. I imprinted on him that if that happened, I would be forced to do as I had always done: hunt down the person in question and put a stop to his unholy acts.

– Then he began… disappearing. He had a lot to do, he said, a lot to take on. And every time he returned he had grown stronger, more powerful. Dangerous. And he courted Abigail, my daughter, my foremost student and fellow teacher. He began changing her, and also the other students and teachers at the center, not the other way around.

– In Katmandu? Malin injected.

A nod.

– In my chosen home, my place of power, where I had chosen to live my life. His presence influenced, perverted the mood at the center. I didn't realize how far it had gone until the end. I had become a content, fat old man.

– The final time I saw him, he was changed, to such an uncanny degree that I couldn't be certain it was the same man. He didn't hide anymore. His features hadn't changed much, if at all. He looked older, but it didn't faze him. But his attitude, his skills…

The exhausted, downtrodden figure in the chair, in the bed released a sore moan.

– He attacked me without forewarning, beat me easily, like he would a little child, right in front of all my students. Almost everybody followed him when he left. He humiliated me and then he broke me.

— At the end, when he held my daughter in his arms, showed me the power he had over her, he gave me a solemn promise: «I'll take care of your son as well, sweet little Louis. He will come for me, desiring revenge for the transgression I've visited upon you. He's already dead. It merely remains to convince him of that fact».

Wind grew in strength everywhere, except on the spot where they sat. In and around the hut silence reigned.

— I'm hunting him, Zahn said low, intensively. — The hunt seems endless, but it isn't. Sooner or later I'll find him. My chances will increase significantly if you train me like you trained him.

— I knew you were coming well before you stepped off the train in Jaynagar, Markham said. — I still have a bit of influence in the mountains.

The Asian mountains.

Zahn realized that this, in a backward way, meant yes.

Markham rose from the chair. The muscles twisted and stretched under the simple clothes. Zahn realized that the man had kept it going, of sorts, waited, waited for him, or someone like him.

The two of them stood in the wilderness. Malin had hidden himself in the hut. Two fires burned, two fires were kept burning, through days and weeks.

— Undress, Markham commanded.

Jeremy didn't move.

— Will you be so kind to undress? Markham asked.

Jeremy undressed, removing every single piece of clothing, until he stood there completely nude in the light and glow of the fire. Markham threw one piece on one of the fires. Zahn shrugged and threw all his clothes on the other. The fire heated his insides. He heated the fire at the fire's core. He sensed it, doing so in beyond powerful ways. And the «Master» had truly nothing to do with it, not as anything but a vehicle for Zahn's wishes. The man knew that on a certain level, and understanding quivered within him.

Markham examined him, from top to bottom, like another might have examined a racehorse. And the other part of it had also begun: the dissection of his soul.

– Remarkable muscles. Almost like…

– Like Joyce?

– As a matter of fact, Markham confirmed pointedly. – I've seen a wide variety of muscle types in my life, but only a few people with this one. There's nothing about it in any modern scientific books, but it is mentioned in the annals of the old Masters. Your patterns are not so well developed as his, though.

A blow that Zahn easily caught.

More blows. Zahn parried them easily.

– But more developed than in others you've met, right?

He avoided another blow and hit back.

Suddenly he was on the ground. It had happened as fast and easy as when Joyce had struck him down.

Markham looked down at him in contempt.

– You don't have more respect than he had.

– Isn't that the reason you're teaching me? Zahn rose with a completely disrespectful grin. – As implied, I'm not seeking to paint fences and such bullshit, but to learn even more ways to kill than I currently possess.

The training began. It continued by day, at night, by the hut, by the fires, in the high mountains. Markham was obviously not the man he had once been, but more than good enough to keep Zahn away. He delivered his doctrine, and dished out physical punishment in exactly the same way, without compassion and mercy, teaching without passion. Zahn clenched his teeth and cursed himself because he needed to clench his teeth.

Zahn didn't really tire. What burned inside him could never be put out, he knew that. But eventually, after being poked and run for days and nights in rows, he collapsed from exhaustion. A few hours later Markham woke him, and it continued. Markham was in a far worse shape, and made sure to get rest whenever possible, while Zahn had to strive and pull trees until haze and red filled his vision… up hills, up cliffs, up steeper hills, and it was as if it would never end.

And then… at the end, at the beginning of another long day of torture… he felt something. He lifted his head. It faded as quickly as it had come, but later, when it rose again, it lingered.

– You shouldn't talk. He spoke to Markham in a relaxed, even tone. – If a fight between us had turned into a prolonged battle, you wouldn't stand a chance. And this in spite of me being far less dangerous now, compared to what I'll be.

And he saw fear in the depth of the other man's eyes.

Days faded, weeks raced. Everything passed by so quickly.

They faced each other again, attacked, parried, attacked. Malin filmed and photographed. He stood still. He stood in the shade, in the middle of a soft breeze. He took the heat. He was sweating.

– Did he ever speak about his parents, his upbringing? Zahn asked.

Markham shook his head.

– He never spoke about himself.

There had been very little talk about Joyce, but more about physiology and other fairly impersonal issues. Talk about very little of what Zahn wanted to speak about. But he didn't let the rage rule him, not to unpremeditated acts, at least. Rage pushed him forward, but exactly as he wanted it. A draw, in a way. And there wasn't any rage, any emotion apart from him. He touched himself here, touched his most deep-felt passions. He pulled half a step back, a quarter of a step forward, danced, danced on the malleable, treacherous ground. And then, abruptly, the solid base of his palm hit Markham's jaw.

Everything happened so fast. And then it was over.

Markham remained on the ground. Far from knocked out, really. But he stared up at his opponent.

– W-what? What you did, now, what did you *do*?

– I hit you on the jaw, Zahn replied dryly and good-humored, with only a slight dash of scorn. – It isn't the end of the world... right?

The man crawled backwards, while sitting on his ass. When he finally managed to get up on his feet, he turned abruptly and rushed away, away from Zahn, as fast as his feet could carry him. A pointed, bottomless hatred lurked at the bottom of the stares he constantly threw at Zahn while he ran off, in an ever more erratic pattern towards the mountain towering above them.

In that moment Jeremy realized several things, including things about himself warming and burning. But the most prominent realization... told him that Arthur Markham had completely and irrevocably... cracked.

It had probably happened a considerable time ago, but now he had, for some reason, passed the point where he was able to hide it.

They could hear him outside the hut at night. Far away, close, as if he was inside the hut, but they couldn't see him. Malin let the tape recorder run.

– A REVENANT walks in my shadow, the old man complained bitterly.

Malin looked more than a little worried at Zahn.

– A revenant is dangerous, Zahn grinned. – A ghost isn't.

But he did feel shock when he occasionally spotted Markham. The complete insanity couldn't be confronted without creating a certain concern. And Jeremy wondered if it had been himself, or Timothy Joyce, who had contributed most to the fall they had recently witnessed. He didn't grieve for Arthur Markham. The guy had been an asshole deserving of everything the world could throw at him.

But… the shock lingered.

Close to a week later, the day after they had decided to take off, thoroughly tired of nightly howls and gawking, the day they set course back to the lower land, when they walked out on the porch in the morning, only one fire burned on the hill. Much, much taller than before. Of the other, they confirmed for themselves, when they took the trip up there and checked, remained neither embers nor ashes.


High flames licked outside and inside the tall building, devoured it in an inferno of enormous proportions. Smoke filled the streets of Tokyo.

Zahn felt the smoke burn, sensed the flames caress him, but he didn't feel the pain. And on one level that pained him more than anything… he did.

Downtown Tokyo looked like a disaster area. People from the special forces following Zahn's lead didn't look too shocked. Everything went in Japan, as long as one could blame a *Gaijin*, a foreigner, a *stranger*.

The elevator had long since stopped working. He rushed up the stairs, ran with a speed and energy that almost made them stop, paralyzed beyond words. They didn't have a snowball's chance in hell of keeping up.

He threw himself into the large hall at the top floor. A hail of bullets hit the wall right above his head. He returned the fire without thought. Two dark clad men collapsed. Still at least ten left. And behind them waited she he had hunted through half of Asia. They didn't stand a chance, she didn't stand a change. The sure thing would have been to wait for backup. But he didn't look back, hardly even looked forward, while advancing further into the hall.

Some threw away their guns and begged for mercy, while falling down flat on the floor. They repeated and repeated *mercy* in English. They cried something different in Japanese, and some other Asian languages, though.

He wondered. But didn't let it faze or stop him. Those who didn't surrender he mowed down. He felt it the moment a bullet hit him, but not where it hit. It didn't stop him.

Fukisawa and the special forces finally showed up behind him, breathing hard, useless.

– Didn't they say... «the demon is coming»?

Fukisawa nodded, with a clear worry visible in his eyes.

Zahn looked around, slightly surprised. There were ten, twelve bodies in the room, in addition to those who had surrendered. There were no more left to fight. Not here.

The last room, the outer, against the street. He rushed on.

Abigael Markham stood by the window, straight in body. Broken, smashed, open. The dark smooth hair had been cut in traditional Chinese style, straight above the brow. She stood there with her arms outstretched and her eyes directed at the open sky.

– GOD IS POWERFUL, she cried to the air. – GOD IS GREAT. Accept well your humble servant.

And then she jumped. Without hesitation, without shaking, before the last, decisive step. She vanished from their point of view. He hurried to the edge, but it went outwards. He couldn't see shit, except the stinking smoke rising from the street far below.

– Find her.

He turned towards Lieutenant Fukisawa with fiery eyes.

– It shouldn't be too hard, the Japanese commented dryly, while looking closer at Zahn. The worry was stronger now. – She has long since hit the streets, so to speak. We may not find all of her...

They found nothing, not the tiniest piece.

The search was extended to include the entire block, far from the window she had jumped through.

– She's alive, Zahn mumbled, as the two searched on street level, between the ruins, turning every rock. – SHE'S ALIVE, damn klutzes.

Slowly but surely a kind of calm settled in their shadows, but the dust took a long time to reach the ground.

He had the honor of seeing Tokyo from the air. He flew a chopper with his escort, out of the city, out of the country. Slightly distant he rejoiced over this fact. He had taken the train to the city, less than three days earlier.

– I'm sorry about this. Lieutenant Fukisawa escorted him to boarding gate 20 at the airport. – The situation escalated totally beyond control, but it's unfair to blame you.

A pat on the shoulder, an unworried grin.

– Don't take it so hard. Zahn grinned wickedly. – I'll be back.


Outside the old mining town of Perth, on Australia's western coastline. The soft wind, the breeze from the ocean emphasized the relative peace inside and outside the small bungalow. Zahn had been invited to dinner in the home of Alexei Stasvej, a well-known Russian immigrant and rebel.

– I spent ten years in Japan, and am still unable to read the headlines. Stasvej spoke fluent English, without the slightest accent. – But he spoke it fluently, both his understanding and execution were close to perfect. I'm sure it's possible for a Japanese to hear he isn't a native Japanese, but it's impossible for everybody else.

Stasvej had been forced to flee from Russia because of his very... unpopular exposure of a number of public environmental transgressions, archived in the file of *national secrets*. He had traveled all over the world and found it wasn't much better anywhere. Australia, for some obscure reason, was one of the few countries where he was still welcome. But he really belonged to a growing number of people without a country, in the early years of the twenty-first century (western, christian time frame).

– We, my group and I, met him and his group outside

Nukamura nuclear power plant, a few weeks before the explosion, during the considerable protests there, before the protests died, as protests tend to do.

– He made an indelible impression on us all, long before he practically eradicated the entire Nukamura City.

The Russian exile cleared his throat.

– Those Joyce has killed to this point are just kid's stuff compared to what he's about to do, what he must do, in order to truly achieve his goal.

– And that is…

– Have you studied modern society, Mr. Zahn, have you seen the poison and insanity everywhere?

He had. It just had never been his business.

– We're fighting a non-violent war, Stasvej added annoyed, in spite of Zahn not commenting on his latest statement, – we can certainly not support his methods. But several people from my group were tempted into joining his, and I must say I don't find that totally incomprehensible…

An even more worried look appeared in the large man's eyes. Zahn pushed him, with a slightly encouraging look.

– There are rumors he has gained access to a new, revolutionary technology… one that allows him to move, through *teleportation,* over huge areas.

– I've heard that, as well, Zahn said pointedly. – But what I've heard is that there's no machine, no technology…

– Oh? The worry grew further, to something resembling fear.

– What I've heard, Zahn said, – is that he's doing it himself. He speaks magical formulas and open holes in the air, passages to distant places.

Zahn had laughed hard the first time he had heard it, and he also enjoyed seeing the other man shrink in his chair.

The conversation ended. Sometimes you got the answer without anyone needing to say it aloud. Zahn rose, shook the man's hand, and vanished through the door. The exile walked with him outside, to see him well off. Here was a very active man, that, in spite of this, had been reduced to being very passive. Not by Timothy Joyce, but by the modern global society and its slick mechanisms developed to keep people in line.

And by his own self-perpetuating fear.

Zahn continued on his long walk.

A medium sized cemetery outside Toronto in Canada. The US border was merely a walk off, out on the lake.

Zahn stared at the withered gravestone, stared both long and hard. Actually, he had a hard time taking his eyes off it, from the faded but clear inscription:

TIMOTHY JOYCE
**BORN/DEAD 1980**
MAY HIS YOUNG SOUL FIND REST

That was all.

It didn't have to mean anything. In all probability he had just spent a lot of time on another dead end. And it was a dead end. But not in the same way as the rest. He more than sensed that, in his very active insides.

He didn't see any point in opening the coffin.

Either there was a dissolved body of a child in it, or there wasn't.

He shook his head, and left the ashes of the dead.

Jeremy Zahn started on the long walk south.

# CHAPTER TEN

## SIX DAYS IN THE CITY OF ANGELS

He returned to the hotel. The darkness descended evenly on
the city, but he still saw the narrow line in the west, where the sea
rolled in.

The group was present at the hotel then. They had been outside
in his absence, and he hadn't expected anything else. He sensed
a certain joy, or expectation, over the fact that he still walked and
breathed. They had had good reason to believe he had taken the
plunge, the great journey. They stared at the woman behind him.
Everybody had stared at her.

– We thought you just went outside to buy beer, Russo
commented with his usual wit.

– I took a slight detour... He pushed Monica forward. – Say
hello to Monica Valdez the younger. She will be part of our team
from now on.

– Hello, Monica said.

– Hello, Caldwell greeted her.

The others mumbled greetings.

More wasn't said.

The others went to bed, with a few minutes of weird mood.
He didn't. That wasn't solely caused by the fact that he had slept
*soundly* only a few hours earlier. He felt infinitely restless. When he
turned to Monica, he saw the same energetic unrest there.

He sat down for a few hours, to browse through new and old
sites about Timothy Joyce and those claiming to be done by him
on the Internet.

She also sat in front of a monitor most of the time. She made
sure he got enough sandwiches, but aside from that she sat there,
entranced by the screen. He saw what she downloaded and
printed out, too. Information about him.

The tingle in the body turned into something, continuous,
constant, as if he wasn't imagining it. He stared at the screen, sat
there calm and collected. Only his eyes moved. And the hands
over the keyboard. He writhed in the chair. It seemed so small

and uncomfortable.

He discovered the blood dripping at the keyboard. It came from his nostrils. He looked at Monica and realized she was looking at him, and he shook his head.

– I tend to have nosebleed when I'm overly excited, he said.

– But you're not… excited, now, are you?

– No.

On the contrary. He had been halfway bored there, watching the screen, while wading through page by page of information, endless information.

He found a set of paper tissues from the drawer and started drying himself, pushing it at the nostrils, in an attempt to halt the worst of the flow. Every time something like this happened it seemed for a while to erupt in a waterfall of blood, every heartbeat sending another burst from the nostrils.

Suddenly he sat there, staring. He had found a site with a web camera. There were many such pages, recording places around the world. A place was photographed in intervals, and after a preset time new images were automatically uploaded.

Zahn stared at the screen. Joyce stood on Santa Monica pier and waved to him.

He looked at the time, visible on the image. The photo had been taken at least eight minutes ago. He breathed, letting all air out of his lungs, forgot to breathe it back in, and sat there panting.

What the fuck was wrong with the shithead? Did he get off by playing that kind of game?

The next image was uploaded. No Joyce. Zahn got an inspiration, and checked another camera, on Venice Beach, and as expected, there Joyce was, smiling some more.

In the bad light Zahn couldn't be absolutely certain that it was truly Joyce standing there. But he didn't really doubt it.

Zahn lifted the monitor, pulled out wires, tore wires apart and threw the monitor at the wall right across the room. It was crushed and sparks flew from the remaining dust. He kicked the cabinet, kicked it so hard that it, flew into the wall as well. The solid metal bent and folded like an accordion. He struck two folded hands at the table. It broke a bit to the right of its center. He lifted a chair and broke it at the floor. And another. And another. There was no pain, aside from the glowing white, insane rage within. He calmed down, slowly, painfully, until he was eventually breathing normally. The rage prevailed. Russo, Wells, Caldwell and Louis rushed into the room, the first three with weapons drawn, Louis with all muscles tensed. They stopped, looking incredulous at the devastation. Monica still sat by her station, the only undamaged in the room. She didn't look particularly worried as she followed Zahn with her eyes, her probing eyes. Zahn left the room with quick steps. No one spoke to him, no one attempted to stop him.

Dawn, dawn of the sixth day. A brief glance at the newspaper dates confirmed what he already knew. He stood on the balcony and looked across the city, the city of angels. The night had flown away, and he didn't feel the slightest bit tired. The volcanic expression of rage had only fueled him, strengthened him.

The floor started shaking below his feet. He realized the entire building was shaking, that all buildings surrounding this one were swaying. The cups on the table rattled.

– This is California. He heard her voice from behind. – We get these minor shakes all the time. You'll get used to it. We Californians don't even stop momentarily in our tasks over such trifles. It will end in a matter of seconds.

Monica came to him, pulled close to him, rubbed sensitive hands across his shoulders, while the minor quake indeed faded.

– I saw you weighing yourself, she said softly. – How much have you put on?

He looked sharply at her. Whatever he had imagined she would be saying, it wasn't anything like this.

– Five kilos, he replied. – Ten pounds. Since last night.

– I rather thought so. It fits my findings.

– What have you found? He asked.

– You've grown the last three years, she said firmly. – You're taller and heavier.

– That's truly crazy, he said, rejecting it out of hand. – No one grows, not in their late twenties, not that much.

– It's not common, but it happens. And it has happened with you. Of that there's no doubt.

She showed him the photographs, those he had already seen in his mind, the folder she had made, the only one in existence. A set of x-rays from the hospital in London, from the London

Metropolitan Police, one from the limited set taken at the Los Angeles hospital, from the LAPD archives, measures and facts collected to give him an LAPD identity-card.

He looked at her with a frown. The facts spoke for themselves, they always did.

– If you keep this up, you'll catch up to Joyce quite soon, she said.

That should have made him feel better, feel exalted. Joyce had always had the advantage of being taller and heavier and stronger.

– What happened when you escaped? She wondered. He had told her all about it, and she had listened in awe. – You're strong…

She reddened.

– … but I don't understand how you could break the ropes. Yours were hardly thinner and weaker than those of the other prisoners.

– My distinct impression was that they were thicker and stronger, he said both distantly and sharply. – Thick and strong ropes cutting skin and sinew.

Muscles and sinew swelling and tightening with the insane rage rising from the depths…

He shrugged. He had hardly been more than semi-conscious.

And he rejected it all with a shrug, rejecting the reality of it. It was just another crazy event in a long, long row.

They sat by the breakfast table. Zahn had already finished one plate and had started on another. No one commented on it.

Caldwell turned to the newcomer in a relaxed pose.

– So, how's the academy these days?

– Pretty boring, mostly, Monica replied. She seemed laidback enough, but very modest and even shy. – We mostly learned theory, redundant theory, and the «real-life» teaching isn't much to brag about either. I'm happy to be given this opportunity.

– You mean you're glad your similarity to the other Monica gave it to you?

– Isn't that how it always is? Monica asked rhetorically, with a flash of a smile. – Small coincidences, decisions made by you or somebody else, may lead you down a completely different path in life?

Otherwise she didn't speak much. Not in the others' presence.

But her observations held a topnotch level, and she noted things he had difficulty seeing, what he carried too tight to his heart.

They stood on the balcony, and watched the town below. He had done so quite a bit lately, both stood on the balcony and watched.

A chopper from some television station hovered some distance from the hotel. They had been given permission to film. This was also a media war.

This was a war.

– It's quite a remarkable sight to see you think, she said, both wondering and ironically simultaneously. – You have one of the most expressive faces I've ever seen.

He didn't have time to reply to her. He heard something, beneath the sound of the chopper, the traffic below. Her eyes widened.

A sound of an engine, deep, in the distance. He registered it, and thought it was funny how a single engine could…

He grabbed Monica, pulled her with him and threw himself and her as far into the room he was able to. In a flash he saw a rocket travel through the air. It hit the building to the right, right in front of the hotel. There was an ear-shattering crack and splinters filled the air in all directions. The pressure wave hit them. Zahn felt his body hit the wall at the opposite side of the room, far inside the building, without quite believing he had been able to get this far in a single leap, but he could, he could. Monica hit him and pushed him even harder at the wall.

Damn, he had wanted to say so much to her out there, how much he trusted her and such. Such craziness.

The world had cracked. Now. If not a long, long time ago.

The sound of the inferno faded, even the inferno itself, reduced to a few, floating pieces of wreckage. A huge hole revealed itself in the wall of the other building. The building had been filled with people. Fine particles in red made a hazy mist outside.

– Damn, he said curtly. – Another morning wasted.

Fire lit her eyes, the laughter returned. She kissed him savagely on the lips. Kissed him again.

The computer she had used still worked, incredibly enough. It showed TV-images directly from the explosion site. These TV-reporters, they were everywhere. They reprised showing the footage of the rocket, and then the explosion itself. Zahn heard the sound of the chopper flying away, to a relatively secure distance.

And then, just then, the chopper exploded in a million pieces. The pressure and the heat caressed the two where they had fallen. He returned her kiss, raw and passionate. The chopper blade hit the wall outside, ricocheted against it and whined towards the street below, to, no doubt, spread death and destruction down there.

Wells stumbled into the room, followed by an uninjured Caldwell. A line of blood ran down his left temple. The screen turned black for a moment, until the studio images took over.

– It seems like we've lost contact with our reporters…

Then the screen once more turned black. And when there once more was a picture it showed footage from inside the castle… Timothy Joyce's castle.

Zahn recognized the stage, recognized the event. The movie of the executions in the old castle was being broadcast. No one could tell or find out where it was transmitted from, but everybody in Los Angeles watching TV saw it. The cameras swept the main hall, the pit, the throne, the stalls, a gladiator arena in miniature. The edited film was first cut as a movie trailer, put together like a series of seemingly unrelated moving images or flashes of moving images, then, after twenty, thirty seconds it «set», turning more lingering. He saw himself, a savage in chains, displayed for the crowd's pleasure. Frances had her badge around her neck. One camera zoomed in on it. It was cut to the catacombs, where she was tied to the rock and recited her oath of allegiance to Joyce, swearing to live a life in his service.

And then back to the hall, back to the arena, to the convicted to death industrial leaders. Words and images and personal information started flashing over the screen.

**CHARGED AND CONVICTED FOR**
**CRIMES AGAINST HUMANITY**
**AGAINST ALL LIFE ON EARTH**

**CLAYTON POWERS**
**TAYLOR LOWELL**
**SHUEN PARKER**
**MARK TOBLATT**

**ELEANOR ROTHRIDGE**
**GRANT STEVENS**
**RUDY PAUL JONES**
**COLE SLATER**
   **DETAILS AVAILABLE ON THE INTERNET**

No details here, not about that last part either. They wouldn't be hard to find, though. They hadn't been so far, and countless sites would keep appearing in his name.

And then it was shown, all of it. Every bloody detail of the executions, until there were only pieces of flesh and bone left on the bloody rock floor.

The ordinary television broadcast returned. CNN, a number of their journalists present in Los Angeles.

The buzz grew in Zahn's ears, sounds caught from close and far away. He rose, pulled up Monica, as she clung to him.

– Let's go, he told them.

Nobody said anything. There was no caustic remark from Caldwell. They picked up Russo and Markham on the way. The two of them had suffered no injuries in the explosion. They wasted some time by allowing a doctor to take a look at Wells, tying a bandage around his head, and then they took the elevator down, down to street level.

Downtown Los Angeles was already boiling, boiling over. Zahn saw it in the very air, in the people he encountered, heard it both internally and externally.

People had just started, in modest ways, to break windows and carry away large and small inventory from the expensive stores' assortment. And some didn't bother to carry or steal anything, but just smashed everything in their way. He sensed the excitement, life's excitement flowing through him. This was Joyce's work. He inspired countless people to do this.

They passed a row of electronic stores. The mayor showed his ugly mug on every television screen. They heard pieces of his speech, heard more than enough.

– … from this moment a state of emergency is declared within the city of Los Angeles and surrounding areas. Please note the curfew from ten PM to six AM. People being caught outside during this time period will be shot without warning. I repeat: Shot without warning. All citizens are encouraged to actively cooperate with the authorities in these trying times…

A hail of bricks made mincemeat of the television sets. Choppers kept broadcasting the message from a somewhat safe distance.

And nothing could any longer be said to be normal, not even what appeared to not have been changed. Everything had changed. And this was merely the start, the first tiny wisps of the wave on its way out on the endless sea. The very air flared with lightning, with… flares.

And in spite of there being rage in bundles, a wrath completely beyond any nine to five life, as had been the case with all the major riots in town, Jeremy sensed… optimism, a grim laughter making it boil within him.

He was able to see them from above. And then… in flashes and the light of flares, he saw from all sides, and they, directed by him, no longer moved like ants directed by a central core.

They found a quiet place, he and Monica, the others just following their tail. Not in the eye of the storm, because there was no longer quiet there. But a pocket, in the air, in time, that could be filled at any time. And they expected and looked forward to that.

Two empty benches. He and Monica on one, the others reluctantly on the other.

– What are we doing here? Wells wondered, clearly cautious, having gained wisdom from previous experience, but obviously frustrated.

– We sit here, enjoying ourselves, Jeremy stated cheerfully, a bit resigned. – This is a great place to sit, isn't it? It reminds me of a place I visited in Australia. A man had found a peaceful spot there. In the middle of the night, in the silence, one could hear everything happening for miles and miles. I took a long walk, sat down on a bench, and enjoyed the night. Alone. I've never felt less lonely.

They all heard it, heard what he heard.

– I grew up in London, he said softly. – In the northern parts of town, in the area around Camden Town. The poverty there was, is, in many ways, just as pronounced as south of the river, in the south east. Like in major parts of this… artificial desert, this tomb. Like in all artificial deserts there's only life on a few, desolate spots.

– Now, you definitely sound like a radical, Caldwell commented without really committing herself.

She never truly committed herself, did she? Dead, like most people. Dead, even though she walked and breathed.

– A radical, huh? Zahn chuckled. – Why don't you keep serving up these clichés, these labels? It amuses me, amuses me a lot.

When he turned towards her, she once again turned to unmovable ice.

– I sound like a human being, Jeremy said very softly. – Like a human being.

He didn't lean forward, didn't look at Monica, but he was speaking to her.

– Society, civilization itself, has become an almost irresistible force, a mastodon of an irresistible force, a shell easy to peel, the moment its center is shaken. But for that to happen, it needs, as I've started to believe, an equal counterforce, another irresistible, minor power peeling the rotten apple and making mincemeat of it…

– Some manage to get away, sort of, Monica said, with bright eyes. – Either by becoming a public servant or a criminal. But it is, in truth, the same thing, an illusion, a mirage they're selling us, to keep us leashed.

– So, you prefer the chaos, the unrest, then? Caldwell sniffed.

– But it is *fun*, isn't it? Zahn countered. – Can't you feel the energy, the irresistible conviction that you're alive, no matter what they might throw at you?

He could just as well be speaking to a dead cat.

He could, feel the fire, in every nerve, inside, outside, along a crooked line. Despair was always there, because she never could. How could she? In spite of moments of danger, she had lived a safe, uneventful life since the cradle. No thought, no action, beyond what society demanded of her. The moment she had seen Timothy Joyce in full bloom, her dearest convictions had been rocked to the core. But it had merely sent her deeper into isolation, into denial.

Monica stared at him. He returned the stare, with a look, a fire, an underbrush of despair.

And you? He told himself. Where are you?

He had begun a Journey three years earlier. The reason no longer mattered. He had seen the world, seen all its parts, from the disgusting to the horrible, to its glory, life in every single point of the air, of the Earth. He could never go back, neither to the place nor the person he had been, because that place, that person no longer existed.

A group of people danced around the corner. They danced, with tables and chairs in hands, food and wine in their bags. It seemed like they were preparing a party, away from the immediate noise and insanity of the big city.

A group of police officers rushed them from the opposite side. They waved their weapons and shouted with insane mugs at the smaller, unarmed group. All the happy people froze, prepared for the worst, but totally helpless. They looked behind, for a possible escape shortcut around the corner they had turned a few seconds earlier, but from there a platoon of heavily armed soldiers ran at them. It didn't look good.

That was the moment the police officers and the soldiers started howling and screaming. Blood stood in straight, horizontal lines from their bodies. Round after round of bullets hit them. They howled in utter panic, attempting to strike back, return the fire, but there was nothing to fire on. Wherever the bullets came from, those who fired them hid behind full proof cover. Both groups were caught in a murderous crossfire and in a matter of seconds they crouched dead and dying in the streets. A machinegun sputtered, shot hole in a window and all the dolls on display there, before the man died and the finger slipped weakly from the trigger.

Silence reigned anew. Zahn and bunch had sought cover behind the base of a statue, in a relatively secure position, never quite sure how secure it truly was, fearing a hail of bullets would come their way as well.

But there were no more bullets. Zahn rose and approached smiling the more or less paralyzed, spontaneous party arrangers on the opposite side.

– My friends, he greeted them heartily. He felt absolutely deliciously wild and crazy. – You've brought food and wine, we bring only ourselves.

– Sometimes that's enough, one of the men said, slightly

nervous, but without being visibly bothered by the bodies lying in heaps and pools of blood merely a few steps away.

– Perhaps we should move away a bit, though, Zahn suggested.
– The flies might be quite a bother eventually, I guess...


– I hear you were witnesses to the shooting, his highness, the mayor snarled.
– That's correct, sir, Caldwell admitted, clearly ill disposed.
– Why, then, didn't you do anything?
Springsteen was also present, but didn't say anything.
– Do what? Zahn wondered, gently and ominous. – Return fire at a superior force, with a superior position? We were lucky they didn't decide to execute us as well.
– But what about the group of looters? Why didn't you *arrest* them, damn it?
– Arrest them... sir? There wasn't a single piece of evidence they had stolen anything. For all we knew they could have planned a picnic well in advance. Should we *arrest* them for bad timing... sir?
His Highness said no more. Eventually he waved them off, denied them the joy of being in his presence.
They heard everything on their way out, they couldn't avoid hearing it. Neither could the rest of the headquarters.
– I have no intention of taking the blame for this, the mayor shouted to Springsteen. – That burden is yours, and that of your incompetent subordinates.
Springsteen cackled. The mayor paled.
– Have you ever taken the blame for *anything?* Springsteen stepped slightly closer to the other man, who paled further.
– You believe everybody is like you, that they're paralyzed by the thought of public condemnation. You, sir, are a fart, a tiny shit that I, at any time, may choose to wipe off my heel. Do we understand each other?
– P-perf-fectly, the parrot croaked.
This in spite of the fact that the poor mayor no longer seemed to fathom anything.
– How many of the partygoers would you say had a rather sparse wardrobe? Caldwell asked Zahn coquettishly and spirited.
– They were eighteen, he replied. – At least fifteen had holes in

either pants or jackets or both.

– You've got such a *fabulous* memory.

Caldwell shook her head in admiration, more excited than Zahn had ever seen her.

The unrest continued outside. They saw it, heard it. And they saw it on big screens at a bar nearby. It had become entertainment, a sports event, surpassing everything else, a gladiator battle with blood, hits and death like in the very old days.

Russo was drinking hard, and he turned even more jovial than he usually was.

Previous riots in Los Angeles and other places in the United States had mostly been unexpected or at least started abruptly. The authorities hadn't been prepared. This time the army units deployed «to support local authorities in the drug war» stood ready to step in.

And local and federal forces, attempting a pinching maneuver, attacked the «troublemakers» and everybody joyfully carrying goods from the local vandalized store, with both clubs, guns and anything else at their disposal. Teargas was spread from choppers. Water cannons cleaned the streets.

But in spite of this the uniformed forces were unable to restore control or order. The unrest, this time, had spread far beyond the ghettos and poor areas. Desperation spread and several shots were fired. People also returned the fire, but then the soldiers instantly did them in, demolishing one or two blocks in the cleanup process.

Noise faded eventually, or at least lessened somewhat. But that was caused just as much by the fact that many had gone home with today's catch and barricaded themselves in tiny apartments.

And at any time, new, local battles or *quarrels* could erupt.

The group had returned to the station. They sat in a room, without anything to do, while the unrest continued raging outside, raging practically unabated.

Russo knelt on the bathroom floor, his head buried in the toilet bowl, puking his guts out. Wells had gone searching for another toilet. There had been a bit too much beer for him, as well.

And the time had just passed twelve noon.

– This is a disaster, Caldwell raged. – We're denied all operative effectiveness, just because the government is unable to uphold Law and Order.

– We haven't exactly been that effective in that regard ourselves, Louis said, quite down.

They watched the television screen all the time. Or at least they never stopped glancing at it. Changing channels was no longer any good. Everybody broadcast either from Los Angeles' chaotic streets or features connected to what happened.

– It's quietest when the wind blows.

– What are you saying, Jeremy? Monica wondered.

– The places I've been where one can sit on a bench or a log, far from concrete and brick, asphalt and glass, I always sense the silence best when the wind blows.

He shook his head, sheepishly, but not embarrassed. He smiled teasingly to her with hungry eyes. She and her hungry eyes returned the teasing smile.

– Six megahertz, he said. – That's' the frequency of the silent wind. It drowns all the tiny, distracting sounds. The brain interprets easier one sound than many. One no longer hears a slamming door, the sound of someone walking on shingle far away.

– And that… is the scientific explanation, always so damn insufficient.

She heard it, heard the wind blow, the eternal wind, at all its levels, irresistible.

And she also heard all the small sounds. It was enough just to listen. She didn't really need him to tell her this. But… it pleased her to hear him say it anyway.

– Something will happen soon, Zahn said. – I know that.

Something would happen soon. It was only a matter of time. He had been convinced of that a long time ago, a certainty that had only strengthened with time. Jeremy Zahn sensed the calm in the chaos and confusion. He had never done that before. He sensed the calm in the wild, the wild in the calm.

Suddenly the studio anchor appeared on the screen. He pushed a hand at one of his ears, while evidently listening breathlessly through the other.

– We've just achieved contact with one of our crews, he said excitedly. – They're right at Pershing Square with our world-renowned colleague, David Kelly, who has agreed to do this job for us…

Pershing Square, wasn't that in the Financial District? Yes, a fairly long distance from the fighting, which had yet to reach the areas where the rich lived, well outside the central parts of the city, or in Downtown Financial District, where many worked.

– … with a… yes… they have contact with a group calling themselves Beyond civilization - the Second Wave. Yes, and I'm told we'll be witnessing quite dramatic scenes. Over to you, David.

The image shifted, an unsteady camera, an excited David Kelly, an open square, decorated and spared no expenses, one of the Financial District's prestige projects.

– Good afternoon, people of Los Angeles, viewers in United States and the rest of the world. What you will be witnessing in a moment is something unique, something completely new in history, an urban guerilla group fighting in the open, in what can be called America's most significant regions. We're immediately passing the word to Kevin here.

A nervous, virtually beardless boy appeared on the screen.

– It's good of you not to make any prolonged monologue there, David, he sniffed. – We don't have much time.

He looked away briefly, before once again staring into the camera with a rigid, intense look.

– We don't need much…

He signaled. The camera turned towards a significant group of boys and girls, of all races, and a ten or so beaten and bloody police officers of all races, bound hands and feet, dressed in remains of uniforms.

– LINE THEM UP! Kevin ordered with the impressive voice of a drill sergeant.

The officers were pulled and pushed to the nearest wall. For every tiny attempt at resistance on their part, strikes and kicks hailed on them from their keepers. They stared at a distant point with empty eyes, not really realizing what was happening, protesting weakly.

They were lined up. Most stood still. A few attempted to jump away on legs tied together. They were kicked and beaten until they were back in the line.

– WE IN BEYOND CIVILIZATION HAVE CONDEMNED YOU TO TORTURE AND DEATH, Kevin shouted. – THIS AS A TINY PAYBACK FOR THE SUFFERING YOU, BEING A THOROUGHLY UNJUST AND DESTRUCTIVE SOCIETY'S FAITHFUL SERVANTS, HAVE VISITED UPON OTHER PEOPLE AND ON ALL LIFE ON THE PLANET.

The boys and the girls directed their pistols, revolvers, machineguns and crossbows at the condemned and fired. The murderous salvo reduced the somewhat living flesh and bones bodies to a heap of blood and shattered tissue.

– It's Joyce! Louis cried out. – He's behind it all, it's his fault.

– Oh, grow up! Monica threw at him in contempt, and he shrunk under her scorn.

It turned quiet again. Caldwell's eyes widened.

– And then there's just one more thing…

A smiling Kevin placed himself at Kelly's side and put an arm around his shoulders. Still smiling he put a barrel at the man's temple and pulled the trigger. The camera fell to the ground. The screen turned black.

Later there were extensive reports of police officers being placed before walls, and executed, at several locations around town. It was like a breaching of a dam… and all the water flowed through it simultaneously. A city, a society stretched to the breaking point through centuries of oppression finally snapped at the seams.

Steps in the hall. For some reason Jeremy looked at his watch. It showed 01.32 PM.

Wells entered the room, as usual with Russo in tow.

– We have a positive identification, he said excitedly. – After a bank robbery Joyce, Talbot and Monica escaped out on the highway, with a number of accomplishes…

He paused dramatically before continuing:

– We've got him!

# CHAPTER ELEVEN

## BEFORE NOW

Paris in spring. A female nurse.

– He stared at me, she whispered. – He stared at us all, before making his… choice.

– Tell me more, Jeremy encouraged her. – Also your own thoughts, before, during and after the attack.

– Well, he had just killed a human being. The alarm hadn't yet sounded, but it did the moment he appeared in the hall among us. He seemed totally relaxed. Even when he killed Henrique, it didn't seem like he did anything but wave his hand, as if he… waved t-to *us*. I recall my own thoughts about the woman. Seven dead and she was alive, I told her how lucky she was, I made a weak attempt at comforting her. No one had counted on him coming to kill her. The guard outside her room was purely routine. The woman told me, told me what he had told her: «I'll let you live a few more days, Jeanne, but I will come and visit you at the hospital, and then your time is up». He was really speaking to the air, he didn't approach her or anything, but he spoke to her. It's meaningless, isn't it, so totally meaningless?

– Perhaps, Zahn said non-committal. – Did you ever hear from him?

– Once, she whispered. – At least I think it was him. I've never told anyone, because it seemed so insane. «I need physicians, I need nurses, Janette, are you able and willing»? «No», I replied. «A pity», he said, and hung up.

– You should have asked him to see a shrink, Zahn mumbled.

– Pardon, Monsieur?

– Nothing important, please go on.

– That's all, she said shyly, bathing in the glow of his very direct stare. – Well, I have to say I never liked Marc Delon very much…

– Neither did I, he said to the air.

– … but if everybody should do this or similar things to entertainment hosts they didn't like, then there would be chaos and unrest everywhere, so that won't do, will it?

– So true, Miss Garnier. – So very true. Thank you very much for your help. You're both a bright and skilled nurse.

– Thank you so much, Monsieur, she said gratefully, and overwhelmed with shyness, she had to turn away.

When she dared to look once more, he was gone.


The Norwegian mountains. Large, numerous, desolate. The desolate landscape could work its toll on a person, if one allowed it. Or it could raise a person up, if one allowed that. After a long drive through sparsely populated areas, he arrived at Jotunheim, the home of ogres and gods and everything, where there was hardly any population whatsoever. After turning off the main road he had to drive for over an hour on a washboard of a shingle road, through a turnpike road (where he didn't pay shit), in order to reach the beginning of the National Park area, a parking lot filled with cars. Driving was prohibited in the park, except for the Tourist Board officials. There were no buildings anymore, except for the cabins run by the before mentioned Tourist Board, who had a monopoly on virtually all things up here.

Zahn had prepared himself thoroughly. He had read on the Internet, on the website of Phoenix Green Earth, and others, what the monopoly led to. He had brought a sack filled with food and a small tent. The prices on food and housing were sky-high here in the wilderness.

And he would be less vulnerable.

He liberated from the car the bike he had rented in Fagernes, the last outpost before the wilderness, where one could get fairly inexpensive food and supplies, and biked the remaining distance to the cabin. He knew it would have taken him an hour at high speed to walk. He wasn't in a hurry, really, but to conserve one's energy didn't hurt. He had read that the energy consumption increased dramatically after just a few hours movement at this altitude. One ate twice as much as usual, and he had already had quite an increase in appetite lately.

The road twisted and turned further into the mountains. Dust rose from the dry shingle, and could be seen for miles. But he didn't care. An observer could lurk on any of the many peaks around him, easily observing everyone approaching. Some things were not worth worrying about.

Water was on the left. Sounds of streams reached him from everywhere. Melted water flowed from the mountains, where there was still eternal water and ice. No longer eternal. It boiled here, like it did everywhere on Earth. These days, more than ever. But here as well, in these enormous heaps of stones and at the mountaintops, where there could be no major human settlement. He could see the narrow path in front of him, so easy to lose sight of. His feet touched the ground, of rocks, ice and hard soil. He biked on, keeping his rock-hard focus, concentration, but he was also moving higher up, in the even wilder mountains.

He moved through many levels, many new straight stretches. In spite of the bike, it took time, before he spotted the cabin Glitterheim, and the other buildings down the slope, before he rolled the last remaining distance to the yard.

After making sure he had secured the bike to the solid fence, he grabbed the rucksack and headed inside. He carried only one set of clean clothes with him. Except for that he had filled the sack with food, basically roasted chickens and a lot of fluid. He carried the tent from a strap around the sack.

Whatever was wrong (if anything was indeed wrong) turned evident fast. The man behind the counter and the maid carrying a tray… looked at him.

– There you are again, sir, the man said in passable English. – I'm sorry, I've yet to spot the man you described.

Zahn didn't say anything. He hadn't been here before, but he kept his mouth shut. Both the man and the maid, who had quickly disappeared through a door, had a worried flash in their eyes. He couldn't say if he or something else, someone else caused it. No, it wasn't anything dramatic. The man was mildly worried, not scared.

– Will you need a room today, sir?

Zahn shook his head and walked into the lounge area. The furniture held a seemingly sober quality… but in a flash he recalled what he had read about classic Norwegian standard. It had quite the price tag attached to it and this was an entire house filled with the same, expensive stuff. The entire shit was meant for loaded foreign tourists. He shook his head and smiled to himself. He even recalled where he had read the stuff about the furniture. That had been two months before Joyce had struck in London. Jeremy and Gwen had been on another of their many mandatory visits to her parents. And he had read about the prices on the web. The warnings had been quite accurate.

They had a guestbook here. It was placed on a table by the wall, a bit off from the rest of the tables and chairs. He sat down and started turning the pages, slightly distracted, before he began looking for names. Major parts of the words were incomprehensible to him, naturally. People from all over the world had passed through this place. Quite a lot of the greetings had been written in English, though. Nothing of interest. But then he stopped turning pages.

«To Gwen and Monica, two great girls I met in the middle of nowhere. In their company I experienced the highest mountain».

The signature didn't tell him anything. The time and date the guy had written indicated he had been here early yesterday morning. It could be fake, of course, but other times, before and after fit.

Then

he sat there, staring.

He stared at his own name, his own signature. Written a few hours after the homage to Gwen and Monica. This was insane. He recognized his own signature... didn't he?

He grabbed the pen and wrote his name, close to the other. It wasn't a resemblance, but an exact copy. Calligraphy, the science of handwriting certainly wasn't a subject he had firsthand knowledge about. He knew the basics. Each person had his or her unique writing, like a fingerprint, somewhat easier to copy, but not without extensive practice.

A shrug. For the thousandth time he kicked himself for allowing himself to be dragged into another act of the game Joyce played.

So, the trail he had followed had been genuine. *Probably*. Monica and Gwen were here in the mountains somewhere. In that case, what were they doing here? What interest did they have in this remote location? He laughed softly. What interest did they have in any location?

An hour later he had «climbed» even further up. He felt like he had walked forever, but it didn't really seem like he was moving at all. The mountain in the distance looked no closer. He knew the tallest peak was Glitretind. There was not much chance of them still being at the top, but he didn't see it as impossible either. He wanted to see what they saw, to walk in their shoes. There was no longer any lack of patience in him. The hunt would continue, until it ended.

He had feared the thin air, the high altitude would tire him quickly, but it didn't. Aside from his increased appetite, it didn't affect him much. He kept the speed without trouble, with a lot of strenuous moves, jumps from stone to stone, and such. He noticed this clearly when he began the actual ascension, when the enormous heap of stones seemed to stretch on forever, and the «trail» could only be seen by following the occasional red paint, when he passed a bunch of people with far less baggage than himself.

The trail was definitely not well marked. He got lost, truly lost several times, but always seemed to get back on track.

The landscape seemed to constantly shift and change around him.

After a while he began wondering if he was truly off course, if one of the peaks ahead, with ice on top, could really be Glitretind. He wasn't tired. Intellectually speaking he knew he should have been close to exhaustion, to the point of collapse. He grew extremely hungry, but the fatigue didn't bother him. It merely hid in the background, like a grumble. It didn't reach the surface. He wolfed down an entire chicken, without feeling full. An entire chicken. He remembered a time when he had had trouble eating a half.

He drank water. To actually feel the fluid flow down his throat had felt great before, too, but never anything like this. He sat with his back to a rock, enjoying the experience of the sun in his face, the silence, the sound of the musk deer close by. A fabulous sight. In a place with hardly any growth, they found what little there was.

Two older men, evidently veterans in these parts, stopped in front of him. They greeted him. He greeted them back.

– You're off track, they told him after an exchange of a few polite remarks. – You can walk to Glitretind from here, but you're actually closer to the opposite side of the mountain at this point, closer to Spiterstulen and the cabin there.

He nodded. The information didn't exactly come as any surprise

to him. He had walked for about four hours, one and a half hour
longer than he had been told was necessary to get to the top.

– There are signs, one of the men, obviously a guide, an
employee, told him. – Didn't you see them, just beyond
Glitterheim? You should never have crossed the river.

He should have seen them, but he had been too focused on
what awaited him, what was ahead.

A grin crossed his face. He had walked well over half the
infamous route to Spiterstulen, and he didn't feel any worse than
after a walk in, the park.

– Your prices stink, he stated suddenly.

– It's the distances… the other said, suddenly very defensive.

– Bull - shit, Zahn rejected his words. – You decide everything
up here. You have monopoly on travel, on trade and housing and
defend it with environmental concerns. Disgusting, if you ask me.

They hurried on, now, scared and ashamed, completely unused
to people speaking their honest mind. About anything.

He moved on, continued towards Spiterstulen, on the infamous
route. The surroundings, the ground he walked, reminded him of
a natural stone desert, one unlike any city… and infinitely more
marvelous. And around it the mountains reached for the sky.
It was… precisely how he had imagined it, as if he had already
passed this way a thousand times.

When he reached Spiterstulen well into the afternoon, he didn't
bother walking all the way to the cabin, but started raising the
tent immediately. The advice given on the webpages was to finish
raising the tent before the evening or even late afternoon set in,
in the hope of avoiding a gigantic gnat attack. He had never liked
gnats much, so that advice sounded more than sensible to him.

The gnats already buzzed in the air around him. He could
sense, could see them, as tiny shadows in the air. Even when
they swarmed one hardly saw them, if they weren't at a certain
angle to the light. They would wait, until he was distracted, until
everything was ready for the sneak attack, and then the bloodbath
would begin.

He put together the tent, a simple process, with a few strained
moments when everything should be balanced. It was far
easier than he had imagined, even though he had never done
it before and the process had only been explained to him, not

demonstrated. He had visualized everything when the clerk in the sports store had given him his detailed description, committed every word to memory, and also more. He had imagined what he was actually seeing now, when he experienced everything in present tense. He had always had a fabulous memory, but now he began suspecting that couldn't be all, that there had to be more to it.

Then his attention was once again drawn to the gnats, drawn to their movements. They didn't fly close to him. He stopped. When he charged them the entire swarm fled. And he didn't see them again. He grinned and shook his head. They clearly didn't like him more than he liked them.

The tent stood there, before him, ready for use. He hauled all the equipment inside and crawled in himself, pulled the zip tight, in case the gnats should change their collective mind. He rested on his back, thinking about it, thinking about them. On a camping trip he had made to Darthmoor, as a boy, they had certainly not fled from him, but on the contrary loved his blood, every single, juicy drop they could get. He hadn't been camping since.

He wasn't sleepy, so he decided to go on a smaller expedition before darkness fell. But darkness fell, and he didn't walk further than to the cabin, going inside it. Somebody played a guitar in there, and people sang. Neither the tune nor the singing attracted him that much. He sat within the other hall, with others who didn't exactly enjoy the performance. Nobody here resembled Joyce. Nobody made his suspicion rise. He entered the room where the «entertainment» took place. The man who played the guitar and was lead singer (he sang horribly false and the tune reminded Zahn of a dusty Nashville piece), sat on a stool in front of a selection of listeners and participants evidently enjoying themselves, the food and the cheerfulness of it all.

Zahn spent an hour, two, there, until he grew sleepy enough, and then returned to the tent. He had another chicken, without thinking it through. It, like the previous, didn't seem to fill up any major space in his stomach. It tasted even better. Every single grain of spice they had spiced it with tasted great. And independently of that, he also sensed the original taste. This hadn't been a wild animal and he more than suspected that. But the overwhelming feeling of knowing made up for the taste of enclosure and imprisonment. He saw it, saw it all. It drifted in his head and he turned dizzy, and he saw even more. He rested on his back and listened to the nature outside. Inside, outside. Somebody approached with a terrain-breaching vehicle, with music thundering from speakers. It distracted Zahn considerably. The roar from the river almost overwhelmed the music, but in spite of that the music distracted him... considerably. But they would rise early as well the next morning, he knew that, and even though he wanted to take action, he held back.

He rested on his back, feeling the ground beneath him and listened, listened to the silence, listened for it, without fear. Without the old fear. He knew he would hear if anyone approached, hear the sound of weapons approaching, everything... not fitting in up here. Half asleep, with his eyes closed, he saw more than he had in his entire life prior to this moment.

Next morning, he hardly felt the weight of the sack. He had thought it felt light yesterday, but today he felt like it was filled with feathers. Glitretind rose before him, clouded in mist, clothed in ice. It reminded him of Kilimanjaro in Africa. There was no resemblance, but to his inner eye they intermingled, becoming one.

People walked up and down all the time. It wasn't seen as a big deal. But to him it was, as he stood at the top, a top clouded in mist. One couldn't see much, not with the eyes. The last stretch hadn't been that hard, even walking through the snow, through a landscape permeated in gray. But the journey here had been long. And he stood at the top of the world and looked at it.

And he looked further up.

He celebrated the ascension with another chicken, and another, on the way down. And he drank, drank lakes of fluid. And it seemed to dissolve within him.

For a moment there, there had been sparks around him, and he had drawn the gun and sought cover behind a rock. He stared at people coming and going, and who evidently hadn't noticed, didn't notice a thing. What had he seen? The air itself? Dancing and singing around him? The next would have to be that he saw a flying saucer levitate above him, and do a summersault in his honor…

He returned to Glitterheim late in the afternoon. His feet burned, he didn't imagine that. He had probably blisters in more than one place. He had expected to feel exhausted, but he didn't. Or: He had expected to feel exhausted… and therefore he did. The last chicken had been consumed an hour earlier. He had stopped under the rug of mist, and looked at the valley, the stone desert below, slightly unsteady on his legs the last few hundred steps to the cabin. Legs didn't feel tired, but they didn't work like they were supposed to. He felt the weight of the sack on his back, the imbalance of it. When he stopped in front of the signposts, he confirmed to himself that the guide hadn't been lying. The signs were right, and he had walked more than four times longer than he had originally planned.

The bike wasn't where he had put it. It didn't necessarily mean that much. He didn't really fear it had been stolen. There could be a number of reasons why they had moved it. It, and also other bikes, had been there the day before.

He walked right to the dining room. Most people had already eaten, and there weren't many there then. It served him well. He ordered the largest deep plate of soup they had, asked for a bigger one, with something he hoped was a charming smile, and got it. The huge jug of water was free. Water was still free in the countries with large amounts of rain. He poured salt in the soup and hardly noticed it, drank a glass of water, drank another. Drank another. When the deep plate was empty there wasn't more water left in the jug either.

– I'm looking for two women, he said in the reception. It dawned on him that he couldn't recall going here. – I was here yesterday as well. You hadn't seen them, but I know they are in the area.

– Yesterday, sir? Who did you talk to?

– I spoke with you, Zahn aped sarcastically.

– Are you sure you're in the right place, sir? The cabins can be quite similar…

– This is Glitterheim, right? Zahn bent forward. The man nodded mutely. – I was here yesterday. I'm looking for two women and a man, I gave you photos. Did you perhaps play too much country music here, too, yesterday?

The man looked completely uncomprehending at him.

And at the wall they had still kept yesterday's date. Negligence or...

– You don't believe it is that easy, do you? He said aloud. – You must do better than this.

Zahn shook his head and laughed scornfully, before moving into the lounge. He sat down and turned the pages of the guestbook. And froze in a twisted, rigid position.

He didn't find his name there. Not the name he had never written, and not the one he had written the day before. And even worse: The other signatures and anecdotes from yesterday had also mysteriously disappeared. The signings... stopped little less than twenty-four hours ago, with the brief, pleasant note:

«To Gwen and Monica, two great girls I met in the middle of nowhere. In their company I experienced the highest mountain».

Memory, all the instincts he might possess (for what they might be worth), told him this had to be the same book. But neither instincts nor reason seemed to work for him lately. He grabbed the pen, while taking himself through everything in his head. The problem was simply that there wasn't anything to go through. Nothing solid. Only what he always found in his search; Ghosts and Shadows. And they danced, danced in the air. And the atonal music drew and scribbled, in the air, as well as inside his head, curls that had to be done by a toddler, because they were so simple... and incomprehensible. A shaking of the head and a shaking hand holding the pen, brought under control by an internal snarl. He scribbled his name once again, in an angry move. The hand rested on the paper afterwards, didn't move. He sat there, unmovable for a while, with the pen in his hand.

He realized he didn't understand more now than before, that he hadn't found anything really tangible, since the day he left London.

Delphi, Greece. A long bus drive from the capital Athens. The walk up to the temple and the round place, in the stinking heat. Tourists whirled around him, incomprehensible. People he thought he had direct access to one moment, had vanished into the whirling sea the next.

– Hello, Jeremy, he heard Joyce greet him. – You won't find any oracle or fortuneteller here, but if you look hard and long enough, you might find one elsewhere.

Zahn drew the gun, drew it up and out, so no one could avoid seeing it. People screamed and threw themselves to the ground, while others ran mindlessly off. The line of sight improved dramatically. He turned, froze. There, by Apollon's temple. A figure appeared close to the wall. Zahn pulled the trigger, the figure disappeared. Zahn rushed over there. Nothing. He swore mutely. No blood, no sign that a human being had stood here.

Jeremy whirled around and stood face to face with David Kelly, who had followed him, that shit. Jeremy's finger shook on the trigger.

– Did you hit him? The journalist cried out, excited and wild in eyes. – Was it him?

– Nothing here, Zahn mumbled. – Nothing more, nothing less.

– I heard him speak to you, Kelly mumbled as well. – As if he stood very close.

And the mirage dissolved in the dry air.


He arrived in Los Angeles late at night, a fine, dry evening. Everything seemed relatively peaceful. He sensed how the charged air tickled his skin. He didn't need to convince himself it was truly happening. He knew it was. Just like he knew nobody else sensed anything. He walked to the police headquarters, strolled through the main entrance, stopped in front of the desk.

– Hello, he politely greeted the man behind the desk.

– Hello, was the rude reply from the sergeant behind the desk.

– My name is Jeremy Zahn, he said politely. – I'm a former inspector with the London police, now with Interpol.

– *We want you in,* Bass Perlman had said to him in Paris. – *As long as you're not broadcasting our alliance, there shouldn't be any problem.*

– I've good reason to believe that Timothy Joyce has chosen this town as his next target, and I would like to speak to the Chief.

– So, you would want to speak to the *Chief,* would you?

The Sergeant puffed himself up, from his initial arrogant posture to incredible proportions.

– Listen you flabby, wagging tail dog, Zahn murmured, without raising his voice. – You have the impression you're all powerful behind that desk of yours, but if you don't get the finger out of your ass pretty soon, as in immediately, I'll personally see to it that you're flayed alive. I'll be doing it myself, as soon as I get the opportunity, and I'm confident it will come soon.

The sergeant's double jaw shook. He couldn't utter a word, but he got moving.

He knew that the man in front of him meant every word he said. He had never truly known fear before, until now.

– I'll get on it right away, sir.

Zahn was shown into a dusty pre-office office. He didn't expect trouble. Impolite and thug-like behavior worked every time, and at least far more often than the usual sheep-tactics.

A TV was on further down the hall. Zahn walked there, as if in a daze. The words and later the images didn't register in his immediate consciousness at first, but then he recognized the voice, recognized the face, recognized Gwen, and rushed forward to the assembly in front of the screen.

– This message will be repeated three times, she stated for the second time. – This is the second time.

– PEOPLE OF LOS ANGELES, LISTEN CAREFULLY. YOU ARE HEREBY NOTIFIED THAT YOUR TOWN IS YOURS NO LONGER.

He stared and stared. It was impossible for him to take his eyes off her. He knew her. He knew her not.

She was dressed in a red brown, tight uniform. A Guevara cap on her head. The direct look stared back at him. The surroundings behind her were hardly more than mist, indistinct, without solid matter.

– It has in truth never belonged to you, of course, but from now on you won't even be allowed to keep the illusion that it's yours. From this moment on, it belongs to TIMOTHY JOYCE and his warriors. His first decree is that the officers of the Los Angeles Police Department shall stay away from the old storage building, where we have been gathering lately. All uniformed personnel moving closer than fifty *meters* from the building's outer walls will be summarily executed. In other words, you'll already be condemned to death the moment you transgress upon the stated border. The death penalties will be executed, no matter how long time it will take and with whatever means necessary. If you value your lives, you will obey the order of the city's new leader. You and the other subordinates will be given subsequent orders on a later occasion.

The screen turned black.

# CHAPTER TWELVE

## SIX DAYS IN THE CITY OF ANGELS

Those who don't understand an intense and vivid story will always feel disappointment, feel empty at its end, at its beginning… because they can't grasp the big picture, because they didn't realize what was really going on.

Or perhaps they will, on the contrary feel vindicated because they can be surprised, can still feel wonder in a world almost devoid of it. Perhaps they will start thinking and act their true will, and start grasping the big picture.

The man walking alone through the small park didn't hide himself, but his face rested in shadow. In his shadow, two steps behind him, walked a figure, a powerfully built male, covered in cloak and hood. In a very conscious walk, the lead man took his time to reach his destination. He felt excitement, he had little trouble admitting that to himself. This would be his second major act, his first public appearance, the culmination of many years of work. He had no trouble admitting his excitement to himself. He embraced it.

He knew he wasn't insane, he had been given ample proof of that, even though a small doubt always lingered. But what he most of all felt, was close to unlimited joy. The laughter came easy. He knew what was going to happen.

They waited for him by the small tower, one of the city's most famous landmarks. A peaceful spot surrounded by trees, bushes and a lawn, a trifle of a «green lung» in the endless gray outside.

They looked curiously at him, filled with expectation, but not in worry and fear. Not yet. Jimmy Swain, Pauline and Penny, Lorna and Joey, almost everybody from Venice, everybody he had caught in his web. They were nine, almost what would be his entire inner circle.

His face changed again. The body grew bigger, broader. Their eyes widened. They understood, and those who didn't understand feared to the point of wanting to understand. Power was the only thing they understood. And now they stood face to face with a Power they could hardly imagine. The power he would show them, push down their throat.

– You wanted to say something, Lorna? He asked kindly.

She who had led the gang who had first approached him in Venice slowly shook her head.

– No, she stated in a very definite manner. – Absolutely not.

– Good, he said cheerfully. – We have a lot to do. First, we will pay a visit to the bank, after a slight detour.

He smiled brightly.

– But that's merely a formality. The world is at our feet.

– Is it dangerous? Penny asked, very cowed, with a thin, innocent voice.

– No. He shook his head. – This won't be dangerous. I can tell you that you will all survive the day, and that you will not be captured by the big and ugly cops. To join me, that is dangerous, but this…? This will be like a walk in the park. Come, and I will lead you into the wilderness.

And they followed him, in a haze, in an ever more aware reality, to the parking lot right outside the «green lung». Three large cars turned towards them. Powerful engines roared under hot hoods. All the cars had a lot of room behind, a lot of room in front. Monica sat behind the wheel of one, Gwen of the other. Another left the driver's seat of the third, leaving it to Timothy.

– This is the time for our first, great show of strength, he cried, and his words penetrated deep within them. – Big things await us.

And they all entered the cars. And the vehicles roared and started moving, moved out on the gray line of speed, of corrupted freedom, coffins on wheels. They suspected what would happen. They forgot their old lives, remembering themselves. They had never felt more alive.

The chopper blades cast shadows on the ground, cut the air with their sharp edge. The Los Angeles police, the city's SWAT team, the military had never had more birds of prey flying above the city before. Right below roofs, highways, nooks and crannies whirled by. Timothy Joyce and his coconspirators led on with an entire caravan of police cars, «civilian» and military vehicles on their heels. His cars clearly had the greatest speed and the greatest speed potential. One saw it, how the three vehicles in front slowed down, allowed those chasing them to catch up, and then increased the lead again. This was most unusual, as the LAPD had a reputation for having an advantage over the city's speeders. This time they chased cars far faster than their own.

But the authorities and bunch still had numbers and logistics on their side. Ever more choppers and cars joined the hunt, and roadblocks were put in place. The path leading to downtown was blocked in its entire length, another first in Timothy Joyce's honor. Zahn sat in the lead chopper, with Monica and a slightly nervous pilot. Springsteen barked orders constantly, clearly… excited.

– Is everything in place? He screamed into the mike.

– Not quite yet, Chief, the reply reached him through the com-system. – We're having a bit of a problem coordinating everything.

LAPD, the army, SWAT, CIA, FBI and added to the mix representatives for several domestic and foreign official and semi-official bodies of influence. Zahn grinned.

Bullets hailed down there. Nobody treated this with the caution that was, after all shown, during an ordinary car-chase or manhunt. But the bullets had no effect. Bullets hitting the wheels had no effect whatsoever.

– In case you're wondering, I will strongly advice you not to use explosives, Springsteen said dryly. – Our dear mayor isn't very happy about the dregs that have visited our proud city the last week, but he will be even less so if we start blowing up his roads and drivers.

A neutral car in the line of fire suddenly sideslipped. If one looked carefully one could spot lines of blood on its blue hood.

– Stop firing, Springsteen roared. – STOP FIRING!

The car somersaulted and exploded in an inferno of gas and sparks.

– It doesn't matter anyway, he mumbled.

Nobody commented on that last remark.

Ten years. Joyce had spent ten years ticking off virtually every possible powerful body and servants around the world. Many of them had sent their representatives to the city, waiting for an opportunity like this, exactly like this. Had even the Man with a Thousand Faces and Thousand Escapes a chance to get away from this?

– Half an hour ago they robbed three banks in a shopping mall, Springsteen cried. – They killed indiscriminately and threatened their way into the vaults, subsequently to kill indiscriminately again on their way back out. But the alarm went off and patrol cars coincidently passed by when they left the parking lot. The patrol cars were fired at with grenades and had to withdraw, but a surveillance chopper keeping its distance followed and referred position and direction. The wonders of technology…

Was Zahn mistaken or did he hear irony in Springsteen's voice?

Two patrol cars charged from an incoming road and tried to block the path for the three escaping cars. They were swept aside and there were hardly dents on the other cars. The patrol cars were totaled.

What car was Joyce in? Was he in any of them at all anymore? Had he ever been there at all? But if he really was down there, he had guaranteed an ace up his sleeve, a plan, a way of predicting the highest possible number of alternatives.

– He's on his ways to Downtown, Zahn shouted into the mike. – He has an agenda there. Bulletproof chassis, puncture proof tires… He has no intention of running on foot on the highway.

But perhaps later. He could disguise himself and slip away in the crowd, but he hadn't done so during the robbery. It couldn't be classified as one of history's most obscure robberies. He wanted attention, he wanted this.

– He wants this! Zahn cried out aloud.

Monica looked fascinated at him.

– What the FUCK are you saying? Captain Lasko's voice was heard through the speakers.

– He wants *this!* Zahn emphasized. – The robbers weren't discovered by chance. It wouldn't surprise me if Joyce himself pushed the alarm. Everything we see here is another thorough and well-planned operation… a Joyce operation.

– That's bullshit, Lasko laughed scornfully. – No one gets away from us on the highway. No one!

– You idiot! The only thing he has to do is to disguise himself and slip away in the crowd. Do you want to arrest all the thousands of spectators, just to be safe?

He had never seen eye to eye with Lasko. Was he wrong or was there a smirk in good ol' Springsteen's expression? Perhaps he also secretly was fed up with the antics of his aide...

Monica unwrapped a map, deliberately, eagerly, just as he had always pictured her.

– He *is* on his way to Downtown, to the Financial District, she pondered.

Zahn looked out of the window and down again, as a reflex, pulled the line backwards, pulled the line forward. He relieved her of the map. It didn't really tell him much. If Joyce turned off the road now, he would come to the place she had pointed at, to Pershing Square or close by. But he could turn later and still reach it easily enough... Even with half the American police authority on his heels, half the world's police authority everywhere else.

Since Timothy Joyce had first appeared, one had wondered about what he wanted, what his goal was. He didn't behave like a common robber, or a common terrorist... or anything. There was a number of criminals, local kings and hoodlums ravaging various places around the world, often with their private army. But they didn't run such a public race. And they didn't operate across the world. How many people had Joyce really under his command? He had had time to build his resources while doing his public shadowboxing.

Here in Los Angeles one asked the following question: What was his agenda here, what was his ultimate goal? What would he do *this* time? He had already done bigger things here than in most other places he had honored with his presence. This represented the end station to him... or, on the contrary, the departure?

The point car turned off the highway, abruptly, violently. The two others followed suit. Smoke rose from whining tires. And then there was a crack on the road behind them, a powerful explosion shaking the entire area. And another. One could see it easily from the air. At least one imagined one saw it, one at the departure point, one at the highway itself. Those leading the chase kept driving straight into the enormous hole or stopped abruptly on its edge. They had no chance of getting around it, no chance of getting any further, beyond the wreckage of cars... from which people were dispersed everywhere.

– Turn back, Springsteen said calmly into the mike. – The wrong way, if you have to. Get the shithead.

The many aerial engines, both from law enforcement and from the press, easily kept up with the runaway cars.

– They're heading towards Downtown, a pilot exclaimed amazed. – Are they insane or…

– They're not running away from something, but towards something.

– What do you mean, there's no roadblock? They heard Lasko shout.

A pipe appeared from the third car, a *bazooka*.

– FLY AWAY! Zahn shouted.

A chopper dissolved in flames. And another one, until they got far enough away.

– Bank of America, Zahn exclaimed. – Get people to surround the bank, make an iron circle around the building. He must not be able to enter it. Evacuate the personnel.

Monica shook her head. Communication had died, as suddenly as the flowering of a bomb. A jamming device? Damn, was there anything that bastard hadn't thought of?

– Delay tactics, he mumbled. – Nothing else. Get us down, get us all down.

But everything happened so fast now. The tall buildings in the Financial District seemed to grow up from the very ground. And the cars had come so close, much too close to the Bank of America building.

The fountain at Atlantic Richfield (ARCO) Plaza in front of the bank, in Flower Street sprayed the chopper as it landed, a rough, unsteady landing. Zahn threw himself outside, before it had settled properly, closely followed by Monica. The three cars charged around the corner, from the opposite side, from Sixth Street. Police officers and others charged from all sides. The cars stopped abruptly in front of the bank's main entrance. Zahn spotted Joyce, he spotted Gwen, spotted Monica. The others wore masks covering their faces. Some carried equipment, but most were armed to the teeth. Monica Valdez froze by his side. He pulled her with him when he threw himself behind cover. The large machinegun, a newer version of the M16, started playing in Joyce's capable hands. A moment later bullets flew back and forth on the plaza. Grenade launchers sent deadly payloads through the air. Huge holes opened up in the ground. Bodies were blown to pieces. Police officers died in droves. All of the robbers evidently had far more experience than even the SWAT team. Joyce stood in the middle of the bullet hail, and fired one deadly salvo after another. He seemed immortal where he stood. He was pushed back. Blood stood in a straight line from the powerful body. He rose again, and ordered his coconspirators with him into the bank. The fire exchange had possibly lasted ten to fifteen seconds. Not more than that. They vanished inside. Several were hit, but no one fell. Zahn charged forward, ignoring shouts of warning, and kept running until two large officers jumped at him and pulled him down. More reached the three and helped pull him back, behind the quickly raised barricades. More police cars arrived. Choppers landed. Trucks stopped not far away. The noise, overwhelming, paralyzing didn't stop. The forward charge, however, did. People moved, kept moving, but not forward. More barricades were put in place. From the bank there were a few screams, incredibly enough heard through a crescendo of noise, in which Zahn could never recall having experienced its like. The stage set slowly. Marksmen chose their positions, on rooftops, behind corners, in windows, behind cover. Weapons, binoculars, pointed looks were directed at the bank, to little or no use, naturally, and it did indeed seem a bit ridiculous. Zahn almost laughed while leaving the front row. Once again Joyce had them all exactly where he wanted them.

The tall Bank of America building. The low, interconnected one by its side, where the bank itself was situated. One saw... wasn't there welding fire in there?

– They're welding the access ways, one cried. – The thorough bastards.

Monica showed Zahn the construction plans for the area. He had no idea how she had gotten hold of them this fast. He hadn't been wrong about her. She was a rare jewel.

There were many access tunnels in the area, a fact Joyce undoubtedly had studied carefully. Zahn gritted his teeth, as the smoke and dust slowly but surely set on Atlantic Richfield Plaza, while one of largest number of «varied» uniformed people the world had ever seen surrounded the area. Figueroa Street, above the bank was just as filled up as Flower was.

The stage was set.

– Get our best negotiator here, Lasko barked. – Get him five minutes ago.

– A… negotiator? Zahn laughed short and sharp, a snarl of a sound.

He looked around, studied the street, the place, saw it for what it was. He hadn't been here before, had perhaps subconsciously avoided it.

His eyes stopped by one of several signs.

PRIVATE PROPERTY

And further down:

PRIVATE PROPERTY

And so on.

There were no benches here. No plants. He looked up at the gang bridges, high above street level, where the businessmen, the masters could move undisturbed between the various tall buildings. Up there, there were plants, green «lungs» and trees, of a sort. He had heard they had had problems with homeless here earlier, that they had eliminated that problem now. The streets here, on street level, had quite simply not been constructed for people. Or rather: Had been constructed to keep people away, a dead, sterile place, completely devoid of life.

He looked towards the bank again, where he could spot implications of life inside. A suspicion, a fleeting thought appeared and vanished again, then, as fast as it had come. He could almost sense how Joyce felt it in there. Almost.

Monica stood right behind him. He shook his head. She always managed to get close without him noticing it. He had to get used to the thought.

– You're not the only one having fun these days, she commented. – Springsteen is also walking around smiling.

– *Smiling?* Well, the old geezer hasn't experienced much in the sense of excitement for years. I guess he gets loads of it now.

– Did you notice he smiled in the chopper as well?

She was sharp. He hadn't been wrong about her. Not at all.

– He has one of the world's most wanted people surrounded in his city. Perhaps it isn't so strange that he's smiling.

He had smiled. And it had been a strange smile, something… skewed, something that didn't belong. And the potbelly? Hadn't it quite simply vanished?

Or had it always been there, never been there, and he had just never noticed?

He looked up again. The street, this part of the city had a bit of the futuristic image, where the world at present time was headed, a world where segregation had been done everywhere. The rich, the powerful, the successful at the top, the poor, the world's outcasts, the unwanted at the bottom. He shook his head. One didn't need to look to the future for that. One saw it easily here, everywhere, a bit less obvious, in the present-day world.

Monica held his fisted hand.

– It's more sideways today, she said softly, harshly. The ghettoes and the wealthy areas are on the same level, at each other's side, but it's just as far up. To somewhat escape poverty and oppression, one must either be a servant, preferably an eager one, or become more ruthless, greedier than the people one despises. Before one knows it, one has become one of them.

He saw Springsteen approach, with the twisted smile in place.

– Some place this, the Chief said cheerfully. – There are no homeless here, not one. And on Pershing Square, a few years back, there were tons of them. But they removed them. And they sought here. Here, where everything was removed. Benches, everything green, everything making it a place to stay. A perfect image of the future, don't you think so?

– Not my future, Zahn stated lightly.

– I hear you, Springsteen grinned. – But the future comes anyway, doesn't it? It can't be stopped, can it?

Zahn shook his head, as the man wagged off. In the week he had known the somewhat celebrated mix of a policeman and a politician, he had never seemed weird before.

– Perhaps he sees himself as a future governor or mayor or something, Monica wondered. – One might go nuts from less.

Jeremy grinned to her. She returned the grin.

The negotiator arrived, leading a formidable team, both in expertise and size. A provisional tactical headquarters was established a bit down Flower Street.

Springsteen waved Zahn and Monica to him, and they followed him into the tent.

– Zahn, Springsteen cleared his throat. – Say hello to Chief Negotiator Cole Meeks. Meeks, say hello to Jeremy Zahn.

Meeks, a huge guy, towering over Zahn, reached out his hand. Zahn clutched it hard, in order to save his own. The tactic sort of succeeded. It did hurt, but his hand wasn't left like a wet spot on the ground.

Lasko entered the tent, excited and quite *busy,* as usual.

– We have access to new, old and alternative schematics. We know all access routes, and we're covering them all.

– Those not already welded shut by Joyce and his people, you mean?

Zahn couldn't and didn't want to hide the sarcasm.

– Uh… Lasko pulled himself together before continuing. – We're also covering all the windows and bridges, and we have full control over the roofs. I've been told our friends in the army have full control in the air, in case anyone wants to come to their leader's aid. We even have people down in the sewer.

– That's a man who knows the position as Chief will be available soon. Monica had the great skill of being able to speak low, and yet be heard. – We have a special name for those at the academy…

– We're also working on accessing the bank's surveillance systems, the Captain finished, clearly more sober, indicating he had heard her.

– Excellent, Captain, Springsteen praised him. – But for the moment I think we should leave the floor to Chief Negotiator Meeks.

– Of course, sir, Lasko said rigidly. – Just one more thing, sir… Springsteen nodded encouragingly to him.

– A small group of Joyce-disciples has gathered on Pershing Square, sir.

– Oh, let them gather, let them make fools of themselves. We have more pressing concerns than to play nanny.

Springsteen nodded to Meeks, who straightened to his full height, an impressive sight. He didn't just attract attention, he demanded it.

– What we will strive for here, the huge man began, very confident, – is to achieve *contact,* a kind of common ground or understanding, so to speak. It will be a fairly more challenging task than it usually is, concerning who is at the opposite side of the table. But even Timothy Joyce is human. He would rather engage in a conversation than to cause bloodshed… especially since his own life is on the line. It's important, if not necessarily essential to avoid… negative associations in that regard and also generally speaking. Remember this, if anything makes it necessary for you to answer the phone. I can tell you one thing: This will be a learning process to him as well. He's no longer in a position of having the upper hand.

– Are you certain about that, Chief Negotiator Meeks? Monica asked. – I've heard he has been in tight spots before, and he has easily walked away from them.

– This time we won't move in without having a complete list of all personnel, Meeks said rigidly. – We're checking the hostiles *and* the hostages, anybody within a mile's radius of that building. Believe me, I've been told from the top that we don't need to spare any expenses.

The nervous «busyness» in the room was slowly muted, to a lower, nervous buzz.

– I'm ready.

Chief Negotiator Meeks sat down in the chair, and dialed the number to the bank.

It lasted well and long. Nobody picked up the phone. The ringing tone echoed strangely in the tent, loud and edgy.

Meeks was about to relent, and redial, when the phone was picked up on the other side.

– This is Gwen, sounded the loud and clear voice. Jeremy shook. – What can I help you with?

– Are we speaking with Gwen Talbot? Meeks asked pleasantly.

– Is that you, Meeks? Gwen exclaimed excitedly in the other end. – Chief Negotiator Meeks? You're one of my great heroes, sir. I've read about you since I went to school. So big and mighty and manly…

– What we want to know is…

– Yes, «we» are speaking with Gwen Talbot, she sang.

– Gwen, we would like to speak to Joyce, Timothy…

– Why didn't you just say so then? TIMMY, THERE'S A PHONE FOR YOU.

Zahn chuckled and clenched his teeth at the same time. Another damn scene.

– Timmy will be here in a moment.

It was another voice, another woman. Jeremy saw, felt, how Monica Valdez froze at his side. He didn't hold that against her, feeling fairly frozen himself.

– Are we speaking with Monica? Meeks asked hoarsely.

– My name is Monica Valdez. The soft voice lingered in the room. – A pleasure, Cole.

– I would like to tell you something, now, Monica, Meeks said, while drying sweat from his forehead with his sleeve. – I don't think you're completely honest with me.

– *Are you certain about that, Chief Negotiator Meeks?*

Jeremy tried hard not to look at the Monica Valdez present in the room. He failed. The rest of those present certainly failed. She seemed strangely calm, like a wax doll.

Meeks pulled himself together and once more focused on the conversation.

– I would very much like to speak to Timothy Joyce, now, he said.

– Joyce here.

More wondering, over something indefinitely *familiar* in the infamous man's voice, something impossible to hide.

A headshake. Jeremy didn't get it, couldn't get it.

– Looks like we have a situation here, Mister Joyce…

– The grass is GREEN. THE NUMBER IS NUMBER, THE BEEF IS RED AND JUDGMENT DAY IS AT HAND

Joyce cried with a totally unrecognizable voice.

– DANCE, DANCE TO THE PIPER'S FALSE TONES. WALK IN CIRCLES, UNTIL THAT'S ALL YOU CAN DO

– W-what? Meeks finally said.

– It doesn't mean anything, Zahn shrugged. – He's just yanking your chain.

– But shouldn't the HONORED Chief Negotiator REALIZE I'm yanking his chain; Jeremy?

– Listen… Meeks attempted.

– LIFE IS LIKE A CEMETERY, Joyce sang.

Everything turned deadly silent, until Joyce spoke again, suddenly, shockingly, with completely normal voice.

– Oooops, sorry, for using such words. One shan't do that, shan't one, such negative loaded words?

– No, one shan't, Meeks said, very aggrieved, totally broken, all juice having been sucked out of him.

– But life *is* like a cemetery, Cole, Joyce pointed out. – It's inevitable, when everybody within its gates believe themselves dead. I'm gonna fix that, fix that, too. But it's too late for you, Cole, you're dead - dead - dead - dead - dead.

It cracked loud, several times. Meeks shook when the bullets hit him, when he was shot to pieces in front of everybody. Everybody drew their weapons and started firing in the direction they thought the bullets were fired from, firing wildly. Many were hit, both in east and west, north and south.

– Cease fire! Lasko shouted. – CEASE FIRE!

A bullet snarled right by his ear. They heard the sound of ricochets, of windows breaking, of pain-filled screams.

It turned silent again. Deadly silent.

Jeremy stared paralyzed at the ruckus around him, at the bloodbath.

– Anybody attempting to turn off the connection, even approaching the switchboard or does anything elsewhere to turn it off, will be shot without further warning. I control the vertical, I control the horizontal.

– Where did the shots come from? Lasko shouted. – I WANT TO KNOW WHERE THE BULLETS CAME FROM

Nobody approached the switchboard. Not even after the tent had been checked for holes and stitched, and all angles had been thoroughly checked, did anyone dare approach it.

– Good! Joyce stated. – Now, we're approaching an understanding here…

It seemed like he was actually in the room, by their side. They felt his presence.

– You're all gonna die, but not quite yet. Come, dear friends, let's go outside, to continue our conversation there.

They were told through their radio links that something was happening. They couldn't make out the words, because all the operatives shouted and screamed simultaneously.

They almost collided with a man on his way in, on their way out.

It happened in front of the bank in Sixth Street. People rushed out on the stairs. Everybody wore masks, but it was clear some of them were forced to do so. Some bank employees were recognized after descriptions and clothing, but it was impossible to be sure.

And then television broadcasts were cut and the events at the front of the bank supplanted the previous images. Some channels had been broadcasting from the events already, but they had no control over anything anymore.

– We could have left this place now, the powerful voice thundered. – You couldn't have stopped us without major casualties.

Silence, dead and numb greeted his confident statement.

– But we like it here, we enjoy all the attention. We're attention-hungry like hell.

A local newspaper had called him an attention-starved demagogue.

– You're all gonna die! He shouted. – But not yet. One is in a hurry, though.

A man in SWAT-uniform fell from a roof high up. They first saw it on a monitor, and then they looked up. He didn't scream. Blood flowed from him as he fell like a rock. There was no thunder when he hit the sidewalk, but they experienced it that way.

– What fools you are! Haven't you even considered the possibility of me having people in your ranks? You've heard it before: you're not safe from me anywhere.

Eyes flickered nervously all over the place.

– Let me start by calming your fears. At this point we'll just take care of the overzealous among you, like the meatball over there. He was about to fire. We can't, unfortunately, keep you all from firing simultaneously. If you start firing now, if SWAT decides to storm later, I can tell you that you, they will be completely safe. We won't fire at you or them, but at the hostages. That's a solemn promise.

And then he stood there, at the front of the bank. The cameras zoomed in on him. He stood there, alone, completely unprotected.

– Don't fire! Lasko spoke into his cell phone. – I repeat: Don't fire!

Timothy Joyce had their complete attention. They were all pulled into his vortex.

– What value have you? He asked rhetorically. – You're no more than ghosts restlessly wandering the world and thus I'll treat you. The sand is pouring in the city of angel's hourglass.

Everybody shook like ghosts.

– This is one of many gathering points of the world's Destroyers, Joyce cried with the loud, clear voice. – There are no homeless here, because the Destroyers don't want to witness the human tragedies resulting from their actions. There's no dirt here, because they don't want to be reminded of their destruction of the planet and life on it. Well, we're gonna remind them, and keep reminding them, until we've eradicated their kind from the surface of the Earth.

He left no doubt that the word «demagogue» did fit him. He played on it, letting his «critics» stew in their own fat, strangled by their own words.

Zahn was sweating. He felt like he was drowning in his own sweat. His nose itched, in a sensation very much resembling pain, but there was no blood.

– We've taken control of your broadcasting system, because we wish to present our own version of what's happening. Those ruling the various channels and their journalist lapdogs belong to the fourth, *supporting* estate. They're nothing but a propaganda tool for the tyrants. We'll expose prejudice, we'll fuck up old, accepted truths. We all exist in a thoroughly unjust, unequal and destructive society. There are no extenuating circumstances anywhere. All nations, all private and public authorities are participating in the oppression. All servants, all participants are guilty of propagating the destruction of Life on the planet. No one is innocent! Or to say it differently: Innocence has become just another commodity, as naiveté is increasing dramatically. We'll put a stop to all of it. Most people have, to this point, had the opportunity to ignore the monstrosity of the present-day world, deny its very existence. From this moment on, that will no longer be an option.

He turned his back to the crowd and returned to the bank with calm, collected steps. The hostages were pulled back in, as they screamed hysterically.

And from Pershing Square, hundreds of meters away, people of many different «kinds» had gathered, and a joy-filled triumphant roar rose from that crowd. The cameras caught it. From above, from their midst. There was dancing and everybody heard the music, even those who didn't hear it through the ear.

Deaf and dead people rose and walked this day.

And everything had been broadcast and uploaded on the Internet. One didn't need to be a genius to realize that. And it would remain, and it would be copied time and time again, until it would be impossible to actually remove. There were tons of Timothy Joyce sites and pages out there already. Their number wouldn't decline with this.

Zahn heard the music. He dried his upper lip, but there was no blood.

– What the HELL, Lasko exploded. – When did they get to be so many?

– It seems like they have rushed in the last few minutes, sir, an aide told him. – Do we remove them?

Lasko looked at Springsteen.

– Do it, by God, the Chief muttered. – In case you've missed it, martial law has been declared in this city. Put them on a train out of the city, out of the state.

– Those resident, too… sir? The aide wondered.

– Everybody, absolutely everybody. Springsteen dismissed him in a violent gesture. – Take as many as you want from our forces here. We tend to step on each other's toes anyway.

It seemed like the building had swallowed Timothy Joyce and the others. There had been no further communication or sound or sign of life from there.

Time passed slowly. A shadow passed in front of the sun, passed a shiny glass tower nearby. Nothing happened in there, nothing happened out here. The world held its breath awaiting Timothy Joyce's next move.

Those inside the tent stared at the phone and communication equipment, at each other. No one in their right mind moved close to it, no one felt tempted.

Lasko, during his prolonged pacing, never ventured close.

– What is he planning? He mumbled. – He must know he's without chances.

He looked up.

– Is the SWAT team ready?

– Right away, sir, he was told.

The hostages' fate had been decided the moment Joyce took them hostage. The response was well established: One didn't negotiate with terrorists. One had to give the impression that all possibilities had been tried first, but then the attack would commence. And any attack, any act meaning the end of Timothy Joyce had long since been approved at the highest level. At this moment the SWAT team prepared to attack from below, above and from all sides. They only awaited the final signal, approval.

Zahn imagined he saw David Kelly out there, a shark just as greedy as those swimming the seven seas. But this particular shark floated on his back and was eaten by the small fishes.

A sergeant approached in a rush.

– We have video feed, sir, he reported excitedly, turned to Springsteen.

– Excellent, Springsteen replied lazily. – Let's take a look.

New wires, moving, writhing snakes were pulled in and attached to monitors, Equipment was set up in a hectic, nervous frenzy, so unlike other police operations.

Images started flickering on the screens. Indistinct, in flashes at first, then crystal clear. This bank had spared no expenses when it came to security. One could see the counter, the entire entrance and hall, the hallway to the vault. People started raising their brows. Expectant looks faded and the worried expression was confounded. It would never more go away.

– But where are all the people? Wells was unable to hide his astonishment and deep, deep despair.

Caldwell said nothing. The lower lip shook in the tanned face, the tanned face having an ever-grayer subtext.

There wasn't a single human being inside the bank.

– Are there blind spots? Caldwell spat.

An employee they had dragged in shook his head.

– None, he assured them. – The surveillance system was designed for situations like these. And all the cameras should be connected. I don't...

A roar rose from outside. They rushed out and almost collided with another aide on her way in.

– They're coming out, she gasped. – The hostages, I mean. Some wear masks, but they don't carry weapons, and I do believe it is the hostages...

234

Music started thundering then, thundering clear and distinctive. Zahn recognized the tune instantly: Bad Moon Rising by Credence Clearwater Revival.

– WHAT THE HELL IS THIS? Lasko shouted hysterically.

Nobody heard him. Zahn saw his lips move like in an absurd theater.

And it was.

The music faded, but the impression of it strengthened, like a resonance inside an enormous echo-tunnel.

They halted on the stairs, the hostages did, staying on their feet, but not really steady. Ties were loose.

Strangely enough, more upset than they, were the people «greeting» them. All ties that bind were loose in front of the Bank of America building this day.

– LISTEN CAREFULLY, Lasko shouted through the bullhorn. – FOR YOUR OWN SAFETY, MAKE NO SUDDEN MOVES.

Everything moved slowly, so infinitely slow. Fingers shook against triggers. If Joyce had appeared from open air and said BOOM just then, a true hell would have erupted, of bullets, blood, stain and death.

After almost a minute of «preparations» the hostages were led down the stairs, to the relative security in the police officers' protective custody.

Not many seconds after that SWAT executed their impressive coordinated attack. No shots were fired. All the spectators and viewers glanced uneasily at each other and wondered about that…

Until the impressive attack force reappeared outside. They seemed confused, as if they didn't know exactly where they were.

– The premises are secured, sir. A sergeant greeted Lasko. – It's… empty.

They already knew it would be, but yet stared at the man with their evil eye.

Jeremy couldn't tell exactly how he felt just then. Paralyzed, approached a correct description. He joined the small group of superiors inside the bank.

They could confirm what they had seen on the surveillance monitors. There had been no loop system, a series of repetitions of the same footage or any other trick in the book, but the incredible truth. They wandered through a landscape gray and remote, exactly as it usually looked outside.

– The hostages, do we still have them in custody? Lasko barked into his radio. – Are we running a *thorough* background check?

– Yes, captain, a humble voice replied. – We suspected the same you did, sir. We're not letting them out of our sight and we're running a *thorough* background check. Everything has checked out so far, but we keep digging and...

– No matter what you may or may not find...

The Captain paused only a moment.

– Arrest them, Lasko said flatly. – Keep them in custody, under constant surveillance. I don't care what you charge them with. It won't be a problem. There's martial law in this city.

Later... Perhaps no more than half an hour, hour, but it felt long, long. They went through the videotapes, tape by tape, frame by frame. They saw Joyce and bunch charge into the bank, they never saw them leave, not anywhere.

Everything seemed normal. Everything had been caught on tape. They focused on the last few critical minutes. Everything looked normal. Everything was normal, damn it! Joyce and subordinates didn't say goodbye. They left the hostages where they had placed them. Arms were bound, not the legs. Then they headed for the vault. Every single one walked into the vault. And there... they vanished without a trace.

There was no camera inside, but not any other way out either.

Zahn entered the vault with a small group. They didn't find anything in there, not a single sign that there had been people there. Everybody looked at each other, with a mix of bewilderment and paralysis. Zahn knew he was unable to conceal his own, total loss of everything.

– Make sure that some people keep watching the tapes, he ordered. – Ask them to look for signs of tampering or whatever might seem strange. Ask them to report it, understand.

– Yes, sir, Caldwell replied, very down and out of it.

Jeremy looked at Monica. He couldn't interpret her expression. He never could.

He sat in the cafeteria at the police headquarters, with his small pack. He hadn't changed clothes. Neither had Monica. The scent of blood, of greased sweat lingered, tore in the nostrils. The other four seemed rudely refreshed in comparison. The scent of perfume and soap sickened Zahn.

Nobody spoke for a long, long time.

– After this I willingly admit I'm tempted to believe the rumors about Joyce... that he has paranormal abilities.

Wells sat there, despairing, enraged.

– He's so incredibly skilled, Caldwell said focused, very focused. – So clever that he can make weak souls believe and believe in anything.

Wells sent her a poisoned look, but he was unable to put any strength in it.

The evening had just come, without them noticing anything. The darkness leaned hard on them, through the large windows, like eyes, giant eyes in eternity.

Not much more was said. There wasn't much to say.

Herbert Ross, from the technical department finally approached them. They managed to straighten a bit in the chairs.

– The surveillance tapes haven't been tampered with, he stated. – We can say that with ninety-nine percent certainty.

– That is always something, Louis fired at him, flippant, and completely out of character.

– But there *is* something, the technician said. – Not necessarily anything instantly useful, but...

– Give it to us.

Monica leaned eagerly forward.

– Okay, we had linguists listen to recordings of his speech...

No name was mentioned. There was no need.

– Earlier, when linguistic experts have been analyzing his speech, they haven't been able to discern much, other than that his English was too mixed, too diluted, too influenced by countless accents and other languages to discern its origin...

– And now? Jeremy and Monica stared at each other.

– Now the picture has suddenly turned that much clearer, Ross said. – There are still many accents and languages in the mix, but now we can tell with fairly high certainty that he's English.

– Not Canadian? Monica asked.

Zahn had told her the entire story, everything he knew. She knew just as much as he did, now. At least as much as he knew he knew.

– Definitely not. The results are fairly unambiguous. He has grown up in England, more specifically in London, a bit to the north, in Camden Town.

It turned silent, but now the wheels had started turning once again. The rollercoaster rose and fell.

– Now, that's what I call impressive research. Monica whistled.

Jeremy didn't say anything. He didn't know what to say. Cold *didn't* trickle down his spine. He knew that, he would have felt it if it did.

The phone rang. Everybody stared at it, but nobody moved. It stood a few steps away, by the cash register. Finally, Caldwell rose and took it.

– Caldwell, she said curtly.

A strange, scared expression grew in her face, before she carried the phone to the table and handed it to Zahn.

– It's for you.

– Zahn.

– Is it mercy or disgust keeping you from putting her to sleep, Jeremy?

Timothy Joyce sat there by his side. The voice whispered into his ear.

– WHAT THE FUCK ARE YOU TALKING ABOUT?

He half stood, half sat while shouting into the mike.

– Think about a number, the cultivated, pleasant voice continued, as if Zahn hadn't spoken, hadn't screamed his lungs out.

– *What?*

– Think about a number, Jeremy, any number.

– Okay…

*Delay him. Delay him to hell and back.*

– Have you done it?

– Y-yes

– Okay, now, this is what you're gonna do. *Don't* say it aloud, but walk to the plate on the adjacent table. Under the plate you'll find an envelope. Okay?

– Okay, Jeremy said weakly.

– Excellent. We'll soon see each other again, Jeremy. Until then, enjoy yourself, huh.

There was a click. The insane conversation had ended.

Zahn hung up. Like a sleepwalker he rose fully and walked the four steps to the other table. He lifted up the plate. There was an envelope beneath it. He lifted it up, and held it on a straight arm, right out from his body, walked back and handed it to Caldwell.

– I thought about 43, he stated.

Caldwell hesitated, but opened the sealed envelope and reached into it with the thumb and index finger, and when she pulled them back up, she held a note.

**I knew you would think about forty-three**
it said with large black, printed letters.

He knew how this trick was usually done. It was dependent on the fact that the man who was the subject of the trick eventually told what number he had thought about. Then the magician would prove he had known about it all the time.

In advance there had been placed notes with numbers from one to ten in various locations around the room.

But now... Jeremy hadn't told anybody what number he had thought about until after he had picked up the envelope.

Frustrated, and with a rising sense of hopelessness he left the room.

A while later Ross carefully stepped into his office.

– We attempted to track down the place he called from. First, we found Alcatraz, then Phoenix, Arizona, then Perth, Australia, Rio de Janeiro, Cape Town... it's no use, I'm afraid.

They came one by one, chasing a direction in life. His direction. Everybody but Monica. Nobody told her what to do.

– Lots of fingerprints on the envelope, Caldwell commented, totally out of it. – Every single one belongs to Joyce, or the prints previously identified as his. He has never bothered to hide them, has he? They're even visible...

The computers hummed and buzzed, the brand new, supplanting those Zahn had... wasted, but no one used them. They sat still. Monica stared at Zahn. He stared at her. Everybody else either stared at the wall or out of the window, the broken windows that nobody had done anything about.

– He didn't kill them, Zahn said aloud. – Why didn't he kill any of the hostages?

Monica looked at him. She understood that he didn't ask a rhetorical question... or that he did.

– He has rarely displayed any reluctance to killing…

– Perhaps he didn't deem it necessary? She said.

And he caught her eyes. Not with suspicion, but rather with a kind of wild joy.

And then suddenly, from empty air:

– The prints were visible… he exclaimed, – weren't they…

Monica stared fascinated at him, as she virtually saw how the mind worked in there. How it analyzed, projected, lived.

He grabbed the envelope from Caldwell before she managed to give it to him. He pushed one key on the keyboard in front of him, made the screensaver disappear. The bright background of the Word program appeared. He tore the two halves of the envelope apart, put one at the top of another and pushed the paper at the screen. The screen lit a small, square area, surrounded by the fat fingerprints.

The letters appeared, clear, distinct, the right way, instantly.

## MIDNIGHT

No more, no less.


They drove well over the speed limit through angel city's streets. Zahn drove on red lights, against one-way signs, across sidewalks and through no-drive streets.

– Do you plan on outdoing our friend Joyce here? Russo joked.

– We're not going to make it, Caldwell complained.

– We are gonna make it, Zahn stated.

There were hardly any people outside. Or cars racing on, even through darkened streets. Almost no one defying the curfew. Most people behaved like nice boys and girls.

Mist lingered in the air after the day's heat. The night's heat clung to them, dry and tight.

Midnight. The old storage building appeared in their line of sight, lit by watt on watt of blinding electrical light. Where it began it would also end. Where it ended it would also begin. Zahn looked at his watch. Only a few minutes left.

Soldiers and police officers surrounded them the moment the car stopped. They were recognized almost instantly, and everybody pulled back respectfully. The six left the car.

– We're going inside, and we're going alone, understood?

– That's just as well, sir, the sergeant cleared his throat. – Not a mouse would be able to slip through the tight perimeter we've established here. There isn't a soul in there.

The small group separated from the crowd, from the honor guard outside, and stepped into the lion's den. Nothing had changed since the last time they had been here. Nothing suggested there were other people present.

Zahn walked the point. But he also saw them from behind, from the sides, simultaneously. He studied them.

These people had come close to him, lived with him, through hectic, intense days and nights. They knew him better than any others.

The moment they stepped inside they knew things weren't the way they were «supposed to be». Torches burned on the walls, like they had done that night. Drums beat, like that night. Caldwell wanted to turn and walk back out. Jeremy stopped her.

– No public servants have done this…

– So, you think he has walked right by almost two hundred officers and soldiers, and lit them, is that what you're saying? And the drums… the drums are the s-same. I saw him sit there and beat the drums, I saw him dance many steps away… *and it happened simultaneously.* And he looked at me. He smiled to me.

She pulled free of Zahn, and led on further inside, further up. Deep into the forest, Jeremy thought. High on the mountain.

They saw no direct traces of the battle. But they smelled it. It had penetrated the very walls, the foundation. A pungent stench they didn't sense through the nostrils, but through the mind. It could never truly be removed, but would last until the very end of time itself.

After retracing the gauntlet run, where an infinite number of people had fought and died, they reached the upper floors, beyond the stairs, the blue carpet, discolored in several places, now, the dark panel, where shadows constantly hid and hunted. The two doors that had been closed. Open now. Cold torches, all over the walls, not there before. The group pushed on. Zahn walked point now. Nobody could say when he had retaken the pole position, when he began leading them even deeper, ever higher. And then, when they had crossed over half the distance to the non-existing doors, a torch was lit. They heard a hissing sound, shook and locked their attention on it, on it and the other torches. Suddenly every single one of them was lit simultaneously.

– Chemistry! Caldwell spat. – A cheap trick!

Her voice shook.

They stood there, unmovable like statues, their guns pointing straight forward. There was no one to aim at, no one to fire at. They moved on, carefully, step by step, as if they feared that the floor at any time would vanish beneath them and the abyss reveal itself.

The other room, almost an exact copy of the first. The steel door had also been removed. The third room, where everything had changed. A banner was displayed above the opening.

WELCOME

it said.

Over the door opening, where there was no door.

Did they imagine things or did a fire flare somewhere ahead? Flare and vanish in a moment. And they could glimpse the demonic face, glimpse it even clearer than in their waking and sleeping dreams, every small second of the day and night.

Russo pulled the trigger, more like a reflex than anything else, than any expression of a conscious, deliberate act. The bullet hit nothing, but faded into the shadows and the mist.

Everybody clutched their weapons, spreading out, slipping through the opening in the wall one by one. Nothing happened. They slid through the darkened, no longer well-equipped offices. The bright room awaited them at the end of the hallway, beyond the stairs. *He chose the room first. It took time. Caution while turning every corner took time. A desk and a chair were placed at the center of the floor, a TV and a DVD-player in the shelves. A recording camera four, five steps closer, in front of the desk. Joyce had a strange stance on interior decoration. But he had been shown to have a strange stance on virtually anything. He wasn't here either. Not physically. Not now. He was here.*

– This was removed, right?

Good old Wells. Reliable like few others. One could always trust him to be predictable, to point out the obvious.

A newspaper on the floor, close to the shelves.

– It's the same equipment. Monica looked under the player and recorder, the TV. – The serial numbers are the same.

– And how do you know this? Caldwell said doubtfully.

– I went through the reports, checked the inventory, memorized details.

Zahn nodded to her in acknowledgment. She did all right, clearly a natural at this. She would do good further on, as well, under pressure.

He looked at his watch.

– A few seconds left, he said aloud.

There could be a bomb here. The sound of grains of sand flowing howled in his mind now. But he didn't think so. He felt convinced there was none… here.

He grabbed his own arm. It hurt, more now, than before. He had felt the pain in his body the entire day. There were no marks or wounds, but his entire body hurt.

Monica stared at him, with her increasingly direct and passionate look.

They heard a click then, heard it clearly, freezing in their tracks, their frozen tracks.

Midnight (in the firing line).

Zahn almost laughed. Bomb dogs, experts had walked through this place up and down, back and forth for ages, everything totally useless, a totally useless effort. If Timothy Joyce wanted to place a bomb here, he would. And no one, no one in the entire world or beyond, could stop him.

Everybody stood still. They realized if the worst happened, they had no chance of getting away.

The player turned itself on, the screen as well.

Jeremy Zahn's face appeared on the screen.

– Hello, Jeremy, we meet again.

Jeremy stared at himself. He sat there in the same worn clothes he wore now. And he seemed like himself in all ways.

– What trick is this? Caldwell exploded.

She turned incredulous towards Zahn as he stood there, on his spot, and studied the screen with intense, staring eyes.

– This hasn't happened, he mumbled. – This has never happened.

– If I were you, I wouldn't care much about it, Caldwell said, suddenly very soft spoken. – Everybody can see it isn't you but

Him there.

Everybody put away the guns, but the hand holding the weapons held on to its rigidity, the feverish eagerness raging through their bodies.

Timothy Joyce sat there. He didn't look like Timothy Joyce. He didn't even resemble him. But Timothy Joyce sat there, and he spoke to them through the recording. They had to pull themselves together several times, and look at the chair where the recording showed he was sitting, to convince themselves he didn't.

– You wonder, Jeremy, he said softly. – You cannot stop wondering. You've asked yourself time and time again, during a thousand lonely moments, how I can be so confident, how I seem to know everything that is gonna happen… Well, the answer to that is simple: I've seen everything from the other side, and I've thoroughly enjoyed myself.

The voice changed… levels, changed tone, turned both hoarser and deeper. *And the face began changing,* to his own, demonic features. Small signs at first, like flowing water or mercury, like metal, like flesh. But during ten, twenty seconds Timothy Joyce had supplanted Jeremy Zahn in front of the camera. Gasps and incredulity echoed through the room. The first few seconds one saw Joyce appear. During the last few one saw Zahn fade.

– It's only yesterday since I thought of myself as what I am, but since that yesterday eternity has passed. And passed again.

All that time passed and passed again.

– *Of course,* you were important to me, Jeremy, how could you not be?

Joyce smiled. Zahn had never, even remotely close, seen a smile like that. Never, ever. It was just a pale reflection of what he saw when he once in a while looked at himself in the mirror.

– You're finally realizing it, now, what I've seen and experienced, because you've experienced it yourself. «To find oneself, one must let go of oneself». I believe, know you're ready for that now. It has taken a very long time, but finally you're ready.

The image faded, the background strengthened itself. The chair stood there, empty.

It turned deadly silent. They realized the drums didn't beat anymore. They couldn't tell when they had stopped, when someone had stopped beating them, when someone had turned off a recording. The police officers and soldiers outside hadn't heard anything. They still stood still outside, like statues in a forest of fog. The fairy tales as they had originally been, rough and bloody.

– This is what he does, Louis exclaimed with a shrill voice, in bottomless despair. – He cuts you, cuts deep, until there's nothing left. He's Satan, the devil incarnated, in human form.

– I thought you were a somewhat sensible youth, Caldwell sniffed. – To express yourself this way and even partly believe it, is beyond nuts.

Wells placed himself between them all, bloated and unusually wild in the eyes.

– RELAX, he howled. – RELAX, GOD DAMN IT

To see the usually so calm, relaxed Wells so completely out of it shocked the others, and it did something to Jeremy. He felt the pressing need to laugh.

– Relax, Wells blew, Wells admonished. – Can't you see beyond his illusion, beyond the deceit, to the purpose behind it? I don't really see what all the excitement is about. This is merely another fine performance, another bag of tricks from our clever enemy. And not even a very original one. One can do anything when it comes to special effects in today's world. Martians could have landed on the lawn outside the White House and nobody could have proven a thing. Not without a public dissection of the Martians in question.

– Joyce basically said the same, Zahn said. – In London three years ago.

Everybody stared at Wells.

He was clearly ill at ease. And funnily enough, guilt was written on his face.

– You don't think that I… you don't think…

– Just the fact that we think you might be Joyce, shows how far we've come in our paranoid understanding of reality, Caldwell soothed him.

It hadn't been Joyce who had said it, had it? Zahn frowned. But Todd Winston. What had Joyce said? He had talked about people, emphasized it, how they could form their own fate. About the Game, about the Enemy, about the Illusion used to keep people down?

Remove them, from their true will.

He suddenly realized it, in a flash of understanding.

There was no illusion, no substance to it. Everything he had seen had been real... everything beyond the illusion.

He had long since realized it, he realized, and at the very least since he saw the first, few seconds on the screen. It gurgled in his palate. He touched his upper lip again and blood wet his fingers. His nose was bleeding again.

He remembered the moment... the moment... a gnat bit him, and fell to the ground, dead in an instant, filled with his blood, his boiling blood.

Pain cut through him. In a moment he stood there, crouching. *Growing pains*. The scenes, the visions flooded him, and he let them. He went through thoughts, events, conversations in his mind, saw what was hidden, hidden in broad daylight. What he hadn't realized, what he hadn't remembered, with his memory, what he should have remembered now appeared very obvious, so obvious that he had evidently been suppressing it earlier. All the pieces of the puzzle. Another, much bigger puzzle revealed itself. He started laughing.

A door slid open in his mind. A velvet curtain he quite simply brushed aside. Sherlock Holmes... of course. Improbable. He he... The expression of paralyzed incredulity and wonder never quite disappeared from his face.

– «How often have I said to you that when you have eliminated the impossible, whatever remains, however improbable, must be the truth?»

– What was that, Zahn? Russo wondered.

– I quoted from the Sign of Four by Arthur Canon Doyle, Zahn enlightened him.

Monica smiled, a joy-filled, intense smile. The others stared at him, as if they didn't have a clue of what he was talking about. And they hadn't.

– Do you know what? He laughed and shook his head. – I've just realized that I, the last three years, during all that prolonged moment in time, during my entire life... have chased myself.

– This isn't the time for philosophical layouts, Zahn, Caldwell pointed out sharply.

– No, you don't understand…

Zahn dried his tears, and straightened, rose to his full height.

They didn't understand. How could they?

– Then you might enlighten us, us primitives, about what we don't understand.

He turned towards Caldwell, focusing for a moment only on her.

– Lieutenant, I've got bad news for you. It's about your friend, the Chief. He allowed it to sink in, waited for the worry to manifest in her face. – I've always thought he was a bit… weird, a bit too much a prototype, a character, but now I'm certain.

– What are you talking about? She asked incredulous.

And afraid, very afraid.

– Springsteen and Timothy Joyce are the same man. He enlightened her.

She stared at him, before breaking in laughter.

– It can't be true. She stared at him, sweaty and swollen in the face. Suddenly her intense and frequent face and body treatments meant nothing. – What proof…

– I'm not sure if they've always been the same, or if Joyce, at some point, slipped into Springsteen's life, but Joyce has been Springsteen since I arrived in Los Angeles. Of that I'm certain. You'll have your proof, count on that.

The thoughts kept grinding through his brain, through his mind, thought upon thought, a chaotic whirl of Life and Fire. And it made sense. For the first time he could remember.

What would happen if he didn't act upon his intensions? Would the world be turned inside out? Would he wake up in an office somewhere, where he would «remember» this as a half-forgotten dream, and then return home to Gwen, his devoted wife? He shuddered, he grinned. They stared at him with a mix of worry and impatient irritation.

The old uncertainty left him. The quivering unrest he had felt his entire life, the drive inside would remain forever.

– He's here, he said flatly and calmly drew the revolver.

– Where?

Caldwell and the others shook. They turned their backs to him, drew their own guns slowly, uselessly, and stared desperately into the shadows.

He fired from the hip, shot her in the neck. The bullet erupted between her wide eyes. Russo and Wells weren't able to react much either, before he put two bullets in each of them. Russo managed just about to focus two swimming eyes on him, before collapsing dead on the floor.

Louis whirled around and charged. Monica kicked out and sent him right into the wall. He fell and before he regained his center she bent down and quick as lightning sent an elbow in his chest. In quick, merciless moves she struck against muscles and limbs, stunning him effectively and ruthlessly. He lay still, conscious, but paralyzed.

She pulled back, looked at Zahn, awaiting his move. Zahn walked to the boy, sitting down on his heels, by the boy's side. He read understanding in the boy's eyes. And also something else.

– I've decided to let you live, Zahn said. – Therefore, you owe me a life. You belong to me for the rest of your life. You're my slave. Every single word, the smallest gesture from me you will obey and execute, eagerly, without hesitation. You're just an empty shell I may choose to fill.

There was indeed nothing there, in the boy's empty eyes, as a shiver passed through him and he knelt before the man towering above him.

– But don't despair too much. There are compensations. You will, for instance, be reunited with your sister. You and dear Abigail will serve me side by side.

He walked to Caldwell, looked down on her lifeless shell.

– I'm looking forward to the bank robbery. I'm looking forward to fucking you.

He thought about the events at the casino. Anticipation riled him.

Then he saw the shimmering in the air clearly for the first time, an opening, a portal in Space and Time itself. He didn't in any way control it yet, he knew that. So far, at this point, everything was instinct and run by the drive inside. It didn't matter. He knew he would learn.

He heard the sound of flowing sand, he sensed the shaking in the ground.

– The San Andreas fault-line, he said aloud.

Monica's eyes widened, in shock, in anticipation, joy and

admiration.

The two looked back at Louis. He was still kneeling, with lowered eyes, lowered body. She laughed short and sharp.

– Come, Jeremy said. – We have much to do.

He walked first into the pulsing shimmer. Monica walked right behind him. Louis followed faithfully two steps behind. They didn't actually see anything special, just followed in his footprints, but the world changed around them, too. The sound of the threatening rumble faded. Night turned to bright day. The sun flowed through the dusty windows. The recorder, the player and the TV stood on exactly the same spot.

– This is fantastic, Monica exclaimed. – This is absolutely incredible.

She checked. No disk in the player. It was in the camera. Everything was ready, ready for the recording.

The time on the player showed 01.32 PM. The newspaper gathered dust where they had found it, not where they had moved it.

– What does Memory tell you? She asked eagerly.

They looked at the considerable number of uniformed guards outside. No one had any chance of seeing them from their current position.

– I recognize several of them. They're the same who are on the lists for the earlier duty… not on this evening. I think we can safely assume we're at the same place we left, but earlier in the day.

She took it all in, silently, in stride, with shiny eyes.

– Nobody was reported, he thought aloud. – We won't be seen.

– We're at the opposite side of town right now. She stared at him, couldn't take her eyes off him. – And also somewhere on the highway…

His eyes were drawn to the chair. He walked to it and sat down in it. She walked to the camera, looked through the lens.

– Are you ready? She asked uncertain.

– I'm more than ready.

She pushed the REC-button. The recording began.

– Hello, Jeremy, he said tonelessly, – we meet again.

It started a bit hesitant, uncertain, even though he knew it wasn't revealed in the recording. But then the words basically came by themselves. He hardly needed to pick them from memory. The voice changed tone, turning hoarser, deeper at the same time. Something that didn't surprise him. Neither did the words flowing from his mouth like vinegar spiced with honey. Or the other way around. No matter, he hardly sensed the bitter taste anymore. It was behind him, a distant, half-forgotten memory. The expectant smile wasn't programmed. When it appeared, exactly where it was supposed to, it was totally spontaneous. He felt small stings in the skin when his face began to change. A slight concentration, and it happened. Timothy Joyce's familiar face appeared.

He rose, after the well-done recording. Monica removed the disk from the recorder and put in the player. An added push and the timer was activated, programmed to make the player turn itself on exactly at midnight.

And perhaps was another timer activated then, as well.

He saw his new appearance, his new Self, in the looks the two sent him, in a mirror later, up the stairs, in the office where he had had one of his encounters with himself. Physically there were no similarities with the person he had been. Everything was changed. But in movements, behavior there would always, inevitably be common traits. He should have seen it before. And he had. But it hadn't occurred to him, because he hadn't wanted to realize it.

With a casual stroll, he descended the stairs, returning to the two waiting below.

– It's accomplished, he shouted from the rooftops. – And the seventh day he called Judgment Day.

Monica started laughing, stopped for a moment, and laughed even more.

– We are The Dead, he said calmly. – The shadows are our valley. We Live, in a world of dead.

The portal appeared in the dark hallway, bleached by the sun, enhanced by the shadows, at his disposal.

A person who could appear wherever he wanted, move across vast distances, one moment be in front of somebody, the next behind them.

And all the rest, everything lurking below the surface, only waiting for him to explore.

He understood Timothy Joyce's reputation now. He understood

it perfectly.

He understood so much.

He would meet Gwen again, meet her in a completely new way.

He was looking forward to so much.

He would never believe in inevitability, but he did believe in Fate. Others might not create theirs, but he did.

He had been stupid, focusing on exercise, weapons. A weapon, in itself, was useless. The true power was in the human will. The will to act on one's beliefs, one's desires, a human's true will.

In the three seconds, the three years he had slept he had learned the truth about what he was. He was Life and Fire, and the wild beast in the forest, a power beyond everything, beyond anything the present-day world had to «offer».

He took Monica's hand, leading her into the shimmering passage. Louis lurked silent and moody behind them. The world turned gray, shimmering in colors, pale and glowing simultaneously. His vision turned real.

– I love you, Jeremy… Timothy.

She was the first to call him that, the first of many. It didn't shock him, like it would have done only a short while ago.

He thought back on the life of Jeremy Zahn. It hadn't been all that much, not at all, and now it was done. Life started now.

He had felt it awaken inside for a while, the deep contempt for anything inhuman. He had heard the sound of flowing sand. He saw the city of Los Angeles, and also the state of California, fall into the ocean.

He sensed the changes come, also from within, towards who he most of all wanted to be.

The pain was behind him, now. Everything else was ahead.

The long walk was done. The long walk continued.

Destiny waited at the other end of the tunnel.

I will praise me, for I have fearfully and wonderfully made
myself!
My soul knows how marvelous are my works.
I was aware when my very bones were formed,
Growing secretly inside my Mother's body
As a plant's root grows beneath the earth.
I knew me before I was born.
The nights of my life were all written in my book
Before they had ever begun.

Timothy Joyce

Amos Keppler
1997-07-20 – 2000-07-23
215. Night 12055
In the year of the Abyss

Printed version ready 2010-06-24
185. Night 12065
In the tenth year in the time of
The Twilight Storm

Paperback version ready 2019-07-07

«Never be afraid to go too far, because that way lies the
truth».

Proust

Other published and upcoming novels by **Amos Keppler** from **Midnight Fire Media**:

**The Janus Clan** - (ten chapters about the Wild Man in the modern world, a world balancing on a razor's edge):

**The Defenseless**
**The Slaves**
**Birds Flying in the Dark**
**At the End of the Rainbow**
**Lewis of Modern York**
The Werewolf of Locus Bradle
The Valley of Kings
Eye in the Sky
The Iron Cage
Phoenix Green Earth

## The Defenseless

The two rivers meet and join in the city of Denver, becoming one...

The two dark brothers, growing up with their sister Linda in a mundane, average suburb, a place well entrenched in modern United States and the world, have since their moment of birth been at odds with the world... and with each other.

Mike and Ted Cousin are not who they are. There is a mystery here, one of birth and upbringing, one of fate. Violence and death, blood and fire follow them all the days of their lives. The fire is resting somewhere inside... waiting for the Spark.

Their parents know something, but are not telling it. The policeman Mark Stewart and their aunt Trudy do, too. Everybody knows something, pieces of the whole, but nobody knows the whole truth, nobody telling it.

The ancient power is returning to the world, a world massively suffering from physical and spiritual poison, on the brink of collapse and a collective tailspin suicide run without equal in human history.

Magick is returning from its long exile. Thus begins the story of the wild beasts rising from their ashes.

The Spark is struck, horrible and terrifying.

First book of ten in the Janus Clan series: Ten stories of the wild man in the modern world, forty years of wandering, before the Phoenix is rising from its ashes.

Hardcover ISBN 978-82-91693-08-8
Paperback ISBN 978-82-91693-26-2

# ShadowWalk

The world is changing. They know this, in their core of cores, where everything moves and shifts. Night and fire have followed them all the days of their lives.

What they carry inside has always scared them, always intrigued them...

They have always felt different, apart from the crowd. And here, now, they get the confirmation they have always wanted, always yearned for, that they are truly different, a breed apart. The metamorphosis begins. Their minds, their bodies are changing in shocking and unpredictable ways, as what's on the inside is brought to the outside. And as they themselves are changing they are also changing the world.

Danger awaits them, Life awaits them, in the small, backward New England town. Magick and Mystery may be found beneath unturned stones.

People, young and old, are descending on the small, insignificant town of Northfield, New England.

Boys and girls, students at the school of Life, Seekers, yearning for what's different, what's hidden.

They're seeking within and without, high and low.

And here, in this dusty, remote place they're finding it, turning the stone, finding the strength within themselves to be themselves, to break out of confines, to the world beyond. And in time, after the initial, tentative steps, pushing down paths new and undreamed of.

And the present-day order sees them for what they are... Agents of Change, a threat to any establishment, any imposed reality. The heatwave, the worst in living memory, is nothing compared to the boiling within the human heart. The Indian Summer heralds the twilight of mankind.

ISBN 978-82-91693-12-5